D0897946

Myths and Fairy Tales in Contemporary Women's Fiction

MYTHS AND FAIRY TALES IN CONTEMPORARY WOMEN'S FICTION

FROM ATWOOD TO MORRISON

Sharon Rose Wilson

MYTHS AND FAIRY TALES IN CONTEMPORARY WOMEN'S FICTION
Copyright © Sharon Rose Wilson, 2008.

First published in 2008 by PALGRAVE MACMILLAN® in the US -
a division of St. Martin's Press LLC, 175 Fifth Avenue, New York,
NY 10010.

Where this book is distributed in the UK, Europe and the rest of the
world, this is by Palgrave Macmillan, a division of Macmillan Publishers Limited, registered in England, company number 785998, of
Houndmills, Basingstoke, Hampshire RG21 6XS.

Palgrave Macmillan is the global academic imprint of the above companies and has companies and representatives throughout the world.

Palgrave® and Macmillan® are registered trademarks in the United
States, the United Kingdom, Europe and other countries.

ISBN-10: 0-230-60554-0
ISBN-13: 978-0-230-60554-1

Library of Congress Cataloging-in-Publication Data

Wilson, Sharon Rose.
   Myths and fairy tales in contemporary women's fiction : from
Atwood to Morrison / Sharon Rose Wilson.
      p. cm.
   ISBN 0-230-60554-0 (alk. paper)

   1. Atwood, Margaret Eleanor, 1939—Criticism and interpretation.
2. Lessing, Doris May, 1919—Criticism and interpretation.
3. Morrison, Toni–Criticism and interpretation.   4. Feminism and
literature–English-speaking countries—History—20th century.
5. Women and literature—English-speaking countries—History–20th
century.   6. Fairy tales in literature.   7. Myth in literature.
8. Postmodernism (Literature)–English-speaking countries.
9. Sex role in literature.   I. Title.
   PR9199.3.A8Z955 2008
   818'.5409—dc22   2008003369

A catalogue record of the book is available from the British Library.

Design by Westchester Book Group.

First Edition: August 2008

10 9 8 7 6 5 4 3 2 1

Printed in the United States of America.

Transferred to Digital Printing 2009

Dedicated to
Rose Wilson and Stephen Wilson-Brown

CONTENTS

ACKNOWLEDGMENTS

I would like to thank Margaret Atwood and the Thomas Fisher Rare Book Library at the University of Toronto for the use of the Margaret Atwood Papers.

INTRODUCTION

Myths and Fairy Tales in Contemporary Women's Fiction is an exploration of contemporary feminist, postmodernist, and postcolonial women writers' use of fairy tales and myths around the world. This book examines meanings of myths and fairy tales in their work as well as their varying techniques, images, intertexts, and genres. Although the writers represent several different nationalities and different racial, ethnic, and cultural backgrounds, all but one of the works I investigate has been written in a country where English is a major language and is postcolonial literature;[1] that is, literature, including that written by marginalized peoples in the United States, that advances readers and societies beyond colonization. My major contention is that metafairy tales (texts about myths and fairy tales) generally convey characters' transformation from alienation and symbolic amputation to greater consciousness, community, and wholeness. With one exception, this pattern is evident in Morrison's *Beloved;* Lessing's *The Story of Colonel Dann, Mara's Daughter, Griot and Snow Dog,* and *Memoirs of a Survivor;* Rhys's *Wide Sargasso Sea;* Atwood's *The Robber Bride, Oryx and Crake,* and *The Penelopiad;* Murdoch's *The Green Knight;* Ferre's *The Youngest Doll;* Erdrich's *The Beet Queen;* and Hulme's *The Bone People.* In addition, since these texts are postcolonial metafictions at least partly about the power of story, it is in and through story that characters construct a hybrid way of being-in-the-world. Characterization, images, themes, structures, and techniques (e.g., magical realism) portray exiled characters' growth from isolation and polarity to hybridity. Mythic intertexts (texts within other texts) not only dramatize nation-building and collapsing in postcolonial work: In-between beings' engagement in the process of constructing identity, knowledge, and "home" is, in itself, mythic.

I use these terms *fairy tale* and *myth* as they are traditionally used by folklorists. By fairy tales I mean wonder stories, märchen. By myths I mean stories believed to be true and sacred, stories that are etiological explanations of creation and the world. Thus, although these stories may be "myths" in a more general sense, referring to aspects of history or of popular or social culture, I am discussing traditional stories often used as intertexts rather than myth as language, speech, or semiological system (Barthes 11, 109, 111).

Myths and Fairy Tales in Contemporary Women's Fiction refutes some common biases that damage understanding of contemporary, ethnic, postmodern, postcolonial, and women writers. First, fairy tales and myths are too often dismissed as simple decoration that is not an essential part of a text. Second, ethnic writers such as Louise Erdrich, Keri Hulme, and Rosario Ferre are frequently expected to be "purely" ethnic or "native" and criticized for using literary techniques, such as postmodernism, supposedly not only owned by *white, mainstream, apolitical* culture but also destructive of one's own oral, folk traditions (Silko 179n4; During 373; Paravisini-Gebert 161–68). Third, despite the number of world writers who have pioneered and use a postmodernism rooted in their own cultures, some readers and writers are stuck in a conception of postmodernism as American, apolitical, elite, and male (Nicholson 4–12). As I show, each of the italicized terms is problematic: From an international, post-structuralist perspective, either-or dichotomies (binary oppositions) continue to be suspect. Considerable evidence exists that such postmodern techniques as magical realism, or the fusion of magic with realism, may have originated in third-world narrative traditions. According to Stephen Hart, magical realism is an international phenomenon emerging from the trauma of colonial dispossession (6), and Homi Bhabha speaks of it as "the literary language of the emergent postcolonial world" (Introduction 1–7). Perhaps the most relevant and inclusive definition for this book is that magical realism "has become a common narrative mode for fictions written from the perspective of the politically and culturally disempowered, as Native Americans in the United States, women writing from a feminist perspective, or those whose lives incorporate different cultural beliefs and practices from those dominant in their country of residence" (Bowers 33). Wendy Farris states that magical realism "may constitute the single most important trend in contemporary international fiction" (*Ordinary* 42). Postmodern intertextuality also draws from oral as well as literary traditions. Despite the possibility that women or world writers may have invented what is now called postmodernism, some feminist and nonfeminist theorists also continue to see feminism and postmodernism as antithetical (see Greene, *Changing* 1; Nicholson 4–12). Much the same situation continues for postcolonialism and both postmodernism and feminism (see S. Wilson, *Margaret Atwood's Fairy* 26–28). I maintain here that techniques are not intrinsically "male" or "female," "conservative" or "liberal," ethnic or "white," colonialist or anticolonialist and that such essentialist thinking interferes with investigating how authors, techniques, genres, texts, and readers convey meanings in particular cultures.

Fourth, misconceptions about metafiction also distort understanding of fiction tradition as well as the narrative traditions of women, ethnic, and postcolonial writers. The works examined here are, either overtly or indirectly, metafictions. Because these works call attention to themselves—and parts of themselves—as fiction, they are in the genre of metafiction: Whether they are realistic novels, neo-Gothic novels, fabulation, fantasy, science fiction, or romance, each is fiction about fiction, about intertexts (Scholes 145), about the procedures of writing or telling stories, about the relationship between fiction and other fictions, fiction and myth, or fiction and reality, and, in postmodern works, finally about the fiction of "reality."[2] Although most of the texts that I have selected here do not parody straight or conventional fiction to the extent that they become antifiction, *Beloved* is an anti–fairy tale and *The Penelopiad* is an antimyth. Some other metafictions that embed fairy-tale and/ or mythic intertexts, such as Beckett's *Molloy, Malone Dies,* and *The Unnamable* and Atwood's *Surfacing* (S. Wilson, "Deconstructing" 53), are antifiction. In opposition to Jean-Francois Lyotard's philosophical usage of *metanarrative,* where the term often refers to totalizing or legitimating master discourses such as science (xxiii-xxiv), metanarrative here simply refers to narrative about narrative, as metafiction is fiction about fiction (Holman and Harmon 297). Because they are about fairy tales and myths, such metanarratives may also be referred to as metafairy tales and/ or metamyths. Since the pejorative declamations about "the death of the novel" and the defensive rationalization of the "literature of exhaustion" (Barth 29–34) in the 1960s and 1970s, metafiction has been absorbed into postmodernism, and its generic self-reflexiveness has been subordinated to its use of parody and irony. As I show here, recognition of the play of intertextuality helps us see and appreciate subtle metafictions, metafictions never named as such, and helps connect written and oral narrative traditions. It also helps us identify metafictional aspects of all narratives (see Kristeva 66). Although writers of such works are sometimes criticized for doing so, they use, and have often helped to invent and globalize, postmodern techniques such as magical realism, intertextuality, and self-reflexiveness that have been mistakenly identified with antifeminist, western, imperialistic, or apolitical literature.

The writers examined here, postmodern, postcolonial metafictionists, are feminist[3] in social and cultural critiques performed through fairy-tale and mythic intertexts. According to Gayle Greene, feminist fiction, grounded in a belief that change is possible, analyzes gender as socially constructed. As a tool of feminist critique, feminist metafiction can reveal the conventionality of the codes of fiction, how they have been constructed, and how they can be changed.[4] Viewing reworked fairy tales in the genre of feminist fantasy, Cranny-Francis refers to the "metanarrative function" of feminist intertextual revisions, sometimes involving direct reader address and always revealing the ideologically determined discourses encoded in the traditional tales (85, 89, 94). Whether or not the authors here identify themselves as feminist, the works are feminist in the sense of questioning gender role conditioning and of assuming full humanity for females as well as males. They also avoid stereotyping of sexual orientation, race, class, and age. Examining Atwood's "Bluebeard's Egg" (1983) along with works by Anne Sexton, Angela Carter, Joanna Russ, and other writers, Jack Zipes suggests that feminist fairy tales

challenge conventional views of gender, socialisation [*sic*], and sex roles . . . [and] map out an alternative aesthetic terrain for the fairy tale as genre. . . . Created out of dissatisfaction with the dominant male discourse of traditional fairy tales and with those social values and institutions which have provided the framework for sexist prescriptions, the feminist fairy tale conceives a different view of the world and speaks in a voice that has been customarily silenced. (*Don't* xi)

Much the same may be said of feminist remythification. Because recent writers often interweave intertexts in a manner resembling medieval interlace (S. Wilson, *Margaret Atwood's Fairy* 31), their evocation of fairy-tale or mythic patterns (archetypes), such as transformation, descent, and return, identifiable in well-known stories, such as the Grimm brothers', Perrault's, Goddess (e.g., Demeter-Persephone), or Phoenix tales, may pass unnoticed or, worse, be misinterpreted. This occurs even when the authors discuss, and most of their work embeds, fairy tales and myth. For example, although Atwood comments on the powerful women in many tales (Hammond interview 115; S. Wilson,

Margaret Atwood's Fairy 12), most of her critics still assume that she and others use fairy tales only to critique social conditioning (see S. Wilson, *Margaret Atwood's Fairy* 6). Many writers of metafairy tales work in subgenres of romance or the fantastic and may also draw on other aspects of folk culture besides fairy tales or on stories belonging simultaneously to folklore, myth, legend, and biblical or other religious lore. They also draw on other popular culture, for example, ghost, vampire, detective, thriller, true romance, fantasy, science fiction, other literary, television, film, radio, and historical stories alongside fairy-tale and mythic intertexts.

Contrary to usual expectation, rather than critiquing fairy tales' use in female socialization, most women writers use fairy-tale structures, images, motifs, settings, and characters in the same way that they use myths: These old stories resonate as intertexts in their contemporary work. Since märchen exist in considerable variety, and some possess matriarchal elements, scholars too often focus on Walt Disney versions or have read only the sanitized tales popular in the 1950s, in which women were servile, immobile, even in a stupor, and the point of the stories was ruffles (Atwood, "Of Souls" 23). Thus, fairy tales appear to be patriarchal "poison apples" that foster female passivity and victimhood (Daly 44, 90–91).[5] However, tales such as the Grimms' "The Twelve Brothers," in which the King wants to disinherit the brothers so that the daughter can inherit, invalidate the "supposed universal sexism of fairy tales" (Atwood, "Of Souls" 27). Similarly, although no original source can be pinpointed for tales based on oral tradition, because of the popularity of the Grimms and Perrault, scholars of third-world literature may see well-known fairy tales such as "Cinderella" or "Sleeping Beauty" ("Briar Rose") as European and thereby colonialist. Some folklorists may be unhappy with writers who transform folk materials[6] or use literary fairy tales alongside stories directly from oral tradition. Fortunately, literary writers drawing on fairy tales and myth remind us of these genres' richness, both in themselves and in their ability to resonate in contemporary fiction. Fairy-tale themes include unhappy childhoods, dangerous romances, the struggle between individuality and community, the journey toward community, and the celebration of life (Fiander xii, xv, vii). In addition, myths and fairy-tale themes include quests, the relationship of the sexes, the search for identity, individuation, and healing, and the transformation of individuals and their surroundings. Frequently, two main quests in contemporary women's metafiction are the struggle to survive sexual politics and the quest to tell the story—to be an artist creating meaning in the world. The ten major texts

I explore here, novels by Margaret Atwood, Toni Morrison, Louise
Erdrich, Doris Lessing, Iris Murdoch, Keri Hulme, and Jean Rhys
and short fiction by Rosario Ferre, spanning from 1966 to 2005, all
use some of these themes and thus foreground the continuing importance of fairy tales and myths in contemporary culture. Five of them
embed the Grimms' "Fitchter's Bird," depicted on the cover, and
"The Robber Bridegroom," Bluebeard stories in which the woman
outwits and survives both the destructive male and society who try to
kill her.

Postmodern myth and fairy tales, evident in feminist revisionists
who use double-voiced irony and embed and parody a particular tale
at the same time, are also much more important in contemporary fiction than are usually recognized. Sadly, critics and students who insist
on literature's being realist and who treat fairy tales or myth, even re-
visioned intertextual myth, as escaping from "real life" (Murray
88–89, Barthes qtd. Murray 88), are still operating within dualistic
binary oppositions. As Eliade suggests and Zipes later states, myth is a
reality: "myth tells us how, through the deeds of Supernatural Beings,
a reality came into existence, be it the whole of reality, the Cosmos, or
only a fragment of reality. . . . myth sets examples for human beings
that enable them to codify and order their lives" (Zipes, *Fairy* 1).
Folk and fairy tales still present camouflaged mythic motifs and "the
structure of an infinitely serious and responsible adventure" (Eliade
201).

Many other contemporary women writers besides those included
in this book write metamyths and metafairy tales, and they are usually feminist postmodernists. Joy Kogawa's *Obasan*, Margaret Laurence's *The Diviners*, Marie-Claire Blais's *Mad Shadows*, and Anne
Hebert's *Kamouraska* (Canadian); Laura Esquivel's *Like Water for
Chocolate* (Mexican); Amy Tan's *The Joy Luck Club* (Chinese American); and A. S. Byatt's *Possession: A Romance* (English) resemble Atwood, Lessing, Morrison, Erdrich, Ferre, Murdoch, Rhys, and
Hulme's texts in their self-consciousness about themselves and art,
but not all are postcolonial or even political in societal critiques. A
modernist metamyth that influences many contemporary writers of
metafiction and Kunstlerromanen (artist novels) is Virginia Woolf's
To the Lighthouse. A number of other postmodern writers not usually
considered both feminist and postcolonialist, including A. S. Byatt,
Angela Carter, Gail Godwin, Eudora Welty, Joyce Carol Oates, Ur-
sula LeGuinn, Sherri S. Tepper, Barbara Comyns, Salman Rushdie,
Robert Coover, Kurt Vonnegut, and Donald Barthelme, also use
fairy-tale and mythic intertexts in similar ways. In each case, when

works call attention to fairy tales, myths, story-telling, fictional form, the relationship of fairy tales and "reality," and themselves as tales, they are metafiction—metafairy tales, metamyths, or anti–fairy tales or myths—and further attention to their intertexts is in order.

Feminist, postcolonial writers use intertexts in their metafairy tales and metamyths in similar ways that will be developed in the chapters. Because they are within other texts, the texts generally embed and sometimes parody the plot, structure, themes, images, motifs, characterization, and sometimes the language of the intertexts. Some tactics of using and deconstructing myth and fairy-tale intertexts include building a scene on one or more powerful images, reversing the gender to shift females from object to subject, displacing the "truth" of traditional texts and patterns to give voice to the silenced, shifting the point of view from the usual privileged, reliable, third-person narration to unreliable third-person centers of consciousness, using tropes and symbols to enlarge the meaning of the ordinary, and displacing the original plot line of tales so that the silent or marginalized subtext is central. In addition, the feminist, postcolonialist metafairy tale and metamyth explode and open the resolution—what DuPlessis calls "writing beyond the ending" (6); transform, bend, or blend either tones or genres; and use irony as a subversive doubled or split discourse, what occurs when "we speak with an inner reservation . . . as if limiting our own authorship or dividing it in two" (Bakhtin 184). These tales also use language to defamiliarize (Shklovsky 13–22), transgress, and parody these elements; revise or "reverse" the norms or ideology of an intertext in a transition toward the postcolonial; by transgressing the conventions of language and culture, use what DuPlessis calls "delegitimation" (29) to engage readers in joint creation of the text; and remythify intertexts distorted or amputated by colonization, racism, and patriarchy to potentially heal societies. Fairy-tale and mythic intertexts thus foreground sexual politics and other political issues, including those of the postcolonial condition (adapted from S. Wilson, *Margaret Atwood's Fairy* 31–33).

Judging by recent critical studies of fairy tales and myths in women's fiction, the topic of this book commands considerable interest. Because it is an historical overview, Elizabeth Warring Harris's *Twice Upon a Time: Woman Writers and the History of the Fairy Tale* offers no extended discussion of particular writers and does not address myth. Susan Sellers's *Myth and Fairy Tale in Contemporary Women's Fiction,* similarly titled to my own book, explores twelve female rewriters of myth as empowering paradigms. She is primarily interested in applying French feminist theory to different, sometimes lesser-known, writers (Byatt, Weldon, Crow, Cixous, Roberts, Rice, Tenant, Warner, Donoghue, Tepper, Thompson, Carter) than I select and gives little attention to particular tales, especially fairy tales. Perhaps the most similar study to mine is Stephen Benson's collection, *Contemporary Fiction and the Fairy Tale*, which explores five English or American male and female writers in establishing a canon of fairy tales in fiction and includes one of my articles. Benson does not explore myth, nor does Donald Haase's edited *Fairy Tales and Feminism: New Approaches*, which examines cross-cultural texts, including Ferre and Atwood, from the seventeenth and twentieth centuries. Cristina Bacchilega's *Postmodern Fairy Tales: Gender and Narrative Strategies* does not include myth and primarily aims to further knowledge of "mechanisms by which postmodern fairy tales multiply narrative and gender possibilities" (146). See also Stephen Benson's theoretical *Cycles of Influence: Fiction, Folktale, Theory*. Volumes on individual writers who discuss fairy tales or myths include Danielle Roemer and Cristina Bacchilega's *Angela Carter and the Fairy Tale,* my own *Margaret Atwood's Fairy-Tale Sexual Politics,* Sarah A. Appleton's projected *Margaret Atwood: Myth, Fairy Tale, and Legend,* and Lisa Fiander's *Everyday Magic: Fairy Tales and the Fiction of Iris Murdoch, Margaret Drabble, and A. S. Byatt.* Feminist studies of women writers, such as Gail Greene's *Changing the Story: Feminist Fiction and the Tradition,* generally do not include ethnic writers or writers outside the United States and are not focused on myths and fairy tales. Although none of these texts has the same focus as mine, each is recommended for further reading.

Chapter 1, "Atwood's Monstrous, Dismembered, Cannibalized, and (Sometimes) Reborn Female Bodies: *The Robber Bride* and Other Texts," gives an overview of myth and fairy-tale intertexts and motifs throughout Margaret Atwood's work as a basis for discussing myth and fairy-tale intertexts in literature. The chapter then goes on to examine the Grimms' "The Robber Bridegroom" in detail and also briefly treats "Fitcher's Bird" and Great Goddess myth, three of the most significant intertexts in *The Robber Bride* and other Atwood works and in the rest of this volume. *The Robber Bride* is a postmodern metafairy tale, even an anti–fairy tale. Atwood deconstructs not only "The Robber Bridegroom" and "Fitcher's Bird" tales and Great Goddess myth but also traditional narrative structure. All the characters play Robber Bridegroom as well as victim roles. By questioning conventional notions of gender and fiction, *The Robber Bride* also exposes constructions of identity, reality, and order.

Chapter 2, "Fitcher's and Frankenstein's Gaze in Atwood's *Oryx and Crake*," continues the Bluebeard focus of the previous chapter through the "Fitcher's Bird," Frankenstein, and "Robber Bridegroom" intertexts. The connections between the Grimms' "Fitcher's Bird" and Mary Shelley's *Frankenstein* are treated in detail, and Frankenstein and mad scientist films and other literary intertexts (Melville, Vonnegut, Piercy) are briefly explored. In Margaret Atwood's *Oryx and Crake*, most readers overlook how quality of vision contributes to the body politics and human folly depicted in this book. Distortions of vision and blindness jeopardize male as well as female bodies, and even the newly gendered bodies of this Frankenstein's created species. This chapter explores the dangers of penetrating beyond the forbidden door of genetic engineering and hybridity to the possible extinction of the human species.

Chapter 3, "The Writer as Crone Goddess in Atwood's *The Penelopiad* and Lessing's *Memoirs of a Survivor*," explores the woman writer in connection to the Triple Goddess myth, especially the Hecate Crone, who is not only the muse but also the creator in both of these texts. In Margaret Atwood's most recent novel, *The Penelopiad* (2005), the Crone phase of the Great Goddess, discussed in detail, is both parodied and symbolic of wisdom and creativity. Since this Crone, discounted in Homer's *The Odyssey* and Tennyson's "Ulysses" as an aged, faithful wife, is also the voice that tells the story we read, Penelope deconstructs not only Homer's *The Odyssey* but also stereotyped conceptions of women, writers, heroes, crones, and other goddesses.

In Doris Lessing's apocalyptic *Memoirs of a Survivor*, the Survivor's world is breaking down in the way that broken appliances and other technology deteriorate. The Survivor goes through barriers to penetrate not only to her unconscious and the unconscious of the human race, but also to the realm of myth: She rediscovers herself as hero and as goddess, a reflection of the ancient Great Goddess who symbolizes earth, life, wholeness, wisdom, and soul, and is reborn with the world. The transformation is not merely personal, psychological, or limited to the good, the female, the human, or even the present. The dog-cat Hugo, Emily's/ the narrator's parents, Gerald, and even Gerald's children all cross "the threshold" to another, utopian dimension.

In chapter 4, "Mythic Quests for the Word and Postcolonial Identity: Lessing's *The Story of Colonel Dann, Mara's Daughter, Griot and Snow Dog*, and Morrison's *Beloved*," both novels focus on the cultural importance of story-telling. Along with its prequel, *Mara and Dann,*

Doris Lessing's *The Story of Colonel Dann, Mara's Daughter, Griot and Snow Dog* uses the mythic storyteller or *griot*, popular culture intertexts, especially Greek myth and brother and sister folklore, and the characterization, images, themes, structures, and techniques (e.g., magical realism) associated with them, to portray her exiled characters' growth from alienation and polarity to hybridity: These in-between beings are engaged in the process of constructing identity and "home" through story-telling.

Although fairy-tale intertexts have been ignored in Toni Morrison's *Beloved* and the tree on Sethe's back is usually viewed negatively, the "Sleeping Beauty" ("Briar Rose") tale, treated in detail, and Great Goddess intertexts are primary in *Beloved,* which focuses on the need to awake and recognize the story we have been living. Each of the fairy tale's major motifs—the curse and spell, the castle in the forest, the tower of isolation, spinning, the prick, sleeping, and the barrier of thorns—functions ironically in the novel, often in more than one sense. The most obvious curse is, of course, slavery, also this novel's Robber Bridegroom; slavery and the racism on which it is based create the secret jungle that grows within both blacks and whites. For most of the book, house 124 is a symbolic tower of isolation that seems to be spacially separated from the rest of the community. More than the symbol of her dehumanization, Sethe's tree also represents her and society's potential rebirth. As in Lessing's *The Story of Colonel Dann, Mara's Daughter, Griot and Snow Dog,* remembering and telling the story is a key to moving on.

Chapter 5, "Reading Louise Erdrich's *The Beet Queen: Demeter, The Wizard of Oz, The Ramayana,* and Native American Myth," is about *The Beet Queen*'s postmodern use of intertexts. Louise Erdrich interweaves Greek and Fisher King myth, Native American legend, Baum's *The Wizard of Oz,* and stories from the *Ramayana* with fairy tales including Andersen's "The Snow Queen." Critiquing gender roles, she presents a pickled princess, a male fairy godmother, a beet queen dressed in "Thumbelina's nightmare" (329), and several tricksters while deconstructing the gendered white, heterosexual, middle-class romantic myth embodied in "Cinderella." Still, these dysfunctional characters manage to create family, community, and hybridity: home.

Chapter 6, Silenced Women in Rosario Ferre's *The Youngest Doll:* "Sleeping Beauty," "The Red Shoes," "Cinderella," and "Fitcher's Bird," is about Rosario Ferre's short fiction, "The Youngest Doll," "Sleeping Beauty," "The Poisoned Story," and "Amalia" from *The Youngest Doll.* These stories parody values that are simultaneously patriarchal, colonial, classist, and racist and use "Fitcher's Bird" or

Caribbean and European Bluebeard stories, Hans Christian Andersen's "The Red Shoes," and tales from *Arabian Nights*. While evoking a fairy-tale archetype of beautiful, fragile, doll-women who play passive female roles and whose stories end with marriage, "The Youngest Doll" also suggests and parodies the nursery rime about girls filled with sugar and spice. Ferre's "Sleeping Beauty," a metafairy tale that suggests the whole volume's focus on the way we can construct stories—whether mythic, religious, fairy tale, literary, ballet, societal, or cultural—either to constrict or to foster freedom. Unlike Morrison's *Beloved*, which also uses a "Sleeping Beauty" intertext, the Puerto Rican society of this story sleeps on, in bed with dead values.

Ferre's "The Poisoned Story" is a trickster tale in which the stepmother reader, ironically both Cinderella and Snow-White's stepmother, becomes ensnared in the story and, eventually, poisoned by it. In "Amalia," an albino-like child as fragile as her wax bride doll symbolizes inbred, protected daughters of aristocracy, who must stay in their boxes, in the house and out of the sun, forbidden gardens, and their own forbidden internal rooms, to guard white skin and clothing. Although protagonists of "The Poisoned Story" and "Amalia" both die, their lives not only revision that of the folk and fairy-tale characters they suggest but also stimulate readers to critique the gender and cultural roles that trap them.

Chapter 7, "Enchantment, Transformation, and Rebirth in Iris Murdoch's *The Green Knight*," discusses the Irish writer, Iris Murdoch, and her postmodern use of myth and fairy-tale intertexts in this largely ignored work. In *The Green Knight*, the most evident mythological references are to the anonymous medieval romance, "Sir Gawain and the Green Knight"; to the Green Knight myth; to the earlier, associated pagan myth of the Green Man, often a mask of a leafy man's face; and to the also earlier Great Goddess myths on which the other stories appear to be based. "Sleeping Beauty," "Hansel and Gretel," "Rapunzel," and "Beauty and the Beast" fairy tales are also significant. Characteristic of Murdoch's tricky postmodern comedy, parody, irony, and frequent intertextual reversals, the preeminent "green man" in this book is a green woman. Many of the characters experience a rebirth similar to that of the Green Knight, the Green Man, and the fairy-tale characters the novel suggests and reverses.

Chapter 8, "Bluebeard's Forbidden Room in Rhys's *Wide Sargasso Sea*," again focuses on the sexual politics of literary texts and intertexts. In the Caribbean novel, *Wide Sargasso Sea* (1966), Jean Rhys foregrounds subversive fairy-tale elements in the novel's main intertext, Charlotte Bronte's *Jane Eyre*. While sometimes taken as a "Cinderella" story, *Jane Eyre* also shows "Cinderella's" shadow side, the "Blue Beard" (Perrault) or "Fitcher's Bird" story about brides dismembered for opening the door to the forbidden room, in this case both Rochester's past and the place where his Jamaican first wife, Bertha, is locked up. Blending biblical and obeah (voo doo) stories with "Snow White," "Sleeping Beauty," "Rapunzel," both Caribbean and European "Bluebeard" tales, and *Jane Eyre, Wide Sargasso Sea* critiques national, gender, racial, and cultural colonization and anticipates a world beyond colonization.

Chapter 9, "Fairy Tales and Myth in Keri Hulme's *The Bone People*," is about one of the writers of the New Zealand Maori Renaissance, Keri Hulme, who integrates multicultural folklore in *The Bone People* (1984). This apocalyptic and utopian metafiction revises fairy-tale and mythic intertexts to create a vision of a new family and a new beginning for humanity, thus realizing Homi Bhabha's conception of hybridization. Embedding and intertwining Maori, Goddess, Fisher King, Grail, Buddhist, Sufi, and Christian myth (especially creation myth), the "Rapunzel" fairy tale and Syndrome, and fish, hook, stone, spider, web, spiral, maze, crucifix, rosary, phoenix, whirling dervish, Aikido, I-Ching, Yarrowsticks, and Tarot images in a multicultural text that uses both English and Maori languages, she opposes and then synthesizes and hybridizes eastern, Maori, and western religion, folklore, and literary traditions.

CHAPTER 1

MARGARET ATWOOD'S MONSTROUS, DISMEMBERED, CANNIBALIZED, AND (SOMETIMES) REBORN FEMALE BODIES: *THE ROBBER BRIDE* AND OTHER TEXTS

Margaret Atwood, the Canadian novelist, poet, short fiction writer, critic, and children's writer, has written over forty books, been published in over thirty-five countries, received the Booker and Trilium Prizes and the Governor General's award, and even been nominated for the Nobel Prize. Among other themes, her works depict the theme of sexual politics, the political aspects of sexual relationships; and frequently this sex and gender war is fought in the female body and is depicted in myth and fairy-tale intertexts.

Trussed in girdles, overweight, anorexic, aging, symbolically missing heads, feet, hands, ears, noses, mouths, hearts, or breasts or owned by the state, Margaret Atwood's female bodies are controlled and uncomfortable through most of their stories. Conditioned to conform to gender, class, cultural, and social expectations of the past, present, future, often by their internalization of popularized fairy tales and myths, these bodies feel fragmented, silenced, and trapped as they are subjected to both patriarchal and "friendly" gazes. Virtually all Atwood protagonists

suffer "bodily harm." Symbolically dismembered and cannibalized in a phallocentric civilization worshipping what Riane Eisler calls the dominator blade rather than the life-generating chalice (xvii), Atwood's artists, and through them their readers, typically face "massive involvement" (*Bodily Harm* 296) within their own bodies as well as in the body politic. (S. Wilson, "Atwood's Intertextual" 55)

Even the titles of various Atwood texts suggest the body's dis-ease in hostile environments: *The Edible Woman, Bodily Harm, Murder in the Dark*. Atwood's visual art, often designed as an illustration or book cover, includes watercolors of a beheaded Anne Bolyn or Mary Queen of Scots, a bride of Fitcher or Bluebeard, a pregnant termite queen, both black and white Eve/ Persephone snakes, a bound concubine, a woman pushing up from underground, a drowned woman, an angel, several harpies, and a comic strip Survival Woman (S. Wilson, *Margaret Atwood's Fairy* chap. 2). Atwood uses intertexts drawn from both popular and high culture, including early Christianity,[1] the film, literature, opera, ballet, visual art, and especially mythology and fairy tales that portray literal and symbolic dismemberment. Her images of women's bodies both illustrate and critique gender, social, and cultural values in what Susan Bordo calls a global "empire of images" without protective borders (1). Nevertheless, like many of Atwood's intertexts, her works also imply hope for regeneration.

An Overview of Atwood's Use of Fairy Tales and Myths

As feminist theorists including Laura Mulvey and Helene Cixous suggest, the patriarchal gaze can be objectifying, dismembering, and silencing, and Margaret Atwood's females often feel victimized by the patriarchal camera-guns Susan Sontag names (14–15). At the same time, Atwood's female characters must also endure gazes of admiration, envy, resentment, and active malevolence from girls and women often collusive with patriarchal power, as in *The Handmaid's Tale* (1985) and *Cat's Eye* (1988). Like the other writers discussed here, Atwood has used fairy-tale, mythic, and other folklore intertexts to dramatize women's feelings of being monstrous, dismembered, and cannibalized, and she has done so throughout her work. Thus, an investigation of Atwood's fairy-tale and myth intertexts constitutes an investigation of how these intertexts function in the works of many contemporary women writers. Under the surveillance of the office virgins and a society pressuring women to marry, Marian of *The Edible Woman* (1969) finds it necessary to hide amid dust balls under a bed, engineering an Alice in Wonderland descent to an underworld.

As Peter asks Marian to marry him, she feels like one of the animals he kills as she is trapped in headlights, and later, when her head is decorated like a cake and she pretends to be a doll, she imagines him as a Bluebeard or Robber Bridegroom chef sharpening a knife to eat her. Marian has been "fed on 'fantasies of rearranging, transforming, and correcting, limitless improvement and change, defying the historicity, the mortality, and indeed, the very materiality of the body' " (Bordo 2). Thus, even her friend Clara's pregnant body seems monstrous, and Marian finds herself unable to eat until she serves a substitute cake woman to both Peter and her baby bear friend, Duncan. The unnamed Persephone goddess narrator of *Surfacing* (1972), on a quest for both father and mother (who have respectively transformed into a werewolf and a jay), ironically goes with men who photo-shoot dressed up moose and the nude body of one's wife for a film they call "*Random Samples.*" The fairy-tale illustrator of "The Golden Phoenix" who was told that there have never been real women artists,, she has colluded in her own dehumanization and lied to herself so long that she must symbolically drown her body in a lake. Living like an animal and waiting for fur to grow, she hopes that she will bear the first true human being.

Internalized cultural conditioning makes Atwood's ordinary females often seem both monstrous and naive. Joan Foster of *Lady Oracle* is one of Atwood's many parodic goddesses and footless dancers in the Red Shoes that all women wear (see chap. 6). Wanting to write *AND* marry, she suffers from an eating disorder and has so many identities that she must also symbolically drown one of them. As a child, Joan wants to be a ballerina, like Moira Shearer, but is cast as an enraged mothball because she is overweight. She has to confront not only her mother's three heads and double mouth but also her own identity as circus fat lady to release herself from the Bluebeards she creates in her internal maze. Characters in *Life Before Man* (1976) feel their bodies being sucked into a void or the past and stretched between two houses. They attempt to survive by wearing camouflage, covering their mouths with their hands, and hoping for someone to give them salvation. Embedding a *Wizard of Oz* intertext, *Life Before Man* has not only its tin man, scarecrow, and two cowardly lions but also a yellow brick road, headless wizard, camouflaged Dorothy, wicked witch, and internal tornados as well. Before these characters can enter a Technicolor reality and go home, they must leave dinosaur prehistory and glass museum cases and fully inhabit their bodies (see S. Wilson, *Margaret Atwood's Fairy* 165–97).

Rennie Wilford of *Bodily Harm* (1981) is one of many Atwood characters married to death in a world body that matches her own cancerous one. She works for *Pandora* magazine, likes to read thrillers and play Clue, and undergoes strangely equivalent bodily harms: bondage games, a break-in, a mastectomy, and incarceration in a Caribbean revolution. The Grimms' "The Robber Bridegroom" intertext provides the basis both for the symbolic cannibalism and dismemberment she suffers as well as for her eventual ability to speak out about bodily violations, with implications for pornography, feminism, and human rights.

Nowhere in Atwood's texts are women's bodies as controlled as in the dystopian *The Handmaid's Tale* (1985), where the patriarchal, theocratic government color-codes, brands, shocks with cattle prods, and forces women to breed, shovel toxic wastes, or be prostitutes, servants, or, ironically, "wives," now officially confined to the home. This novel's "Little Red Riding Hood," Mother Goddess, and biblical Bilhah is reduced to a womb that must endure pseudo-religious "Ceremonies": the Commander's legalized rape, in order for her to bear a baby or die. Because Offred, like the Robber Bride, finds her voice, supposedly tape-recorded over music, she tells her story and the Gileadean regime dies. In *Cat's Eye* (1988), Elaine becomes both Andersen's Snow Queen and the Grimms' Rapunzel, frozen in a distant tower, after her supposed friends briefly bury her in the ground and she completely loses that time. A magical cat's eye marble, hidden for years in a red plastic purse, and a vision of the Virgin Mary/ Great Goddess help her to heal her internal split.

Atwood's "The Female Body" and its companion piece, "Alien Territory," were written for Female and Male Body issues of *Michigan Quarterly Review* and satirize gender scripts inherited from fairy tales and myth ("Rapunzel," "Fitcher's Bird," Aphrodite), the Bible, literature, and our new mythology: advertising. Also in the volume of flash fictions called *Good Bones* (1992), "The Female Body" presents the female body equipped with fichu, modesty panel, and a head as accessories. "The female body can be a doorknocker or something to hold up lampshades" (also *Bodily Harm*); it sells and is sold. (43). Atwood's illustration for this story in *Good Bones and Simple Murders* suggests an infinite regress of pregnant Pumpkin Women (70), from the nursery rime "Peter, Peter, Pumpkin Eater." If the connections between the two halves of the female brain mean that women listen in to their internal conversations, the brains of men contribute to their mythologizing of the female body, which thus must be trapped, leashed, and chained (S. Wilson, "Fiction Flashes" 32).

The Robber Bride (1993), discussed in the second section of this chapter, typifies Atwood's use of intertexts to show body politics. In this novel, fairy-tale and mythic intertexts parodically pair real bodies with mythic ones, including a full-breasted Minoan snake goddess, Cinderella, Little Red Riding Hood and the Wolf, Frankenstein, Dracula, the Mummy, Jezebel, Nancy Drew, and even the Three Pigs. Real bodies again experience bodily harm: Both ample and petite bodies are symbolically eaten, dismembered, sold, bartered, lost, raped, injured, or killed in wars, denied or filled with food, enhanced with cosmetic surgery, camouflaged, or displayed as commodities in expensive or bargain clothing, desired, envied, despised, abandoned for a spiritual realm, and split in two. The Grimms' fairy tales, "The Robber Bridegroom" and the closely related "Fitcher's Bird" and "Bluebeard," are the primary intertexts; thus, *The Robber Bride* again depicts the fairy-tale dismemberment and cannibalism as well as the "magical" healing that most of Atwood's characters experience.

Grace of *Alias Grace* (1996), based on a real nineteenth-century woman found guilty of murder and literally incarcerated, is, like her psychoanalyst Simon Jordan, a Fitcher or Robber's Bride at the same time as she is the Fitcher and Robber. She is simultaneously seen as a seductive monster, an innocent victim too beautiful to be evil, a sly cat, and a sick person with multiple personality disorder. Wanting to be a lady but subjected to daily physical and mental proddings first as maid and then as prisoner, Grace is more aware of sexual and body politics than many of Atwood's characters. She capitalizes upon her body and the system by playing upon contradictory nineteenth-century stereotypes of women and thus prospering.

The Blind Assassin (2000), Atwood's novel-within-a-novel-within-a-novel, focuses on women's violated, beaten, displayed, impregnated, adulterous, sacrificed, and aging bodies in three dimensions of fiction. It is no accident that a Medusa rules Iris's Tennysonian family estate, Avilion, and that she is likened to various other mythical and fairy-tale characters, including Sleeping Beauty, the Girl Without Hands, Little Red-Cap, Cinderella, Rapunzel, Gretel, Fitcher's Bird, Persephone (Jones 56; BA 417), and especially the mythic Iris. Like Daedalus, Iris is lost in a maze for much of the book.

The novel is narrated by an eighty-nine-year-old woman looking back on the personal and political assassinations of World Wars I and II, and the following years as she writes her personal memoir. Iris also embeds a novel about an affair between unnamed characters who resemble her and Alex and a science fiction story based on pulp comics of the 1930s and 1940s featuring blonde, buxom females being menaced by creatures from another planet. Essentially sold to her much older husband and later beaten by him as he molests her younger sister,

Iris is asleep and frozen in the patriarchal gaze of men with burning heads. Fragmented in her identities as daughter, sister, wife, mother, and lover, her touch is symbolically amputated. In Sakiel-Norn as well as upper-class Port Ticonderoga, "blind assassins" turn "sleeping beauties" into passive, mute, handless maidens (the Grimms' "The Girl Without Hands") incapable of touch or action. The novel's central images are photographs of two sisters' creeping, cut-off hands and the steamer trunk that is this novel's forbidden room. Iris's nameless mother, awarded to a maimed war hero, dies after giving birth to a stillborn child. Laura, this novel's Dido, symbolically sacrifices herself on a burning pyre: White-gloved, she deliberately drives off a bridge because her mute acceptance of rape and abortion has not saved the life of the man she loves (Aeneas/ Alex). Also trying to be an angel but becoming another "assassin," Iris achieves eyes as dead as the glass ones of her fox fur piece. Like the Grimms' Robber Bride and Offred of *The Handmaid's Tale,* Iris regains her hands and vision by telling her story and leaving a steamer trunk of words.

In Atwood's recent and alarming novel, *Oryx and Crake* (2003) (see chapter 2), most reviewers overlook the extent to which body politics contributes to the human folly depicted in this book. As most noticeably in *Life Before Man, The Handmaid's Tale, The Robber Bride,* and *The Blind Assassin,* male as well as female bodies are in jeopardy. In their childhood and adolescence, Jimmy and Crake, this novel's Fitchers, Robbers, and Frankensteins, spend much of their time on pornographic Web sites that commodify women's and sometimes men's bodies. The futuristic society that only slightly exaggerates ours uses not only collagen injections but also NooSkins Beau Toxique Treatment to paralyze wrinkles forever and the Fountain of Youth Total Plunge (175) in the attempt to attain eternal youth and beauty, ensuring sexual attractiveness. Because obsessive sexual activity produces overpopulation, it is no accident that a product called BlyssPluss, providing unlimited libido and sexual prowess and protecting against sexually transmitted diseases, is used to sterilize people without their knowing it and, incidentally, infect them with the virus that may make the human species extinct.

If not for Atwood's newest novel, *The Penelopeiad* (2005) (see chapter 3), we would wonder if Atwood's work, as filled with puns, wordplay, and comic irony as ever, is growing more pessimistic about the fate of human bodies. The suitors call Penelope an old bitch and an old cow, and she is jealous of her cousin Helen's beauty. Re-visioning the Penelope-Odysseus myth and now without a body, Penelope still talks back to both canon and culture that continue to expect men to be waylaid by beautiful goddesses but value women only to the extent that they are beautiful. Not one of Atwood's monstrous, dismembered, and cannibalized bodies, Penelope survives over centuries to critique the empire of body images.

The Grimms' "The Robber Bridegroom" in *The Robber Bride*

Astonishingly, no one has thoroughly explored Margaret Atwood's use of "The Robber Bridegroom" fairy tale in her novel, *The Robber Bride*, whose name slightly amends the title of the tale by reversing the gender of the Robber. Despite clear references to the Triple Goddess myth that is also rarely discussed, "myth" tends to be viewed reductively as escapist from real-life concerns when "we are not yet capable of facing life without magical intervention" (Murray 72–73, 87). As we have seen, Margaret Atwood has used folklore and mythic intertexts throughout her works, including her poetry and visual art; and she presents some of the same themes and intertexts as Toni Morrison and Rosario Ferre do, often in a more comic vein. On a symbolic level, all the characters in *The Robber Bride* are potentially or actually the Robber of life depicted in the Grimms' fairy tale, "The Robber Bridegroom"; they may also be the Robber's victims. Despite differing intentions and illusions, all are "children" of the violence that has characterized human history. As participants in the imperialistic games of power and sexual politics, they are "at war"; in other words, they are what currently passes for human. Thus, the novel operates on personal, national, and global levels. Deconstructing the Grimms' "The Robber Bridegroom" and any simplistic division between robbers and victims, *The Robber Bride* is simultaneously a feminist, a postmodern, and a postcolonial metafairy tale. Also an anti–fairy tale, *The Robber Bride* not only presents multiple versions of reality but also focuses our attention on fairy tale, myth, literature, this book, and all stories, including those we call order, reality, culture, gender, and identity. *The Robber Bride* exposes colonialist constructions of identity, reality, culture, and order.

In addition to the Grimms' "The Robber Bridegroom," some fairy-tale intertexts Atwood has frequently used in other works also recur: the Grimms' "Fitcher's Bird" (Perrault's "Blue Beard"), "Cinderella," "The Girl Without Hands," "Little Briar-Rose" (Perrault's "Sleeping Beauty in the Woods"), "Little Snow White," "Little Red-Cap," "Rapunzel," "Hansel and Gretel," "The Water of Life" (Youth), and "The Wolf and the Seven Little Kids"; and Andersen's "The Red Shoes." The Robber Girl of Andersen's "The Snow Queen," who sets her reindeer free so that they can carry Gerda to Lapland to rescue Kay (*Complete* 67–69), is probably also an inspiration for the gender reversal in Atwood's book. Another major intertext in *The Robber Bride* is the Great Goddess myth, including the three moon phases corresponding to Diana, Venus, and Hecate; the Minoan snake goddess; Medusa; Lamia; and Isis-Osiris-Horus and the servant Kharis.[2] The epigraphs from Jessamyn West, Gunter Grass, and Oscar Wilde; the Beatrix Potter quotation on the original typescript of the novel;[3] and sources, anecdotes, stories, and texts mentioned in the acknowledgements, including James Reaney's "Doomsday, or the Red-Headed Woodpecker," are also important.

Intertexts and allusions identified by critics also function in the novel. As Jacobsen points out, the novel uses such popular culture texts as the folk song "Pop Goes the Weasel," the Avalon myth, the tales of E.T.A. Hoffman, and Offenbach's opera *Tales of Hoffman*. McCombs finds sources in Baum's *The Wizard of Oz,* astrology, numerology, Tarot cards, puzzles, and games. Davidson notes the importance of the song "Clementine" and medieval Ouroboros structure (n.p.); and Potts suggests that the book uses a soap opera plot, comic books, Graves's *The White Goddess,* Euripedes' *The Trojan Women,* Sophocles' *Andromache,* Fisher King legend, "Jack and the Beanstalk," murder mysteries, and horror movies as intertexts ("The White Goddess" 230; "The Old Maps" 283). Jennifer Murray overlooks "The Robber Bridegroom" but mentions "The Three Little Pigs" as a fairy tale (77–78). Since Atwood parodied Harlequin romances in *Lady Oracle,* we might suspect the same in *The Robber Bride;* it is worth noting that since Atwood's *The Robber Bride* appeared, Harlequin Historical Series, No. 455 (1999), features an identical title by Deborah Simmons. Like fellow Canadians Robert Kroetsch, Jack Hodgins, and Michael Ondaatje and Lessing, Morrison, Ferre, Erdrich, Murdoch, Rhys, and Hulme, Atwood uses intertexts that highlight her magical realism. In this and other novels, Atwood creates magical realism by inserting trickster figures, shape changers, demonic revenants, witches, devils, vampires, a potent underworld, real or inverted quests, and actual colonialist history into believable situations.

By focusing on the character Xenia as the villain and restricting Tony, Charis, and Roz to the roles of victims, many readers of Margaret Atwood's *The Robber Bride* (1993) have missed the ironies and paradoxes of Atwood's postmodern and postcolonial metafairy tale. The extent to which patriarchal imperialism is again the setting for the foregrounded "female" evil has been overlooked. Like *Cat's Eye,* Atwood's novel has even been labeled postfeminist or antifeminist.

Reacting against some women's demand for exclusively positive female role models, Atwood definitively reestablishes the efficacy—and eternal appeal—of Lady McBeths (see Atwood, "Margaret Atwood's Address" 11). As in the other poems and novels in which she uses folk, fairy-tale, and mythic intertexts, however, matters are far from this simple. *The Robber Bride* typifies Atwood's use of fairy-tale and mythic intertexts to show power, sexual, and body politics. Exaggerating some readers' expectations of current fiction through the twins, Paula and Erin, Atwood demonstrates not only that females can play every role in a story (see Atwood, "Margaret" 11), but that this story can question all the old stories and any simplistic conceptions of fiction, feminist fiction, characterization, villain, hero, innocence, or guilt.

Resembling the Quebec writers Marie-Claire Blais and Anne Hebert as well as the Puerto Rican Rosario Ferre, Dominican Jean Rhys, African American Toni Morrison, Native American Louise Erdrich, and New Zealand Maori Keri Hulme, in this and other texts Atwood critiques her culture's values, including colonialist, nationalistic, classist, sexist, racist, and literary biases, by re-visioning fairy tales and myths. Although, like these writers, she is criticized for doing so, Atwood also uses postmodern techniques such as magical realism, intertextuality, and self-reflexiveness that have been mistakenly identified with antifeminist, western, imperialistic, or apolitical literature. Postcolonial aspects of *The Robber Bride* have received even less attention than the novel's postmodernism. Since 1995, when I first discussed the novel as postcolonial,[4] only a few critics, including Donna Potts, Shannon Hengen, and Coral Ann Howells, have briefly pursued this topic.

Gayle Greene finds the recent fiction of Atwood, Lessing, and Drabble "postfeminist" in severing the personal from the political and in no longer envisioning writing as re-vision (*Changing* 27); and Shannon Hengen, unconvincingly defining postfeminist to include postmodernism, postcolonialism, and postimperialism (275), also speaks of *The Robber Bride* as postfeminist. Neither feminism nor feminist fiction seems as dead as the term would imply, however, and as we begin to see, writers demonstrate the compatibility of each of these isms. Bouson thinks that in this novel Atwood critiques what Naomi Wolf calls "victim feminism," mistakenly identified with radical feminism (149n1). Despite the popularity of Wolf's blasts among those who fear feminism, Atwood's unreliable narrators are not feminists, and the principal perpetrators of views that women are passive victims still seem to be nonfeminists. Some readers might insist that this Atwood novel portrays stereotypes, such as a beautiful but ruthless female villain modeled on the Snow Queen or Snow White's mother, in addition to helpless female victims. Instead, *The Robber Bride* challenges conventional views of gender, gender roles, and feminism in fairy tales, literature, and popular culture with her intertextual tactics. Reversing the expectation that men are the robbers and that a female villain must be entirely evil, on one level Atwood's novel seems to reverse the frequent commodification of women by commodifying men. Using developing narrators to reduce most of the men's roles to the status of plunder or loot, however, forces us to rethink oversimplified conceptions of power politics. Critiquing the institution of patriarchy that victimizes males as well as females, the novel deconstructs any easy line we might draw between victors and victims or winners and losers. *The Robber Bride* neither calls upon male saviors nor allows us to settle for a traditional resolution: Instead, as Tony the military historian says, "the end is where you . . . see through, to the other side, to the beginning of something else. . . . The end of any history is a lie in which we all agree to conspire" (540). The female voices—unreliable narrators— that might customarily have been silenced in a traditional, third-person fairy tale, such as the Grimms' "The Girl Without Hands," instead narrate Atwood's feminist metafairy tale. *The Robber Bride* revisions the Grimms' tale, Triple Goddess myth, sexual politics, patriarchal parameters of women's relationships, socialized gender roles, the heterosexual romance story, and traditional narrative structure.

In terms of other intertextual tactics, *The Robber Bride* builds scenes of cannibalism on the Robber's eating of the maiden; uses basin of blood symbolism to suggest war and imperialism; opens the resolution to question whether the characters and their society will continue to be Robbers and victims; blends comic and tragic tones and realistic and fabulist genres; uses irony as a subversive antipatriarchal and anti-colonialist discourse; uses language to parody consumerism and imperialism; revises the ideology of an intertext such as "The Three Pigs" in a transition toward the postcolonial; transgresses conventions to tell an unexpected story; engages readers in joint creation of the text; and remythifies intertexts, such as the Great Goddess one, distorted or amputated by colonization, racism, and patriarchy, to potentially heal societies.

The Grimms' "The Robber Bridegroom" ("Der Rauberbrautigam," AT 955),[5] first published in 1812, is one of many Grimms' tales that use Marie Hassenpflug as a source (Zipes, *Complete* 717). The tale is about a maiden who does not trust or love her prospective husband "the way a bride-to-be should" but feels "a secret horror" and "shudder[s] in her heart" when thinking about him. He insists she visit him and his guests on Sunday in the dark forest, where he will scatter ashes. Feeling uneasy, she marks her way with peas and lentils (Motif R145). When she reaches the dark and solitary house, it is "deadly silent" until a voice cries twice: "Turn back, turn back, young maiden dear,/ 'Tis a murderer's house you enter here." The voice comes from a bird in a cage; otherwise, the house seems entirely empty as the maiden proceeds from room to room, coming at last to the cellar, where an extremely old woman, whose head bobs constantly, again tells her she is in a murderer's den: "You think you are a bride soon to be married, but you will keep your wedding with death." A kettle of water is on the fire: "When they have you in their power, they'll chop you to pieces without mercy. Then they'll cook you and eat you, because they're cannibals. If I don't take pity on you and save you, you'll be lost forever" (Hunt and Stern 200–201; Magoun and Krappe 151–52; Zipes, *Complete* 153–55).

The maiden then hides behind a barrel, where she is told not to budge or move, just before the godless robbers return. They are dragging another maiden, whose heart bursts in two after she is forced to drink three glasses of wine: one white, one red, and one yellow (Motif F1041.1.1). The prospective bride realizes the fate planned for her as the victim is chopped into pieces and salted. The hiding maiden is almost discovered when the victim's chopped-off finger (sometimes hand) springs into the air, falling into her lap (in some versions, bosom); but the old woman calls the robbers to dinner and drugs their wine. Both women escape, following the sprouted peas and lentils home, where the maiden tells her father, the miller, everything (Hunt and Stern 201–2; Magoun and Krappe 152–53; Zipes, *Complete* 155–56).

On the day of the wedding celebration, the bridegroom appears with all the miller's friends, and each person is expected to tell a story. When the bride sits still and does not utter a word, the bridegroom says, "Come, my darling, do you know nothing?" She then relates a "dream," finally presenting the victim's chopped-off finger (Motif H57.2.2.). Because the bride speaks, the Robber Bridegroom is executed: it is the groom, not the bride, who marries death.[6] Tales closely related to "The Robber Bridegroom" have similar events. The ancient Greek version of "Fitcher's Bird" features a corpse-devouring death as the murderous husband (Leach and Fried 150); "The Castle of Murder" includes the old woman in the cellar, edible victims, and the tale-telling trap (Zipes, *Complete* 670–71); and "Mr. Fox" features the warning, a woman's severed hand, the Bloody Chamber of "Fitcher's Bird," the bride's tale, and a cut-up groom.[7]

The "Robber Bridegroom" and related motifs, many gender-reversed, figure prominently in *The Robber Bride,* operating simultaneously on personal, national, and global levels and influencing plot, structure, characterization, themes, images, and motifs. Instead of explicit fear of marrying a cannibal (Motifs K1916, G81) and being chopped up and eaten, in this novel the fear is that the robber-cannibal will rob and eat the spouse victim and, quite possibly, the woman from whom he is stolen as well. Not until the end of the book do the other potential robbers, who have felt like robbed victims, recognize their, their country's, and all human beings' capacities for and complicity in colonizing, carnage, and cannibalism. Most scholars and reviewers either ignore the fairy tale entirely (Zimmerman, Hengen, Miller), think that it functions minimally in the novel, primarily in the title "The Robber Bridegroom" chapter or the parodic presentation of males victimized by a female, or think that, primarily, "it adopts the tale's technique of a female victim narrating her story of victimization in retrospect."[8] Rarely do they explore the Robber Bride of the fairy tale as a cunning survivor rather than a victim, or the tale's important connections to the novel, especially its theme of surviving by telling the story. As I established elsewhere, fairy-tale intertexts are much more than allusions in Atwood's texts: "frame narratives echo inner narratives' images, motifs, themes, characterization, structures, and even plots, self-consciously reflecting, and reflecting upon, intertexts" (S. Wilson, *Margaret Atwood's Fairy* 3–4). Bontatibus offers an interesting reading of the tales in the novel through Estes's Jungian analysis but does not address specifics of the intertexts, Atwood's postmodern parody and irony, or her postcolonial uses of them (3, 6). Both the fairy tale and book feature distrust of the robber, path-marking on a journey (Motif R145), a visit to the robber's home, unheeded warning, hiding, passivity, consumption of beverages, heartbreak, amputation or dismemberment, communal eating of precious food, assistance of an elderly "godmother," return to society, communal telling of the crime, presentation of an emblem representing the victim, and, finally, communal punishment/ retribution. Dramatized through split, unreliable narration, most of these motifs occur comically in *The Robber Bride.* The novel also features or parodies motifs from "Fitcher's Bird," the Bluebeard tale about another dismembering groom and the curious "bird" who outwits him: disguise, enslaving touch, falling into an ogre's power (Motif G400), abduction by a monster (Motif R11.1), test-orders, a mysterious door, a forbidden chamber (Motif C611), dismembered bodies, eggs, a stain or mark, power reversal, a decorated substitute (Motifs K525, K521.1), the victims' remembering and rebirth (Motif E30), revenge or punishment of the "murderer" (Motif Q211), and restoration of community.

Patriarchal sexual politics is evident in virtually every scene of *The Robber Bride* and constitutes the main cause of imperialistic "war" on the personal level and in most of the intertexts it embeds. Like the Grimms' closely related "Fitcher's Bird" (Perrault's "Blue Beard") with which Atwood associates "The Robber Bridegroom," their "The Robber Bridegroom" (Motif K1916) is on one level a gender-specific Bluebeard story about marriage as female heartbreak, dismemberment, cannibalism, and death. As we have partly seen, Atwood has used this fairy tale as an intertext in *The Edible Woman,* in *Bodily Harm* (Col. 200, Box 33, BH drafts, Margaret Atwood Papers), and in both a published and an unpublished poem for *Interlunar.* She has used "Fitcher's Bird" in the watercolor reproduced on the cover of this book, *Power Politics, Bluebeard's Egg,* and in connection with "The Robber Bridegroom" in *The Blind Assassin, Oryx and Crake,* and many other works (see S. Wilson, *Margaret Atwood's Fairy*).

"The Robber Bridegroom" is about a person who chops up and eats prospective spouses, the woman in "the cellar" who knows and warns, and the woman who witnesses and tells the story of his crime. On one level, the tale implies that women should listen to their instincts, help one another, and speak out against gender oppression. Conversely, men should be careful about what they do to women, especially regarding unnatural "tastes," lest they be the ones who will marry death. Significantly, not just one man but his whole band and all his kinsmen are implicated, and the woman's relatives are similarly involved. Thus, the tale dramatizes survival problems in a cannibalistic, colonialistic world. Margaret Atwood's revised metafairy tale is also about postcolonial survival.

As in other narratives, character roles in fairy tales and myths are both doubled and foiled and often archetypal. In the Grimms' tales "The Robber Bridegroom" and "Fitcher's Bird," there is both a Robber or a Fitcher and, although she is never called this, his opposite, a Robber or a Fitcher's Bride. In reference to these tales, the title of *The Robber Bride* can refer to a female who takes the "male" role in the tales, symbolically dismembering or cannibalizing her opposite. As the title of Atwood's novel, *The Robber Bride* can also refer to the female, such as Tony—or, theoretically, the male[9]—who is smart enough to mark the path with images of life, listens to the symbolic person in the cellar, escapes from the patriarchal or colonialist Robber's den, and breaks the silence to speak for previous victims by telling her or his own story. As Fitcher's Bride, the person who outwits the Bluebeard figure, such an Atwood character is able to open the forbidden door to knowledge about self and the Other, rejoin the pieces of her sisters, and bring them back to life. Like Zenia, she escapes Bluebeard's castle by disguising herself and leaving a substitute image. In the tales, both the Robber and Fitcher die with their kinsmen in their patriarchal houses. If women can be Robbers or killers, by implication, men, too, might choose the role of the clever Bride. Atwood suggests that as long as female and male play games of sexual and colonial politics, as long as people of either sex choose to remain at war, both Robber Bride and Groom play predictable and interchangeable roles in narratives leading to death. Although Atwood's characterization is as archetypal as in the Grimms' tales and myths, she simultaneously uses and deconstructs not only the tales but also traditional narrative structure, social myth, gender roles, and readers' expectations of novels, fairy tales, history, and reality. Like Morrison and Hulme, she implies that we can construct a better future.

"Fitcher's Bird" and the Parodic Great Goddess

Initially obsessed with holding onto the men in their lives, the three main characters, Tony, Charis, and Roz, choose to see both these men and themselves as innocent and passive victims of a female monster, cannibalistic as in "The Robber Bridegroom" and some versions of the Bluebeard cycle, and darkly powerful, like the old moon aspect of the Great Goddess. Ironically, what mainly makes Zenia monstrous is an ability to appropriate and hold onto men who "belong" to someone else. In short, she is a sexual colonizer. Like the Wizard of "Fitcher's Bird," who is able to get maidens to jump into his basket when he appears (see chapter 2), Zenia seems irresistible. We first see her reflected in a smoky mirror at the Toxique, supposedly returned from the dead:

She looks, as always, like a photo, a high-fashion photo done with hot light so that all freckles and wrinkles are bleached out and only the basic features remain: in her case, the full red-purple mouth, disdainful and sad; the huge deep eyes. The finely arched eyebrows, the high cheekbones tinged with terracotta. And her hair, a dense cloud of it, blown around her head by the imperceptible wind that accompanies her everywhere, molding her clothes against her body, fitfully moving the dark tendrils around her forehead, filling the air near her with the sound of rustling. In the midst of this unseen commotion she sits unmoving, as if she were carved. Waves of ill will flow out of her like cosmic radiation. Or this is what Tony sees. It's an exaggeration, of course; it's overdone. But these are the emotions that Zenia mostly inspires: overdone emotions. (38–39)

Zenia's body is, as Atwood discusses in two interviews, an advertising illusion, constructed in Tony's and other women's minds as what they not only would like to be but also assume they should be ("Margaret Atwood," Ovation). In this sense, she is the debased, ironic goddess of consumerism as well as the Great Goddess.

If you look at the pictures of women that you get in women's magazines, these are obviously dream figures. They are presented as archetypes. . . . [Zenia] is a shadow for the women and an anima for the men. So, she is an aspect of each of the three women. . . . There are three women and each of the women has at least one other self. . . . Zenia has three manifestations. So, that all adds up to nine and nine is the Great Goddess number. . . . You could say that Shanita, the grandmother and Zenia form another triad. ("You Can't Do Without" 208–10)

Like Jimmy and Crake of *Oryx and Crake,* Zenia is both Frankenstein and the monster (Atwood, "You Can't Do Without" 211). Because she is also a symbolic and parodic vampire, illustrated in the cannibalistic passages suggesting the Robber Bridegroom, she possesses the potential for resurrection (Atwood and Beaulieu 96), another goddess attribute.

By comparison, Tony, Charis, and Roz, who all have more than one name and suggest parodic aspects of each phase of the Great Goddess cycle, find their bodies inadequate. Although Tony is a bright academic, a military historian who ironically publishes articles on how different underwear might have affected the outcomes of war, and although she buys her own clothes in the children's section of Eaton's Department store, when she compares herself to Zenia, she still feels frightened and, like Roz and Charis, "sick of [her]self"(39). The intelligent head of this trinity, Tony, as its tiniest member, might also suggest the Virgin or Maiden aspect of the goddess if we do not assume, as does Murray, that the Maiden represents a societal conception of beauty (79). Tony has mole-paw hands, tiny feet, and legs so short that she needs to use her tote bag as a footstool. But as these characters age, they live through each phase of the Great Goddess, even the dark one, and seem "reborn" by the end. Charis, the Spirit of the trinity, who could no longer be Karen after Uncle Vern's child abuse, is wearing a "sagging mauve cotton jersey dress, with a fuzzy

grey cardigan over the top" and, like the other characters, can be seen
as the entire cycle of Maiden, Mother, and Crone:

> Her long straight hair is grey-blonde and parted in the middle; she has her
> reading glasses stuck on top of her head. . . . She resembles a slightly faded
> advertisement for herbal shampoo—healthful, but verging on the antique.
> What Ophelia would have looked like if she had lived, or the Virgin Mary
> when middle-aged. (32)

Charis's naiveté regarding Billy's relationship with Zenia suggests the
Maiden, but she becomes the Mother, of August. In addition, Charis
has the Goddess's oracular powers. Since each of these characters denies responsibility for actions and somewhat humorously contem-
plates killing Zenia, each also has a Crone side. Roz's face, "plump,
with cushiony pink milkmaid's cheeks and dimples," does not go with
the expensive electric blue designer suit that she is packed into and
certainly suggests heart, body, and the nurturing Earth Goddess. But
in addition to her fury at Zenia, Roz chooses to abandon suicidal
Mitch. Although Charis feels Tony's body "is appropriate the way it
is," Roz suggests spike heels or a leg implant for Tony (33) and, like
the others, constantly feels guilty for not living up to societal images.
Using imagery from both "Fitcher's Bird" and revenant lore, Atwood
suggests that each of these characters has a flaw:

> A Zenia knocks on your door and you open it and she says, "Hello, I'm
> Zenia. I would like to come into your life and completely destroy it." You an-
> swer, "No, thank you, goodbye," and close the door. Those three women have
> a weakness in their character. Without this opening, Zenia would not have
> been able to get in. I had to construct each character so that there was a door
> in her character that opened up and let Zenia in. (Atwood and Beaulieu 90)

Zenia inflicts bodily harm mostly through the psychological and emotional games she plays with both male and female characters. As a
trickster magician with secrets, she holds others "in thrall" (187) and,
acting as a Dracula as well as Robber and Fitcher, literally robs the
women of both men and illusions. Tony is afraid that Zenia will leave
her as useless as an amputated hand and thinks she might be appeased
with Fitcher's bowl of blood (199, 15), and Charis feels as if Zenia
has "taken a chunk of Charis's own body and sucked it into herself"
(78). Roz speaks of Zenia only taking one bite out of West before she
throws him away (215). When Zenia tells Roz that she did not own
Mitch, that "He wasn't your God-given property," Roz replies: "But

that doesn't alter the fact that you ate him for breakfast" (510). Ironically, Mitch also took love bites out of the women with whom he had affairs (345, 347), and virtually every other character, including Roz, who becomes thirsty for Mitch's blood (436), is described as a Dracula or Robber cannibal. Even Charis thinks of slipping Zenia on like a flesh dress (463); and although her grandmother, another goddess figure, has healing hands, Charis pronounces her a killer when she decapitates chickens and serves the pet pig for dinner (288–89). Duped at least twice each by Zenia's contradictory life stories, Tony, Charis, and Roz cannot admit that much of what Zenia tells them about West, Billy, and Mitch may well be, if not "true," less fictional than their own self-serving versions of the men and their relationships with them. These supposedly independent women also find it painful to recognize the extent to which they have structured their lives for and around men and patriarchal game-playing.

Perhaps the most painful episode of symbolic dismemberment and cannibalism occurs when Uncle Vern rapes Charis, who at this point is named Karen.

Then he falls on top of Karen and puts his slabby hand over her mouth, and splits her in two. He splits her in two right up the middle and her skin comes open like the dry ski of a cocoon, and Charis flies out. . . . What she sees is a small pale girl, her face contorted and screaming, nose and eyes wet as if she is drowning—gasping for air, going under again, gasping. On top of her is a dark mass, worrying at her, like an animal eating another animal. (300–301)

As Dworkin suggests, "incest is increasingly the sadism of choice, the intercourse itself wounding the female child and socializing her to her female status"; incest victims frequently feel that they have been "split in two" (194). Clearly, the sexual and body politics of *The Robber Bride,* like those of other Atwood texts, transcend women victimizing men or men victimizing women: Atwood presents us with a world culture of dehumanizing violence. The Gulf War is the backdrop of the book, and, ironically staging battles with kitchen spices, Tony frequently recalls the dismemberments of historic battles. Robbers and Fitchers pervade personal, national, and global life.

In this novel, friendship, not heterosexual romance, emerges as the most meaningful personal relationship for the four main characters; and the "gender corral" enforcing traditional, heterosexual, male, and female roles is exposed as "rusty old wire" (528).[10] Ironically, friendship with other women seems to outlast sexual relationships even for Zenia, who quickly writes off Mitch, Billy, and West and asks for the help of Tony, Roz, and Charis. Although it is threatened in a society where women are expected to compete for a man, where their status depends on having one, and where they are supposed to do anything to gain or keep one, the novel ends not with marriage or a new man but with female friendship and Tony's recognition of Zenia as similar to themselves. Tony, Roz, and Charis help and genuinely care about one another. Figuratively, they play Fitcher's Bride and the Great Goddess, especially Isis, who puts the pieces of Osiris back together, by helping one another regenerate. Ironically, despite what Zenia has done to them, they are, as Charis says and West recognizes, her best friends. Although the narrators exist for the most part in separate narrative worlds, just once, in "The Toxique" chapter near the end of the novel, *The Robber Bride* surrealistically dramatizes the interpenetrating consciousnesses, memories, and dreams of Xenia, Charis, Roz, and Tony. Tony, like Charis, feels twinned and, like Zenia, experiences the marching boots of war horrors. Roz dreams she is wearing Tony's sailor dress, and Charis merges with Zenia, seeing herself with power.

In this re-visioning of socialized gender roles, of the Grimms' tales, and of the Great Goddess, Zenia, like the other characters, is more than a powerful Robber or Fitcher and more than a destroying goddess. Responding to suggestions for book club questions, Atwood suggests that Rider Haggard's *She,* featured in her uncompleted doctoral dissertation, might have been the inspiration for Zenia. She also queries whether women might have to "break the rules and operate as outlaws" in society as it is now constructed in order to exercise power and whether women have different kinds of power than men. If Zenia is a trickster, Atwood suggests that she is also a "messenger of the gods" (Margaret Atwood Papers, 26 Aug., 1993, fax to Marly Rusoff). Once called Zilla (RB Holograph, Box 131), Zenia is, in addition, a classic femme fatale, of the Lilith, Delilah, Salome, Siren, Medusa, Medea, and Morgan le Fay variety. Listing literary parallels in French, Atwood associates Zenia with Lady Macbeth, Keats's "La Belle Dame Sans Merci" and "Lamia," Coleridge's Geraldine, Tennyson's Vivian, Thackeray's Rebecca Sharpe, Stoker's Lucy, Wilde's Salome, and Pater's description of Mona Lisa.[11]

In Atwood's *The Robber Bride,* "the story of Zenia" that Tony thinks ought to begin long ago in a tangled undergrowth (3), all of the main female characters parodically and seriously play the Grimms' Robber Bride: All tell stories. As Tony recognizes at the end of the book, "That's what they will do, increasingly in their lives: tell stories" (546), for that is how human beings create patterns in existence. Charis, Roz, and Tony finally tell their stories in a way that rejoins the symbolically dismembered pieces of themselves and their lives; and the fourth character, Zenia, is both muse and subject of their stories. We do not hear Zenia's version of events because Zenia, as both the source and subject of stories—the Great Goddess in both creator and destroyer masks as well as the muse[12]—is Fitcher's forbidden room behind a door her victims open. Finally, Zenia is story, is, literally, body made text. She is also a metaphor for myth, magic, art, artifact, history, puzzle, and all human constructs.

When considering the Zenia-ness of Zenia in her final version of the Zenia story, Charis feels that she chose Zenia to teach her something. Now Charis, absolved and released from her past as segmented Karen/ Charis, is, like Zenia, falling into her own future with a daughter who has also renamed herself (524). Similarly, Roz, revising her story of Zenia to include Zenia's blackmailing of her son, Larry, also begins to foreground her present and future in preparing to accept Larry's gay relationship with Boyce.

It is Tony, the historian, who especially reaches feminist and postcolonial consciousness. She also voices this metafairy tale's postmodern view of reality and both a postmodern and postcolonial view of identity. Aware that Zenia "will only be history if Tony chooses to shape her into history" and that, like folklore, Zenia is "insubstantial, ownerless. . . . drifting from mouth to mouth and changing as it goes," Tony recognizes the impossibility, and futility, either of essentialist identity or of accurate reconstruction and, thus, the arbitrariness of an ending (535–36, 540). Nevertheless, like other Atwood creators, Tony persists in an act of defiance that creates meaning:

> these histories may be ragged and threadbare, patched together from worthless leftovers, but to her they are also flags, hoisted with a certain jaunty insolence, waving bravely though inconsequently, glimpsed here and there through the trees, on the mountain roads, among the ruins, on the long march into chaos. (536–37)

Constructing her own story of Zenia, Tony "stares up at Zenia, cornered on the balcony with her failing magic, balancing on the sharp edge, her bag of tricks finally empty." Imaging the Snake Goddess to invoke and deconstruct the Great Goddess of matriarchy, much as Atwood does in *The Penelopiad*, Tony finally realizes that

> whatever her secrets are she's not telling. She's like an ancient statuette dug up from a Minoan palace: there are the large breasts, the tiny waist, the dark eyes, the snaky hair. Tony picks her up and turns her over, probes and questions, but the woman with her glazed pottery face does nothing but smile. (545–46)

Still, like the male military commanders that Tony spends so much time studying, what becomes of Zenia, who had spent her life robbing and colonizing, is finally not only "a female matter" (531, 545), but a Canadian and a human one.

Lacking personal identity and self-respect, all four women feel alien, without a national identity (see also Rao 174). In *Survival,* Atwood was among the first Canadians to discuss Canada's victim position as a colonized country and to identify the similar deceptions, rationalizations, and game-playing resulting from individual, ethnic, and national colonization. As a victim, a country or individual may displace the cause of the oppression, feel excused from attempting to change the situation, and direct anger against fellow victims and oneself (35–39). As works by Beran, S. Wilson, and other scholars suggest, most of Atwood's texts may be read through these positions, with characters and, by implication, their country, moving from fragmentation and symbolic amputations toward position four, in which one could be a creative nonvictim (Beran 74; S. Wilson, *Margaret Atwood's Textual* xiv). As Potts discusses, all four female characters in *The Robber Bride* demonstrate victim positions but move toward "the potential of the 'hybrid self,' " as defined by Homi Bhabha (Potts, "The Old Maps" 291). In addition to their all feeling like orphans, refugees, and war babies, Tony feels inferior because of her Canadian status, Charis is self-deceived about its security, and Roz (like most Canadians an immigrant herself) is paradoxically alarmed about the growing numbers of immigrants ("White Goddess" 232–34). Charis finds even her "white" Canadianness, compared to the indeterminate ethnicity of Shanita and Zenia, flat and boring. As she points out, her Scottish, English, and Mennonite family (both colonized and colonizing) ended up in Canada through wars. Roz recognizes that national identity is a costume one wears: "the hired help in outfits. The backdrops. The props"; but Torontonians "will do anything to disguise themselves" (102, 107). Although they would probably all agree with Roz that the idea of an aggressive Canadian is laughable (108), it is a Canadian who abuses Charis (a personal violation with profound national and political dimensions), "sweet Canadians" (*Bodily Harm)* who want to murder their "best friend" (referred to in a newspaper as a Canadian), a Canadian—the ballistics expert Gerry Bull—who was developing a Supergun for the Iraqis until he was murdered (35–36), and Canadians who will send their navy to aid the "market expansion" of the United States into the Gulf.

In characteristic fashion, Atwood deconstructs Canada's historic "neutrality," no more likely in *The Robber Bride* than essentialist gender roles, fixed identities, or objective reality. When, at the end of the novel, Tony understates the question of whether "we are in any way" like Zenia (546), she has already detailed comparisons of Zenia to Marius, Genghis Khan, Saddam Hussein, and other colonizers. Recognizing from the novel's beginning that the basin of blood in "Fitcher's Bird" would have been appropriate for Zenia (15), Tony first sees Zenia, back from the dead, reflected in the mirror as she wishes that Charis could see the piles of skulls and pits filled with bodies that go back century through century, as far as you can go (36–37). Zenia is history, and like Zenia, "history is a construct," but "definitive moments . . . change the direction of time" (4). Although history can repeat itself, it can, like a novel, be written and spoken differently. As Tony writes Zenia's ending—the novel's ending—Atwood challenges all of us to write and exist differently. Ready for another story, Tony rejoins the female friends that, she now recognizes, have, like herself, included and been the ever-changing Zenia: both the Grimms' Robber Bride and Robber and Atwood's *The Robber Bride*.

CHAPTER 2

FITCHER'S AND FRANKENSTEIN'S GAZE IN ATWOOD'S *ORYX AND CRAKE*

THE GRIMMS' "FITCHER'S BIRD"

As chapter 1 began to demonstrate, the "Fitcher's Bird" fairy tale appears in virtually every Atwood text, often alongside "The Robber Bride." Atwood's watercolor, *Fitcher's Bird* (see cover), shows the skull-faced substitute bride of the fairy tale. In *The Edible Woman* (1969), Marian imagines that she will open the forbidden door in her Bluebeard's apartment to see her fiancé holding a carving knife. She increasingly feels like food and stops eating. In addition to the men in her life, Fitcher/the Robber represents her consumer society. Similarly, in *Bodily Harm* (1981), Rennie, eaten by cancer (and symbolically by both her physician and live-in lover), meets other Fitcher/Robbers in the middle of a Caribbean revolution and, whether she ever leaves the prison or not, she recognizes that bodily harm is global. *Bluebeard's Egg* (1983), which actually quotes the Hunt and Stern translation of Grimms' "Fitcher's Bird," is a comic treatment of the fairy tale in which the "bird" thinks her husband plays the egg rather than Bluebeard. Sexual politics is dominant as Bluebeard, a heart doctor, symbolically dismembers the many women, including the deluded wife, whom he betrays.

In *Alias Grace* (1996), "Fitcher's Bird," "The Robber Bridegroom," and "The Girl Without Hands," intertexts underline the dismemberment, cannibalism, and male/female conditioning including blood, the forbidden door and chamber, the casket of secrets, a missing hand, Pandora's box, punishment, disguise, trickery, and escape motifs. In this novel about repressed sexuality, class privilege, and gender stereotypes, Grace, like Lady Macbeth, continuously imagines (or says she does) spots of red in her prison that suggest Fitcher's basin of blood. Even a book (the Godey Ladies Book with fashions from the states) is found in bed, covered in blood, "murdered" along with its reader. Neither of the book's unreliable narrators has much self-insight, and both Simon and Grace resist opening doors to forbidden chambers of the self while they are eager to open those concealing the other. Unlike *The Robber Bride* and most of Atwood's work embedding fairy-tale intertexts, *Alias Grace* offers no regrown hands, the only fairy-tale transformation being that of Grace into an accomplished creator. A novel within a novel within a novel, a "maze" seemingly designed to trap readers into confusing characters and plots, *The Blind Assassin* (2000) also uses "Fitcher's Bird" and "The Girl Without Hands" intertexts. By the end of the book, Iris and her protagonist, "Iris," are no longer mute, sacrificial virgins, Blind Assassins, or handless, helpless females. As in "The Girl Without Hands" fairy tale, Iris's symbolically cut-off hand grows back; as in the "Fitcher's Bird" fairy tale, Iris is able to reassemble the dismembered pieces of herself. Fairy-tale intertexts in Atwood's recent and alarming novel, *Oryx and Crake* (2003), are less recognizable than in most of Atwood's previous texts. By studying her earlier use of the Grimms' "Fitcher's Bird" and other intertexts, however, we see again some of this tale's primary motifs. Other important folklore intertexts in *Oryx and Crake* are other Grimms' fairy tales and nursery rimes, biblical references, and the Frankenstein legend, the basis of Mary Shelley's *Frankenstein*.

As a postmodern writer, in *Oryx and Crake* Atwood revisions and deconstructs its fairy-tale intertexts by using techniques such as building scenes on fairy-tale images, moving females from object to subject, displacing the truth of traditional narratives to shift the point of view to a somewhat unreliable narrator, making marginalized subtexts central, and reversing intertexts' norms or ideologies. Atwood uses irony, parody, gender reconfiguraion, self-conscious and developing narrators, and bent and blended tragic-comic tone and genres to depict characters and personas who experience greater awareness, in Jimmy's case a kind of ironic fairy-tale transformation. The novel builds numerous scenes, such as Jimmy opening the sealed door to kill Crake, on the scene of Fitcher's bride opening the forbidden door. Jimmy, who grows in awareness, relates to us an unauthorized story that we are invited to complete. Atwood's door and vision symbolism, writing beyond the ending, and remythification move readers to awareness of

Fitcher's and Frankenstein's menace. *Oryx and Crake* is a superlative
master text in delegitimating—creating an unexpected story (Du-
Plessis 29)—and in transgressing and defamiliarizing language. The
novel's puns, word play, and irony—as in Hott Tots, headsoff.com,
Extinctathon, and Paradice—and defamiliarization of absurd cultural
excesses no longer questioned, surpass all of Atwood's previous work.
Because it uses and sometimes undercuts so many mythic, fairy-tale,
literary, and popular culture intertexts, perhaps *Oryx and Crake*'s
biggest irony is that even absurd language and cultural myths make us
recognize the importance of the language we use and the stories we
tell. Jimmy is ultimately an artist who, like Scheherazade, exists to tell
his story and will speak as long as he lives. Like Fitcher's Bird, he
chooses life rather than death.

Significantly, despite her initial powerlessness, the woman protagonist in the Grimms' "Fitcher's Bird" (AT 311, also "Fichter's Bird")
is a "clever and wily" opponent rather than a victim of the groom who
punishes inquisitive brides. As in Maroon and Anancy (Anansy) slave
tales used in Rhys's *Wide Sargasso Sea,* where the trickster can escape
into the wilds or fly (Emery 39–40, 49–50; see chapter 8), the third
sister escapes through trickery. When the disguised wizard touches a
woman, she is "forced to jump into his basket." The German word
ficht even means to fight or beg. He then carries the woman into the
dark forest to his magnificent house, also suggesting Pluto carrying
the young woman into the palace of death (Atwood, "Of Souls" 36).
Following patriarchal tradition, as in ancient Rome, Fitcher gives the
woman the keys to the house (Leach and Fried 575) and, supposedly,
"everything [her] heart can wish for," but he lays down very explicit
"rules" for her conduct: On pain of death, she may not enter one
room, and she must "preserve" the egg (sometimes a key) he gives
her "carefully for [him]," carrying it with her everywhere. The first
two sisters, who "allow [themselves] to be carried away by curiosity"
and thus oppose his will, are betrayed by the egg's indelible blood
spots (Motif D474.4) from the bloody chamber. In each case, they
are punished with death for breaking the taboo (Motif C920): Their
heads are cut off, they are chopped to pieces, and they are thrown
into the bloody basin with all of the previous interchangeable brides.
The third sister, however, not only safeguards the egg outside the
room, but also rejoins the parts of her sisters' bodies, thereby restor-
ing them to life (Motifs E30, D1884). She is able to fool both the
groom as well as his friends by getting him to carry her sisters to
safety in a sack (reversed in "Sing, Little Sack!" Jaffe and chapter 8,
n. 2), disguising herself as a marvelous bird—the Fitcher's Bird of the

title (K521.1.)—and setting an ornamented skull in the window to represent herself as Fitcher's bride (Hunt and Stern 216–20). Viewing the story comically, Atwood sees the wizard thus transforming from a kind of Svengali into a Ken doll ("Of Souls" 33), a reverse transformation mirroring that of the Bride.[1] While fairy tales are not reducible to rational explanation, the implicit power politics of the tale merits further attention (S. Wilson, *Margaret Atwood's Fairy* 260–70; see also chapters 6 and 8).

Perhaps the most important fairy-tale motif in *Oryx and Crake* is the door to the forbidden chamber (C611.1), behind which literal or figural rooms hold horrifying discoveries, in this case suggesting apocalypse. The door becomes this novel's central symbol. Tales other than "Fitcher's Bird" also present doors, typically two doors hiding menace, such as tigers or death, and the third one treasures, and characters must choose which to open. In folklore, tales about forbidden places, including caskets, chambers, and doors, have a wide geographic distribution, including French Canada; doors may also be entrances to the lower world or the fairy world, they may be guarded by monsters, sometimes magic is necessary for opening, and ghosts may be able to enter closed doors (Aarne and Thompson 526, 222; Thompson VI 224–25). *Oryx and Crake* also uses other motifs from "Fitcher's Bird," such as dismemberment, cannibalism, unwitting marriage to death, death for breaking a taboo, resuscitation by arrangement of members, disguise, the tricked ogre, and punishment of the murderer. Other fairy-tale, nursery rime, and folk allusions in *Oryx and Crake* include "The Robber Bridegroom," "The Wolf and the Kids," "Red Cap," "The Water of Life," "Hansel and Gretel," "Cinderella," "Beauty and the Beast," "The Girl Without Hands," and "The Three Pigs." Mythic intertexts include references to Great Goddess myth; creation myth, including tales about eggs (A 655); female demons, mermaids, and harpies; mythical beings such as unicorns, griffins, manticores, and basilisks; and Pandora. Biblical ones include those about the patriarchal Old Testament God; Adam, Eve, and the snake; the Eden story and the fall from Paradise; and Moses, the burning bush, the Sermon on the Mount, and the Ten Commandments. Literary allusions in *Oryx and Crake* include Shelley's *Frankenstein* and *The Last Man* (see next section of this chapter), Orwell's *1984* and *Animal Farm,* and Defoe's *Robinson Crusoe* as well as *Alice in Wonderland* and *Through the Looking Glass, Gulliver's Travels, Macbeth, Oedipus Rex, Pippi Longstocking,* and *Tarzan.*

In addition to the Rapunzel Syndrome discussed in reference to *The Green Knight* and *The Bone People,* folklore motifs appearing in many fairy tales, such as "Once upon a time," menacing or helpful animals, the golem, unnatural food, the trickster, the robber of life, the casket full of secrets, the abandoned or sold child, the quest, escape, rescue, and the fountain of youth, occur in an apparently realistic context that is, as will be seen, actually dystopian, gothic, and profoundly ironic. As in fairy tales and *The Handmaid's Tale,* the narrator addresses an audience even though he cannot know that anyone will hear him. In this novel, there is no escape by use of a substituted object or rescue by a sister: Like Snowman/Jimmy, readers of *Oryx and Crake* are on their own. Jimmy is the character/unreliable and self-conscious narrator who must prove his worth and pass the fairy-tale test. While he hopes he will win Oryx/Eve, like many of Atwood's narrators he initially marries death: He chooses blindness and accepts a cannibalistic culture. He becomes distracted by games and superficialities and chooses the door to treasure and then the one to attacking animals rather than to authentic humanity. He does not begin to gain knowledge until he is expelled from an infected Paradise (here Paradice) to become a prophet for the Crakers, the created beings who are supposed to replace human beings. Crake, the novel's Adam, Fitcher, and the trickster robber of life, amuses himself with Extinctathon and substitutes a killing microbe for the magic Fountain of Youth (the Grimms' "Water of Life") the pleeblanders seek. Oryx, also this novel's eaten Robber Bride or a dismembered sister of Fitcher's Bride, is the sold child, Eve/snake, Scheherazade, and reversed Cinderella. She is what Eve Sedgwick calls an object of exchange between the two men (524).

Unlike the many fairy tales, such as "Cinderella," in which friendly animals help the hero or heroine on a quest, sometimes leading them to treasure, here the betrayed and abused animals, chimeras[2] who have been subjected to genetic hybridization, get revenge on human beings who lack reverence for other beings or the natural world. Like the pigs in Orwell's *Animal Farm,* the pigoons in this cautionary tale show intelligence and team work: On Snowman's quest to the destroyed compound, they maliciously watch and attack. Here it is humans that not only have built their houses on sand and of sticks and straw, but also have no shelter against the ultimate Big Bad Wolf they have created. Unlike "The Three Pigs" (AT 124A),[3] where the pigs are vulnerable because they built weak houses, the human wolves in Crake's society do not need to blow houses down: The affluent intellectual elite have already broken into the houses of lower beings, including not only pigs but also low-status humans, rabbits, chickens, skunks, raccoons, and even wolves, all now subjected to Fitcher's gaze. They barricade themselves in gated communities called "Compounds." As in the Grimms' "The Wolf and the Kids" and "Red Riding Hood" (Redcap: The Glutton, AT 123, 333), the elite "wolves" use disguise and deception, including false advertising and products, in order to open the doors of their victim's defenses so that they may be eaten, in this case by microbes that produce this novel's apocalypse. Ironically, beautiful Oryx, still an abused Cinderella, delivers the libido-enhancing product that kills, only to be killed by her "prince."

In *Oryx and Crake,* "the Fitcher's Bird" intertext is again paralleled by "The Robber Bridegroom" one. The sexual politics theme may seem absent since it is in the background of this violent, dehumanizing, classist society:

> its main products being corpses and rubble. It never learned, it made the same cretinous mistakes over and over, trading short-term gain for long-term pain. It was like a giant slug eating its way relentlessly through all the other bioforms on the planet, grinding up life on earth and shitting it out the backside in the form of pieces of manufactured and soon-to-be-obsolete plastic junk. (243)

The forbidden door motif begins early in the novel, in the "Once upon a time" when Snowman was Jimmy. For much of Jimmy's life, all women are "doors" to be unlocked with the words "I love you." Jimmy believes in answers, codes, and passwords and continuously remembers and constructs stories about colonialism, societal rules, products, his mother, Oryx, and Crake, but he prefers to watch voyeuristically rather than to see and know. He can parody self-help books but not help himself or others when he gets a glimpse of the forbidden. Even though the Compound people are "sealed up tight as a drum" away from the pleebland cities and are themselves forbidden places to the poor, what appears to be mad cow disease gets in. Jimmy is dimly aware of the dangers of doors being unlocked. Before his microbiologist mother decides to stay home and later to protest the work of OrganInc and other Compounds, she explains that, because "the bad microbes and viruses want to get in through the cell doors and eat up the pigoons from the inside," her job is to make " 'locks' for cell 'doors' " (18–19, 29). He worries about the forbidden door swinging open when his mother leaves home. Looking back on his life before cell doors are unlocked, Snowman imagines hearing "the door of a great vault shutting" while he is watching Oryx float. He feels trapped and "knows they are both in great danger" (43).

When Jimmy wonders whether Crake has told her to have sex with him, Oryx implies that she will close the door on Crake. She is

> a casketful of secrets. Any moment now she would open herself up, reveal to him the essential thing, the hidden thing at the core of life, or of her life, or of his life—the thing he was longing to know. The thing he had always wanted. What would it be? (314)

Even the Internet picture of Oryx (or someone who looks like her) on Hott Totts and Oryx's past is a forbidden door. Crake uses the picture as his gateway to the subversive Grandmasters' section of the Extinctathon playroom that aims to shut down the whole perverse society through terrorism. As head of an outlaw group called MaddAddam, Crake resembles the robbers of life in the Grimms' "The Robber Bridegroom" as well as in "Fitcher's Bird," representing not just one mad scientist but an entire mad segment of an already ruined society.

> Jimmy had a cold feeling, a feeling that reminded him of the time his mother left home: the same sense of the forbidden, of a door swinging open that ought to be kept locked, of a stream of secret lives, running underground, in the darkness just beneath his feet. (216–17)

After Crake has gotten Oryx to spread the JUVE virus all over the world, she ends up on the same side of the door as Crake. Jimmy finally closes the door against Crake, only to open it when he cannot see Oryx, who has lied to him. Crake slits Oryx's throat and Jimmy then shoots Crake and seals the door until he leaves with the Crakers. Jimmy's and his society's blindness and fear of forbidden knowledge, also revealed in his and Crake's Frankenstein and monster roles, are evident in Jimmy's cultivated fish-eyed stare, the RejoovenEssense Compound's "blind eyeball (297), and the ruptured and empty eye sockets of people exposed to the virus.

Some Internet sites, especially "At Home with Anna K," are doorways to Jimmy's love of words and, like those of other Atwood creator-narrators, his decision to collect and shape them into the story we read. Snowman's acceptance of responsibility for the Crakers, his efforts to speak and to create meaningful myths for them, and his one-eyed, then two-eyed, then no sunglasses suggest that he attains some wisdom. His myths about the creation of words and of the children of Oryx from eggs and those of Crake from coral and mango are etiological: Rather than leaving Crakers with chaos, the myths explain basic questions about the origin of life and such matters as why animals cannot talk. His quest back to the Compound and his decision to face the human beings who make Robinson Crusoe footprints on the beach are also "doors" to a possible future. When he returns to the Compound, he expects that "someone—someone like him—is lying in wait, around some corner, behind some half-opened door" (229), and thus recognizes his own complicity in Fitcher games. Still, neither Snowman nor the Crakers suggest the kind of fairy-tale or mythic transformation implied in earlier Atwood texts. None of Atwood's novels is resolved, but in *Oryx and Crake* any transformation of this fallen world resembling our own must, in postmodern and postcolonial fashion, be constructed by the reader. Since Jimmy, like Atwood's Iris, Grace, and Tony and Hulme's Kerewin, transforms himself into the creator who shapes the tale we read, as a reader I construct the possibility of societal as well as personal transformation.

Fairy tales continue to be Atwood's main intertexts, and, as her most recent works indicate, they and the stories in which they may be embedded depend upon a reader or listener for their existence: "Because a story—any story, but especially one that exists in such a vernacular domain—is a negotiation between teller and audience, the listeners are accomplices" (Atwood, *Moving Targets* 187). As in Atwood's 2004 poem "Bottle II," if the writer or tale-teller is a voice in a bottle, the voice depends upon the reader or audience to uncork the bottle and listen.

FRANKENSTEIN'S GAZE: LEGEND, MEDIA, AND FICTION

As early as the poem first published in a rare book, *Speeches for Doctor Frankenstein* (1966), Margaret Atwood has been concerned with creation parables like Mary Shelley's *Frankenstein*. The theme and several images in this poem recur in *Oryx and Crake*. Also published in *The Animals in That Country* (1968) under the title "Speeches for Dr. Frankenstein," it is about an artist who "dared/to attempt impious wonders" but is unable to foresee the results. He loses control over the creation, which is aborted, deformed, and monstrous. "Insane with skill" but wincing "before this plateful of results," by the end of the poem the doctor, not the monster, is the shadow:

You sliced me loose
And said it was
Creation. I could feel the knife.
Now you would like to heal

That chasm in your side,
But I recede, I prowl.
I will not come when you call. (42–47)

In *Oryx and Crake*, most readers overlook the extent to which the quality of this Frankenstein's vision contributes to the sexual politics and human folly depicted in this book. While Atwood's early texts often focus on protagonists' distortions of vision, especially through mirrors and cameras (see S. Wilson, Atwood's "Eyes" 226–27; "Camera Images" 29–32), this image has received little comment in recent texts. As most noticeably in *Life Before Man, The Handmaid's Tale, The Robber Bride,* and *The Blind Assassin,* blindness and distorted vision put male as well as female bodies, and even the newly gendered bodies of this Frankenstein's created species, in jeopardy.

Atwood's little-known visual art again makes this sexual politics tangible. Although the rare book, *Speeches for Doctor Frankenstein* (1966), was illustrated with her friend Charles Pachter's visual art, Atwood created two untitled watercolors, later published as *Frankenstein I* and *II* (1970) (S. Wilson, *Margaret Atwood's Fairy* 48, Plates 6 and 7) for this poem. Suggesting the same kind of dynamics and visual contrast as in *Mary Queen of Scots I* and *II*, where the female figures have a cut-off hand or head, *Frankenstein I* features a robotic male figure (the "monster") without face, arms or hands "holding" a fluid, passive female (Elizabeth). In *Frankenstein II,* showing the dead Elizabeth and mourners watched by the doctor or possibly his "monster," the male and female are separated by different frames and apparently occupy different realities.

In their childhood and adolescence, Jimmy and Crake, monstrous in their own ways, spend much of their time on pornographic Web sites, including Hot Totts, Tart of the Day, Super Swallowers, and Noodie News, that commodify women's and sometimes men's bodies. Significantly, we first see Oryx in the same voyeuristic way that Jimmy and Crake do, as the object of a scopophiliac gaze (Mulvey 440), a silenced, sold child on a kiddie porn show, and she continues to function as an object in this book filled with images of walled, one-eyed, fish-eyed, ruptured, blind, and ultimately empty-socket vision. Jimmy watches Oryx through the peepholes into the Crakers' secret space and the hallway outside Crake's private quarters. After her death, she is reduced to a voice in Jimmy/Snowman's head. Resembling Elizabeth of Shelley's *Frankenstein* and Atwood's watercolors, Oryx is, as previously stated, always part of a Sedgwick triangle in which the central erotic figures are the two men vying for power

(524), and like Elizabeth, it is her body that is sacrificed in this battle. Long before his creature kills Elizabeth to punish Victor, Victor Frankenstein dreams of holding her dead body, which he associates with his mother's (49). In both novels, women are passive objects of exchange. Crake provides Oryx's body to get Jimmy's cooperation. Jimmy thinks that if Crake dies, Oryx will sacrifice herself on a funeral pyre, as Shelley's monster says he will; but as soon as she has spread the virus, Crake slits her throat in front of Jimmy.

It is Oryx's voice that reminds Snowman to watch over the Crakers, gives him a reason for being, and, muse-like, inspires his tale. As one of Atwood's many tricksters, including Zenia of *The Robber Bride,* Circe of *You Are Happy,* harpies, and sirens, seductive Oryx holds Jimmy in bondage to Crake by telling him contradictory stories. It is Oryx who evades answering Jimmy's many questions about her past or her relationship with Crake, and Oryx who, possibly unknowingly, spreads the virus that may make the human species extinct. Both Jimmy and Crake objectify her in the way that she has apparently always been objectified as sold child and sex slave. There is no sign of her returning the gaze or of really seeing.

In *Oryx and Crake,* even war and other violence are recognized as "misplaced sexual energy." Thus, the new humanoid species created by Crake, this novel's principal Dr. Frankenstein, no longer feels lust or jealousy, no longer rapes or wages war, mates cyclically every three years when the females go into heat, and neatly drops dead at thirty. Nevertheless, both Crake and the Abominable Snowman/Jimmy are caught in the sexual politics that drives the novel's plot. Although *Oryx and Crake* is characteristically unresolved, unlike Atwood's other fiction, apart from the transformations we construct, this novel seems to offer no rebirth for either male or female bodies, this time literally dismembered and eaten. One of the profoundly ironic possible endings we are offered is a Wild West shoot-out in which the created beings are unlikely to survive precisely because they are innocent of violence. As in *Bodily Harm, The Handmaid's Tale,* and *The Robber Bride,* sexual politics is not only a metaphor of global disaster but also one of its major causes. Still, this novel that awakens us from our blindness and warns us about our Dr. Frankensteins leaves us in a double bind: Continuing on our current blind path insures extinction, but attempting to eradicate aggression could insure the same thing.

Atwood writes in a speculative fiction and dystopian tradition including Orwells's *1984* and *Animal Farm,* Huxley's *Brave New World,* and H. G. Welles's *The Time Machine* and *The Island of*

Dr. Moreau. As Atwood says, speculative fiction is usually in the romance mode, and *Oryx and Crake* is an adventure romance "coupled with a Minippean satire."[4] She also uses so many canonical and popular cultural texts that *Oryx and Crake* constitutes an overview of literature and culture as well as a critique of ancient and modern values and modes of being. As narrator, Snowman is one of the long stream of narrators from Job (Bible) to Melville's Ishmael (*Moby Dick*) to Shelley's Walton (*Frankenstein*) to Vonnegut's John (*Cat's Cradle*) to bear witness to the human folly and grief that constitute human experience. Paradoxically, these stories of destruction inevitably shape new creations. Melville chooses Job's story, which he associates with Jonah's, for Ishmael's epilogue to his narrative of disaster: "And I only am escaped alone to tell thee" (432). Job, Ishmael, Walton, and John are not only forced to see the wreck of all conceivable projects of vanity but are also self-conscious narrators who must tell their stories, creating art from destruction sometimes paradoxically caused by monstrous creation. Ironically, only Job can transcend human apocalypse and the boundaries of fiction to regain and even double what was taken from him.

Shelley's *Frankenstein* (1817) uses alchemy, golem, creation myth, and Faust legend as well as tales of pride, disaster, and fall in its story of destructive creation. In *Frankenstein*, it is appropriate that we first encounter all three self-conscious narrators in this tale within a tale when they are shut in by ice. From his colonial perspective, Walton sees the created being as "savage" rather than nobly European, as he thinks Dr. Frankenstein is (20–21). Thus, he identifies with the monstrous creator whose quest for the Absolute culminates in a shadow self, a "child," he cannot accept and for whom he feels no pity. Not surprisingly, having never experienced Lacanian parental mirroring (*Ecrits* 5), education, or any kind of "warmth," the being ironically wants to die on a funeral pyre: the symbol of lost love. Shelley's Dr. Frankenstein is not only Prometheus, Faust, and Satan in his cold and prideful striving to create life out of death, but also the archetypal bad father who steals the female ability to create life and who takes no responsibility for his "child" or his actions. As narrators, Walton and Frankenstein are at least as unreliable as the murderous "monster" who admits his flaws and wants to be punished for his crimes. In their abilities to wall themselves in ice, both Walton and Dr. Frankenstein prefigure Vonnegut's creator of ice-nine as well as Atwood's central creator-monster, Crake, who not only remotely designs apocalypse, watches, and then abandons the species he creates, but even gets someone else to distribute the pills that increase sexual pleasure while they kill humanity. As in *Frankenstein* and Atwood's poem, Crake's supposedly perfect species develops in directions he does not foresee. When they make an image of Snowman to call him back, Jimmy recognizes that

Symbolic thinking of any kind would signal downfall, in Crake's view. Next they'd be inventing idols, and funerals, and grave goods, and the afterlife, and sin, and Linear B, and kings, and then slavery and war. (361)

John of Vonnegut's *Cat's Cradle*, who says he should have been Jonah because he was compelled to be at certain places at certain times, ends up telling a different story than the one he had intended, "The Day the World Ended," about the atomic bomb. *Cat's Cradle* is a useful introduction to the absurd universe *Oryx and Crake* penetrates. In *Cat's Cradle*, it is still possible to laugh at science and technology so irresponsible and chaotic that a childish scientist deprived of tinker toys could create both the atomic bomb and ice-nine. Supposed to freeze mud for the convenience of the military, ice-nine gets out of hand and freezes the earth. Defoe's *Robinson Crusoe* (McCombs), Shelley's *The Last Man*, Dodson's *Alice in Wonderland* and *Through the Looking Glass* (Gussow 2), Swift's *Gulliver's Travels* (epigraph), Woolf's *To the Lighthouse* (epigraph), Piercy's feminist dystopia/utopia *Woman on the Edge of Time*, and "mad scientist" films depicting irresponsible experiments in creating or prolonging life also inform *Oryx and Crake*. For example, Marge Piercy's *Woman on the Edge of Time* (1976) anticipates both Atwood's use of multicolored Crakers as a proposed tool for the eradication of racism and social manipulation of language to condition values. Unlike Crake's scheme to create what he advertises as "Paradice" by ending war, aggression, sexual violence and angst, overpopulation, environmental pollution, and fear of aging and death as well as racism, Piercy's utopia also tackles sexism by using *per* as a gender-neutral substitute for *his* and *her* and making all births test-tube ones.

Crake, who suffers from Asperger's disease, resembles the many archetypal mad scientists of film and their parodies:[5] the numerous *Frankenstein*s frequently featuring Boris Karloff (Whale 1931), *The Invisible Man* (Whale 1933), *Island of Lost Souls* (Kenton 1933) and several remakes, *The Island of Dr. Moreau* (Don Taylor 1977, John Frankenheimer 1996), *Forbidden Planet* (Fred M. Wilcox 1956), and *The Fly* (Kurt Neumann 1958, David Cronenberg 1986), whose Faustian efforts to rival God inevitably spell disaster. Like Professor Morbius of *Forbidden Planet*, played by Walter Pidgeon, Crake transcends normal humanity but creates "a Monster from the ID. . . . when . . . machineries for good bec[o]me engines of ill will" (Chapman). While overtly doing the establishment will, his buried resentment over his father's murder helps precipitate the disgust that culminates in his species murder. Crake is even a kind of Dr. Jekyll whose Hyde personality, his dark double, remains hidden behind computer screens and technological experiments (see Stevenson's *The Strange Case of Dr. Jekyll and Mr. Hyde*, 1886 and the many films based on it, including Victor Fleming's *Dr. Jekyll and Mr. Hyde*, 1941). He is also a Dr. Strangelove (Kubrick's *Dr. Strangelove: Or How I Learned to Stop Worrying and Love the Bomb*, 1964), whose "strange love" is his attraction to extinction. More recently, Crake is the evil scientist, Dr. Totenkopf, that Sky Captain (Kelly Conran's *Sky Captain and the World of Tomorrow*, 2004) must defeat. It is Jimmy who, seeming to be The Invisible Man of the film, is left alone with the world Crake creates.

Crake, like his models Prometheus, Faust, God, and Satan, most closely resembles Shelley's Dr. Frankenstein. His complex dome "like a bubble of ice" (228), with watch towers suggesting those of the 1932 film, even recalls the frozen island that mirrors the doctor's inner as well as outer landscape at *Frankenstein's* end. Actually named Glenn and modeled on the Canadian pianist Glenn Gould whom Atwood believes also suffered from Asperger's disease (cited in Bethune 46), Glenn adopts the name Crake, after the nearly extinct red Australian bird, as his username on the secret terrorist site of the video game show, Extinctathon. As his gateway and to irritate Jimmy, Crake uses the picture of Oryx that he has secretly saved since he and Jimmy were voyeurs of Hot Totts, a child pornography site. Like Victor Frankenstein, however, Crake is physically remote and repressed. Although Crake later frequently touches Oryx, an employee acquired through Student (sexual) Services, his touch says, "Mine, mine" (313) and is ultimately as deadly as Victor's.

Ironically, just as Dr. Frankenstein's attempt to create life is doomed by his selection of dead body parts, the species Crake creates to replace human beings is implicitly marked for extinction by being named after their death-obsessed creator. Like Dr. Frankenstein, who defies God by egotistically creating life and working to eliminate the distinction between natural and man-made, Crake and his fellow scientists eradicate the distinction between real and fake, parodying religion by offering the new species as "floor models," to be adjusted to consumer preferences, and the Moses Model rock, which gives water when struck (302, 200). Despite his distrust of religion and efforts to "edit out" religious impulses, including questions about origins and the desire to know the creator, *Crake* is the name by which he is later "worshipped."

As Dr. Frankenstein locks up his creature, Crake locks up not only his new species but also the entire group of antisocial scientists in the RejoovenEssense Compound. As extensions of today's exclusive gated communities, Compounds can be one of the secret, forbidden spaces, including also the Grandmasters' section of the Extinctathon Web site (216), resembling the forbidden doors in the previously discussed Grimms' fairy tale "Fitcher's Bird." Such forbidden doors hide the dismemberment and sometimes cannibalism that function symbolically in "Speeches for Dr. Frankenstein" as well as *Oryx and Crake*. As head of an outlaw group called MaddAddam, Crake also resembles the robbers of life in the Grimms' "The Robber Bridegroom" (see also S. Wilson, *Margaret Atwood's Fairy* 198–228), representing not just one mad scientist but an entire mad segment of society.

Both Crake and Jimmy are monsters in their contrasting ways of seeing without seeing. It is no accident that Crake's dome complex is described as a "blind eyeball" and that it has only slits for windows. Although his pseudo love intensifies Crake's blindness, Oryx admires Crake's "vision" (313, 322). Like other scientific geniuses rewarded by society, Crake is a demi-autistic "brainiac" who ironically functions as a mutant on another planet as he proceeds toward exterminating humanity on this one (174, 193). This victim of the "Geek Syndrome"[6] reduces art to a desire to get laid and dismisses female artists as misguided, but except for competition with Jimmy to possess Oryx and the single-minded effort to eradicate a society obsessed with sex and war games, he seems to feel little human emotion himself.

In addition to sometimes doubling as both the doctor and the monster creation desiring his bride (169), Jimmy is the deformed Igor figure, usually played by Bela Lugosi in early Frankenstein films. Jimmy's deformity is feeling unloved and not good enough and thus obsessed with sex. One of the reasons he is attracted to Oryx is that he thinks that Oryx sees him as he is. She is "the closest she could get to him without becoming food" (315). We first see him as Snowman, another image of cold despite his tendency to sunburn and of the monstrous as in "abominable." He is wearing one-eyed sunglasses after a life of "structured" ignorance and blindness that contributes to the apocalypse: "He'd grown up in walled spaces, and then he had become one. He had shut things out," turned a "blind eye" (184, 260). As a child, he cultivates a fish-eye stare (277). After he sees his mother's filmed execution following a riot scene from a *Frankenstein* remake and other interjections, even the sunrise is "blinding":

Everything in his life was temporary, ungrounded. Language itself had lost its solidity; it had become thin, contingent, slippery, a viscid film on which he was sliding around like an eyeball on a plate. An eyeball that could still see, however. That was the trouble. (260)

After he has allowed Crake to destroy everything he values, Jimmy opens and closes his eyes, realizing that he cannot regain the past and will be destroyed by the present if he looks at it too closely (147). The Crakers see him as a prophet, and in a sense he is a blind Tireseus, warning us in this cautionary tale that we, too, are blind, knowing no more than Oedipus who we are or what the consequences of our actions may be. Jimmy does develop a conscience, recognizing that some lines should not be crossed. He is a time-traveler without a time machine, however, and thus unable to return to his time (106) or to undo the damage he passively watched. As the self-conscious narrator of the book we read and the creator of myths for the Crakers, he, too, is a creator. Allowing his gift with language to be commodified in Crake's service, he still hopes to prevent words from becoming extinct. His head always filled with words and voices despite his knowledge that there are no listeners, he still feels compelled to tell his story.

If Crake and Jimmy are blind Frankensteins and Oryx the object of exchange that fuels the book's power politics, their society is the epitome of a world out of control, created by and creating Frankensteins. This is a society in which the body, "having ditched its old traveling companions, the mind and the soul, . . . has set out on its own adventures" (85). According to Amanda's pleebland roommates, their current society, only slightly more vicious than ours, is monstrous: "It was like a giant slug eating its way relentlessly through all the other bioforms on the planet, grinding up life on earth" (243).

Parodying the Boston Tea Party, global coffee wars rage while many people watch Noodie News, deathrowlive.com, and American crime shows with sports-event commentary. Hedsoff.com plays live coverage of executions in Asia, the Queek Geek Show features the eating of live animals and birds, and nightee-nite.com shows assisted suicides, a program Crake finds hilarious, especially when the show's sad doctor declares life extinct (83). Disastrous world events generate games, such as Kwiktime Osama, Barbarian Stomp, and Three-dimensional Waco. Genetic engineering has deadly effects on the animal world, which seems to refuse being passive objects and enacts its revenge. While wolvogs, dogs genetically altered to guard in moats, are caged in BioDefences and not intended to get out, they and other vicious or toxic new species, such as bobkittens and iridescent green rabbits, take over less dominant forms. Atwood overturns the hierarchy of human over both animal and vegetable worlds with her intelligent pigoons, developed from cloned pigs to supply microbe-resistant human-tissue organs for transplant (see Margaret Atwood Papers, 335, Box 145). They actively gaze, watching for Snowman's return, and organize an attack on him and the few remaining humanoids. Spoat/giders (goats crossed with spiders) and chickens without heads, designed to supply chicken parts for the new fast food, ChickieNobs, represent this "headless" society. Like Dr. Frankenstein's monster, even Crake's supposedly utopian creation, the Crakers, "fall" into human frailty as they begin to evolve in destructive directions of the past.

While the species Crake creates cannot read and does not even understand the concepts of war and rape, it is superior to Crake's fellow human beings in many respects, including its reverence for environment and living beings and its comic communal healing through purring. But these advantages exist because of genetic preprogramming and thus make the Crakers seem less free than the human beings who precede them. Crake does his best to prevent the Crakers from being able to develop civilization, including art, technology, or the kind of human achievements pitted against human atrocities on the game show, "Blood and Roses" (78–79), but they are already dreaming, singing, building a graven image, and beginning to develop in directions Crake thought he had edited out. Thus, even if their innocence does not mark them for extinction, there is no assurance that they will not eventually develop the self-destructive characteristics that lead human culture to death. On the one hand, Crake's motives might be good. On the other hand, he always enjoys playing intellectual games to see whether he can do what he conceives. Not just Crake but other human beings often act without examining consequences. In this sense, all people can be Frankensteins.

Oryx and Crake convinces us that human beings are in serious trouble. As indicated by Atwood's famous "brown box," the press clippings about child slavery, epidemics, disappearing animal species, cloning, polio, climate change, hybrid animals and foods, and "the race to create transgenic pigs" Atwood provided to accompany review copies of the book (Bethune 46; see Margaret Atwood Papers, 335, Boxes 104, 108, 145),[7] the current world already seems hopelessly messed up. Is it really impossible to change? In order to survive, is it really necessary to program sex and death and adapt humans to eat what they defecate? Is it really necessary that, except for different colors, everyone looks alike? At the end of the novel, close to dying from infection and malnutrition, Snowman can still feel rapture at the beauty of the earth and is willing to risk his life to protect the Crakers. He and at least three other human beings face imminent death but are still alive. They still have some choice, and so do we.

CHAPTER 3

The Writer as Crone Goddess in Atwood's *The Penelopiad* and Lessing's *The Memoirs of a Survivor*

Frequently the aged and aging narrators and personas in recent women's literature are viewed as Medusa monsters like the one at Avilion, the Tennysonian estate in Margaret Atwood's *The Blind Assassin*. Looking out from wrinkled and deteriorating bodies, their gazes may indeed seem freezing evil eyes, partly because we are afraid to see, hear, and know what they know, views usually at odds with official or approved opinions. Since they often write the stories we read, we experience these crones as Medusas and witches. We may even be afraid, as May Sarton suggests in "The Muse as Medusa," that their faces could be our own (1690–1691).

As in contemporary women writers ranging from Margaret Laurence, Toni Morrison, and Rosario Ferre to Angela Carter and May Sarton, Doris Lessing and Margaret Atwood's Crone figures are based on myth. Part of the Great Goddess, the Crone is the Hecate and old moon aspect of the cycle, differentiated from the Diana or virgin (new moon) and Venus or mother (full moon) but, like other phases of the Triple Goddess, suggesting the moon in all three of her aspects. Although the Crone is the "old" aspect and may be associated with death, she also suggests wisdom, healing, and rebirth. Other figures representing the dark aspect of the moon include Medusa, fairy-tale witches in "Sleeping Beauty" and "Snow White," female vampires, and werewolves. Discussing the Woman as Nature and Nature as Monster themes in reference to the "bumper crop" of Hecates in Canadian literature, which are often portrayed as ice or rock (Pratt 86–96), Margaret Atwood points out that Hecate or the Crone "is not sinister when viewed as part of a process" (*Survival* 199–201).

Most significantly, the Crone, like Medusa, symbolizes divine female wisdom (B. Walker, *Encyclopedia* 629), often the "all-judging eye of wisdom." For poets, Medusa is an archetype of female creativity, of "powers previously hidden and denigrated" (Pratt 55, 40). Often the Medusa gaze has been considered the artist's ability to impose "beauty and form upon the chaotic flux of experience" (Barnes 32–34, qtd. Pratt 38); thus, the female artist has been seen as the opposite of the nurturing mother and, therefore, a monster. Concerned especially with artists like herself, the mature narrator in Sarton's *Mrs. Stevens Hears the Mermaids Singing* says that "We are all monsters. . . . we women who have chosen to be something more and something less than women!" (155–56). Because the unnamed narrator of *Memoirs of a Survivor* and Penelope of *The Penelopiad* reveal unrecognized female power in their telling of their stories, both may strike some readers as monstrous. As Lessing's title foregrounds, however, they are survivors. They are also artists and creators.

Despite stylistic differences, in terms of intertextual tactics, Lessing's *Memoirs of a Survivor* and Atwood's *The Penelopiad* are similar. Both build scenes on images, such as the cracked-open egg and the murdered maids, from myth or fairy tales. Although goddess myth did focus on females, many readers think of male heroes, such as Hercules or Odysseus, instead of female ones. Thus, the two texts reverse the gender readers expect protagonists to be and give voice to the silenced, especially true for Penelope who epitomized societal constructions of the conventional, conformist female. Using unreliable narrators who admit that they are uncertain and may even be inconsistent about some events, both also undercut the pose of truth, the illusion of reality, that some readers still expect fiction to present, and give us very surprising stories. Their symbolism, of the egg, of the phases of the moon, enriches the experience of readers who have forgotten goddess myth. Both texts "write beyond the ending" by writing from a time beyond the time of their stories, as if the narrators continue speaking after we have closed the books and bend genres and blend tones, as when the maids who will be murdered constitute a chorus line. The books' profound irony and parody critique current culture and narrative tradition and, perhaps more than in most of the writers here, remythify forgotten myth that treats females as well as males with respect.

THE ODYSSEY AND CREATION, GODDESS, AND HERO MYTH IN ATWOOD'S *THE PENELOPIAD*

Margaret Atwood's texts have drawn on the mythic Great Goddess in *Double Persephone, You Are Happy, Lady Oracle, The Robber Bride, The Blind Assassin,* and her visual art; and in her recent novel, *The Penelopiad* (2005), Atwood chooses to have her Great Goddess figure, Penelope, both a parody and a symbol of wisdom and creativity, retrospectively retell and revision the story of Penelope and Odysseus from her Crone phase.[1]

Not apparent until near the end of *The Penelopiad,* the entire cycle of creation, harmony, and balance is suggested by recognizing the writer Penelope as an aspect of the Great Goddess. Just in case some readers have not seen through Penelope's disguise as the faithful wife, the maids present an "Anthropology Lecture," confessing that Penelope and the twelve maidens are really the Moon Goddess Artemis and the twelve moon cycles of a year (163–64) and cautioning that this is not just "unfounded feminist claptrap" (166). An ancient means of measuring time, the phases of the moon coincide with the female menstrual cycle and are the measure of the month: *Moon, menses,* and *month* all come from the same root, meaning "measure" or power (Leach and Fried 743; B. Walker, *Woman's Encyclopedia* 670). Thus, the bow that Telemachus shoots through the twelve ax heads to hang the maids is the old-moon bow of Artemis, the axes are the double-bladed ones associated with the Great Goddess, and the rape and murder of the maids is the patriarchal overthrow of the goddess and matriarchy. Commenting on and even videotaping some of the action, Atwood's twelve maidens constitute a parody of a Greek chorus in being also a chorus line, initially jumping rope and later dancing and singing to music. Characteristic of Atwood's mythologizing, the raped and enslaved maidens are parodic whores with renewable virginity yet at the same time mythic symbols of real injustice and usurped female power.

The Egyptian Moon Goddess, Menos, invented writing (B. Walker, *Encyclopedia* 634), and Penelope, who measures the time until Odysseus's return, "spins" the "thread" of the story she tells us (119, 4), showing her association with another aspect of the Great Goddess: the Morae or Three Sisters of Fate. Like Penelope and numerous goddesses, the Three Sisters weave and, in cutting the threads of life, unweave, as the ancient goddess wove the universe every day and unwove it every night. The pre-Hellenic Penelope is a fate-weaver (B. Walker, *Woman's Dictionary* 161, 163), the shroud that Penelope unravels is called "Penelope's web," and she even jokes about being Arachne. She is a "Veiled One," representing future fate, and saves Odysseus, the beheaded Year King or Hanged Man (Atwood, *Penelopiad* 166–67), because she is reluctant to cut the thread of his life (B. Walker, *Woman's Dictionary* 161). The suitors pursue her as all humans woo Fate but also because she was once the orgiastic fertility-mother (B. Walker, *Woman's Encyclopedia* 782). Penelope's rage over the maidens' execution also suggests the Furies, the destructive or vengeful power of the goddess closely related to the Fates and a remnant of the matriarchal clan system. The Furies or Eumenides resemble snake-haired gorgons in Aeschylus's conception and pursue criminals to punish antisocial acts, especially crimes against mothers (Leach and Fried 347; B. Walker, *Woman's Encyclopedia* 327). So irritated by the behavior of her son Telemachus that she wishes to ship him off to another Trojan War, Penelope thinks the best solution for him might be "a graceful death on my part" so that he would not kill her and be pursued by the Furies, as was Orestes when he killed his mother (110).

In *The Penelopiad,* Penelope has grown from a giggling fifteen-year-old prize in an archery contest to a wise trickster Crone. Handed over to Odysseus like a package of meat, "a sort of gilded blood pudding,"[2] Penelope has to hold her tongue so often that her still having one is a surprise (39, 160). Even within the "family-push-and-pull over whose word was to carry the most weight," everyone agrees that it is not Penelope's (71). As in Tennyson's "Ulysses," Odysseus may "leave to seek a newer world" and take his time getting home at least partly because he is "Matched with an aged wife" (Tennyson 1213–14). We discover, however, that Atwood's Penelope is much more than the archetypal faithful wife of Homer's *The Odyssey,* and Odysseus is not the only clever trickster of this story. Speaking retrospectively from Hades, Penelope reports that the suitors called her an old bitch and an old cow but admits the rumors that she was jealous of her cousin Helen, that she may have slept with all of the suitors—over a hundred—and supposedly gave birth to Pan. Although unlikely, she may even have ordered the deaths of the twelve maids, who were spying for her, to keep them quiet about her activities. Although she does not know everything, she still carries a sack full of words and continues to speak with no mouth because she "like[s] to see a thing through to the end" and "Now that all the others have run out of air, it's my turn to do a little story-making"(1, 3–4). In this postmodern tale, Atwood not only deconstructs Homer's *Odyssey* but also revisions cultural conceptions of crones. True, Penelope weaves and unweaves continuously, but what she weaves is the thread of life, fate, and story. Penelope is creation and story as well as creator.

In Atwood's version, Penelope's stories rival those of Odysseus, the noted persuader, establishing her as an equivalent "crafty cheat." During her long wait for her husband's return, Penelope keeps up the appearance of cheerfulness and hope by bringing up Telemachus on stories of how wonderful Odysseus is. Later, as Penelope and her twelve maids unravel her weaving at night, they tell stories, riddles, and jokes. Penelope's storymaking challenges those of patriarchal myth. As Atwood says in the "Introduction" that reminds us of the *Alias Grace* "Author's Afterword," "The story in *The Odyssey* doesn't really hold water: there are too many inconsistencies" (xv). Regarding the archetypal hero Odysseus, Penelope refuses to fill the role Virginia Woolf characterizes in *A Room of One's Own*: She is not a looking glass to reflect her man at twice his size (60) and does not even heed the injunction never to step between a man and his reflection (Atwood, *Penelopiad* 137). Odysseus is barrel-chested, with legs too short for his body, and this novel puts him on trial for an action barely noticed in the epic: His killing the twelve maidens exposes him as one of the patriarchs, including Perseus and St. George, who symbolically murder the moon-cult or Great Goddess of Matriarchy (165; see Pratt). He and Telemachus actually gloat over locking the women up and taking command of what had been a domestic sphere. Reminding us of how Atwood links and intertwines fairy tales and myths, Penelope even implies several resemblances of Odysseus and Bluebeard (the Grimms' Fitcher), notorious for chopping up successive wives who fail his prenuptial test. Telling her that everyone has a hidden door to the heart, behind which there is a secret that could help one master the Fates and thus control the thread of one's destiny, he jokes that, if she tells anyone about the bedpost rooted in the earth, he "would have to chop me into little pieces" (57–58, 74). Later, he wants to chop the maids into pieces (158, 171). Resembling the way Atwood uses the closely related "The Robber Bridegroom" fairy tale throughout her work, Penelope asserts her power over the threads of destiny by reversing the story to make Odysseus pass her "bedpost test."

For nearly every story or song from the *Odyssey* celebrating Odysseus's heroism, *The Penelopiad* posits a deflating counter story: Instead of a one-eyed Cyclops, Odysseus might have fought a one-eyed tavern keeper over the bill; instead of being waylaid by Circe, Odysseus was sponging off a madam of a whorehouse. The wilder the story, the more gifts Penelope has to provide the minstrels or tellers. Even Penelope's stories about herself deflate her role in myth. She emphasizes that she is twenty years older than the suitors, who make crude jokes about sleeping with her. As for the statue of Modesty erected when she pulled down her veil instead of declaring her desire for her husband, she confesses that she wanted to hide her laughter; and she daydreams about pretending to be modest while doing a man's work so that Odysseus will like her more than her cousin Helen. Like her more famous husband, Penelope is adept at disguise and lies. As in most of Atwood's recent work, there is always "another story. Or several," such as "The Perils of Pauline" narrated by the maids, in which, despite rumors of her immorality, Penelope can appear to be whatever she wishes if she "blame[s] it on the maids." Although she recognizes Odysseus immediately when he returns, she pretends not to and makes him wait. As they reestablish their relationship founded on stories,

The two of us were—by our own admission—proficient and shameless liars of long standing. It's a wonder either of us believed a word the other said.
But we did.
Or so we told each other. (173)

If the stories in *The Odyssey*, "the official version," do not "hold water," neither do those of Penelope, who is, after all, half Naiad and adept at floating in water (2, xv, 9). Penelope's "fishy" connection is even emphasized in Nina Chakrabarti's cover illustration based on Atwood's unacknowledged pen and ink mock cover showing Penelope with a star-fish eye (Atwood Papers, 335, Box 151). Every bit as wise and charming as Atwood's Circe ("Circe Mud Poems"), Siren ("Siren Song"), and harpies ("Bad News," covers of *Good Bones and Simple Murders*), this time it is Penelope's turn to weave and unweave the story, deconstructing reader expectations. But is Penelope's memoir only a record of vengeance, as Ingersoll suggests ("Myth")? Since she is so adept at making us laugh, so persistent about speaking, despite her situation in Hades, and intrinsically part of a cycle, it seems unfair and simplistic to equate her, the Great Goddess, and by association, women writers' revisioning and creation, with destruction or only "the dark side." Who beside Atwood's Circe and Penelope has ever questioned Odysseus's vengeful and unheroic acts, including slaughtering the twelve maids, let alone wondering how killing Trojans can establish him as a hero? Atwood's Penelope is a creator who feels compelled to speak even from the underworld, challenging Odysseus's reputation as a tale-teller by creating in the kind of void Albert Camus describes in *The Myth of Sisyphus*. Atwood's Penelope is not content to be objectified: Turned into a story by gossip (Baudelaire's "Rumour"), particularly since everyone believes that Odysseus's version of events is the true one (2–3). Even in Hades, she cannot bear to be thought of as just another princess married to a hero, another female whose only hope is a man. Focusing on her personal odyssey in *The Penelopiad*, Penelope appropriates patriarchal myth and establishes her own identity as a wise Crone creator. Characteristically, Atwood re-visions old stories, in this case Homer's canonical story, in a postmodern manner, emphasizing how history, myth, and reality—yet other stories—are all constructions. Like Scheherezade without a mouth, Penelope is an archetypal woman writer: She creates, changes, and perpetuates a world and herself for as long as she speaks.

LESSING'S *MEMOIRS OF A SURVIVOR*

Doris Lessing, born May Taylor in Persia (Iran) in 1919, grew up in Southern Rhodesia (Zimbabwe), moved to London, and like Margaret Atwood, has won the Booker several times and been nominated for the Nobel Prize. Although Doris Lessing uses myth, fairy-tale, and other folklore intertexts throughout her work, from *The Grass Is Singing* to *The Sweetest Dream* and *The Cleft*, this significant subject has not received the attention it deserves. Critics have noted some references to Greek mythology, Sufiism, and other religions, have applied Jungian and Laingian psychological approaches, and have commented on Lessing's characteristic tendency to puncture "fairy tales." Often, the myths and fairy tales discussed tend to be metaphoric, as in happy endings or idealistic dreams, rather than those to which folklorists refer: the stories people tell to explain reality (myth) or the fiction that pictures its wonders (märchen) (Leach and Fried 676). Scholars of myth recognize that myths are etiological: They explain the cause or origin of natural phenomena and the fundamental enigmas of human existence (Harris and Platzner 37); contrary to contemporary usage that makes *myth* synonymous with *false*, myths are or were believed.

For Lessing, myths are particularly useful because they can communicate beyond words, through their form, a technique with which she has been particularly preoccupied in parts of *The Four-Gated City, The Golden Notebook, Briefing for a Descent into Hell, The Memoirs of a Survivor, The Marriages Between Zones, Three, Four, and Five,* and *The Cleft.*[3] According to Lessing, "Words are contaminated, full of traditional associations . . . [and] connected with factions. . . . *Memoirs of a Survivor* is the direct result of my meditating about the inadequacy of language. I write as in legends or fairy tales" (Torrents 66–67). With *The Memoirs of a Survivor* (1975) she was attempting "an autobiography of dreams, in dream form. . . . In part I was writing an autobiography in terms of metaphor—behind the dissolving wall is the most ancient symbol you can probably find. I always use these old, hoary symbols, as they strike the unconscious" (Tomalin174). As Lessing notes, although several critics point to autobiographical aspects of *Memoirs,* including the problematic mother-daughter relationship behind the wall (Tiger, *Ages* 14) and the way that each of the characters in the book represents a part of the narrator as well as of Lessing (Perrakis, *Journeys* 42), few have taken her words very seriously (Tomalin174; Rousseau 148), especially about writing metaphorically, as in fairy tales and myth. Psychologists such as Jung and Marie-Louise von Franz use the same techniques to analyze myth, fairy tales, and dreams; the connections among the three in Lessing's work should receive greater attention. In *Memoirs,* the work the narrator does behind the wall resembles the "work" of psychoanalysis and productive dreaming. To go forward, this time the narrator (and by implication, all human beings) must not only relive the past—hers, Emily's, Lessing's, Edwardian England's, and ours—through mythic symbols, actually seeing and understanding its oppressions and repressions, but also step out of it into a new future. Thus, the flawed characters, including child criminals, transform and become part of the whole.

Like *The Penelopiad, Memoirs of a Survivor* remythifies goddess myth. Both are about the power of the woman artist, the Crone, and survival through words. While *The Penelopiad* also parodies goddesses and heroes, *Memoirs of a Survivor* suggests the need for a mythology that reverences nature and a beginning beyond industrial collapse.

Early reviews of *Memoirs of a Survivor* were "mainly confused or hostile" (Sullivan, "*Memoirs*" 157–58). As Gayle Greene asserts, most readers expected realism and missed the point (*Doris* 142; 252n3). They particularly found the conclusion, which is a new beginning, obscure (Rubenstein 238) or unsatisfactory. Malcolm Cowley and Victoria Glendinning attack the novel's conclusion as a "'cop-out,' a 'fairy godmother' deus ex machina" (24; 1405). However valuable their comments may be, most critics manage to avoid entirely any discussion of the black iron egg, and many even ignore the "she" that the narrator is incapable of describing.[4] Using a Jungian approach, Rubenstein thinks the egg symbolizes the narrator's "state of psychological pregnancy" that produces a child, Emily (223), but, of course, Emily appears long before the black egg does. Sullivan feels the ending "posits a mystical solution" (*"Memoirs"* 157–58), and Rashke compares "the inadequacy of this ending" to the conclusion of Eliot's "The Waste Land," "which returns us to the text in order to find a way out of a seemingly inescapable wasteland" (44).

"The Waste Land" parallel is pertinent since this canonical Eliot poem, like *Memoirs,* uses folklore and myth intertexts (for Eliot, primarily the Fisher King and vegetation myths) to expose the breakdown of the British class structure, western technology, and modern civilization and depicts fragmented values, identities, and institutions. Indeed, *Memoirs of a Survivor* could also be read as a retelling of the Fisher King myth, this time with a "Fisher Queen" or goddess hero. Both texts link personal physical illness to societal and world disharmony. Beginning with the metaphor of a mythic sea journey (3), also used in *Briefing for a Descent into Hell,* Lessing uses "The Sorcerer's Apprentice" to show endless tasks becoming futile and chaotic, a "poltergeist" to symbolize destruction of order, "The Pied Piper" to suggest people's willingness to follow hypnotic leaders, "Hansel and Gretel" to suggest the human "capacity to eat and eat and never be filled" (142),[5] "Beauty and the Beast" to imply the inseparability of the human and the animal, Demeter-Persephone and Edenic myths to express the yearning for a lost green world, and hero myth to show an individual battling and overcoming the "monsters" of urban decay. *Memoirs* also uses dystopian and utopian traditions to depict the collapse of empire (M. Green 36–37), the realistic novel, and the hierarchies of patriarchal structures as well as the beginning of new forms and a new world. Lessing's unnamed city, like Eliot's, is unreal and falling down. Lessing's narrator is even a kind of Tiresias, watching and recording the death and, though debatable in Eliot, rebirth of the world. The Survivor makes it clear that several old worlds have ended and that life is a continuous process of re-creation. The tone of the final pages is reverential, even miraculous. Perhaps because of fantastic elements and paradoxical mythic images, few people seem to recognize this novel's optimism.[6]

As Lessing says, "behind the dissolving wall is the most ancient symbol you can probably find. I always use these old, hoary symbols, as they strike the unconscious" (Tomalin 174). The egg is *Memoirs's* chief ancient symbol.[7] Anyone familiar with what are usually called creation myths—prehistoric explanations of the origins of the universe and of particular cultures and countries—does not find them a "cop out." Often repeating globally with variations, these myths signify truths beyond any words. Why, then, do many readers not find the egg meaningful?

For one thing, since most of *Memoirs* is an apocalyptic dystopia, filled with images of decay, chaos, fragmentation, world breakdown, and collapse, readers may overlook or minimize the utopian elements: The novel is not about the end of the world, as M. Greene asserts (142), but about its new beginning. Also, despite the famous Diana (Artemis) of Ephesus, whose many breasts resemble eggs (B. Walker, *Woman's Encyclopedia* 204–205), many readers associate eggs, where they still recognize the symbolism, with a male creator or with fertility stripped of power and wonder in patriarchal societies. Mythologically, eggs represent the earth, life, or the seat of the soul (Leach and Fried 341) and are the mystical symbol of the goddess or creatress, "whose World Egg contains the universe in embryo" (B. Walker, *Woman's Encyclopedia* 270). In India, Egypt, Greece, and Phoenicia, the creator and humankind emerge from the Cosmic Egg (Leach and Fried 1184; see also Motif A641, Thompson, *Motif* 6: 246).[8] Some mandalas, which are maps of the universe, are oval or egg-shaped (B. Walker, *Woman's Dictionary* 10). An egg can appear as a shiny ball; and in African folklore, an egg can transform into a house (Thompson, Motif F878, D469.1.1). According to Carol Mitchell, stories about the universe being born from an egg are properly cosmogonic rather than creation myths, and generally the birth is parthenogenic, from a female deity without a consort. The goddess has been associated with birds since the Neolithic period, and since the upper Paleolithic one, the egg is a symbol of wholeness, life, death, and rebirth (10–11, 21, 25).

Another dilemma is that, although preceded by images of yellow and white, including white egg shells and egg, the egg at the end of *Memoirs of a Survivor* is black, not golden, red, or white; and, rather than being "natural," it is made of pockmarked iron, a material associated with the manufacturing and technology that figures largely in the collapse of civilization depicted in *Memoirs*. The few critics who do discuss the egg at all (Newman 3–4; Sullivan, *Memoirs* 160–61) omit any reference to its being both black and iron. The 1981 David Gladwell film even finds it necessary to replace the black egg with a large but ordinary-looking white one. Since in many cultures black is identified with death and mourning or the devil rather than life, its use in *Memoirs* could be paradoxical or ironic. On the other hand, black is the color associated with the Hecate Crone aspect of the Triple Goddess. A black egg could also suggest the Orphics since it was the Great Goddess of darkness, Mother Night, who stands for the darkness of the womb and the archetype of the unconscious, which first brought forth the World Egg, identified with the moon (B. Walker, *Woman's Encyclopedia* 270; *Woman's Dictionary* 34, 207, 347). Black is frequently used in Ukrainian Easter eggs, which suggest rebirth, and in India black is protective against spirits. Also, in the Hindu tattvas for classifying the elements, the fifth element, spirit, is a black or indigo egg called Akasa, the Void. From the elements and colors, including black, all the world can be created. Petronius's zodiacal table has an egg-shaped goddess at its hub. A substitute for the Logos, the Cosmic Egg carries all Arabic numerals and alphabetical letters combined with an ellipse to show that all is contained within one form at the beginning (B. Walker, *Woman's Dictionary* 106, 5).

Iron, used in charms and taboos, may also be protective against sorcery, evil spirits, or dragons and is sometimes sacred; Hindu women wear iron wedding rings, and iron has been used for thousands of years as a healing agent in magnetic therapy. Especially relevant to the egg's pockmarked quality and the novel's concluding miraculous tone is iron's association with meteorites, which Aztecs and Egyptians called a "marvel from heaven" and Babylonians "heaven fire" (Leach and Fried 241–42, 528). Evoking Greek creation myth from Hesiod's *Theogyny,* Lessing's iron egg marks the end of the Iron Age of Humanity (Newman 4) and becomes the egg of creation from chaos and darkness. The Ages of Man include gold, silver, brass, hero demigods, and iron ages; the iron egg suggests the annihilation of evil humanity in the present (Hamilton 63, 69, 70). Paradoxically, as Morgan says, the egg can also mean a cyclical return—I would call it a rebirth—of a different Golden Age than the one Hesiod envisions, that of the Great Goddess, who creates new world harmony ("Iron"). In Hamilton's account of the Golden Age, only men exist before Pandora, the first woman, who comes to release plagues on human kind (70). Earlier, however, Pandora was part of the Great Goddess, possibly an underworld goddess associated with Hecate (Leach and Fried 843), and, typical of the way that patriarchy reversed goddess myth, she may have released not plagues but benefits to humanity when she opened the box or jar. On an individual as well as cultural level, *Memoirs of a Survivor* promises present and future wisdom to those willing to follow their Crone selves through the walls of consciousness to integration.

In Lessing's revisioned creation myth, the Cosmic Egg requires human coconstruction: The narrator mirrors her creator. Without the narrator's journey through the wall and without her work to clean and order the chaos—work that matches that of the painter and gardener—presumably this egg could not open. As well as being a witness to the death and rebirth of the world, Lessing's unnamed narrator is an active participant in its re-creation.

Echoing and implicitly commenting on narrators and narrative tradition from *Moby Dick* to *Cat's Cradle,* the writer narrator is a self-conscious artist who retrospectively records everything to do with "that time" and the generalized unease of "it" (5) in fantastic, postmodern metafiction that refuses reduction to the realistic and rational. For a twentieth-century narrator, she is partly reliable in the sense that she tries hard to render truthfully what happens. Despite transmutation to "another key," however, she is either not privileged or refuses to take advantage of privilege to go beyond ordinary mortal limits. She frequently uses the word "perhaps," admits that some things are beyond words, and even says that she is not sure what she saw (212). More frustrating for readers still expecting Western rationalism (Greene, *Doris* 141) and realism rather than the novel's magical realism (see chapter 4) is the use of major motifs, including the color white and the concept of pattern, in opposing ways to mean either the stale, conditioned, and mechanical behavior of puppets or the fresh, clean, and vital activity of free and responsible beings. For example, the color white appears in the smothering, trapped, personal world of the nursery—"an interminable plain of white"—where repressed parents teach their children to obey the same patterns, including gender conditioning, hierarchies, and institutions that confine them (130, 133,136). But it is also the white of the egg that marks the pure, natural cleanliness and order of the vital world that emerges only when the narrator makes her mythic journey into and through the wall.

> Gradually, the narrator senses that something was going on behind the wall of my living-room. . . . [, that] there was a room behind that wall, perhaps more than one, even a set of rooms, occupying the same space as—or, rather, overlapping with—the corridor. (8)

She compares looking at or thinking about the wall to "holding to one's ear an egg that is due to hatch. . . . I even found that I was putting my ear to the wall, as one would to a fertile egg, listening, waiting." She notices a yellow stain, a yellow pulsing, on this "empty" wall. When sunlight hits the wallpaper, which has been painted over with white paint, she discovers a half-obliterated pattern of flowers, leaves, and birds under the paint, suggesting trees, a garden, and colors of an underworld. Instead of being dragged under the earth, like Persephone, or going down a rabbit hole or "through the looking-glass," like Alice, the Survivor goes through the wall of her flat to discover rooms and gardens of another world that she has longed for and always known and a similarly familiar, androgynous "someone," the exiled but rightful inhabitant of the rooms, in white painter's overalls. She admits that this face might be a shadow or mirror of longing, reflecting back the person she sees at the "end" (11–14). Later, she encounters also a destructive presence and notes a continuous destruction and re-creation. While she mainly watches and records in the world outside the wall, in the personal realm inside the wall she experiences the shut-in stuffiness—cold father, untouching mother—of past family life, including Emily's and her own. In the freer impersonal realm, which momentarily feels like "the inside of a cleaned out eggshell," she cleans, paints, and orders. One of the rooms the narrator discovers is the octagon of a mandala that suggests the narrator's equilibrium or reconciliation of opposites (Raschke 50). It is here, for the first time, that the creator/ narrator sees people matching pieces of old material to the carpet, bringing the carpet's design to life—a process that must go on always and a scene that recurs in flashes at the end of the book, inside the Cosmic Egg (78–79, 212). As Phyllis Perrakis suggests, this matching is an analogy to both the interpretative process and the experience of reading the novel (Letter; see also "Journeys" 41). As the Survivor later realizes, it also suggests a mythic knowledge beyond words.

When they are not enclosing the nursery, broken junk, filth, or the endless "hunger" of "I want, I want," the walls through the wall continue to be associated with eggs and the color white, just as this realm's growing world is identified with nature: unpoisoned forests, grass, flowers, gardens, and streams, part of the one Presence and the Whole (98–99). Immediately after seeing the white sugarhouse that suggests the cannibalism of the "Hansel and Gretel" fairy tale and the neediness of consumer society's alienated people, the narrator hears Emily crying while her white-clad mother complains about her filthiness and bathes the child in alternately freezing and scalding water. Anticipating the conclusion, the narrator briefly steps outside walls into freedom and encounters a brilliant white egg as big as a house, poised lightly on a lawn and being touched and smelled not only by Emily and June but also by her father and mother (142–45). Then, however, she finds herself back in a dark passageway. Throughout the

book, eggs and their suggestion of creation, purity, order, and harmony counter apocalyptic destruction, decay, filth, and chaos.

The book is written in the future that occurs after the novel's end,
demonstrating a "writing beyond the ending" before this postmodern strategy in women's fiction was named[9]: The dystopian world
"ends" with the step first into a folding up world inside the giant
black egg and then into "another order of world altogether." Resembling the cycle of the seasons in the Demeter-Persephone myth, it
ends with the onset of winter after many of the hordes depart for "Silence and cold," with no word ever coming back. Four-year-old Dennis and some other children kill a man, asserting, like Golding's *Lord
of the Flies,* primal evil, the decline even of tribal order, and, one of
many folklore motifs in the book, the desire for a savior (207,
210–11). After waiting and finally seeing the "hidden pattern" on the
wall, Emily, Gerald, Hugo, and the narrator walk into the wall for the
final time. Now, rather than a white egg, they encounter a glossy
black egg paradoxically of pockmarked iron, that, like a meteorite,
journeys from another world and reflects them, as well as little Dennis
and Emily's officer father and "laughing gallant mother." It breaks
"by the force of their being there." Out of it comes

a scene, perhaps, of people in a quiet room bending to lay matching pieces of
patterned materials on a carpet that had no life until that moment when vital-
ity was fed into it by these exactly answering patches: but no, I did not see
that, or if I did, not clearly. . . .

Although previous "new starts" failed because of conditioned patterns, the transmutation to "a different order altogether" is final and
triumphant: The marvelous World Egg breaks, "the last walls dis-
solve," and everything is possible. Each character fulfills what had
only been potential: It is "Emily, yes, but quite beyond herself, trans-
muted, and in another key, and the yellow beast fitted her new self: a
splendid animal, handsome, all kindly dignity and command" (212).
The creator/ narrator reaches the end of simultaneous heroic and
artistic journeys:

the one person I had been looking for all this time was there: there she was.
No, I am not able to say clearly what she was like. She was beautiful: it is a
word that will do. I only saw her for a moment, in a time like the fading of a
spark on dark air—a glimpse: she turned her face just once to me, and all I can
say is . . . nothing at all. (213)

Using images that transcend the limits of language, the Survivor has penetrated not only her unconscious and the unconscious of the human race, but also the realm of myth: She rediscovers herself as hero and as "goddess," apparently a reflection of the ancient Great Goddess who symbolizes earth, life, wholeness, wisdom, and soul, and is reborn with the world. The transformation is not merely personal, psychological, or limited to the good, the female, the human, or even the present: The characters constitute passengers on a kind of Noah's Ark, another mythic reference. The dog-cat Hugo, Emily's/ the narrator's parents, Gerald, and even Gerald's children all cross "the threshold" to another dimension.

Both Atwood's *The Penelopiad* and Lessing's *Memoirs of a Survivor* revision the roles of the Crone and the woman artist. Atwood's Penelope becomes more than a faithful but uninteresting, old wife whom Odysseus can ignore while he sojourns with beautiful goddesses during the twenty years it takes him to return home. A clever trickster, Penelope sends words through time to retell Homer's story and reminds readers that the Great Goddess is not just "feminist claptrap" but did exist and that myths, even when parodied, continue to provide meaning and pattern. Lessing's Survivor, also no longer young, is the intelligence that records the fall of civilization and its new beginning, again showing the continued relevance of myths—especially Great Goddess myths—that give order and pattern to existence. Like Atwood's *The Robber Bride* and Hulme's *The Bone People,* both texts also demonstrate the power of the female artist.

CHAPTER 4

MYTHIC QUESTS FOR THE WORD AND POSTCOLONIAL IDENTITY: LESSING'S *THE STORY OF GENERAL DANN AND MARA'S DAUGHTER, GRIOT AND THE SNOW DOG* AND TONI MORRISON'S *BELOVED*

Doris Lessing and Toni Morrison are among the many contemporary women writers to shape profound new myths and fairy tales by drawing on the old great stories. Toni Morrison, an African American born Chloe Woffard in Lorain, Ohio, in 1931, won the Pulitzer Prize and then the Nobel Prize for literature in 1993. Doris Lessing, born May Taylor in Persia (Iran) in 1919 and a white daughter of British expatriates, grew up in southern Rhodesia (Zimbabwe), later moved to London, and like Margaret Atwood, has won the Booker several times and been nominated for the Nobel Prize. She also received the Prix Médicis. Disregarding the considerable stylistic and thematic differences in their work, both write about racism, sexism, and colonialism and both use similar intertextual tactics.

Like other writers in this book, Lessing and Morrison use mythic and fairy-tale plots, structure, characterization, images, themes, and motifs in *The Story of General Dann and Mara's Daughter, Griot and the Snow Dog* and *Beloved*. They also build upon or parody intertexts by creating scenes based on myths and fairy tales, evident when Dann remembers Mara and himself escaping the ogre, Kulik, and when

Amy views the blooming tree on Sethe's back. Both displace "truth" and give voice to the silent in undercutting authority and allowing both slaves and those who have never had homes or been allowed to develop healthy self-concepts to speak. Both communicate through such tropes as weather and colors to make their worlds deeply symbolic, and both use subversive irony, as when Snow Dog is more "human" than Dann and when, in Morrison's world, Beloved is not allowed to be loved. In both books but *Beloved*, especially, language defamiliarizes subjects—environmental collapse, fall of empires, slavery—few people want to recognize and moves readers toward the postcolonial and cocreation of the text. As in a number of Lessing's recent works, language in *The Story* is that of the ancient *griot* (storyteller), who tells us what we need to know in order to survive. Language in *Beloved* is poetic, choral, from the collective unconscious, unique, but also necessary to human survival. Genres and tones bend and blend, and intertexts are remythified.

Despite the major role myths and fairy tales play in creating their postcolonial visions, and despite both authors' discussion of folklore and reference to it as influential in their work, in neither case do these aspects of Lessing's and Morrison's works command sufficient attention.

The Power of Story in *The Story of General Dann and Mara's Daughter, Griot and the Snow Dog*

Since Doris Lessing grew up in a colonized culture, southern Rhodesia (Zimbabwe), it is no accident that her characters have to struggle to survive spiritually and even physically in worlds of clashing values. Although Lessing is usually perceived as a member of the colonial elite rather than one of the colonized, and although she shared the privileges of "whiteness," for much of her life she was still "a colonial" living in Africa rather than the "home" country and, thus, a representative of a supposedly second-rate culture. As Margaret Atwood, among others, has described, colonials are conditioned to feel low self-esteem and have an inferiority complex (*Survival*), even the kind of failure complex Martha Quest and Mary Turner represent, about being colonial rather than truly "English." Lessing has actively opposed colonialism, imperialism, and institutionalized racism throughout her career. Nearly all of her work (e.g., the *Martha Quest* and the Canopus series, *The Grass is Singing, Mara and Dann, The Story of General Dann and Mara's Daughter, Griot and the Snow Dog*) is explicitly or implicitly critical of both literal and secondary or meta-phorical colonialism.

As in *Memoirs of a Survivor* and *Marriages Between Zones Three, Four, and Five,* Lessing's narrators often watch themselves and their worlds of clashing cultures fall apart spiritually and physically before they can take action to cross physical and psychological borders and construct new hybrid identities. According to Homi Bhabha, "It is in the emergence of the interstices—the overlap and displacement of do-mains of difference—that the intersubjective and collective experience of *nationness,* community interest, or cultural value are negotiated" (*Locations* 2). Both a postmodern and postcolonial writer, Doris Less-ing uses popular culture intertexts, especially myths, fairy tales, and folklore, and the characterization, images, themes, structures, and techniques (e.g., magical realism) associated with them, to portray her exiled characters' growth from alienation and polarity to hybrid-ity. Mythic intertexts not only dramatize nation-building and collaps-ing in Lessing's work. Her in-between beings' engagement in the process of constructing identity, knowledge, and "home" is, in itself, mythic. It is in and through story that Lessing's characters construct a hybrid way of being-in-the-world.

As we have seen, since Lessing's texts sometimes leave "realistic," chronological, and linear time for a mythic one, although characters may worry about aging (*The Summer Before the Dark*), suffer injury or illness, or have difficulty taking care of themselves (*The Diaries of Jane Somers*), the journey toward wisdom is often as spiritual as phys-ical, sometimes involving movement through walls of the mind and the appearance of mythic beings, including goddesses. Her metafic-tion, including *The Golden Notebook, Marriages Between Zones Three, Four, and Five, Memoirs of a Survivor,* and *The Story of General Dann and Mara's Daughter, Griot and the Snow Dog,* sometimes uses self-conscious, developing, partly unreliable narrators who practice writ-ing as a means of ordering, growing, and knowing.

The Story of General Dann and Mara's Daughter, Griot and the Snow Dog (2005) is a sequel to Lessing's 1999 novel, *Mara and Dann,* a more compelling story centered on a strong character. Mara's perspective grows in a traditional way as she experiences near starvation and death, alternating kinship and isolation, home and not-home, and identity and split on her and her brother Dann's quest for a better place, a place further north. According to Mona Knapp, Mara

is an ice-age Martha Quest who, . . . not wanting to change the world if she can just watch it go by from a safe place, is as unable to challenge her environment as was Mary Turner in the 1950 novel *The Grass is Singing*. With her very small personal voice, Mara brings fifty years of Lessing full circle. (366)

In this novel and its sequel, however, although the environment appears to rule everything as much as colonialism with its racism, sexism, and cultural conditioning ruled the worlds of Martha Quest and Mary Turner, the only realities are change and loss and the attempts to save knowledge, construct home and kinship, and tell the story. Mara, formerly Princess Shahana, is a much more sympathetic character than Dann in either book, and, if the two volumes are taken as the beginning of a series, the memory of her and her values provides the second book with most of its few glimmers of hope. It is Mara who notices that women are not free, that tribes such as the Mahondis will die out, that power rules relationships, that people mistakenly believe what they have will continue, that the truth will not be believed unless someone has experienced it, and that people and "cities are as temporary as dreams" (*Mara and Dann* 361). It is Mara who learns to value the uniqueness of different kinds of people, hears the flowers screaming for water (143), worries about species becoming extinct, and tries to pass on learning. With Lessing's advancing years, after "the sweetest dream" of Marxism and the end of the British Empire, the destruction and re-creation of the world in *Memoirs of a Survivor*, and her excursions into space fiction, her perspective has broadened so that, like Mara, Dann, and later Griot, she tells what she has seen, revealing all tyrannies and triumphs and even life on earth as short-lived. As early as her 1988 interview with Claire Tomalin, she speaks of how her interviewer (and readers) have not seen what she has seen, including "the angry and destructive hoards" of migrating people depicted in *Memoirs*, and take as permanent ideas or structures, such as the white regime in Rhodesia, that suddenly vanish (Tomalin Interview 174–75).

The Story of General Dann and Mara's Daughter, Griot and the Snow Dog more completely deconstructs the happy ending both novels explicitly discuss and any expectation that there can be a stable home, identity, ethnicity, nation, or planet. A cautionary tale resembling oral narrative (Tiger 23) and set thousands of years in the future, this novel will probably be even less popular than *Mara and Dann*, which has received almost no critical attention, because it denies readers what many of us want: well-defined characters in recognizable life-situations, comfortable themes, and an eventual happy resolution. We still do not want to know about global warming with its melting ice caps and violent weather changes and, like most of the characters of this book, we would rather live in either the past or the future than see the unpleasant present evident here. According to Theresa Crater, Lessing wrote *Mara and Dann* in part as a Sufi teaching story, "a corrective to the massive spiritual illness of the 1990s (17). Some reviewers blame one or both books for being didactic (Review *Kirkus* 1249) or repetitive (Korenowsky 114). As Hazel Rochman says of *The Story*, "one must slog through endless generic journeys in a future world to get to the personal relationships that matter" (32).

Unlike *Mara and Dann*, narrated through Mara's consciousness, in *The Story*, the main center of consciousness is Griot, another self-conscious narrator who makes this novel truly a story about a story, a metafiction about creating, recreating, and synthesizing from the midst of destruction. This futuristic novel about loss and grief begins with Dann's view in third person of what he sees as he travels in Ifrik, apparently what is left of Africa following global warming, the melting of ice caps, the flooding of cities, the dissolution of empires, the loss of cultures with their heritage of accumulated knowledge, and the mass migrations of diverse people of many races and languages. As Virginia Tiger says, the title is cumbersome and the characters are stick figures, with perhaps the best-drawn one—certainly my favorite—being Ruff, the Snow Dog (23). These characters are, however, archetypal, representing positions and values and suitable to the romance form evident in science fiction, fantasy, and folklore.

In her "Author's Note" to *Mara and Dann*, Lessing speaks of her conscious reworking of a very old tale about the adventures of a brother and sister found in most cultures of the world (vii). The repetitive and fantastic struggles of both this novel and its sequel suggest folklore, including fairy tales and myth. Lessing has previously referred to brother-sister incest or extremely close relationships in *The Golden Notebook*, with Maryrose and her brother. As Abel suggests, Anna's perception of Saul as brother "sets her free from her futile round of self-destructive relationships" (121). In folktales, both the brother and sister may be heroic (Thompson VI 100–101, 709), but, as in *Mara and Dann*, often there is a loyal, clever sister and an alternately loyal and betraying brother. Both books' motifs of starvation, struggle for survival, cannibalistic greediness, and archetypal characters suggest AT 327A, the Grimms' "Hansel and Gretel," about abandoned orphans trying to outwit ogres and find their way (see chapter 7). The Grimms' "The Juniper Tree" and the similar Scottish tale "Applie and Orangie" (AT 720; Dorson 37–40) feature children eaten and reincarnated as birds and a punished stepmother. Tale Type

450 also features a brother and sister who escape a cruel stepmother to live in a forest. Some of the related tales have sisters who search for or rescue brothers, brothers who betray and rescue sisters from the devil, and brothers who magically transform. Sisters in fairy tales, folktales, or myths may be driven from home or become cannibals, may rescue or be rescued by their brothers, may plot against them, or may work with them to heal the king (Aarne and Thompson 551, 580). In the Russian tale, "Sister Alyonushka and Brother Ivanus," thirsty orphans alone in the forest remain loyal and rescue one another from transformation, drowning, and a witch (Russian Crafts .com/tales). In traditional stories, the earth may be formed from the murder of the first brother and sister, the moon and the sun or vice versa may be sister and brother, the ocean and his sister may give birth to rivers as offspring, and a brother may impregnate, eat, or flog an unchaste sister, win his sister's suitor test, or kill the sister's husband.

In these tales incest, often involuntary, occurs worldwide, and, as stated in *Mara and Dann,* such marriage between brother and sister was practiced among the royalty or higher nobility in Egypt, Persia, Peru, Siam, Ceylon, Wales, Burma, Hawaii, Uganda, among Greek deities, and is recorded in Genesis. Incest between brothers and sisters was more commonly forbidden because it could cause tragedy, such as drought, could prevent one from entering Paradise, could make one bear insect children, or, as Mara suggests in *Mara and Dann,* could make them malformed or like sinister doubles (Leach and Fried 165–66). Sometimes, as in the Santal Parganas aboriginal Indian story "Kora and His Sister," their blood and even the smoke from their burned bodies refuse to mix, indicating that never again should a brother and sister marry (Ashliman). In the Lithuanian tale, "A Brother Wants to Marry His Sister," when all her relatives conspire to make her marry her younger brother, the beautiful sister asks the earth to open and swallow her. She marries the lord of the underground instead of her brother (Ashliman). Although orphaned Mara and Dann refuse to form a doomed dynasty based on intermarriage of their extended family, Dann seems never to adjust to losing what he believes is his "true bride" and mourns Mara throughout most of *The Story.* In addition to folklore narrative patterns and character types, Lessing also uses mythological motifs, including a relative's treachery, kindness and unkindness, the false bride (Kira), magic in hair (Leta), escape from an ogre (Kulik), quest for a savior (Dann), and escape from deluge as one of many world calamities (Leach and Fried 478; Aarne and Thompson 152–53; Thompson I).

Our supposed hero of *The Story*, Dann, previously Prince Shah-mand, worshipped by Griot and Ruff the Snow Dog, is regarded as a great leader, thought to possess magic, and, as in *Oedipus Rex* and the New Testament, expected to be a savior. He is so incapacitated by Mara's death, however, that he seems to be a parody of a hero. Like most epic heroes, he is on an Odyssey of sorts, complete with a "witch" who detains him on an island (94), and it takes him a very long time to return from war to a home that is no longer home. Like *The Mwindo Epic* (Zaire, collected 1956), *The Story* does imply a code of proper behavior: Interpersonal relationships are as important as heroic deeds, and all forms of life deserve respect (Rosenberg 440). But after Dann gambles away his sister in the previous novel, it is other characters, especially the Mara muse and, ironically, Snow Dog, who model human behavior. Like many of Lessing's characters, Dann's identity is multiple rather than singular or simple: Both slave and ruler, he is split between Dann and the Other One, but unlike Anna in *The Golden Notebook* and the Watcher in *Memoirs of a Sur-vivor*, he cannot heal his split or penetrate the walls that block his in-tegration. His grief, parallel to that of Griot, who cannot remember family or home and has never loved, of Tamar, who cannot remember her mother, and of Snow Dog, whose parents drowned, is the poison that interferes with healthy growth. Dann's friends, Durk, Marianthe, Kass, Shabis, Leta, Daulis, Ali, Griot, his niece Tamar, and Snow Dog, accompany him on his multifaceted quest. His estranged wife, Kira, with her daughter Rhea, plays this book's "look at me" windup doll who is ill on poppy but, unsurprisingly, not only wants Dann to lick her foot but also wants to rule all of Tundra. Except for Kira and Rhea, the characters gradually become aware that they all "have to play their parts . . . until the story is finished." Thus, in a sense, be-cause they move "from one bad dark place to a better—from the Farm to the Centre, and then to a good place—," Tamar can say that they live "happily ever after" (280–81) even though Dann laughs. But home and identity in this book cannot be simply attained and held. In *Memoirs of a Survivor*, the narrator tells us that everything al-ways changes, but few of us have experienced the extent to which change and loss are the only constants in *The Story of General Dann and Mara's Daughter, Griot and the Snow Dog*. The only possible home and identities are those brief moments of coming together with family and friends, including Snow Dog and the memory of him, in the long journey called life and story.

Griot's name means mythic storyteller, and it is he who creates pattern by finding his voice, the tuneless growl or howl that attracts animals to listen, "his tentative voice, which seemed that it wanted to learn something" (276). In a world of broken nations and empire, roaming hordes, and fragmented individuals who often have to keep part of themselves locked up or pacified with poppy or alcohol, Griot performs the classic role of the storyteller or Griot, in this case in a mock-epic story without the dragons of *Mara and Dann* or other heroes. As the Griot accompanies Mwindo in the Nyanga tribe's *The Mwindo Epic* along with a band to sing his praise while the hero accomplishes feats, Griot in *The Story* sings of Dann's postcolonial journey and at last has a life purpose. As Mara taught Dann in the preceding volume, as maps, books, and carvings teach how things were "a long time ago," and as Dann teaches Mara's daughter, Tamar, Griot helps everyone see, know, and remember. He also loyally allows Dann to take the credit for everything Griot does, including building an army from multiracial people united only by their red blankets. Dann never finishes his journey and, even at the end, as he and Mara assumed they would do at the end of *Mara and Dann,* wants only to continue walking. In addition to its archetypal characters representing positions and values, typical of this romance form is a possible new beginning at the "end" (writing beyond the ending): Although it would be stupid, Rhea might come as head of an army, and another kingdom might attack, quite possibly in a sequel to this novel. As in *Beloved,* perhaps the story of the journey beyond colonialism and empire never ends. According to Ashcroft, Griffiths, and Tiffin,

> Most post-colonial writing has concerned itself with the hybridised nature of post-colonial culture as a strength, rather than a weakness. . . . it emphasizes how hybridity and the power it releases may well be seen to be the characteristic feature and contribution of the post-colonial, allowing a means of evading the replication of the binary categories of the past, and developing new anti-monolithic models of cultural exchange and growth. (183)

The postcolonial world of *The Story* interweaves opposing ideas, as of returning to a Mahondi dynasty, building unity among diverse elements by providing food and red blankets, forming a new empire, avoiding the molded conformity of the Hadrons and the Hennes soldiers, both critiquing and reverencing different cultures and power structures, and just moving on. Thus, it illustrates what Homi Bhabha calls postcolonialism's "inscription and articulation of culture's *hybridity*" (38). As in Toni Morrison's *Beloved,* the possibility of cultural hybridity comes through a story based on historical and folklore intertexts.

GODDESS MYTH AND "SLEEPING BEAUTY" IN MORRISON'S *BELOVED*

Like most of the other authors in this volume, Toni Morrison inter-weaves myth, biblical, folklore, and fairy-tale intertexts in all of her novels. Although some readers would not consider North American writers postcolonial, Morrison powerfully critiques U.S. colonialism of both past and present, the system of patriarchal racism, sexism, and classism that has not only denied the freedom, self-determination, and even humanity of African Americans, but has sometimes literally colonized the bodies and property of people who live within its territories and borders. Orally transmitted folklore is important in all African American literature, including Morrison's work. As Ridley states,

verifiable traces of West African myth, religion, and aesthetic criteria that early slaves could hold in memory and transmit orally have survived in the oral traditions of expression that segregated black communities have developed in America. (153)

Critics have recognized Morrison's use of anti–fairy tales, flight and quest motifs, and trickster characters in her early works.[1] Morrison herself frequently discusses her fairy and folk references in articles and interviews, saying she wants her "fiction to urge the reader into active participation in the non-narrative, nonliterary experience of the text." She admits that she tries "to incorporate into [her] fiction . . . the major characteristics of Black art," one of which is "the ability to be both print and oral literature: to combine those two aspects" so that one "hears" the story and participates "in the same way that a Black preacher requires his congregation to speak, to join him in the sermon," or that "a musician's music is enhanced when there is a response from the audience" ("Rootedness" 341). She avoids literary references "unless oblique and based on written folklore," and she briefly discusses how, in *The Bluest Eye, Sula, The Third Life of Grange Copeland,* and *Tar Baby,* she tailors the tale ("Hansel and Gretel," "Goldilocks and the Three Bears," "Tar Baby") to characters' thoughts and actions "in a way that flags him or her and provides irony, sometimes humor" ("Memory" 387). In order "to confront a reality unlike that received in the West, [my work] must centralize and animate information discredited in the West . . . information held by discredited people, information dismissed as 'lore' or 'gossip' or 'magic' or 'sentiment' " (389). She regrets that folklore, "a little subject in the academy," is perceived of as "illiterate" (Caldwell 243).

Readers may also overlook the political implications of *Beloved*'s magical realism, or realism infused with the magical or the spiritual and fantastic. A term used by Franz Roh to describe German artists of the *neue Sachlichkeit* (new objectivity), magical realism portrays "the imaginary, the improbable, or the fantastic in a realistic or rational manner (Drabble 607; see also Zamora and Farris's Introduction). Remarkably diverse from text to text, magical realism often presents magical images, objects, or characters, such as Beloved and the tree on Sethe's back, that may emerge from incongruous contexts. Implying that the world may have a magical dimension that radiates, magical realist texts are often political, expressing "a world fissured, distorted, and made incredible by cultural displacement." (S. Hart and Ouyang 4, 2; Boemer cited 6).

The two most important types of folklore intertexts in *Beloved* are goddess myth and fairy tales. Although in 2008 no one has yet studied fairy tales in *Beloved* and few people explore the great significance of goddesses in this book, these patterns, interwoven with other intertexts, including their transformations or reversals, help create the magical realism that makes this novel so compelling. Embedded African American folklore includes folk tales, legends, myths, verbal formulae, praise names, and songs. The novel builds on traditional trickster stories; tales of "badness" such as the Sango myth (Ridley 154, 158); tales of slavery; the myth of the North as free; tales of succubi, shape-shifters, demons, and the vagina dentata (T. Harris 3, 13, 155); Morrison's own family ghost and other stories (Blake 188; Caldwell 242); other revenant and vampire tales; and sermons. Arthurian and other legends, including those of the Lady of the Lake and Morgan Le Fay, are important intertexts in *Beloved*. Biblical stories include those about the Good Samaritan (Carolyn Mitchell 28), Seth (Mayer 192–93), Abraham's sacrifice of Isaac, the Trees of Knowledge and Crucifixion, Christ's crucifixion and resurrection, Lot's wife, and various beloveds. Historical intertexts of the United States are also significant.

Goddess myth in *Beloved* includes tales of a killed child's resurrection; other African, Greek, Egyptian, or variant myths such as that about Seth, a mother who cuts off and replaces her son's "contaminated" hand (S. Wilson, *Margaret Atwood's Fairy* 363); and stories about the Libyan snake goddess Medusa and Egyptian equivalent Maat; Egyptian Hathor, Isis-Osiris-Horus and Osiris-Set or Seth;[2] African Yemaya, Oshun, Erzulie, Triple Goddess Neith, and the Asenath of the Bible (B. Walker, *Woman's Encyclopedia* 721). Middle-Eastern Astarte-Adonis, Greek and Roman Demeter-Persephone or

Kore, Eurydice-Orpheus, Medea, Lilith-Eve-Mary,[3] and Goddess Tree of Life myths are all central in *Beloved*. Morrison literally bases the novel on the true story of Margaret Garner (1853–1873), a mother who tried to kill all four of her children and succeeded with one when the slave catchers came (*Toni Morrison: Profile of a Writer*). But this story became a legend, and Morrison links it to myth and folk tales. Since Great Goddess myth occurred virtually everywhere in the ancient world and the Goddess was the basis of all life, Great Goddess figures in different cultures are much alike, generally viewed in a trilogy or with seven aspects. Sethe's attempt to save Beloved by killing her evokes both the Demeter and Isis myths as well as trickster cultural heroes. As Demeter, the mother whose sorrow over her daughter's absence causes the world to become barren, the goddess attempts to make the king's son immortal by putting him in the fire to burn away his mortality. The Egyptian Isis performs a similar action on the royal child of Byblos, and the Phoenicians may have also performed this ritual to protect children against evil (Stapleton 66). Isis also resurrects Osiris after he has been chopped into pieces. When Beloved dies, Sethe's world, like Demeter's without her daughter Persephone or Kore, no longer has color. Although she tries to repress memory, Sethe, like Isis, reincarnates her beloved. Like Kore or Persephone, the maiden abducted to the underworld, Beloved can only remain in the world a short time. Beloved also becomes pregnant, suggesting the mother phase of the goddess. Amy-Denver-Beloved, Sethe, and Baby Suggs variously combine to suggest the Triple Goddess cycle,[4] also evident in African folklore, of maiden or Virgin (Diana), Mother (Venus), and Crone (Hecate). As Trace suggests, they symbolize "being and becoming, growth and decay, life and death" (17).

We actually see Sethe in all three goddess roles, as a young woman making love to her husband among the cornstalks, as a mother risking everything to get baby Denver across the river to freedom, and as the dark Crone killing her child Beloved. By the end of the book, we also see the cycle beginning anew, with Sethe symbolically dying and beginning to live and love again, recovering herself at the same time that she and Paul D. recover the ability to care for another and that Denver rejoins the community. Throughout most of the book, Sethe is Mother Goddess, Denver the maiden, and Baby Suggs the Crone. Because Beloved comes back from the dead, she is a revenant or ghost, never meant to stay but the stimulus for change and for the continuation of the cycle. Sethe, the mother who is raped rather than honored and whose milk is stolen rather than used to nurture the child of her flesh, bears the Goddess Tree of Life on her back.

Numerous goddess figures inform the characterization and imagery of *Beloved*. The theft of Sethe's milk is one of the most powerful scenes of the book and clearly evokes the Egyptian mother goddess Hathor, who was worshipped as a cow deity from at least 2700 B.C. and personified the Milky Way, which was viewed as the milk flowing from the udders of a heavenly cow. The mother of Horus and often depicted as nursing him, Hathor is also supposed to greet the souls of the dead in the underworld and give them food and drink. In her seven aspects, Hathor becomes deities of fate, appearing at birth to cast lots determining the infant's future life (Leach and Fried 485), the dark Crone aspect that Sethe also seems to possess. Hathor also becomes associated with the war goddess Sekmet, with Aphrodite (goddess of love and beauty), and with Isis. Like other Great Goddesses, Isis represents eternal life/resurrection and healing and is Lady of the Green Crops as well as Queen of the Underworld, and she, too, precedes Mary in art depicting her breast-feeding. When, at the end of the novel, Paul D. collects Sethe's symbolically amputated pieces, and she reciprocates with his, she is enacting the way Isis collects and puts together the scattered pieces of her husband, Osiris (Leach and Fried 529). Since the African goddess Erzulie ruled over rivers, streams, lakes, and waterfalls and Sethe must cross a river to get home, Sethe is also associated with the Haitian and Yoruban Erzulie, who is beauty, sweetness, love, and sensuality and who mediates between the divine and natural world (African Goddesses). The name *Sethe* can also suggest the river of forgetfulness, Lethe, one of the rivers over which the dead shades traveled on their way to Hades, and the Styx, the border of the underworld. Since the child Sethe kills, Beloved, arises from water, she suggests the Yoruban Mother of the Sea and all life, Yemaya, and the goddess of the rivers sustaining life, Oshun. When the beautiful and pregnant Beloved's water breaks, she also connects with Hathor, who was a herald of imminent birth, as when the amniotic sac breaks. Like Hathor and Isis, whose heads were chopped off by Horus and replaced with that of a cow, doubling Horus's own beheading (Leach and Fried 485, 529), Beloved was beheaded. Because she stimulates change, Beloved is also playing the Yoruban Oya, Goddess of the Winds of Change, who clears the way for new growth and does what needs to be done (African Goddesses, Hathor).

Important in Islamic, Jewish, Native American, and Christian religions as well as the Goddess one, and figuring in Asian and Celtic myths, the Tree of Life that Sethe wears offers immortality. The goddess Hathor was a tree spirit of sycamore groves. For Guiana Indian tribes, the wonderful tree bore all the food plants (Leach and Fried 1123; see also chapter 8). Trees also suggest ancestry and heritage, as in family tree. In Christianity, there are the Trees of Knowledge and the Trees of Death (see also B. Walker, *Woman's Dictionary* 53, 459). Ironically, Sethe's tree, which seems to bloom, is vengefully carved into Sethe's back by white racists who deny that African Americans are human and want to punish her. As in Rhys, Erdrich, Atwood, Murdoch, and Lessing texts, trees and the green world in *Beloved* are richly mythic, ranging from Beloved's mother's hanging and Sixo's ironic "crucifixion"—while singing and laughing—in trees, to Baby Suggs's sermons in a clearing surrounded by trees and Denver's Emerald Closet of trees that suggest home. Critics often view Sethe's tree of scars somewhat negatively, as a symbol of slavery, death, and repressed pain; as the need to shed blood to move past suffering; as the loss of her mother and the loss of mothering in her; as Sethe's guilt and sins; and as evidence that "she has only been able to read herself through the gaze of others" (Greenway 4–5, 7; Henderson 87). According to Henderson, although a white woman and a black man read the scars differently, the scars are an inscription of the master's code. They "function as signs of ownership inscribing her as property, while the mutilation signifies her diminishment to a less-than-human status. . . . the scars function as an archeological site or memory trace" (86–87). Hardly this simple, such a view seems to accept the white masters' estimation of Sethe's worth and it discounts the symbolic "blossoming" indicating Sethe's gradual growth beyond victimization, her recognition that she, scars and all, is her "best thing." Although Greenway finds Sethe's suffering and redemption positive in terms of Christian faith, Mark Ledbetter conflates the tree of life and the tree of knowledge but recognizes the broader mythic power of this image:

This sculpted tree is the tree of life, whose fruit, in this case cherries, gives the knowledge of the gods to those who consume it, in this instance Paul D, and perhaps the knowledge that there are no gods to those who disfigured bodies must bear the tree and its fruits. And such news is frightening to the body-politic, a world where white men are the gods. (45)

Sethe's Tree of Life reminds us of Sixo's finding freedom in punishment, where his "body disfigurement imposes his identity as a black man on a white man's world, and reduces their world, not his, to ashes" (Ledbetter 46). Not only is Sethe representative of her gender and the ancestral African past (Greenway 6): She and her blooming

Tree of Life symbolize a re-visioned myth of transformation, healing, and rebirth for Americans and everyone who can remember, truly see, and move on. Like the degraded goddess figures and the Tree of Life, the trees in *Beloved* never let readers forget the possibility of life beyond slavery's wasteland.

Along with goddess myth, the "Sleeping Beauty" intertext is primary in *Beloved*. Although the Grimms' "Briar Rose" and Perrault's "Sleeping Beauty in the Woods" are the best-known versions of this tale type (AT 410), variants of both tale and the sleeping motif, including a Negro West Indies version, exist in most places in the world (Aarne and Thompson 138–39). In "Briar Rose," a child reaches adulthood despite a wise woman/godmother or grandmother witch's curse. A king and queen who arrange a feast to celebrate the birth of their child invite only twelve of the thirteen wise women to the celebration because they have only twelve golden plates. The one who is not invited wants revenge and makes an evil spell so that the princess will prick her finger on a spindle and die. The last wise woman amends the sentence to a sleep of one hundred years. Although the king orders all spindles in the kingdom to be burned, on her fifteenth birthday the princess discovers a tower and unlocks a door to a room where an old woman is spinning. When the princess touches the spindle and feels the prick, she is overcome by a deep sleep. Gradually everyone in the palace falls asleep and a briar hedge encloses it for a hundred years, until a prince discovers that he can easily enter. When he finds and kisses the princess, she awakes, they marry, and "they lived happily to the end of their days" (Zipes, *Complete* 186–89).

Each of the tale's major motifs—the curse and spell, the castle in the forest, the tower of isolation, spinning, the prick, sleeping, and the barrier of thorns—functions ironically in the novel, often in more than one sense. The most obvious curse is, of course, slavery, this novel's Robber Bridegroom; slavery and the racism on which it is based create the silent and secret jungle rather than the forest that grows within both blacks and whites (198–99). Even when Sethe has left the book's first ironic castle, the Sweet Home neither sweet nor home, racism's enigmatic spell continues to color the book's every action, scene, and setting. Like Sweet Home prior to schoolteacher—where slaves were not beaten, male slaves were regarded as men, and no one thought of escape—for most of the book 124 Bluestone Road, the other ironic castle, seems to exist outside of time and space. After the book's unthinkable handsaw "prick," the ghost-ridden 124 is also a symbolic tower of isolation that seems to be spacially separated from the rest of the community.

Beloved, the main reversed princess of Morrison's anti–fairy tale, has been "sleeping" in the underworld, with Denver awaiting her awakening in the present, as Sethe, Halle, Paul D., and the other slaves "sleep" too long at Sweet Home. Unlike Stamp Paid, who courageously braves the thorns protecting the sweet berries that miraculously feed the entire community, for most of the book Sethe, Paul D., and even Denver continue to will the metaphoric briars that interfere with awakening, individuation, wholeness, and integration into the community. Although Baby Suggs's preaching initially signifies her power and wholeness and inspires the whole community, she finally takes to bed. Even the "charmed" Denver recognizes "the downright pleasure of [ghostly] enchantment" (41, 37). If Sethe earlier assumes the godmother role in "Sleeping Beauty," associated with the goddess Moera or Fate who spins and severs the threads of life (B. Walker, *Woman's Encyclopedia* 302–3), she, too, plays Sleeping Beauty. She beats back memory and the past by spinning what she perceives as destiny. Recalling the mandala image associated with the goddess as she spins around the room, "turning like a slow but steady wheel," Sethe circles Paul "the way she was circling the subject" of Beloved's death (159, 161).[5]

Mandalas may be symbolic diagrams, often considered maps of the universe, or "simple, personal expressions of feeling or awareness." Although circular mandalas "frequently refer to the cyclic view of life, nature, fate, time, or all of these combined in the symbol of the Goddess" (B. Walker, *Woman's Dictionary* 10), at this point Sethe prefers to remain asleep. Despite the possibilities of their sleeping or dormant powers,[6] the characters of the book, like Sleeping Beauty and Rapunzel, are isolated and entrapped in something more fearful than a tower, more like the caged box in a trench, "that grave calling itself quarters," in which the chained Paul D. was lowered along with other prisoners (106). Although healing power is associated with the mandala, Sethe, Denver, and Paul D. are not able to rejoin amputated pieces and make their world bloom until they face the past, leave their towers, and tell their stories.

All folklore uses similar motifs, including the abused child and the great goddess or godmother who may come to the child's aid. Related fairy-tale intertexts including "Cinderella" (the Grimms' "Ashenputtel"), "The Juniper Tree," The Handless Maiden (the Grimms' "The Girl Without Hands"), "Hansel and Gretel," and "Fitcher's Bird"—about abused children or women and displaced goddesses sometimes called witches, fairy godmothers, angels, or sisters—critique patriarchal, colonialist society in *Beloved*. As Marie Louise

Von Franz notes, female power in patriarchal society has often seemed frightening and, thus, female images have been polarized (*Shadow and Evil* 105). Although the dark aspect of the goddess, the witch, including the Sethe perceived by neighbor children in *Beloved* and the resident of the Gingerbread House in "Hansel and Gretel," is notorious for harming children, as a godmother the goddess returns to help abused children or heal decapitated or dismembered women. As in the Grimms' "The Girl Without Hands" and other folklore, in *Beloved* a child is cut to protect her from the devil; in the tale, an angel later helps the girl regrow her hands. As in "Fitcher's Bird" or "The Robber Bridegroom" and Margaret Atwood's texts, where those who go beyond Bluebeard's "forbidden door" are amputated, dismembered, and sometimes cannibalized, in *Beloved* those who, in Baby Suggs's words, "don't know when to stop" (104) also reap what they sow, whether they are the white people Baby has in mind or Sethe, who ironically also has to learn this lesson. When Denver drinks Beloved's blood along with Sethe's milk, and when schoolteacher and his nephews steal Sethe's milk, vampirism and the cannibalism of the Grimms' "The Juniper Tree" are also suggested. Ultimately, it is the institution of racism that is the Robber Bridegroom canibalizing the characters and society. Trace notes that some goddesses, including Kali, represented in the book as "the sow that eats her farrow, . . . [and] life itself, the universe," are also cannibalistic (25). As in the Grimms' "Fitcher's Bird" or "The Robber Bridegroom" (see chapters 1 and 2 for summary), where the patriarchal and colonialist wizard or robber marries the death intended for his victims, in *Beloved* as in history we are all married to our national past. Tragically, Beloved, whose death and resurrection as a flesh and blood vampire-ghost symbolizes the effects of slavery, cannot be magically healed.

Despite their abilities to survive as tricksters in hostile worlds, all of the book's major characters suffer mythic and fairy-tale amputation. All are "in pieces," as at times, the narrative, with its alternating self-conscious, third-person, undramatized single narrators, anonymous multivoiced narrators, and centers of consciousness or reflector narrators may suggest. Beloved's sliced neck, held on only by Sethe's grip, and Paul A's hanging and decapitation foreground these amputations. Symbolically lacking eyes, like many readers of the book, Sethe no longer sees clearly and deliberately beats back memory. Like the black and white beginning of Victor Fleming's film, *The Wizard of Oz* (1939), after "the misery," Sethe's reality even lacks the colors that are all Baby Suggs wants to see. Nearly all of the characters want to avoid caring about anyone or counting upon anything and, thus, are symbolically heartless. Baby Suggs's heart breaks, and, like *The Wizard*'s Tin Man, Paul D. has a rusted tobacco tin in place of a heart (72–73, 104). He has also "shut down a generous portion of his head" (41). Symbolically mouthless, Sethe as well as Paul D. seem to wear the bit, the cruel device that prevented slaves, including Paul D., from speaking or telling their stories. Similarly, Denver stops hearing because she cannot bear listening to the story about her mother killing Beloved to keep her from the slave catchers. Afraid to act and thus symbolically handless, characters frequently sit bowed over, with their hands dangling between their knees.

Other apparent intertexts in Morrison's novel are "Beauty and the Beast," with Beloved playing both (see chapter 7), and, as mentioned, L. Frank Baum's *The Wizard of Oz,* which supplies Denver's "emerald closet" or bush house and all of the characters' search for home. The novel includes a nightmare inversion of the milk scene from Steinbeck's 1939 novel *The Grapes of Wrath,* where an act of communal giving in the earlier novel is replaced with a theft that becomes rape. Beloved also reconfigures the events on the river raft in Mark Twain's *Huckleberry Finn* (Carolyn Mitchell 34), where the white girl Amy, who is going east rather than west, helps Sethe give birth. In addition to myth and fairy tales, the abandoned child theme seems to draw on the Frankenstein legend, including Mary Shelley's *Frankenstein* (see chapter 2); and Beloved's ascent from the underworld of the unconscious, the past, and hell seems to reverse the folklore motif of descent to the underworld. In addition to amputation or dismemberment and abandonment, Morrison also uses the folk motifs of the trickster caught in his/her own trap, the journey, the quest for a lost love, and the heroic quest.

The "spells" break by being reversed. Beloved redescends into the water, Here Boy returns, and Denver, who had voluntarily imprisoned herself in her own tower or underworld, leaves 124 without leaving her mother. Unlike Howard and Buglar, who chose not to hear their mother's voice as they left, Denver regains both ears and mouth and reintegrates herself and her family into the community. Although Denver initially thinks that, like Persephone, she has "lost" her mother (266), she grows into a young, independent woman by rejoining the world, having a job, learning, and possibly falling in love. Paul D. and Stamp Paid are hardly "representatives of patriarchal authority in the novel" (Trace 18), surely a role that schoolteacher fills. For Paul D., "his coming is the reverse of his going" when he no longer escapes but goes through absence by returning to 124, Sethe, and Denver (263, 270). He recognizes that Sethe is, for him, what the Thirty-Mile Woman was for Sixo, an Isis figure: She "is a friend of my mind. She gather me, man. The pieces I am, she gather them and give them back to me in all the right order. . . . Only this woman Sethe could have left him his manhood like that." Although Sethe had never had any plan except for escape and has retreated into the same bed as Baby Suggs, she, too, "opens her eyes." With Paul D.'s help, she recognizes that she is "her best thing." Joining hands, they develop plans for the future (38, 272–73). Once the characters decide, as Paul D. does, to put their individual stories next to the stories of those they love and those who have had similar experiences, we can recognize the magnitude of Morrison's achievement. For it is she who has collected the personal, communal, fairy-tale, mythic, and biblical stories and made the separate parts come together.

The book implies that in the years since slavery, the United States has not only been afraid to confront the Medusa of its history, and to tell, listen to, and let go of its stories; it has even cultivated a "spell" and "briars" to hide its actions from itself. Resembling the characters in this and other feminist, postcolonial metafairy tales, we cannot rely on a prince to rescue us but must rescue ourselves, sometimes with a little help from our friends, families, and artists who, like Morrison (*Toni Morrison: Profile of a Writer*), undertake this job for us. Finally, pronouncing itself metafiction and an anti–fairy tale, the book breaks its own spell with the magical incantation of verbal formulae. It repeats, with slight variation, this ritual phrase three times: "It was not a story to pass on. . . . It was not a story to pass on. . . . This is not a story to pass on" (274–75). Paradoxically, *Beloved* permanently embeds, and yet releases us from, the story of slavery and its sequel, racism, by opening the deterministic pattern of a supposedly "finished" plot, that of history. Contrary to many views of fairy tales and some views of *Beloved,* both tale and novel are profoundly positive.

In both *Beloved* and *The Story of General Dann and Mara's Daughter, Griot and the Snow Dog,* there can be no instant fairy-tale transformation. The quest for full postcolonial identity in these metafictions is dependent upon telling the story, which continues.

CHAPTER 5

ERDRICH'S COMMUNITY AS HOME: *THE WIZARD OF OZ, THE RAMAYANA,* AND GREEK AND NATIVE AMERICAN MYTH IN *THE BEET QUEEN*

Like feminist, postcolonial writers including Atwood, Lessing, and Morrison, Louise Erdrich uses traditional folklore, including myth and fairy-tale intertexts, in order to push beyond a colonialist position. Native American and German and born in 1954, in Little Falls, Minnesota, Louise Erdrich grew up in Wahpeton, North Dakota, where her parents worked for the Bureau of Indian Affairs. A novelist, poet, short-story writer, essayist, and critic, she won the Best First Fiction Award from the American Academy and Institute of Arts and Letters and the John Simon Guggenheim Award in 1985. In *The Beet Queen* (1987) especially, she comically and parodically revisions myth and fairy-tale intertexts, critiquing the majority culture's colonialist, nationalist, classist, sexist, racist, ethnic, religious, and literary biases. Unfortunately, as we have seen with Toni Morrison, ethnic writers of the United States, including Native American Louise Erdrich, experience what Homi Bhabha refers to as the postcolonial position of being "in between" in terms of identity and nationality, but are not always read as postcolonial. Analogies between postcolonials and oppressed U.S. ethnic groups in terms of this oppression, including acculturated low self-esteem, racial and ethnic prejudice, loss of religious and cultural identity, and other forms of what would usually be called colonization by a dominant group, are too obvious to be ignored. Like other indigenous peoples all over the world, Native Americans established their own nations before European settlers arrived. They can argue very persuasively that another nation is indeed colonizing them. As John Rowe states, "It goes without saying that in the contemporary US Native Americans remain the repressed contents of an imperial cultural consciousness that has only recently been addressed directly" (197).

Similarly, the postcolonial practice of postmodernism is often read as a flaw in ethnic writers. Despite the number of world writers who use and have even pioneered a postmodernism rooted in their own cultures, some readers and writers are stuck in a conception of postmodernism as American, apolitical, elite, and male (Nicholson 4–12). Erdrich is now recognized as "something other than a fine 'ethnic' or 'Native American' novelist," and her *The Beet Queen* has been considered "an engrossing and breath-taking novel," achieving a "unified, total effect" through metafictional devices (Editor 178; Chase 169; Rubins 14–15). Leslie Marmon Silko and many others, however, accuse Erdrich of privileging style and language over Native American culture and politics: "Self-referential writing is light-years away from shared or communal experience that underlies oral narrative and modern fiction" (Silko 179). Apparently oversimplifying postmodernism as an exaggerated combination of formalism, surrealism, and modernism, Silko finds Erdrich's prose

an outgrowth of academic, post-modern, so-called experimental influences. The idea is to "set language free," to allow words to interact like magic chemicals in a word sorcerer's pristine laboratory, where a word and its possible relationships with other words may be seen "as they really are, in and of themselves" without the tiresome interference of any historical, political or cultural connections the words may have had in the past. Any characters or plot are imagined within a world that answers only to "itself," the inner created world of the novel or poem itself. (179)

In the notorious controversy following this review, Susan Castillo sees Silko's argument, particularly her suggestion that Erdrich is ambivalent about her Indian origins, as "devastating" and views Silko's conclusion as "the verbal equivalent of a hand-grenade" (2). According to Silko:

The Beet Queen is a strange artifact, an eloquent example of the political climate in America in 1986. It belongs on the shelf next to the latest report from the United States Civil Rights Commission, which says black men have made tremendous gains in employment and salary. This is the same shelf that holds The Collected Thoughts of Edwin Meese on First Amendment Rights and Grimm's Fairy Tales. (Silko 179)

Ironically, by referring to Grimms' fairy tales as one of the unreal artifacts that belongs on a shelf, Silko reveals a widespread bias against one of the folklore intertexts that makes Erdrich's work distinctively cross-cultural. Although no original source can be pinpointed for tales based on oral tradition and variants exist all over the world, the popularity of the Grimms and Perrault lead scholars of third-world literature to see well-known fairy tales such as "Cinderella," which includes at least one Native American version (Leach and Fried 799; "The Algonquin Cinderella"), as European and thereby colonialist. Ethnic writers who use fairy tales may be seen as selling out or being ashamed of their own culture, fostering native and female passivity and victimhood (xiv), or diminishing stories directly from oral tradition by using them alongside literary ones. Because Erdrich is German as well as Native American, some critics think she cannot speak for first peoples. Despite the many prizes she has received, Erdrich is often not included in anthologies of Native American literature or read as Native American. Because critics sometimes see Erdrich as nonpolitical (J. Rowe 201) and The Beet Queen as silent on the issue of race (Meisenhelder 45) and with few or no significant Native American characters (Catt 71), they tend to ignore this text when characterizing Erdrich's main themes and character types, sometimes falling into the essentialism of assuming that her work does or should present fixed ethnic, communal, and personal identity. Although The Beet Queen only seems to concentrate on the European immigrants important in Erdrich's heritage when readers ignore Mary and Celestine's mixed backgrounds and the novel's other Native characters, Erdrich's The Master Butcher's Singing Club (2003) and Tales of Burning Love (1996) have focused on Argus's immigrants. If we do read Erdrich as a Native American German, postcolonial, feminist postmodernist, we are able to recognize the extent to which she uses intertextuality along with trickster characters and magical realism to develop a new, very political, hybrid discourse.

Like Toni Morrison, Zora Neale Hurston, Rosario Ferre, and Keri Hulme, Louise Erdrich interweaves oral narratives with written ones, sometimes achieving an oral quality in her fiction for readers/listeners capable of hearing her differing narrators. Her four-volume series about the Anishinabe (Ojibwa Chippewa) in North Dakota illustrates the metaform so prevalent among contemporary women writers. Love Medicine (1984, rev. 1993), The Beet Queen (1987), Tracks (1988), and *The Bingo Palace* (1994) all comment on one another as well as call attention to themselves and their intertexts as art. *Tracks* achieves a fully oral narrative situation in which the principal narrator, Nanapush, modeled on the Ojibwa trickster and culture hero Nanabozho or Nenibush, addresses his granddaughter, Lulu, and, implicitly, his reading audience to insure the survival of the family, the tribe, and Nanapush himself. Ironically, the "tracks" of the title refer not only to those of the tribe and animals on the earth, but also to marks on papers, including those establishing identity, ownership, and meaning, and those appearing on the pages of this and other books. Celebrating indigenous magic through other tricksters, the water monster Misshepeshu, Windigoes, and manitou, Nanapush is simultaneously both postmodern, unreliable narrator and postcolonial Prometheus. *The Beet Queen* occupies a central position in the tetralogy by using folklore motifs, images, and patterns in a multicultural context.

Again borrowing and parodying plot, structure, characterization, themes, motifs, and images from her intertexts, Erdrich uses similar tactics to those of Atwood, Lessing, and Morrison. Her memorable magical realist scenes often build directly on mythic or fairy-tale images, as in her parody of Sita's kidnapping in *The Ramayana* and of goddesses and fairy godmother's association with the Tree of Life. She shifts females from object to subject, enlarges meaning with names of places (Argos) and people (Sita, Canute) that are mythic and symbolic, writes beyond the ending, blends genres (romance, epic), reverses the norms of intertexts to parody, ironize, and tell unexpected stories, and remythifies amputated old stories.

Critics have almost completely ignored the role of myth and fairy tales in *The Beet Queen* (1987). In this novel, Erdrich interweaves Goddess, Greek, Danish, Fisher King, biblical, and Native American myth, Baum's *The Wizard of Oz,* stories from the *Ramayana,* allusions to *Alice in Wonderland,* and such folklore motifs as flight—return, abduction, escape, orphans, ripped–open hearts, cannibalism, animals, disguise, and falling with fairy tales including the Grimms' "Hansel and Gretel" and Andersen's "The Little Mermaid," "The Red Shoes," and "The Snow Queen." Erdrich presents a pickled princess, several witches, a male fairy godmother, a beet queen dressed in "Thumbelina's nightmare" (329), and several tricksters while deconstructing the gendered white, heterosexual, middle-class romantic myth embodied in "Cinderella." She also uses elements of tarot cards, fortune-telling, yarrow sticks, and popular romance and detective stories and juxtaposes biblical and shamanic intertexts (Rainwater 407) in a postmodern manner.

The Beet Queen, a parody of a heroic epic, both uses and parodies mythic and fairy-tale structures, featuring inner and outer quests from innocence, ignorance, or chaos to experience, knowledge, or pattern, and, as in *The Wizard of Oz,* home. Tree of Life images, cyclical patterns corresponding to the seasons (Rainwater 416), Fisher King motifs of sickness to healing, drought to fertility, and blindness to vision, and ironic fairy-tale transformations also occur.

As in *Beloved* and *Wide Sargasso Sea,* tree images frame the book. No Garden of Eden, Argus is a dry plains area with sparse vegetation. As Karl and Mary enter Argus to look for their uncle and aunt's butcher shop, they encounter "one tree, weak, a scratch of light against the gray of everything else, tossed in a film of blossoms." Suggesting Sita near the end of the book, like a sleepwalker Karl stands "stock-still among the branches" until he tears a branch from the tree and the petals drop like snow around the attacking dog. Later, blight attacks the tree where the branch was pulled off (1–2). As indicated in "The Branch," the Tree of Life important in Goddess, Islamic, Jewish, Native American, and Christian religions and figuring in Asian and Celtic myths (Leach and Fried 1123), here guarded by a dog rather than a snake or dragon, offers immortality. But Karl is expelled from Argus, breaking apart the remainder of the Adare family and subjecting him to sexual assault, suggesting the Tree of Knowledge and the Tree of Death that are often associated with the Tree of Life. Instead of cutting off his feet as in Andersen's "The Red Shoes," Fleur uses this same apple branch in making casts for Karl's feet after he falls from the boxcar.

Trees are also important to Adelaide, Mary, Sita, and Celestine. Having escaped her family by flying off with The Great Omar, Adelaide sends Fritzie a postcard picturing a man standing in the branches of "The largest Live-oak in So. Jacksonville, Fla.," precipitating Mary's postcard, "An Aerial View of Argus," depicting "brown dots of buildings, bare streets, and puffs of green trees surrounded by a patchwork of dull brown fields" and announcing the death of all of Adelaide's children (56, 58). The postcard suggests the maze with no exit that Mary knits into Dot's sweater (277), and Mary imagines Adelaide looking but unable to find her in the aerial view. Disappointed that the box holding her family jewels is empty, Mary predicts Sita's frail beauty as what "could be broken off a tree by any passing boy and discarded, cast away when the fragrance died" (21). When she has a dream of Sita by Sita's Mountain Ash tree with orange berries, Celestine recognizes Sita's illness, and Sita's guest bedroom even has pictures of a tree in all seasons. By the time the dead Sita decorates her yard's poisonous yew bushes, associated with immortality, we recognize that, for most of the book, there is no Tree of Life in this Waste Land.

As part of their sickness, characters in *The Beet Queen* are trapped by rigid gender and sexual roles that dehumanize, paralyze, and separate them from other people, their families, and their cultural heritage. "Erdrich both critiques white America's ideals of masculinity and femininity and suggests underlying similarities between racial and gender oppression in American society" (Meisenhelder 46–49). Thus, recognizing gender colonization helps us recognize the racial and ethnic colonization in the book. "Getting shot apart is what [Russell Kashpaw] live[s] for all his life." For all of his heroism, "scars and stripes," and adherence to a masculine ideal (111), the decorated former football player is reduced to a "dead" stuffed Indian saluted by American legionnaires in the Beet Queen parade. Sita Kozka, of Polish heritage, assumes that what she and other Argos people eat is inferior to French food. Resembling her aunt Adelaide, who had assumed that "with her figure and good looks, she could find work in a fashionable store," both satisfy the feminine ideal, as Helene Cixous views it ("Castration" 480–83), by being laid out as Sleeping Beauty dolls, resembling many of Rosario Ferre's characters.

As in Greek mythology, *The Wizard of Oz*, "Cinderella," and many other fairy tales, family structures in *The Beet Queen,* symbolized both by web and branch images, are broken and dysfunctional. Characters initially seem "fated" to bear the punishment of previous generations and revisit negative inherited patterns in mazes of their own construction. Argus is ironically not only suggestive of Argusville, close to Fargo, North Dakota, but also of Argos, the center of the Mycenaean empire in ancient Greece associated with the heroic Odysseus, Jason, the Argonauts, and the murdered Agamemnon, and a plains area afflicted with drought. The people of Argos, the descendants of Danaus, were the Danaans of Homer's *Iliad*. Argos is also the dog with a hundred eyes told to watch Io, and, in a sense, the novel's multiple narration, including aerial views that reduce characters to "dots" on a map, simulates a hundred perceptions of fragmented characters and a fragmented reality. Cut off from his family and unable to find them in his visit to Argus, Karl and Mary's brother Jude worries that "when the parade was finally over and [the crowd] drew apart he would disperse, too, in so many pieces that not even the work of his own clever hands could shape him back the way he was" (315). Ironically, Jude, named after the patron saint of lost causes, comes to Argus because of a year-old letter Sita never mailed that Celestine discovers as she thinks about black holes. These holes suck everything into them, including objects that survive people (277–78). They, like the pre-Hellenic Greek world of revenge rather than law, the brick of accident that crashes through Mary's window and later hits Sita, and the donkey of destiny that Dot attacks in her school play counter the book's more positive pattern of the family web that can sustain characters caught in traps.

By having sex with Celestine James, Karl, a bisexual who parks his car in a position for easy escape, ironically helps create the constructed family that will replace his, Mary's, and Jude's fractured one. Lacking a fairy godmother herself, "witch" Mary tries to counter "witch" Shumway by playing godmother to her niece, Karl and Celestine's child, Dot (186); and Wallace, a homosexual who invents "Pfef's poor dead sweetheart" (159), also assumes Fisher King, Wizard of Oz, Emperor of the Emerald City, witch, and godmother roles (304) in this novel's constructed family of humanity. Not a fake like the Wizard of Oz, Wallace has a good heart and a vision of the green world Argus can be if it grows sugar beets. Ironically parked in Lover's Lane without the lover he dreams of, Wallace imagines prosperity: "Before him, like Oz, the imaginary floodlit stacks of the beet refinery poured a sinking smoke straight upward in twin white columns" (110). It is his lover Karl that claims to and does perform miracles in dust bowls with the air seeder, eventually used in Argus at the end of the Beet Queen celebration. As *The Wizard of Oz*'s Dorothy is brought up by uncle and aunt, Mary Adare finds her uncle and aunt Kozka not in the House of Atreus but in the House of Meats after her mother breaks the family tree and abandons her and her brothers. Mary is herself also an "auntie M." to Dot (an abbreviated Dorothy). Although none of the characters reaches Oz., Wallace, Karl, Mary, Celestine, and Dot do survive a tornado and together establish home.

Critics seem not to have recognized either *The Beet Queen*'s multiculturalism or Erdrich's use of a *Ramayana* intertext, one of two great romantic Hindu Indian epics credited variously to Tulsi Das or Valmiki and the basis for some of the novel's most hilarious events. In Vedic mythology, Sita, literally furrow, is the beautiful Goddess of Agriculture who is adorned with lotuses. In the *Ramayana,* she is the human form of the Goddess Lakshmi and, as wife of Rama, is the embodiment of conjugal affection and purity (Leach and Fried 517, 924, 1015). Parodying the shape-changing Ravana's abduction of Sita, who establishes her faithfulness to Rama by a fifteen-year ordeal, *The Beet Queen* features Sita's brother-in-law kidnapping her from her wedding with Jimmy, who refers to Sita with names of desserts. When Erdrich's Sita, a superficial slave to fashion who feels superior to relatives and spouse and makes fun of Indians, is blown like tumble weed into an Indian bar on the reservation, with dress turned inside out over her head, the patrons remark that "It's a fucking queen" (100). In the *Ramayana,* Sita calls upon Mother Earth as witness to her purity; the earth opens, and Sita disappears, leaving the disconsolate Rama to go to heaven. In *The Beet Queen,* the twice-married Sita dramatizes the fate of societally conditioned Beauty Queens who lose their identities. Tied to her image in a mirror, she is Snow White's stepmother rather than the *Ramayana*'s duty-bound Sita. In addition to Sita, Fleur (50), Adelaide, and Dot are also described as princesses and Mary and Celestine as unable to meet the requirements, but there is no reward in being a queen of beets. First silenced like the Little Mermaid and then preserved by pharmaceuticals to be the real Beet Queen wearing Adelaide's queenly red garnet necklace, Sita parades dead in a House of Meats truck. She is a parodic combination Snow White-in-coffin—the Grimms' "The Glass Coffin"—and eternally Sleeping Beauty. Even her supposedly elite restaurant, Chez Sita, likened to the ship of the dead, is associated with the underworld. Similarly, the beautiful Adelaide, who abandons life as a mother to fly away on an adventure with the Great Omar, crashes and leads an unfulfilled life "wearing" red shoes. Experiencing sequential fits of rage with wordless screams, she breaks glass and cuts her feet in her silver birdorama trap (232). Ironically, it is Karl, another "queen," who, in Sita's crazed vision, descends into the earth as a parodic Persephone and Hindu Sita, symbolizing an eventual rebirth of Argus in which Erdrich's Sita is unable to participate. According to Erdrich's *Blue Jay's Dance,*

A woman has to be her own hero. The princess cuts off her hair, blinds her eyes, scores her arms, and rushes wildly toward the mouth of the dragon. The princess slays the dragon, sets off on her own quest. She crushes her crown beneath her foot, eats dirt, eats roses, deals with the humility and grandeur of her own human life. (104)

Erdrich's nontraditional women—Fleur, Mary, Celestine, Dot—and, for that matter, nontraditional men—Wallace, Karl—all tricksters to some extent, are the book's simultaneously parodic and real heroes.

Athough discussed in the other volumes of the tetralogy, even Native American myth in *The Beet Queen* has received little attention. Fools, culture heroes, creators, shape-changers, and survivors often compared to animals and ruled by erotic impulses, most of the novel's main characters are tricksters as defined in Native American myth. Similar to Hansel and Gretel (AT 327) and evoked by Mary and Karl's journey to Argos is the native story of The Deserted Children featuring a boy and girl who flee, are carried across a stream by a water monster, are tied to a tree, and end up with lots of food (Thompson, *Folktale* 360). Fleur Pillager, the powerful female trickster said to transform into a bear and to sleep with the water god, Misshepeshu, rescues Karl, binds his feet with parts of a magic tree, and heals him when he makes one of the novel's many transformative falls, this time from a boxcar but later at the Minneapolis convention, in Celestine's kitchen, and in the festival's dunking pool. As he begins to have a stroke, Celestine's twin, Russell, has a vision of the Native road to death with his dead sister Isabel signaling for him to follow. Desiring Russell, Mary dreams of waiting for a horned lover (79; Motif A131.6), the horned god of Irish, Egyptian, and Native mythology as well as many mythologies' devil. In addition, ice images in this as in other Erdrich novels, including icy hands, hearts, and brains, such as Mary's Wendigo (as well as Snow Queen) brain of ice after her mother leaves and her brother is stolen (15), are connected to Wendigo, a giant skeleton of ice who embodies winter starvation. The playground "miracle" of Christ's (Mary's) face formed in ice in Mary's accident on the slide (40) is especially important. Most significant to the novel's major web and destiny motifs are Spider Goddess stories evoked by Mary's knitting of a sweater for Dot that seems to be a trap or maze without exit. In classic mythology, Arachne (also Clotho, Athene, Moera) is the Fate-Spinner; and similar Native American (plains, southwestern, western United States), Hindu, Scandinavian (B. Walker *Encyclopedia* 957–58), and Ghana myths exist. In Native tales Spider is a helpful creator or trickster, often a grandmother (Leach and Fried 1074) related to the Great Goddess. She weaves the universe every day and unravels it every night. The world is supposed to end when her web is finished. In a Pueblo version, the goddess begins creation by spinning two threads, east-west and north-south. She makes people of the earth from different-colored pieces of clay, and her two daughters make the sun and moon (B. Walker, *Woman's Dictionary* 162–63, 419–20). In a Cherokee tale, Grandmother Spider steals the sun, giving light and fire to her part of the world (Erdoes and Ortiz 155). These spider stories suggest fate, creation, destruction, and re-creation in *The Beet Queen*.

Other mythic, folklore, or fairy-tale connections include Mary's role as Cinderella, stepsister to Sita, Mary's seeing Dot as Atlantis,

touching waves with an iron scepter; the baby Dot's birth in a blizzard suggesting the Grimms' "Little Snow White"; Dot's comparison
to Atalanta, female hero suckled by a she bear who excels in foot races
and might have gone with the Argonauts; Dot's acting like the Queen
in *Alice in Wonderland* by wanting to chop off the heads of her court
attendants; and Dot's face like a stopped *Wizard of Oz* tornado. The
butcher Cannute's name, recalling the Danish and English King who
commands the tide to go no further but is soaked, and reference to
the trickster Loki are also important. Even the sewing machine that
Adelaide ships Mary so that she would "always have a skill to fall back
on" (60), is described as "a little black mechanical dragon, with one
busy, murderous fang" (141). Paralleling these parodic references are
mock religious and mystical images and visions, including Mary's implied comparison to the Virgin Mary, the chipped statue of the Virgin
Mary nearly thrown like a brick, Mary's hands that glow in the dark
after she uses a cleaning solvent (77–78), Mary's genuine predictions
(e.g., Dot's birth in a blizzard), Karl's picture of himself as burning
like Lucifer, and Karl's sexual abuse by "Saint Ambrose."

It is in Dot's hair that Celestine finds the web symbolizing the
threads or connections that tie all the characters into a postmodern
constructed community and suggest a pattern to their existence: "A
web was forming, a complicated house, that Celestine could not
bring herself to destroy" (176). Webs of the Spider Goddess suggest
alternatives to the Donkey of Destiny story that replaces the story of
Christ's birth, to the red brick of accident, to the black holes that ob-
sess Mary, and to other etiologies in which people search for meaning
(217). Although Spider Goddesses may be linked to destruction, the
destruction is part of re-creation and rebirth. Characters who have
never "fit" anywhere transform into a family through the threads that
link them. Square-bodied Mary, with black hair that did not come
from her mother but from an unknown but probably Indian father,
becomes part of Dot's family. Karl, who has always "traveled light,"
finally recognizes a need for community and culture: "I give nothing,
take nothing, mean nothing, hold nothing. . . . I wanted the whole
world of people who belonged to each other and owned things and
cooked food and remembered old songs" (317–18). He comes home,
saves Wallace from drowning, and rejoins his community. Dot repli-
cates her grandmother's escape with the Great Omar by flying away
from the Beet Queen Festival: "There is a thread beginning with my
grandmother Adelaide and traveling through my father and arriving
at me. That thread is flight" (335). Although her family's eyes seem
to set traps, she reverses the aerial view of Mary's postcard: On a plane

loaded with Karl's seeder, she helps to seed the clouds that finally bring rain to Argus—fertility to the Waste Land—and returns to a now magnified earth, drawn by the magnetic power of her mother's love.

Subjected to biblical flood and Fisher King drought, Argus is parodically saved by the sugar beet; and the portrayal of the sugar beet, complete with its own queen, float, and fertility festival (Storhoff 348) telling its story, is one of the book's primary examples of magical realism,[1] a technique that, contrary to some expectations, fuses the real and the magical, essentially making the real magical rather than presenting the unreal. Not just events, but images and characters, including the cow eye diamond, Mary's ice and hand "miracles," Karl's sinking into the lawn, Sita's sage brush entrance to the bar, Sita's dead body on her yew bush, Mary's dream of wild plums ripening and falling as Dot is conceived (143), Dot's birth in ice, and Dot's return to earth are magically real. In Erdrich as in other magical realists, the magical realism contains an irreducible element of magic, gives a strong sense of the phenomenal world, engages the reader in attempting to reconcile two contradictory understandings, merges different realms, "disturbs received ideas about time, space, and identity," and is, therefore, political (Farris, *Ordinary* 7)—in this case by critiquing gender roles, conformity, materialism, and prejudice. Through its postmodern intertexts, *The Beet Queen*'s ordinary, flawed, but transforming characters gain mythic resonance.

CHAPTER 6

SILENCED WOMEN IN ROSARIO FERRE'S *THE YOUNGEST DOLL:* "SLEEPING BEAUTY," "THE RED SHOES," "CINDERELLA," "FITCHER'S BIRD"

"THE YOUNGEST DOLL" AND "SLEEPING BEAUTY"

In her collection of stories, *The Youngest Doll* (1976), Rosario Ferre uses fairy-tale and other folkloric intertexts to critique her native culture's colonialist, classist, sexist, racist, and religious biases. Since scholars are used to identifying postcolonialism with countries once colonized by France, Spain, or particularly England, it may initially seem strange to speak of a person from Puerto Rico, once colonized by Spain but now a U.S. territory and still subjected to U.S. imperialism, as a postcolonial writer. As we have seen, however, economic and racist exploitation among subjected peoples within a particular country, including that of Native Americans and African Americans, is increasingly being identified as colonization; where cultures are evolving beyond colonial consciousness, we may identify them as postcolonial, in Puerto Rico especially still a fluid condition in-process rather than finally achieved. Here I am also extending *colonization* to include parallel forms of "imperialism," such as that based on sexism, class, and religion. Resembling texts by Louise Erdrich and Toni Morrison, Ferre's work does proceed beyond colonization and colonial consciousness, and she does so by writing feminist, postmodernist, metafiction that extends readers' cultural and fictional frames.

Rosario Ferre attacks patriarchal and racial colonization in her fiction. Ferre was born into a country that has always been a colony, first of Spain and, since 1898, the United States. With a history of slavery and now "the only country in the world which is still attached to the United States without being fully integrated as a state nor fully autonomous," Puerto Rico was one of the first areas of Latin America to experience "the full effects of global Americanization," including emigration from the land to the cities and then to the United States (Franco ix). Ferre's mother came from the former sugar baron aristocracy, and her father's family became wealthy by doing business with Puerto Rico's largest employer, the U.S. government. Her grandfather and his four sons founded the Puerto Rico Cement Company, which supplied cement to the U.S. government for building the Roosevelt Roads Naval Base. Later, her father became governor of Puerto Rico. Ferre broke with her family's politics and social class by joining the Partido Popular Democratico and, briefly, the Socialist Party and displeased her family by divorcing two husbands, getting a Ph.D., and becoming a feminist writer satirical of socially assumed roles.

Both bilingual and bicultural by her own admission (Hintz 175), Rosario Ferre generally translates or is a cotranslator of her own fiction. She suggests that, "In a way, all writing is a translation, and in this sense the translator can be said to be a shaman." She speaks of herself, sometimes living in exile in the United States, as an Ophelia adrift in the canal between Puerto Rico and the United States. Both as a Puerto Rican and as a woman writer, she is at home on neither shore, in neither past nor present, but uses "the water of words" in the "crevice in between" ("On Destiny" 154–55). It is this from this "crevice in between" that Ferre's feminist, postcolonial consciousness emerges.

As we have seen, feminist, postcolonial writers frequently use traditional folk and fairy-tale intertexts in subversive ways. Like Jean Rhys (Dominican), Rosario Ferre parodically re-visions folk and fairy tales sometimes mistakenly considered exclusively western. By writing texts that call attention to fairy tales, story-telling, fictional form, the relationship of fairy tales and "reality," and texts as tales, these writers create metafairy tales. Although sometimes criticized (Paravisini-Gebert 162) for appealing to international audiences with postmodern techniques such as magical realism or magic feminism,[1] intertextuality, and self-reflexiveness that have also been mistakenly identified with "white," "male," western, imperialistic, or apolitical literature, they have actually helped invent and globalize these techniques.

In addition to making fairy-tale, mythic, and opera allusions in *The House on the Lagoon* (1995), Ferre frames this and a recent metafiction,

Eccentric Neighborhoods (1998), within the Latino oral tradition, popularized by Gabriel Garcia Marquez, of epic family histories. But her much earlier stories, which she wrote in Spanish rather than English for a smaller audience and then later translated into English,[2] are unforgettable masterpieces. The volume, *The Youngest Doll*, translates thirteen of the original fifteen stories in *Papeles de Pandora* (1976) and one story from *Las dos Venecias*. In *The Youngest Doll*, Ferre gives a distinctive Puerto Rican flavor to interlacing intertexts including "Bluebeard" or "Fitcher's Bird," "Sleeping Beauty" ("Briar Rose"), "Cinderella," "Little Snow-White," "Red-Cap," "The Snow Queen," "The Red Shoes," "The Pied Piper," the Bible, *A Thousand and One Nights, Don Quixote;* Ovid's *Pygmalion*,[3] ballet, family folklore; phoenix, Pandora, and Midas myths; and golem and trickster stories,[4] including Anancy ones, that cross racial, national, and cultural borders.

Ferre parodies every aspect of her intertexts, including plot, theme, characterization, image, and motif, sometimes writing anti–fairy tales. Her tactics include building ironic scenes on powerful fairy-tale images, such as the prince's kissing Sleeping Beauty, reversing females from object to subject but ironically still not allowing her females to speak, and displacing the "truth" of traditional stories, deflating reliable narrators through a variety of innovative print, font, and epistolary techniques. Ferre also uses subversive motifs and symbols, including the colors white and red and dolls; open resolution; blended genre (satire, magical realism, tragedy); defamiliarized language; irony; reader cocreation, to the point of the reader feeling "poisoned"; and delegitimation. Unlike other texts I am examining, "Sleeping Beauty" in *The Youngest Doll* offers no remythification, no healing, and little hope for either character or this colonized Latino culture.

All of the stories in *The Youngest Doll* are implicitly informed by a re-visioned Pandora myth, and this time Pandora is a Puerto Rican writer who infuses, not the ills of mankind, but the ink of feminist passions into the Caribbean and the world. Although not mentioned by name in the stories, Pandora, like Medusa, was originally part of the Great Goddess worshipped all over the world prior to patriarchal religion. Like Medusa, whose beauty and goodness were "reversed" when patriarchal religions subordinated female deities, Pandora is a symbol of patriarchal usurpation and perversion of female power. Since Medusa also signifies consequent female rage, it is appropriate that one of the stories in *The Youngest Doll*, "Sleeping Beauty," appeared in the volume *Reclaiming Medusa*, ed. Diana Velez.

"The Youngest Doll" and "Sleeping Beauty" are particularly interesting for their parody of values that are simultaneously patriarchal, colonial, classist, and racist. While evoking a fairy-tale archetype of beautiful, fragile, doll-women who play passive female roles and whose stories end with marriage, "The Youngest Doll" also suggests the nursery rime about girls filled with sugar and spice. In another story in this volume, "Marina and the Lion," the aristocratic protagonist dresses as a doll for a costume party and is even put in a cellophane box. Based on a story one of Ferre's aunts told about a relative (Hintz 136, J. Franco xi), "The Youngest Doll" illustrates the role of Ferre's own family folklore in building an oral, vernacular voice for her first published work. In "The Youngest Doll," the sting of patriarchal, racial, and class violation never heals but, hidden under gauzy folds of a maiden aunt's skirt, must be dragged around in a monstrous leg concealing an angry river prawn, apparently black in Puerto Rico. As the past breaks up "with the same impassive musicality with which the crystal chandelier crumbled," this representative of the aristocracy makes dolls to mark each year of her nieces' lives. Eventually, each doll has ivory porcelain hands and face made from a wax mask of the girl's face covered on both sides with plaster, "like a living face sheathed in two dead ones." The doll's glass eyes are imported from Europe but submerged in the local stream "so that they would learn to recognize the slightest stirring of the prawn's antennae." Unlike previous dolls filled with the "guano brains" of gourds, the life-size wedding dolls, "sentimental ornaments that should not threaten the grooms," are filled with honey. These last dolls are given to each girl on her wedding day with these words: "Here is your Easter Sunday" (*Youngest* 3–4).

When the last, youngest, niece marries the son of the doctor who has chosen to finance his son's education by not healing the aunt's literal and symbolic wound, "the youngest doll" is "born." This doll, however, is warm and looks through pupils made from the aunt's diamond eardrops. Like a doll, the youngest niece becomes a silent and motionless balcony ornament confirming her bourgeois husband's marriage into society. But she does not, as some critics believe (Hintz 128), turn into a doll. After her husband pries out the doll's eyes, she realizes that he possesses not only a paper silhouette, but also a paper soul. When "a sisterhood of pious ladies" offers him money for the doll's hands and face, which, ironically, "they thought would be perfect for the image of the Veronica in the next Lenten procession," he digs up the house grounds looking for the doll, which has supposedly disappeared (*Youngest* 5–6). Invested in shallow societal roles, this and other paper men and women can't tell the difference between aristocratic women, saints, and the seemingly demure dolls, significantly with white or ivory faces marking class and race, who replace them on balconies overlooking sugarcane fields. But this doll is filled with the river prawns that symbolize patriarchal rape and enslavement to a monstrous role. It remains warm with the aunt's and later her niece's suppressed rage and revenge: Ironically this doll insures the rebirth of the youngest niece and creates vision in colonized or empty eye sockets by turning colonizing imagery against several kinds of colonizers.

Ferre's "Sleeping Beauty" (Grimms' "Briar Rose," AT 410) is perhaps the most overt example of a metafairy tale that suggests the whole volume's focus on the way we can construct stories—whether mythic, religious, fairy-tale, literary, ballet, societal, or cultural— either to constrict or to foster freedom. (see chapter 4 for a summary.) Although some of the vulgar language and shocking passages have been deleted (Hintz 175–91), the English translation of this story still uses different type fonts, as in the Spanish version of "The Poisoned Tale," and spaces, as in Spanish versions of "When Women Love Men" and "Mercedes Benz 220SL" (Hintz 182), to mark changes in narrative voice. Since each voice ironically comments on the others and, by implication, the story and its intertexts, "Sleeping Beauty," perhaps Ferre's most self-reflexive story, is an anti–fairy tale. Like "The Youngest Doll," "Sleeping Beauty" centers on a violated woman, this time an artist forced to choose between traditional female roles and dancing. Maria de los Angeles is a convent-educated victim of marital and patriarchal rape who, in the Spanish version, prostitutes herself (Hintz 180) and, in the English version, commits adultery to end her "Red Shoes" dance. Although we read anonymous letters Maria writes her husband, brief passages of undramatized narration about her, and letters, social columns, and her mother's captions and bridal newspaper clippings in her wedding album, we have only six italicized sections of her interior monologue. We never hear her speak to us or anyone else. Helene Cixous, one of Ferre's major influences (Hintz 37), points out that Sleeping Beauty and other well-known fairy-tale princesses are always passive, found in bed, never standing up or awake for long. Because woman is decapitated in a masculine economy, she has no tongue. Prince Charming teaches the Law of the Father (Cixous, "Castration" 481, 483, 486).

Unlike the princess that viewers of Disney's "Sleeping Beauty" may expect, Maria de los Angeles, or Mary of the Angels, resembles most of the successive wives of the "Fitcher's Bird" (Grimms) or "Blue Beard" (Perrault) fairy tale: She marries death rather than living happily ever after and is even buried in a designer wedding dress and veil. In "Fitcher's Bird," the Grimm brothers' fairy tale embedded in the works of Charlotte Bronte, Gustave Flaubert, Jean Rhys, and Margaret Atwood, the groom or husband dismembers brides who dare to do the forbidden, in this case open the door to the room containing the bodies of the bride's sisters (see chapter 2). Thus, in feminist revisioning, "Fitcher's Bird" can be "the other side" of the "Cinderella" or "Sleeping Beauty" stories, implicit also in the "Giselle," "Coppelia," and "Red Shoes" intertexts of Ferre's story.

Ferre's ironically reversed "Sleeping Beauty" actually refers to three ballets, at least three fairy tales, and Cupid mythology. The "Coppelia" ballet is about a woman who pretends to be a dancing porcelain doll in order to capture the interest of a man, and, as in both "The Sleeping Beauty" ballet and fairy tale cycle, she and her lover live happily ever after. Both the "Giselle" and "The Red Shoes" ballets, like Hans Christian Andersen's rather different "Red Shoes" fairy tale, depict women whose desire to be free ends tragically. "Giselle," also the subject of a Margaret Atwood poem, "Giselle in Daytime," is the romantic Adolphe Adam ballet based on the tragic Theophile Gautier story and legend recorded by Heinrich Heine. Giselle attempts to kill herself, and both she and her lover die at the end of the ballet.

The main image in the Andersen tale, the ballet, and Powell and Pressburger's 1948 film, *The Red Shoes,* starring the red-haired Moira Shearer, is female amputation. In Andersen's tale, the girl who wears red shoes to church has her feet chopped off, and the feet in the red shoes go dancing away into the woods. Although dancing originally suggested the Goddess's cosmic creation and was important in religious ritual for centuries, it later became associated with witches and devil-worshippers, who often wore red. About the sixth or seventh century, Christian churches outlawed ecclesiastical dancing for being "too sensual and too much enjoyed by women" (see S. Wilson, *Margaret Atwood's Fairy* 126). In the ballet and film, a woman artist must choose between marriage and dancing: The price of wanting to dance is losing her feet.

In Ferre's story, too, the Church, Maria's parents, and her husband disapprove of Maria's dancing. Although the Beautiful People are willing to pay $1000.00 a ticket for a charity performance of Maria dancing in "Coppelia," and her husband later profits from her dancing, they all think she should be satisfied with a safe marriage, either to the church or to someone who will help her produce a male heir. When Maria, Ferre's Swanhilda, disguises herself as the porcelain doll Coppelia, she dances away from the man and out of the theatre, but as Giselle, Maria becomes trapped in the wedding aisle. As Sleeping Beauty, when Maria awakens with a kiss, she discovers that she is pregnant. Resembling the protagonist in Atwood's *Lady Oracle,* which also uses a "Red Shoes" intertext, she still opens the forbidden doors and does the forbidden dance. Maria de los Angeles dyes her hair red to resemble the circus trapeze artist, Carmen Merengue, who would never marry, is uninterested in being a lady, and rejects her privileged role as pampered mistress to return to the freedom of the circus. Also resembling the red-haired ballerina of *The Red Shoes,* Maria defies church, husband, father, and position in society by staging her death: Dancing nude on a tightrope in exaggerated white pancake makeup and false eyelashes, she awaits her killer.

Commenting on Ferre's use of cosmetics in "When Women Love Men," another story in *The Youngest Doll* volume, Debra Castillo notes that, along with race, cosmetics "serve as the fundamental visual clues of social class" (159):

decent women wear alabaster powder and subtle perfumes to emphasize their porcelain-doll-like fragility and helplessness, while strident colors underline the robust sensuality of their rivals. (164)

Since "few other options beyond the ritualistic are even remotely conceivable," Ferre's female characters frequently state rebellion through

a revolutionary use of makeup. . . . Instead of making themselves up for a man, they are making themselves up as a form of emancipation that serves along the way as a potent demystification of the myth of everlasting love in its conventional forms. (159)

Much as the Mexican writer, Rosario Castellanos, reverses the usual stereotypes to make cooking revolutionary in "Cooking Lesson," the artificial faces Ferre's characters create release them from roles dictated by class, race, gender, and nationality.

With action that has been described as "gynocentric" (Hintz 131), Ferre's "Sleeping Beauty" is, nevertheless, about more than constrictive gender roles and more than the colonization of female bodies. Don Felisberto deliberately makes Maria de los Angeles pregnant in order to advance himself in her father's company by producing a male heir. But even he recognizes that he is essentially a hired stud, viewed as socially inferior to his wife, her family, the BP's or Beautiful People, and the SAP's or Super Adorable People, who model themselves on U.S. filmstars, emulate U.S. fashions in showers, weddings, and clothing, and attend U.S. universities. Ironically, even the Academy of the Sacred Heart, where Revered Mother Martinez had hoped to marry Maria to the Divine Husband, is reduced to a colonized BP setting when Maria's father supplies it with Frigid King air conditioning from Connecticut. In "Fitcher's Bird," the husband, along with all his kinsmen, is duped and eventually marries death. At the end of Ferre's "Sleeping Beauty," Maria's husband kills her and also dies, but the patriarch, Fabiano Fernandez, has charge of his blue-eyed grandson and is bribing his way into heaven. Unlike the characters of Morrison's *Beloved*, which also uses a "Sleeping Beauty" intertext, the Puerto Rican society of this story sleeps on, in bed with dead values.

As Debra Castillo suggests, Ferre's "silenced and objectified women" comment not only on the muting of women and women's issues in Puerto Rican society, but also on the Puerto Rican situation in general: Puerto Rican youth have forgotten Spanish and have never learned to speak English. In Ferre's words, "They are becoming mute" and committing "cultural suicide" (qtd. Castillo 159; *Youngest* 163). According to Hintz, Ferre writes the English translation of her *Youngest Doll* stories to raise the consciousness of her fellow non-Spanish-speaking Puerto Ricans (Hintz 184). Thus, the silencing of women in Ferre's fiction is a symbolic silencing that can signify colonial, class, religious, racial and national as well as gender silencing. Like other writers of feminist metafairy tales, Ferre begins the development of postcolonial consciousness in a colonized society.

"The Poisoned Story" and "Amalia"

As folklorists are establishing, folk motifs and tale-types occur around the world. While variations in orally transmitted folklore are culturally distinct and significant, similarities and differences provide a means of speaking across cultures. For example, Flowers notes that West Indian folk stories are frequently about tricksters and include devil-spouse and animal-spouse motifs, often with a similarity to the Bluebeard type. As stated previously, the forbidden room motif "is an obvious favorite among West Indian storytellers" and can be found with almost any other type or motif. Of the four main divisions of West Indian folk tales she finds (the animal-trickster—Anancy, Bre-nancy—the etiological, the picaresque, and the magic story, 601–7), most of Ferre's stories feature magic and tricksters. She often uses, parodies, or subverts well-known fairy tales and folk motifs, including "Bluebeard." "The Poisoned Story" and "Amalia" are particularly interesting for their parody of patriarchal, aristocratic, and bourgeois values.

Ferre's "The Poisoned Story" is a trickster tale in which the stepmother reader, ironically both Cinderella and Snow-White's stepmother, becomes ensnared in the story and, eventually, poisoned by it.

Her very act of turning the pages written with poison guave ink prepared by her stepdaughter Rosaura, with the help of Rosaura's ghost mother, causes Rosa's apparent death. The Rosa-Rosaura story is what happens to Cinderella, Cendrellon, or Cenizosa after she attains the female, capitalistic dream, which does not include getting her own work published, and turns into her stepmother. Intertwining "Little Snow-White," "Red-Cap," and "Fitcher's Bird" ("Blue Beard") intertexts and characteristic motifs with "Cinderella," it is also what can happen to the Anancy trickster when he becomes she. In addition, "The Poisoned Story" uses motifs associated with the tale-types, including the cruel stepmother, doe's heart substituted for human one, disguise, punishment for female curiosity, murder by poisoning, marriage to death, the abandoned child secretly cared for by the mother, the transformed mother as helper, magic power from the mother, the dead mother's friendly return, cooking of magic fruit, and juice turning to blood. In addition, it uses the motif of the magic story (Thompson D1266.3) and reverses the execution escaped by story-telling motif (Thompson J1185). Like the dragon deceived into listening to a tale to enable the hero to cut off his head (Thompson K835), Rosa apparently dies before the tale she is reading—ironically about Rosa and Rosaura—ends. Like many of Ferre's female characters, both Rosa and Rosaura are unable to write and live their own, new stories.

The Cinderella and Cap o' Rushes tale-type (Arne Thompson 510, 510A), possibly originating in Asia, generally features a once-wealthy, rather than always poor, heroine abused by her stepmother and stepsisters. Often she stays on the hearth, and sometimes she flees the father who wants to marry her. Other important features are magic help, meeting the prince, having to prove her identity as the true bride, marrying the prince, and sometimes demonstrating the meaning of loving salt. Often the dead mother returns to help the girl; and the story usually includes a magic wand, tree or other objects; disguise; transformation; and recognition. Although the best-known Perrault "Cinderella" ("Cendrillon") ends with two morals, the first about a woman's graciousness and kindness being more important than beauty and the second about not neglecting godmothers and godfathers (see Zipes, *Beauties* 25–30), the ball is only for "people of quality." Cinderella would never have attracted the attention of the prince or the court without beauty and fine clothes, and, as commonly recognized, the story is about her attainment of money and status. Although Perrault's Cinderella moves her stepsisters to the palace and arranges marriages for them, in the Grimms' "Cinderella" ("Aschenputtel"), their treatment of Cinderella is avenged: They are so eager to fit the shoe that they cut off parts of their feet, and pigeons peck out their eyes (see Grimm; Zipes, *The Complete* 91–92). "Cendrellon" is a Creole Cinderella picture book in which Cendrellon, the man she marries, Paul Thibault, who "is like a prince," her *nannin* or godmother, and everyone we see is black. Distinctive features in this story include pink embroidered slippers, a mahogany wand the nurse inherits from her mother, narration from the point of view of the nurse, and, unlike the Perrault version, Cendrellon's renunciation of magic and fine clothes as prerequisites for passing the prince's marriage test. We know nothing about the fate of the stepsisters. Instead of a moral or a "living happily ever after," the tale ends with the storyteller's address to the audience, asserting that she knows the story "because I was there. I danced the *gwo-ka* and ate nine helpings of chocolate sherbet and came away only to tell you this tale" (San Souci n.p.) Nevertheless, the story is still partly about status and money, also implicit in major motifs of the tale-type (see Zipes, *Complete* 121–28; Pourrat, "Mary-in-the-Ashes" 7–14; Rooth; Dundes).

Flowers lists fifteen Puerto Rican versions of "Cinderella" that probably also influenced Ferre. In these tales, the Cinderella character, like Ferre's Rosa, is often a good seamstress and maid; and a witch rather than a godmother usually helps her. Often, fathers wish to marry their daughters, and the tales do not always feature princes and happy endings. In one version, after Cinderella marries the prince and the stepmother moves in with them, the stepmother throws Cinderella out of the window and she turns into a duck. Later, she turns back into a princess. In one unusual Puerto Rican variant, the prince becomes insane when Cinderella slips away and the ball ends abruptly (e.g., "Maria la Cenizosa," "La Cenizosa," "La Cenicienta," "Cenisosa," Flowers 170–74). In another, the Cinderella figure, like Ferre's stepmother, is actually named Rosa and is a good daughter. Although she is rewarded with warm tears, clean hands, and gold-droppings from her hair when she puts a witch's house in order, her sister, Carmen, suffers a reverse fortune ("La Cenizosa"). One Puerto Rican Cinderella even blackens her face and works as a bootblack until she is recognized by a ring in a cake ("Los Tres Trajes"). In several of these tales, sisters or stepsisters are cursed with tails growing out of their foreheads or filth coming out of their mouths (Flowers 170–74). Ferre seems to use the revenge or curse, the disappointing prince, and the unhappy ending of some of these stories in her own re-visioned Cinderella tale.

Ferre also uses a "Little Snow-White" intertext in "The Poisoned Story." "Little Snow-White" (AT 709) features a maiden with skin like snow and lips like blood, a jealous stepmother, a poisoning, a prince's resuscitation, and the stepmother's death. Often, there is a mysterious housekeeper, dwarf helpers, a poisoned comb, poisoned clothing, or a glass coffin. In Puerto Rico, where Flowers lists nine versions (243–45), the stepmother-witch may open a diabolical book to bury the girl or stick a pin in the girl's head, robbers or swans may help her, and she often marries a robber (Hansen 81). Throughout *The Youngest Doll*, Ferré re-visions this and other fairy tales by exposing hidden racial, gender, and class implications. Many of this volume's dolls have snow-white skin; and the "cannibalistic" bourgeoisie, who frequently "poison" everything they touch, sport blood-red lips and missing or black hearts.

The Red Riding Hood or The Glutton tale-type (AT 333), including a Puerto Rican version ("La Caperucita Roja," Flowers 127), features the wolf's disguise as a mother or grandmother, his deception and devouring of the girl, and the victims' rescue. As in many versions, "The Poisoned Story" makes the mother figure, here stepmother, ambiguous by doubling the wolf and grandmother. Even more subversively, the "heroine" turns out to kill the "hungry" "bad mother."

As previously mentioned, Bluebeard tale-types (AT 311, 312), including the devil-spouse, animal-spouse, and forbidden room motifs, are popular not only in Europe, but also in West Indian folk stories (601–2). Long before Perrault's "Blue Beard" and the Grimms' "Fitcher's Bird," "The Third Calendar's Tale" in *Arabian Nights* and the Sixth Tale of the Fourth Day in the *Pentamerone* depict the consequences of entering a forbidden room. The Grimms' "The Robber Bridegroom" (AT 955), featuring cannibalism as well as dismemberment, is closely related. Ferré is probably familiar not only with the Grimms and Perrault, but also with Puerto Rican and other Caribbean versions of Bluebeard tales and with similar stories including some of the same motifs. As in many Bluebeard stories, including the Grimms' and Perrault's, one Puerto Rican version features three daughters. A fisher promises a giant the first thing he meets on returning home, and the giant wins the first daughter, whom he kills when she enters a forbidden room. The giant kills the second girl, too, but the youngest resuscitates them, in this case with the help of her horse and dog ("El Pescador y sus tres Hijas," Flowers 85). She escapes and marries a prince. In another Puerto Rican version, a girl who has been bathing is kidnapped by a black man who places her in a box and commands her to sing. Her mother recognizes the girl's voice and fills the box with dirty water, which later sprays on the King and causes the man to be killed ("Los Zarcillitos de Perla," Flowers 83). Sometimes, as in a Puerto Rican and two Haitian versions, the murderous husband is the Devil, often with gold or silver teeth; he may also be a giant, pirate, troll, Death, or even The Thing (Haiti). In another Puerto Rican version, a woman is kind to a horse that tells her how to revive her sisters, and she is also able to revive and marry the prince. When the Giant causes the prince to fall asleep magically, he carries off the princess, whom he plans to boil in oil. She succeeds in removing the enchanting ball, however, and the prince and soldiers awake and quarter the giant (Hansen 27). Not all Bluebeard stories end happily for the woman, though, and this is the kind of ending Ferre selects for "The Poisoned Story." In one, also Puerto Rican, a nameless king is really Blue Beard. Although a visitor, rather than his wife, opens the forbidden room, he kills his wife. "This is the punishment that comes to the disobedient" ("El Caballero sin Nombre," Flowers 86).[5] In reference to Ferre's satire, we might say that this is the punishment that comes to the woman who rejects culturally approved gender, class, and racial roles. As we are beginning to see, "The Poisoned Story" interweaves "Cinderella," "Little Snow-White," "Red-Cap," and "Fitcher's Bird" intertexts and characteristic motifs. Instead of being about a beautiful, upper-class girl who is denied her rightful place in society by her stepmother, as in most "Cinderella" stories, "The Poisoned Story" is actually about a lower-class woman, ironically the stepmother, blamed also in "Little Snow-White" and "Hansel and Gretel." Instead of being the sweet "doll-heroine" assumed in well-known versions, Rosa is a plump, ambitious, somewhat crude woman, "hungry" for status and profit. Here Cinderella literally goes "from charwoman to gentlewoman, first wallowing in mud, then wallowing in wealth. But finery does not a lady make" (8). Used to domestic work without animal or dwarf helpers, Rosa is an excellent seamstress who capitalizes on the desire of bored bourgeois women to be beautiful. She sees them and their husbands as "a plague of vultures," hypocritically "scalping" the land and posing as pro-American while hoping to "graze once again on the poor man's empty guts" (13–14), an image of cannibalism suggesting "Little Red-Cap" and "The Robber Bridegroom." The "quality" folk gossip about Rosa, as they mock the speech of the kind washerwoman-nurse in *Cendrellon*. Ironically, although Rosa is a reader and critic of this story without a heroine, the story belongs primarily to her rather than Rosaura, the beautiful daughter about whom we know little except that she does no work and gets revenge on her stepmother. As in some Puerto Rican versions, Ferre's "Cinderella" implies a possible incestuous relationship between Rosaura, the upper-class Cinderella, who is mysteriously sad, and her father Lorenzo, the unsatisfactory

"Prince," whom she is determined to please. Don Lorenzo is a member of the sugar baron aristocracy whose house, a fantasy world with ghosts, termite-ridden floor, and cellar chicken coop and pigpen, symbolizes the criollo past, including its resistance to the U.S. invasion.

Again ironically, the lower-class stepmother, Rosa, who resentfully "work[s] her fingers to the bone in order to keep them all fed," doubles both Rosauras, the dead mother and the aristocratic daughter who lives in a storybook world instead of working, in a name suggesting Little Red Riding Hood's cap, the blood in the snow and red-hot shoes of "Little Snow-White," the bloodstained egg or key of "Fitcher's Bird," the crimson bougainvillea vines Rosaura hides behind, the red book Rosa reads, the color of its guava ink, and its resemblance to blood. Gender-marked red, often the color of a victim, these females all lose their ways in stories. Even the father, who gives his daughter a gold-bound storybook every year for her birthday, the last one bound in doe-heart's skin recalling "Snow-White," ends up selling his own heart or land and dying after he becomes a storyteller. Seduced like other poor people into welcoming the Yankees, reliving "Gone with the Wind" (another "scarlet" story), and preaching the doctrine of "salvation through style," in middle age Rosa still gets punished for being Puerto Rican and not being a socially approved Cinderella: She becomes Snow-White's ample-bodied stepmother. Increasingly numb and dizzy as she reads the poisoned tale after Lorenzo dies and she disinherits Rosaura, she also becomes Bluebeard's wife, curious to open the forbidden room of the deceptively diabolical story and then to know its end. Thus, she is ready to be chopped up by Fitcher and eaten by the Robber Bridegroom or Red Cap's "wolf." Significantly, Rosa recognizes that the story festers "in some remote corner of [her] mind, poisoning [her] with its dregs of resentment" (16). Not suited by age, class, skin, figure, or manners to be a true bride or "snow white," Rosa is thereby not a candidate for resuscitation. In many ways, Rosa is also the trickster tricked. As Hyde points out, with rare exceptions, such as Aunt Nancy as a variation of Anancy and the female Coyote, tricksters are male, probably because they belong to patriarchal mythologies. Female tricksters may have been ignored or suppressed, and some scholars believe that trickster stories reveal gender differences (335–39). Like the aunt in "The Youngest Doll," who gets revenge on the son of the doctor profiting from the wound he perpetuates rather than heals, the three female tricksters in "The Poisoned Story" are also victims of a classist, patriarchal, capitalistic culture.

Rosaura, the other Cinderella/Snow-White of "The Poisoned Story," is also a Sleeping Beauty (AT 410) and Rapunzel (AT 310), an archetype of passivity and isolation like her day-dreaming mother. Significantly, "she lives with her head in the clouds" until she makes her mother's recipe for guava compote, sees her dead mother "waft in and out of the window several times, on a guava-colored cloud," puts her birthday book under her pillow, and dreams that one of the tales in it will destroy its first reader (13–14, 17). Although she manages to trick her stepmother, nothing in "The Poisoned Story" suggests that her "ending" will be any better than that of her mother or Rosa.

Like Margaret Atwood's *Murder in the Dark,* "The Poisoned Story" also manages to tease readers into the possibility of being murdered. It begins with an epigraph from *One Thousand and One Nights* about a King who is poisoned as he turns the blank pages of a story. Although the King recognizes that there is "nothing written," the story is, nevertheless, poisoned (Zipes, *Arabian Nights* 7). In addition, the epigraph may suggest Scheherazade, also of *One Thousand and One Nights,* whom Ferre describes as one of her earliest heroines: Scheherazade uses the story as "a powerful weapon to defeat death. The epic of Scheherazade is not only that of the storyteller; it's more precisely that of the woman storyteller" (qtd. P. Hart 97). Whereas the story poisons the King, Scheherazade is able to defeat death by prolonging her stories. Thus, Ferre not only ironically reverses the story of Scheherazade as she does many of the fairy tales and myths she uses in *The Youngest Doll;* she also provides layers of intertextual resonance.

On one level, like *One Thousand and One Nights* and such postcolonial metafiction as Danticat's *The Farming of Bones,* the story asserts the power of the storyteller, of story-telling, of language, of speaking and expressing the feelings repressed by so many of Ferre's characters, especially her females. On another, it suggests the way we may all be "poisoned" by what we read, hear, and believe, particularly if these stories enforce gender, class, racial, historical, national, and other political conditioning. Whether Rosaura, the mother, or Rosaura, the daughter, or an anonymous story teller has written the story Rosa attributes to a small-town writer, it also literally expresses women's repressed anger or poison, including that of the female storyteller. Rosa counters the first narrator's version with her own experience as a servant who rises in class by marrying her master and starting her own business. Thus, she, too, becomes a storyteller, her narration contradicting that of the "two-bit," small-town writer who makes her laugh. Instead of creating her own "truth" by rewriting the plot in the way that Atwood's Circe and Penelope do in *You Are*

Happy and *The Penelopiad,* Rosa questions mostly the sequence of events rather than the events themselves. She becomes obsessed with defending her efforts to gain money and status. Thus, the story she reads eventually poisons her as, by implication, many of us are poisoned by patriarchal, capitalistic tales. Clever though she is, Rosa, representing the aspirations of Puerto Rico's real poor, is still poisoned by the old aristocracy and the dreams of money and glamour they inspire and foster.

Unlike Rosa and other lower-class workers who survive for a time by taking advantage of patriarchal and aristocratic dreams, most of Ferre's aristocratic women resemble dolls. In addition to playing roles in "The Youngest Doll" and "Sleeping Beauty," doll motifs, including the magic doll (Thompson D1268), figure prominently in "The Poisoned Story," "Mercedes Benz 220 SL," "Marina and the Lion," and "Amalia." People can become dolls and dolls, conveniently without voices and unable to move unless they are mechanically wound, can, or are supposed to, substitute for people, another global folk motif (the golem) with culturally specific Puerto Rican implications. Like the cheap dolls imported from Taiwan in "Amalia," these aristocratic dolls must live "predestined lives, caring for the tea tables and the flowered vases, the china and the matching table linen, being gracious hostesses to the colonels, the ambassadors, and the foreign ministers" ("Amalia" 50). As previously noted, race and even cosmetics "serve as the fundamental visual clues of social class" (D. Castillo 159) in Ferre's stories and, by implication, in Puerto Rican society. As we have seen, in *The Youngest Doll*'s title story, the youngest, aristocratic niece attains her only freedom by leaving the last life-sized, ivory-faced doll in her place. In "Sleeping Beauty," Maria de los Angeles goes from being a Coppelia doll to a low-class circus performer. Opening the forbidden doors and doing the forbidden dance, she dyes her hair red and dances nude on a tightrope in exaggerated white pancake makeup and false eyelashes. The artificial faces Ferre's characters create can release them from roles dictated by class, race, gender, and nationality.

In "Amalia," an albino-like child as fragile as her wax bride doll symbolizes inbred, protected daughters of aristocracy, who must stay in their boxes, in the house and out of the sun, forbidden gardens, and their own forbidden internal rooms, to guard white skin and clothing. This nameless girl is doubled with her wind-up doll, Amalia, with whom she is "one inseparable being." She knows that in the forbidden garden, one of this story's forbidden rooms, she can at last be herself, but "this is going to be all the way and to no avail. This time

I'm going through with this to the end": She has no escape (47). Like the aristocratic women of "Marina and the Lion," "The Youngest Doll," and "Sleeping Beauty," she still defies the roles dictated by her class. Marina of "Marina and the Lion" chooses to wear a doll's dress and even display herself in a cellophane-covered box, like Snow White in her coffin; but her masque, like the cement dust that encases the garden, keeps her life "shining and distant as if covered by a coat of varnish" until she dies (65). In contrast, as well as being Snow White, the twelve-year-old girl in "Amalia" is one of this volume's Pandoras, Eves, and brides of Bluebeard, curious to possess secret knowledge and willing to pay its price. Although visitors seem to mistake her for a mechanical doll as she greets them at the door, and although she may appear like "a rag doll" after she has been in the sun, she will not be a replica of her mother, as her mother is of her brother, or a doll slave to him. Dressed all in white, confined to the house, and told to avoid dirtying herself like Lessing's Edwardian child in *Memoirs,* she disappoints her mother by lying on the floor "like a common slut" (48). Early in the story, she enacts her rebellion through her dolls, naming the three plastic ones predestined to be hostesses after the three maids who adore Gabriel, the singing and dancing chauffeur. She pretends that it is Amalia who becomes shameless, feeling she is free and can do whatever she likes, lifting her skirt, dancing, engaging in unladylike behavior, and becoming Gabriel's slave. Having come to life, Amalia apparently defies the class rules forbidding her to visit floors other than the one to which she is assigned in the dolls' "summer palace." The girl says it is Amalia who dyes the skin, hair, and eyes of the blond groom doll to resemble the black chauffeur, Gabriel, even exchanging his General's uniform for that of a chauffeur, and embraces him in her box. The girl, however, is also a Snow White without a rescuer. Her only prince is the uncle who puts his hand on her breast at her confirmation ceremony. After her uncle locks the door, marooning her and Amalia outside, she is also unable to escape by leaving a doll substitute, like Fitcher's Bird. She happily dies in the sun in the forbidden garden, with her eyes as wide open as those of her melting doll, because she finally eats the forbidden fruit of the knowledge she craves. It is her General uncle and the house of aristocracy, not the curious woman, that the servants dismember as they dance, and the servant Gabriel, not the uncle who dresses like an archangel, who holds the flaming sword.

Although protagonists of "The Poisoned Story" and "Amalia" both die, like Maria in "Sleeping Beauty" and, in some interpretations, the youngest niece in "The Youngest Doll," their lives not only revision that of the folk and fairy-tale characters they suggest but also stimulate readers to critique the gender and cultural roles that trap them. In my interpretation of "The Youngest Doll," a smart trickster, resembling Fitcher's "Bird," is able to outwit the patriarchy and survive the entrapping classism, racism, and sexism. Like other writers of feminist metafairy tales, Ferre foregrounds sexual, racial, and class politics, including those of the postcolonial condition.

CHAPTER 7

Enchantment, Transformation, and Rebirth in Iris Murdoch's *The Green Knight*

"Gawain and the Green Knight," "The Green Man," "Hansel and Gretel," "Sleeping Beauty," "Rapunzel," and Other Tales

Dame Jean Iris Murdoch, Anglo-Irish and born July 15, 1919, in Dublin and died in 1999, studied with Ludwig Wittgenstein at Oxford and became a fellow of St. Anne's College, Oxford, in 1948. A philosopher, novelist, playwright, and poet, Murdoch was awarded the International Mann Booker Prize for Fiction in 1978. The novels of Iris Murdoch do not always receive the acclaim that they deserve. Too often the twenty-six novels, extending over a thirty-year period, are considered traditional or antimodernist (Gordon 115; Duddy 2287) rather than postmodern, and the unreliability and irony of the third-person centers-of-consciousness are often overlooked by philosophers who quote characters' dialogue to represent Murdoch's own views. Murdoch's work has been limited by oversimplifications, such as the usual expectation that she always uses realism and refers to objective reality. In addition, she is thought to write tragedy rather than comedy (Lesser 15), be antifeminist or nonfeminist (M. Rowe, Review 352; Fiander 8, 10–11),[1] and is treated as English rather than as an Irish woman who has been influenced by Irish writers and sometimes takes what is today called a postcolonial position (Gerstenberger 79; M. Rowe, "Dame" 316–20; Weese 648). Since most of Murdoch's characters feel enchanted, under a magic spell, and awaiting rescue or salvation or assuming that they are able to rescue someone else, her myth and fairy-tale intertexts have particularly suffered from insufficient attention.

According to Conradi, Murdoch's references to fairy tales are only decoration for the plot and "contribute to . . . atmosphere." He sees her use of myth as "deliberately incomplete, throw-away, and provisional" with "more the feeling of delighted play or joke than of any palpable symbolic design on the reader" (11, 126, 250). Elizabeth Dipple thinks that Murdoch's allusions to myth result in "overplotted, tricksy" novels (3). Although Murdoch characters use myth and fairy-tale roles to deceive themselves that their lives are fated or scripted and that they are enchanted or imprisoned, paradoxically, myths and fairy tales also suggest transformation and rebirth. Comically, their transformations, like their love relationships, may be transitory. Nevertheless, most do awaken to see more clearly and do keep striving for goodness. Myths and fairy tales are stories and stories in Murdoch's texts ultimately suggest art, a way of creating meaning in a mysterious universe.
According to Murdoch,

I think that people create myths about themselves and are then dominated by the myths. They feel trapped, and they elect other people to play roles in their lives, to be gods or destroyers or something, and I think that this mythology is often very deep and very influential and secretive, and a novelist is revealing secrets of this sort. (Bellamy 138)

Thus, the novelist or artist is in a sense the master magician. Slaymaker suggests that myths "provide fictional frameworks to support [Murdoch's] notion of the incomprehensibility and impenetrability of human action and motivations" (166). Myths frequently portray quests, for escape from a labyrinth or trap, to defeat or kill monsters, to defeat death, to become a hero, to win a prize. Regarding fairy tales, Lisa Fiander suggests that Murdoch's novels challenge and celebrate fairy tales' prescriptions for social engagement. Fairy-tale themes include unhappy childhoods, dangerous romances, the struggle between individuality and community, the journey toward community, and celebration of life (Fiander xii, xv, vii). In addition, fairy tales are about the search for identity, individuation, and healing and the transformation of individuals and their surroundings. Thus, myth and fairy-tale intertexts, hardly just decoration, convey the images, characterization, themes, and structures of Murdoch's novels. These "novels" are actually closer to the genres of romance, fabulation, and the fantastic, with an interesting interlay of the money, manners, marriage, and morals tradition of the English novel.

Contrary to what most critics believe, although Murdoch admires traditional nineteenth-century Russian and English realistic novels and speaks of herself as a "traditional" writer, she does not necessarily write novels like Tolstoy and Dickens and is, in fact, only too willing to admit that she does not (Sagare 698).[2] Instead, like the other contemporary writers examined here, she creates deceptive postmodern works that question her culture's master texts, including Plato, capitalism, Marxism, Christianity, and some canonical literary works. Despite/ because of her philosophical exploration of Plato, the world of her novels, filled with flawed human beings, lacks Reality and the Good. She deconstructs national, social, and cultural myths, as of fate or free will, and substitutes the concept of social construction for fixed concepts as of gender, identity, reality, or truth (Holman and Harmon). Stuck in a postmodern world of shadows and illusions, her characters still experience magical epiphanies that sometimes help them transform:

A novel is a drama about people who are in some kind of confusion or illusion but are seeking enlightenment, freedom, seeking happiness of course, which we all seek, and the novel describes a drama which ends in catastrophe, falling back into illusion, or acquiring greater illusion or becoming more sensible, more enlightened or more free or something of this kind." (Sagare 698)

Throughout her work, Murdoch's self-conscious centers-of-consciousness and first-person narrators chatter continuously about the stories they have been living and congratulate themselves on entering "reality" at the same time as they begin another fiction. Most readers have completely overlooked this metafictional dimension of her fiction, probably because it is almost totally dramatized and the implied author is at considerable ironic distance from the narrators. In *The Unicorn,* for example, Gerald and Effingham self-consciously comment on the life narratives which, by implication, are little different from the fiction we read. In their thoughts and dialogue, they reveal an awareness of choosing "art" over "reality," of creating and participating in aesthetic patterns or stories that may distance them from things as they are (S. Wilson, *Self-Conscious* 94–95). In *The Green Knight,* some characters do penetrate beyond illusion and use art to quest for enlightenment. In addition to metafiction, double-voiced irony, and self-conscious narration, Murdoch also uses other postmodern genres and techniques: antifiction, intertextuality, magical realism, parody (Holman and Harmon), and open-endedness or writing beyond the ending.

Murdoch's next-to-the-last novel, *The Green Knight* (1993), has attracted almost no critical attention but beautifully illustrates these postmodern techniques. Her fiction is nearly always metafiction, or fiction about fiction, and her narrators continuously call attention to their telling of stories. While Murdoch does not generally use full-fledged antifiction, which parodies traditional plot, structure, characterization, and even theme, her narrators do tell stories, such as of Lucas's killing a mugger, that, like Atwood's *Surfacing* and *The Robber Bride*, unravel as they proceed. Regarding postmodern open-endedness, Murdoch's plots are detailed and ingenious, and the novel gives an impression of every plot thread being tied together. But Murdoch makes no effort to explain Harvey's gothic incident in Tessa's house, probably an encounter with one of the women Tessa is attempting to help, but never spoken of and never related to the main action. Like the actions of Tessa, Emil, and Clive, the Adwardens, Cora Brock, and Lucas outside of the main events, this event stands for the external world which cannot be perceived objectively but continues to be there, regardless of what happens to the characters we know. Finally, *The Green Knight* uses mythic and fairy-tale intertexts, my focus here, in a postmodern manner.

In addition to displacing the truth of traditional texts and shifting the point of view, intertextual tactics in *The Green Knight*, parodic until the end, include scenes based on mythic or fairy-tale intertexts and gender reversal, such as the sleeping Harvey being awakened by a kiss at Peter's party; symbolism that enlarges the meaning of the ordinary, such as Moy's cutting off her braid; writing beyond the ending to involve readers in plotting events beyond the book; genre blending; transgressive and ironic language; and surprising remythification, as when Moy realigns her personal world as she places the rock where it belongs. Fortunately, the two scholars who do discuss *The Green Knight* do briefly explain either a few fairy-tale or mythic references. Fiander notes "Hansel and Gretel" in reference to Harvey's fear of abandonment, "Cinderella" to characters aided and impeded by families, animal bridegroom tales, and "Beauty and the Beast" (see Fiander). Frankova briefly discusses "Sir Gawain and the Green Knight" and Green Man myth.

Many of the mythological and fairy-tale references are motifs or images that connect to "The Green Knight" and the Green Man. As Murdoch says, "The mythology, if you like, is made by the people in the novel themselves. . . . There are certain general patterns—for instance, the idea of an ordeal: somebody has to undergo an ordeal in order to become enlightened or even to succeed" (Sagare 705–6). Ordeals—tasks to be performed or contests—figure not only in "The Green Knight" and the Green Man, but also in many of the book's other intertexts: the Grail, Lochinvar, St. George and the Dragon, Perseus, Minotaur, Odysseus, Philoctetes, and other myths and on some level in most fairy tales, such as "Hansel and Gretel," "Cinderella," "Beauty and the Beast" and other animal bridegroom and monster (ogre) tales, "Blue Beard" or "Fitcher's Bird," "Briar Rose" ("Sleeping Beauty"), and "Rapunzel." Another general pattern is the quest, and Murdoch's characters are always questing for meaning, identity, goodness, love, metamorphosis or transformation, salvation, and a new era. Other mythic and fairy-tale motifs include spells and potions, sleeping, falls, injuries, dismemberment, enchantment, transformation, rescue, salvation, and healing. Other intertexts include those about the Great Goddess, Valkyries, Sibyls, the Delphic Priestess, Moira (fate), Silkies, Leda and the Swan, Circe, Daphne and Apollo, Andromache, and wizards. Literary (*The Tempest*), and biblical intertexts (Abel and Cain, Christ, Lazarus, Angels, Mephistopheles) also function in the book. Murdoch admits that she wanted to be a painter and, at the time of the interview, still wanted to be one (Lesser 13). References to painting, such as Rembrandt's *The Polish Rider* and Carpaccio's two *Saint George and the Dragon* paintings in this novel, are everywhere in Murdoch's work, and she recognizes that some of her visual images "carry a mythological charge." They and characters' surroundings are also symbolic, as everything is, because "people make things symbolic for themselves" and surroundings are "charged with emotional significance" (Lesser 13). Magical objects and talismans—the bat, Peter's magic ceremonial sword (umbrella with hidden knife), characters' masks at the birthday party, the Anderson house (Clifton), Moy's stones, and Moy's braid—are also important.

In a book titled *The Green Knight,* the most evident mythological references are, of course, to the anonymous medieval romance, "Sir Gawain and the Green Knight," a poem that is already "a fusion of Celtic myths and Norman French stories" (Frankova 77); to the Green Knight myth; to the earlier, associated pagan myth of the Green Man, often a mask of a leafy man's face peering out of foliage that is displayed in European churches and pubs; and to the also earlier Great Goddess myths on which the other stories appear to be based (see Miyares on *The Green,* 185), in which the goddess represents "Nature,

Fate, Time, Eternity, Truth, Wisdom, Justice, Love, Birth, Death"
(B. Walker, *Woman's Encyclopedia* 346). The poem has a self-
conscious narrator who draws attention to his telling of "as surpass-
ingly strange a tale as ever Britain spawned" (Raffel 49). It is about
Arthur's "perfect knight" of the round table, Sir Gawain, first con-
vincing Arthur to let him take Arthur's place and then accepting a
challenge to exchange blows (play the beheading game) with the
Green Knight. The Green Knight has green hair and skin, a green
horse, a green axe, and green clothing, is associated with the green
chapel, and is often referred to as the green man (Raffel 52–61).
Gawain has characteristics of the Celtic sun god, including a diadem
of golden hair, resembles Cuchulainn, Lug, and Gwri, and his
strength waxes until midday and wanes afterwards (Leach and Fried
442–43). After Gawain cuts off the Green Knight's head, the Green
Knight picks up his head and says that he will return the blow in a
year and a day's time, at the Green Chapel on the New Year. On the
way to the chapel, Sir Gawain stops at Sir Bertilak's (Bercilak's) castle,
where each agrees under the Gains game to give one another whatever he receives each day. While Bertilak is hunting, Gawain is
tempted by his host's wife, who gives him kisses, which he passes on,
and a green girdle or belt supposed to protect his life, which he keeps.
At the Green Chapel encounter, the Green Knight, who is also Sir
Bertilak, slightly injures Gawain on the third blow because Gawain
does not tell the truth about the girdle, but he pardons Gawain for his
love of life and Gawain keeps the girdle as a reminder of his sin.

The whole event is Morgan (Morgana) le Fay's test of Arthur's
knights and, in goddess myth, her presiding over the death and resurrection of the rival year-gods as they behead one another in the life cycle (B. Walker, *Woman's Encyclopedia* 674). Morgan, related to
numerous river and lake goddesses, valkyries, and mermaids (Leach
and Fried 746–47) as well as the Crone or Fate aspect of the Great
Goddess (Moira-Moy in *The Green Knight*), dwindled in power by
the late medieval romances, when she became Arthur's sister. Morgan
ruled the Fortunate Isles where valkyries, associated with Aleph in the
novel, ushered dead heroes to the afterlife (B. Walker, *Woman's Encyclopedia* 675, Leach and Fried 746). The poem is about "chivalric
virtues, temptation and chastity, goodness and truth. . . . The mysterious double figure of the pagan/ Christian Green Knight/ Bertilak
lends the poem an enigmatic quality" (Frankova 79), and, more significantly, appears to be the basis for the Peter/ Lucas doubling in
The Green Knight. The poem and Green Knight myth link to
pre–Christian Green Man myth, found in the many cultures through-

out the world that depict foliate heads (including those of Dionysus, Osiris, Bachus, Al-kadir, and Jack in the Green),[3] because, like earlier goddess myth, both suggest the cycle of life, from death to rebirth to death and rebirth each Spring. Thus, the Green Man celebrates life and suggests fertility and Nature. He is also connected to the end of time, is the voice of inspiration to artists, and can come as a white light, a gleam, or an inner mood (Anderson). These themes, character types, images, and the mysterious tone translate to Murdoch's book and intertwine with other mythic, fairy-tale, and folklore intertexts in this metafairy tale beginning "Once upon a time there were three girls. . . . And they lived at the bottom of a well" (1).

Characteristic of Murdoch's tricky postmodern comedy, parody, irony, and frequent intertextual reversals, the preeminent "green man" in this book is a green woman. It can be argued, however, that many of the characters experience a rebirth similar to that of the Green Knight or the Green Man and thus also enact these roles. Beginning in an urban Waste Land reminiscent of T. S. Eliot's (partly based on Grail and other vegetation myths), Camus's *The Myth of Sisyphus,* and Sartre's *Nausea,* where many characters feel "shipwrecked" (327), empty, hollow, wounded, and without purpose, most experience the growth and rebirth of the Green Man and the Green Knight. At the beginning, Peter is a confused manic depressive who almost dies, Lucas seems suicidal to his friends, Clement is deceived and tricked, Harvey is crippled and longs for a home, Bellamy longs for religious meaning but masochistically gets no further than punishing himself, Moy is drowning, Louise is passive, Sefton and Alethea seem caught in routine, Joan wants to be rescued, and all await a parodic apocalypse. Virtually all feel they have been enchanted by a spell, are unfree, and are asleep. They seek magical transformation and salvation. All experience comic deaths and rebirths.

The Green Knight and Green Man intertexts interlace with fairy-tale, biblical, other folklore, and literary intertexts. The obvious Green Knight, Peter Mir, dressed in green and symbolically decapitated like the Green Knight, is actually a decoy, ironically dead at the novel's end. Thought of as a psychoanalyst and sorcerer or magician, and immediately the center of the book's social circle, Peter has an aura of power and prestige that is deflated when we discover that he is an escaped mental patient and butcher-fishmonger. The last name of Peter Mir, a man bent on revenge and punishment for a blow on his head which was assumed to have killed him, ironically means world peace. His first name suggests Simon Peter, the apostle of Christ, Czar Peter the Great, Robin Hood, and Peter Pan, who never grows up. Both

Robin Hood and Peter Pan, like Robin Goodfellow and Puck, have historically been associated with the wild Green Man. Peter is also the minotaur in a maze of confusion (led by a green girdle), Odysseus, Lazarus, the biblical Saul and Paul, Mephistopheles, Mr. Pickwick, the beast of "Beauty and the Beast," a healer, a scapegoat some readers will identify with Jesus, a pirate, an artist, and Eros, who symbolically shoots arrows of love (through his "special" drink/ potion) that apparently affect each of the main characters except Tessa and Lucas, who are not present at the party. In the second encounter of Murdoch's Green Man and Green Knight, Murdoch varies the myth by having the Green Man symbolically beheaded twice. Like the sun aspects of Gawain and the shafts of light (imagination) linked to the Green Man, Peter is associated with light the second time he enters the green world when, depending upon the viewer, a star or plane falls, he burns, he is hit by lightening, or he turns into an angel. Since Peter remembers his Buddhist religion when he is hit on the head for a second time with the baseball bat, he regains his Green Man reverence for life and plans charitable activities for the future before he dies in the mental hospital. Peter's unexpected clean stabbing (an ironic butcher cut) of Lucas with the hidden dagger causes no harm but completes the ritualistic cycle and indicates to Lucas that Peter is an artist.

Other male characters also share aspects of Gawain or the Green Knight in that they are comically associated with knights, warriors, or Trojan heroes and function within the book's cyclic design. Lucas Graffe, the ironic Gawain of the book, whose first name suggests light, Lucifer, and luck, ironically lives in an always dark house. He is another Prospero sorcerer or wizard and secret Bluebeard, the ringmaster, Mephistopheles, and Abel who prides himself on absolute power over his brother. Although the reference to *Beowulf* suggests that this "shadow-goer" may enter the light (422) and both Harvey and Sefton feel that there is more to Lucas than we see, he seems to win the Lady of "The Green Knight" or Beauty without reforming his monstrous behavior. Ironically, his life is spared without his demonstrating a love of life. Clement, a Harlequin buffoon, Polonius, and juggler whose name means *merciful, gentle,* is the "parfit gentle knight" (11). He dreams that Lucas is offering him the Grail but fears it is poisoned (84, 87). Interestingly in a book by an author who thinks that Plato is the greatest philosopher, one of the Popes named *Clement* attempted to reconcile Platonic and Christian ideas (www.behindthename.com). Referring to Peter as the Green Knight and Lucas as having had an ordeal (implying that Lucas is Gawain),

Clement recognizes that the two are linked and that perhaps justice is greater than the Grail (456). Comically and ironically, he cannot recognize either the allusion to his being the supposedly murdered "third man" in the melodramatic shadows (C. Reed) or the actuality that his brother tried to kill him. Still, by the end he wakes to action in marrying Louise. Harvey Blacket, whose first name means *battleworthy*, is called Lochinvar after the poem about a knight carrying off a bride. He and Sefton-Sophia—history, order, and wisdom, masked as a Bishop and sibyl and linked to the amber necklace's qualities of luck and self-healing (Holistic Qualities of Gems)—do eventually decide to marry, but through much of the book he is crippled and immature, a Sleeping Beauty under a spell or curse and asleep in a fairy tale. He also looks like a Greek *kouros* and feels like an abandoned Hansel, the snake-bitten Philoctetes, a puppet, and an androgynous Ariel, creator of illusions. Probably the most comic of these questers, and reminiscent in his self-deceptions of *The Unicorn*'s Effingham Cooper, is Bellamy James, so unfocused and masochistic in his obsession with guidance, angels, and salvation that he causes Father Damien to lose his faith. Reunited with dog Anax (overlord, king) and forming a new relationship with Emil by the end, he finally manages to act in saving Moy from drowning. We know little about Emil except that he is German, rich, gay, initially in a relationship with Clive, writes books about art history, and appears to be more stable than the other characters.

On the other hand, Moy or Moira Anderson, whose first name means goddess of fate, who is part of the Great Goddess, and who is considered a witch in the novel, actually represents the Green Man and the Great Goddess in her oneness with the earth. According to S. Wilson,

Contrary to what many feminists believe, folklore actually preserves information about the Great Goddess (Gimbutas, *Civilization* 226) and many other fairy tales ([besides "Cinderella"] e.g., "The Sleeping Beauty" or "Briar Rose")) (Von Franz, *The Feminine* 20) are Goddess stories; the real moher of Ella (Hel or Helle) was the earth. The "fairy godmother" of later versions of "Cinderella" (Motif F311.1) represents "the dispossessed Great Goddess in retirement underground" and is still associated with the tree of life. (Walker, *Woman's Encyclopedia* 168; Von Franz, *Interpretation* 9–10; S. Wilson, *Margaret Atwood's Fairy* 20)

Initially stuck in Clifton like a Rapunzel tower or Sleeping Beauty castle, feeling like a "hump-backed dwarf" (386), and close only to her beloved, Rembrandt's painting, *The Polish Rider,* she and her sisters ("the Vestel Virgins," 49) must, like the other characters, wake up from routines to experience life. Attacked by a swan, explicitly recalling the myth of Leda and the Swan, Moy is trying only to protect a duck and does not seek, as in Yeats's well-known poem, to put on the god's knowledge and power; instead, she worries that she may have hurt the swan. Moy wishes she had been the prince in "Sleeping Beauty" and awakened Harvey with a kiss. She is, however, the real Beauty of the book in being good, being the first to recognize Peter's goodness , and finally in representing the union of Beauty and the Beast. Privileged for a time with powers of telekinesis, one instance of the novel's real magic and use of magical realism, at the end Moy turns into a silkie (selkie, silky—in Shetland and Orkney Island myth, a seal who can take off its skin) and back into a person before she returns the conical stone to its original site. As Aleph recognizes early in the book and Moy repeats at the end, symbolically Moy is a girl on the land and a silkie in the sea, and the silkies are *her* people (16, 467). She is also able to commune with stones, spiders, and Anax and has reverence for all life. Rather isolated within her family early in the book, Moy cuts off her Rapunzel braid, becomes part of a new family with Bellamy and Emil, and is on the way to becoming one of Murdoch's special Buddhists. Peter's gift of a lapis lazuli necklace suggests psychic powers, the opening of a third eye, total awareness, and balance (Holistic Qualities of Gems). Significantly, she is the book's main artist. In love with Rembrandt's *The Polish Rider,* she sees him as "brave, innocent, chaste, good," a knight on a quest (20). Seeing Carpaccio's paintings of St. George and the dragon and also thinking of Perseus, she takes the side of dragons rather than captive princesses and thinks that princesses "should be careful and not make themselves attractive to monsters" (203), the fate apparently in store for Aleph-Alethea (Truth), who also plays Andromache chained to a rock (112), Beauty of "Beauty and the Beast," the Lady of "The Green Knight," and a military Bluebeard (208), signifying the secret room of her relationship with Lucas. The diamonds Aleph receives from Peter are associated with strength, eternity, and peace.

Moy's mother, Louise, who wears a moon mask and, like Aleph, is identified with a sacrificial victim, is also associated with a phase of the Goddess ("the great mother figure" 371) and does signify happiness once she overcomes her symbolic paralysis and Rapunzel inability to reach anyone. Joan, the doubled mother/ witch of "Hansel and Gretel," who ironically makes Harvey feel abandoned but sleeps in his bed and interferes with his becoming an adult, is Circe masked as a Delphic priestess (207). Apparently lacking anyone else that she can manipulate or lean on, she ends up with Humphrey Hook, a man earlier spoken of as the last recourse. In keeping with the novel's amazing transformations, enigmatic Tessa Millen, a feminist who runs a woman's shelter and is also a sibyl, a body guard, "Hitler in knickers" (5), and the witch of "Hansel and Gretel"—whose body is the delicious house—becomes a medical student.

As is beginning to be evident, other myths besides the Green Knight and the Green Man and numerous fairy tales help shape the meanings of *The Green Knight.* Jeanne-Marie Leprince de Beaumont's "Beauty and the Beast" (AT 425C), the more famous tale, is based on Gabrielle-Suzanne de Villeneuve's earlier, longer "The Story of Beauty and the Beast" (Zipes, *Beauties* 231–32). De Beaumont's version is especially relevant to *The Green Knight* because the tale is about the superficiality of beauty: Character, virtue, and kindness rather than good looks or wit create happiness. As all of Murdoch's works, both fiction and philosophy, suggest, goodness is what matters. Although Beauty's father is wealthy and her three sisters become arrogant and proud, he loses his money and the family is forced to be farmers in the country. When he is notified that his merchandise is safe and will journey to recover it, Beauty, unlike her envious sisters, asks only for a rose. The father becomes lost while returning home and enters the Beast's apparently deserted palace, where he finds food, a bed, and clothing. While leaving, he plucks a rose, only to be scolded by the Beast and told that he must die in three months unless a daughter takes his place. He returns home with a branch of roses, Beauty leaves with him in order to take his place, both he and the Beast are delighted with "the goodness of Beauty's heart," and the father reluctantly leaves. Beauty grows to respect the Beast, who does not eat her but wants to marry her, and recognizes that, although an ugly monster, he is "very good." Because she sees her father's grief in the Beast's magic mirror, she goes to see her father again and stays longer than a week, during which the Beast nearly dies. Beauty returns to the Beast's palace, does not find him, and sees him unconscious in the garden from fasting in his grief. Beauty realizes that she does love Beast, he transforms into a prince "more handsome than Eros," the two sisters become statues until they recognize their faults, and Beauty and the Beast marry. Their relationship is based on virtue (Zipes, *Beauties* 233–45).

"Beauty and the Beast" underlies *The Green Knight*'s characterization, themes, and motifs. Although this group of middle-class, educated people is mostly prosperous, they all feel a void in their material existences that fills through love. As Beauty prefers a rose to riches and realizes her love for the Beast in his garden, many of Murdoch's characters find healing and greater consciousness being in nature (the park, the sea, the second time on the bridge). Symbolically, Moy, like Beast and All Fur (Zipes, *Complete* 263), is able to remove her animal skin disguise (Thompson Motif K521.1) and, like both Beauty and Beast, dedicate herself to a quest for the good.

In addition, the Grimms' tales, "Rapunzel" (AT 310),"Briar Rose" (Perrault's "The Sleeping Beauty in the Woods," AT 410), "Hansel and Gretel" (AT 327A), "Fitcher's Bird" (Perrault's "Blue Beard," AT 311), and "Cinderella" ("Ashenputtel," AT 510, 510a) are among the most significant. "Rapunzel" and "Briar Rose" signify a movement from isolation to relationship. Both take place in towers cut off from other people but surrounded by green nature. The tower in "Rapunzel" lacks doors and stairs, and the witch/ sorceress strives to keep her treasured maiden for herself alone, paralleling the father in "Briar Rose" who encloses his daughter and cuts her off from the world to keep her safe from the curse. Although Clifton, the Anderson house, tall and narrow like a tower, is sometimes a center for social activities, most of the time each character occupies a separate room, and Louise certainly wants to keep her daughters and herself safe after their father dies. In "Rapunzel," because a woman covets Mother Gothel's private garden and steals some of the rapunzel plant, she loses her daughter. The witch insists on justice, like Peter Mir, and confines the girl in a tower. The girl still sings, as do Murdoch's Anderson sisters. When Mother Gothel discovers that a prince has been climbing up Rapunzel's hair, she cuts it off, exiles Rapunzel to a desolate land, and traps the prince climbing on the cut off braids. After the prince jumps off the tower and blinds himself on thorns in failing to rescue the princess, he wanders for years until he finds Rapunzel and the twins she has given birth to and regains his sight (Zipes, *Complete* 46–49). Harvey always feels that he is wooing a princess when he is in Clifton, but he initially pursues the wrong princess. Aleph is apparently already involved with Lucas, and Moy, who ironically considers becoming a nun even though she thinks she loves Harvey, never lets down her hair to him. She finally renounces Rapunzelhood by cutting off her braid and chooses to be an artist and a Buddhist. Harvey and Sefton plan to establish their own family.

Variants of the "Briar Rose," "Hansel and Gretel," "Cinderella," and "Fitcher's Bird" tales (including West Indies versions already discussed) exist most places in the world (Aarne and Thompson 138–39). "Briar Rose," "Cinderella," and "Fitcher's Bird" are about marriage, both "Briar Rose" and "Hansel and Gretel" are again partly about maturation to adulthood, and "Fitcher's Bird" is an upside down "Cinderella" story in which the ogre groom is caught in his own trap. *The Green Knight* is also about maturation and marriage in pursuit of happiness and a good life. Most of "Briar Rose's" major motifs—the curse and spell, the castle in the forest, the tower of isolation, the prick, sleeping, and the barrier of thorns—function ironically and parodically in Murdoch's novel, often in more than one sense. In "Briar Rose" a child reaches adulthood despite a wise woman/ grandmother witch's curse. A king and queen who arrange a feast to celebrate the birth of their child invite only twelve of the thirteen wise women to the celebration because they have only twelve golden plates. The one who is not invited wants revenge and makes an evil spell so that the princess will prick her finger on a spindle and die. The last wise woman amends the sentence to a sleep of one hundred years. Although the king orders all spindles in the kingdom to be burned, on her fifteenth birthday the princess discovers a tower and unlocks a door to a room where an old woman is spinning. When the princess touches the spindle and feels the prick, she is overcome by a deep sleep. Gradually everyone in the palace falls asleep and a Briar hedge encloses it for a hundred years, until a prince discovers that he can easily enter. When he discovers and kisses the princess, she awakes, they marry, and "they lived happily to the end of their days" (Zipes, *Complete* 186–89).

Moy, too, has a birthday party (16th) and has a gift-bringing visitor, not initially expected, who changes the course of everyone's lives. Depending upon how one counts, the number of standard invitations might even total twelve. According to Joan, "Harvey ought to be the prince who hacks his way through the forest, but he can't be, he's *in* the castle!" (11). Harvey, both prince and parodic princess in *The Green Knight,* is "green" in the sense of naïve and innocent and certainly feels cursed, under a spell, asleep, and isolated, especially when he has to bypass Circe witch Joan and sibyl witch Tessa (334, 133). Still, Fiander's assumption, that in Murdoch's universe love means loving without too much knowledge (xiv), seems oversimplified. While his pursuit of Aleph always seems barricaded with thorns, when he shifts to Sefton, who has already awakened him at Peter's house, he has the knight's experience of "Briar Rose": It is as if "the beautiful flowers opened of their own accord [to], let him through" (Zipes, *Complete* 188). Disregarding the pun on *prick* that one is tempted to connect to Harvey and Sefton's first sexual experience, both prince and princess Harvey and Sefton, who have known one another nearly all of their lives, so suddenly become aware of one another that

Harvey has to tell Sefton to "Stop, stop, wake up" when she assumes Harvey must be in love with Aleph (421). Several other characters— Peter, Moy, Bellamy, Clement, Louise—play Sleeping Beauty to the extent that they do not awaken to a real life purpose until late in the novel. As Louise says when she thinks she will descend into old age without romantic love, "for so long I was paralysed as if asleep" (336).

The Grimms' "Hansel and Gretel" and "Fitcher's Bird" (Perrault's "Blue Beard") both take place in a forest, as does "Briar Rose"; and, along with "Cinderella" and Green Man myth, thus suggest an origin in tree myth. The three tales involve trickery, betrayal, resourceful- ness, and animal helpers; and both "Cinderella" and "Fitcher's Bird" involve transformation. "Hansel and Gretel" is about a child's move- ment from abandonment and anxiety about independence (Bettel- heim 98) to self-sufficiency. It is also about famine and greed, and some versions of "Fitcher's Bird" are about unnatural hunger— cannibalism. "Fitcher's Bird" also explores each person's "secret room," sexual politics, and transformation. *The Green Knight* is about all of these themes. Many of Murdoch's characters feel abandoned or unloved in childhood, resort to trickery and even betrayal, are greedy or covetous, and manage to keep parts of themselves secret. Some, such as Joan and Tessa, play games of sexual politics, and some man- age to transform. Meals at Clifton are ritualistic (309), may be offered instead of sex, and sometimes humorously puncture melodramatic di- alogue, as when Aleph offers Harvey a prosaic lunch right after he suggests they are experiencing "a special moment in time . . . like sal- vation" (264).

In "Hansel and Gretel," a woman convinces her husband to aban- don two children deep in the forest when there is a famine. Although once they manage to find their way back by stones Hansel has dropped, the next time the birds eat the crumbs he hoped to follow and they are lost until a white bird leads them to a house made of bread, cake, and sugar. The mother's double, a wicked witch on a crutch, takes them in but plans to eat them, especially Hansel, whom she puts in a cage and tries to fatten up. Gretel manages to push the witch into the oven prepared for Hansel, releases Hansel, and they re- turn to the forest, where they are helped across a river by a white duck. They return home to their father "and they lived together in ut- most joy" (Zipes, *Complete* 64). Specifically again Harvey, but, as stated, many of *The Green Knight*'s characters, feel abandoned, Lucas by his parents when they have a "real" son, Clement by his brother Lucas, Joan and Louise by Clement, Bellamy by God, and Anax by

Bellamy. Harvey, whose parents do leave him alone and hungry for affection, humorously plays the wicked witch on a crutch as well as Hansel but learns to take responsibility for his actions. Although *The Green Knight* is not really moralistic because of the parodic undercutting, all of the characters resemble Gretel in using their wits and moving beyond self-obsession to concern about at least one other person.

"Fitcher's Bird" is the Bluebeard tale about a wizard who enchants girls into jumping into his basket and dismembers them when they open the door into a forbidden room with dead bodies. This tale, associated with animal bridegroom ones (Fiander 73), is obliquely suggested by the wizard-like power, which sometimes seems mock-gothic, that Lucas and Peter exercise over other characters. Restitution for a wrong committed is the theme not only of "Gawain and the Green Knight" but also of animal bridegroom tales (Fiander 68). Lucas, the "ringmaster" who seems to manipulate everyone behind the scenes without feeling anything for anybody, remains a mysterious ogre. Fiander suggests that Lucas is a borderline psychotic (67), and he certainly behaves in a beastly way to everyone. In opposition to "Cinderella," where a girl in the ashes rises in fortune to become a princess, the third sister in "Fitcher's Bird" discovers the underside of a fairy-tale marriage: She outwits the wizard by not getting her egg bloodied in the forbidden room, disguises herself as a marvelous bird, uses goddess power to re-member her hacked-apart sisters, and survives while the wizard is punished. Comically in *The Green Knight*, Lucas secretly succeeds with successive women, appears to murder without consequence, and gets away with the beauty. Aleph's family worries that he may destroy her. Peter, who is his own secret room, dies before he is able to carry off a maiden. Sexual politics, between men and men as well as men and women, emerges in dominance-submission games between Magnus and Bellamy, Lucas and Peter, and Joan and Clement. Moy seems to possess the third sister's, the Green Man's, and the Great Goddess's power to heal and resurrect. Symbolically under the well at the beginning of the book, she emerges from "drowning" at the end.

To a greater extent than in some of Murdoch's early novels, most of the characters of *The Green Knight* do experience a comic rise in fortune to celebrate life, and in most cases, even though sudden, these characters' epiphanies show greater awareness. While human instead of perfect, their happiness appears genuine rather than illusory and likely to last longer than their previous experiences. Although still young, Moy shows great insight and capacity to do good. Clement and Louise have known one another well for a long time and seem to have realistic expectations, and Harvey and Sefton will continue school and postpone marriage for a while. Tessa has chosen a useful career, and Aleph acts on a dream. Less can be said about the chances of Bellamy, Lucas, and Joan, but each is at least in a relationship and not mired in self-pity or selfishness.

Murdoch's fairy-tale and mythic intertexts thus are integral to every aspect of her novels: They supply the unforgettable, magically real images—the bell in *The Bell,* the sea monster in *The Sea, The Sea,* and, in *The Green Knight,* the shaft of light surrounding Peter as he is "beheaded" for the second time and the conical rock returned to its place on a hill beside the sea. They reveal the comic and parodic but still likable characters who spend their lives questing; they depict ways of creating meaning in a mysterious postmodern universe.

CHAPTER 8

BLUEBEARD'S *FORBIDDEN ROOM* IN RHYS'S *WIDE SARGASSO SEA*

THE GRIMMS' "FITCHER'S BIRD" AND THE DESECRATED GREAT GODDESS

Jean Rhys, born Ella Gwendolen Rees Williams at Roseau, Dominica, in 1890, of a Creole mother and a Welsh father, later lived in England, Holland, France, and Austria, once working as a chorus dancer. She won the W. H. Smith and the Heinemann Awards and is now, somewhat ironically, often considered a canonical writer. In *Wide Sargasso Sea* (1966) Rhys not only foregrounds subversive fairy-tale elements in the novel's main intertext, Charlotte Bronte's *Jane Eyre*, but also creates a dark postmodern and postcolonial metafairy tale of her own. While sometimes taken as a "Cinderella" story, *Jane Eyre* shows "Cinderella's" shadow side, the "Blue Beard" (Perrault) or "Fitcher's Bird" (Grimms') story about brides dismembered for opening the door to the forbidden room. In *Jane Eyre,* the forbidden room is literally the place where Rochester's Jamaican first wife, Bertha, who is and does the forbidden, is locked up. As an unusually sensitive reader of Bronte's novel as well as writer of her own text, however, Jean Rhys recognizes that the forbidden room in *Jane Eyre* is also the hidden, repressed, and silenced selves of the novel's three central characters, Rochester and Bertha's unspoken past lives,[1] and, in the nineteenth century, the forbidden subjects of female individuation, sexual politics, and colonization. Thus, in *Wide Sargasso Sea* Rhys also uses the Bluebeard story to open the forbidden rooms of both English and Creole masters' West Indian houses, including cultural, racial, sexist, and economic recriminations and abuses. In addition, by giving voice to the "white cockroach," who may unconsciously both critique and collude in colonialism (Ciolkowski 340), Rhys also convincingly conveys the discomfort of the Creole's in-between position, alien not only to English, Carib, or Spanish colonizers but also to immigrant slaves and Arawak natives of Jamaica or Dominica, at home nowhere. Blending Caribbean folklore—Arawak legend, Anancy trickster tales,[2] Maroon escape narratives (Emery 39–40, 49, 57–58), obeah—and biblical and mythic intertexts with plot details from *Jane Eyre* and "Bluebeard," *Wide Sargasso Sea* critiques national, gender, racial, and cultural colonization. Because *Wide Sargasso Sea* is about the events leading up to Bluebeard's dismemberment of his bride and her setting fire to the house of patriarchy, it is about patriarchal dismemberment of females and simultaneously retaliatory and revolutionary female rage. In addition, the Rochester figure, a younger son forced, like many nineteenth-century English aristocrats, to marry a wealthy foreigner, also represents England as an imperialistic and colonial power. Thus, the novel is about colonial power politics and the beginning of postcolonial identity.

Despite some critics' assumption that *Wide Sargasso Sea* is modernist, this novel is one of my best examples of a feminist, postmodern, postcolonial metafairy tale and metamyth. Although its intertexts other than *Jane Eyre* have been relatively ignored, with virtually no attention to fairy tales, *Wide Sargasso Sea* also effectively illustrates intertextual tactics. Since Rhys chooses a character voiceless in canonical literature, more than any other writer in this book, she shifts the point of view and thus shifts a female from object to subject, also giving the English patriarch and colonist a point of view but not a name. She builds a number of scenes on mythic and fairy-tale images, such as Antoinette's dream of flying home to her Tree of Life and the Rochester character's drawing of the Bluebeard castle to which he will confine Antoinette. She uses the door trope and symbol to suggest the small choices that may lead to traps and focuses attention on the Bertha subtext that most readers of *Jane Eyre* ignored until recently. Again blending tones and genres, with the gothic and surreal or magical real displacing the romantic, this novel demonstrates writing beyond the ending in making Antoinette's "end" different from that of the intertextual character on which she is based, in itself a major instance of postmodern irony. Defamiliarizing language by setting the book in a culture "alien" to British imperialism, the metafairy tale reverses the ideology of traditional English literature, engages readers in co-creation of the text, and remythifies debased goddess, Anancy, and Arawak myth and forgotten Bluebeard tales.

Since *Jane Eyre* embeds a "Bluebeard" and several other folklore intertexts, *Wide Sargasso Sea* incorporates these intertexts along with plot, motifs, characters, and themes from Bronte's novel. The two best-known versions of the Bluebeard story, both of which Rhys probably knew, are the Grimms' "Fitcher's Bird" (see chapter 2) and Perrault's "La Barbe Bleue," in the Three Sisters Rescued from the Power of an Ogre cycle (AT 311 Rescue by the Sister). The Giant Killer and His Dog (Bluebeard) (AT 312) is also about Bluebeard. "Fitcher's Bird," the recently translated Grimms' tales, "Bluebeard" and "The Castle of Murder," the anonymous English "Mr. Fox," and Perrault's "Blue Beard" all have the motif of a forbidden secret chamber (C611) containing the dismembered bodies of previous "brides." Perrault's "La Barbe Bleue," which ends with the wife becoming rich and marrying a man much more worthy than Blue Beard, is from *Histoires ou contes du temps passe* (1697) by Charles Perrault but published under the name of his son, Pierre Parrault Darmancour, to mask his own identity (see Zipes, *Beauties* 17–19, 31–35). Long before Perrault, the "Tale of the Third Calender" in The Arabian Nights' Entertainments and the Sixth Tale of the Fourth Day in the *Pentamerone* depict the consequences of entering a forbidden room. The Grimms' "The Robber Bridegroom" (AT 955), featuring cannibalism as well as dismemberment, is closely related (see chapter 1). "Variants of folklore types do, of course, appear all over the world" (Aarne and Thompson 102–103), and Rhys, who alludes to fairy tales and other folklore in her autobiography and novels (e.g., *Smile* 16, 23; *Voyage in the Dark* 60), was probably also familiar not only with Jamaican and other Caribbean versions of Bluebeard tales, but also with similar stories including some of the same motifs.[3] For example, Flowers notes that West Indian folk stories frequently include devil-spouse and animal-spouse motifs, often with a similarity to the Bluebeard type. The forbidden room motif "is an obvious favorite among West Indian storytellers" and can be found with almost any other type or motif (601–2). Sometimes, the murderous husband is the Devil, often with gold or silver teeth. In one Jamaican version, Mr. Bluebeard is a witch and knows when his wife enters the forbidden room. Her brothers, also witches, know there is trouble when the life token of water turns to blood, and they rescue her just in time. In another Jamaican version, after the cruel aunt's dog, Tiger, confines a girl to a cave, her brothers shoot and quarter him. In two other Jamaican stories in this cycle, one features a snake Bluebeard ("Yellow Snake"), and in the other, the Bluebeard thinks no one can escape without his cock crowing ("The Brother and his Sister"). In one version from

Dominica, after a godmother causes a girl to disappear as she combs her hair, the brother revives the girl with liquid in a vial and kills the witch ("Frere la avec Nenene Panda"). In two others, the hero cuts off the devil's seven heads or burns the devil in oil (Flowers 82–92).[4] In a Basque version, the youngest sister even kills Bluebeard herself with a saber (Leach and Fried 150). Not all Bluebeard stories end happily, though. In a Puerto Rican version, a nameless king is really Blue Beard. Although a visitor opens the forbidden room, he kills his wife. "This is the punishment that comes to the disobedient" ("El Caballero sin Nombre," Flowers 86). Thackeray, Anatole France, Silvia Townsend Warner, John Fowles, Margaret Atwood, Anne Hebert, Jay Macpherson, Vladimir Nabokov, Malcolm Lowry, Daryl Hines, Angela Carter, Kurt Vonnegut, and Susan Fromberg Schaeffer, among others, have all written Bluebeard stories (S. Wilson, *Margaret Atwood's Fairy* 259; see Zipes, *Spells* for some of these).

"Fitcher's Bird," like most fairy tales, is generally considered a story of initiation or a cautionary tale, warning women to guard their "eggs" for their prospective husbands, thereby testing their faithfulness to the man's orders "or, in a broader sense, to him," and possibly implying the destructive aspects of sex, jealousy (Bettelheim 300–301), or the animus. As Margaret Atwood points out, "egg" in German also means testicle ("Of Souls" 36), so that men are also warned to protect their "eggs." However, some interpretations seem to disregard or minimize not only sexist violence but also the male's deceptive kidnapping of the woman, against her will, as in the Demeter-Persephone myth. Such interpretations also disregard women's "status" as prize or property in numerous fairy tales. The disguised wizard, who seeks pretty girls, begs for food. His unsought "touch," that causes the innocent girls' captivity and death, is not simply sexual initiation but patriarchal exploitation. Like "The Robber Bridegroom," this tale is hardly gender-neutral, as Bettelheim (226) and others have traditionally viewed fairy tales. As I suggest elsewhere (S. Wilson, *Margaret Atwood's Fairy* 260, 14, 349), neither do fairy tales, this one in particular, necessarily depict women as victimized in the way that some feminists have suggested (see Daly 44, 90–91, 151–52, 266; Gilbert and Gubar 36–44). If this tale, like texts that embed it, contains a theme of sexual politics, it is also political in a larger sense, particularly when embedded in works in which Bluebeard and his wife or fiancée differ in class, ethnic, national, and cultural identities.

Recent feminist critics of *Jane Eyre* have become interested in Bertha, "the mad woman in the attic" (Gilbert and Gubar) and the

Caribbean wife of an English younger son who marries this Creole heiress in order to gain a fortune. Sandra Gilbert notes that the central conflict of Bronte's novel is between Bertha and Jane, that the third floor has numerous locked doors, and that Rochester treats Jane as a possession, joking about attaching her to a chain (476). But the Bluebeard motif and subplot in *Jane Eyre* has elicited little comment. Ironically, most readers continue to forget Rochester's first wife and his explicit racism, sexism, and ethnocentrism in order to enjoy the Cinderella story of the second wife. Bronte's text does, however, both explicitly and implicitly reference "Fitcher's Bird," and Rhys uses or reverses the same motifs. When Mrs. Fairfax first shows Jane the third floor of the Rochester estate, Jane sees it as "narrow, low, and dim, with only one little window at the far end, and looking, with its two rows of small black doors all shut, like a corridor in some Bluebeard's castle" (93). Later, Jane hears "snarling sounds" from behind the concealed door before the blood-soaked Mason emerges (183), enters the room to see Rochester tie "the clothed hyena" to a chair (257–58), and hears how the "intemperate and unchaste" woman that once attracted Rochester is "shut up" (270). When Rochester hears "the sweet wind from Europe" whisper to him of hope, he then "buries" the "monster's" identity and connection to him in England. He roams Europe seeking "the antipodes of the Creole" in "inferior" mistresses who resemble the "slave" he previously purchased (271–74). "The Robber Bridegroom" fairy tale is also suggested when Rochester "seem[s] to devour [Jane] with his flaming glance." Jane, fearing that he might regard her like her predecessors and insisting that she cares for and respects herself, resists him (274, 279–80). Later, of course, when Bertha sets fire to the house that has imprisoned her and that blinds and maims the colonizing master, he is free to marry the newly rich English governess. Resembling many characters who break taboos in folk tales, including tricksters caught in their own traps, Rochester ironically suffers the same fate as one of the victims of the English Bluebeard: He loses his hand.[5]

Despite the way the "Fitcher's Bird" intertext highlights the power politics of both Bronte and Rhys novels, critics seem not to have noticed the significance of the Bluebeard fairy tale in *Wide Sargasso Sea*. Still, the novel embeds most of the major motifs from "Fitcher's Bird": the maiden's abduction by a monster or ogre, her unwitting marriage to the ogre or cannibal, the forbidden room, a stain that will not wash away, death for breaking the taboo, the tricking of the ogre, disguise, escape by use of a substituted object, rescue, resuscitation, and the punishment of the ogre and his kinsmen, usually in a fire that destroys both the house and the society it represents. Related motifs in both tale and novel include a forest setting, secrets, more than one bride, disguise, the door, the room that hides his unknown self, dismemberment, male ownership and control of the house, a male ogre who gets caught in his own trap, a female rescuer, and fire. The more sophisticated Perrault version also focuses on the fear Blue Beard's difference—his blue beard—inspires, dwells on Blue Beard's wealth and the estate's elegance—including gilt mirrors—and offers two morals about female curiosity and male jealousy. Ironically, the Perrault conclusion entirely undercuts the man's mastery: "And whatever color his beard may be/ it's difficult to know who the master be" (Zipes, "Blue Beard" 35).

Characters, images, and settings of *Wide Sargasso Sea* connect to "Fitcher's Bird." Resembling the practice of other postmodern and postcolonial literature, *Wide Sargasso Sea* ironically reverses or revisions some fairy-tale elements; and their motifs are often metaphoric or symbolic. Perhaps most significant for her twentieth-century metafairy tale, Rhys gives the Caribbean bride her own name, narrative voice, history, and setting. This includes a house in the Windward Islands that belongs to Antoinette before she loses all her property by marrying an unnamed English colonizer, the book's Bluebeard. Since this man without identity is also based on the Rochester of Bronte's novel, I will call him Rochester. Alternating female and male first-person narration to double as well as foil her characters, Rhys interlaces biblical, obeah, mythological and other folklore intertexts with "Fitcher's Bird" in her novel.

Among other global fairy-tale and folklore motifs in *Wide Sargasso Sea* are marrying a "prince" ("Cinderella"), losing one's identity or soul in a mirror or other reflection ("Snow White"), meeting a threatening "wolf" in a forest ("Red-Cap"), "sleeping" through life ("Sleeping Beauty" or "Briar Rose"), being isolated in a "tower" ("Rapunzel"), and dancing in the red shoes marking female sexuality ("The Red Shoes," see chapter 6). In *Wide Sargasso Sea*, both "Cinderella" and the Creole variant, "Cendrillon" (AT 510, 510A), function ironically. Rochester is not Creole, like Cendrillon, nor is a mahogany wand used to make him as kind as Paul, the prince figure. Cendrillon, unlike Antoinette, renounces spells so that their love is genuine (San Souci). In some versions, Cinderella resembles the third sister of "Fitcher's Bird" and escapes by dressing in an animal or human skin. Like Snow White's stepmother and both Jane and Bertha in *Jane Eyre*, both Antoinette and her mother lose their identities or souls in a mirror or another reflection. Both Rochester and Antoinette double one another in experiencing a split self, most evident when Antoinette looks into a gilded mirror near the end of the novel and is both her Coulibri self and the ghost of *Jane Eyre*. Whether the frightened little girl Rochester meets in the forest represents Antoinette's childhood self in her first dream (Baer 141), the power dynamics certainly resemble those of "Little Red-Cap" (AT 333 The Glutton): He embodies the patriarchal, colonialist "hunger" that threatens not only the obeah magic suggested by the flower offerings (Emery 41), but also Antionette's and the Caribbean's green world, including its orange tree symbolic of female power.[6] Reversing "Sleeping Beauty" (AT 410) and "Rapunzel" (AT 310) when Antoinette's husband turns out to be no prince, Antoinette begins to sleep away her life in total isolation. The color red, associated with Antoinette's red dress, fire, and "the stain" of female menarche, not only recalls the full-moon phase of the mythic Great Goddess but also recalls early Christian strictures against female sexuality suggested in Andersen's "The Red Shoes" (Motif D2061.1.2; S. Wilson, *Margaret Atwood's Fairy* 120–29).

Antoinette's favorite painting of the blue-eyed Miller's daughter, representing her dream of being an English girl, "exactly like other people," implies several other fairy tales, including the Grimms' "The Girl Without Hands" (AT 706). A disguised incest story about a Miller who sells his daughter (sometimes a sister) to the devil but "protects" her by cutting off her hands and expelling her from her home, this tale often features slander and uses some of the same motifs (T411.1) as in some versions of "Cinderella." It is suggested both when Richard Mason, Antoinette's stepbrother, sells her to Rochester, refusing any further responsibility, and when Daniel Cosway, Antoinette's illegitimate, colored half brother, slanders her. The first fire destroys this painting, representing the conditioning partly responsible for causing her to desire an identity she can never have, being English, and, thereby, colluding in her own colonization. In addition, it destroys the parrot whose beak is linked to obeah rituals (Emery 43) and any security she feels as a child. As the final page of the novel shows, however, the second fire restores Antoinette's childhood paradise, including garden, tree of life, pool, painting, parrot, and Tia, representing part of her Caribbean identity. When the fire destroys the nightmare, rather than fairy tale, that England has become (36–37, 190), it suggests the growth and restoration that the Girl Without Hands experiences in a magic garden and sometimes in a tree.

Rhys also uses mythic and other fairy-tale intertexts. The Perseus-Medusa myth, one of several about patriarchy's suppression of matriarchy and worship of the Great Goddess, is suggested as Rochester decides to "decapitate" the power of the sensual "monster" who does not feel and think as he does. Rochester's imprisoning of Antoinette in a cold, dark place recalls the Greek myth about Hades's abduction of Persephone to the underworld. Spivak reads the mirror imagery through the Narcissus myth and connects Rochester to the Freud and Oedipus myths (242–45). Significantly, in the Grimms' "The Robber Bride," the tale closely resembling "Fitcher's Bridegroom," the bride's act of telling the story saves her and causes the ogre's punishment. By telling the bride's story in *Wide Sargasso Sea,* Rhys creates a feminist, postcolonial text.

Motifs from Antoinette's narration suggest "Fitcher's Bird." Forest, secrets, stain, door, and room motifs begin early in *Wide Sargasso Sea.* As a child, Antoinette lives with her mother Annette and brother Pierre at Coulibri, a wild Eden with its own garden, tree of life, and snaky orchids. Her mother hopes only when she passes a looking-glass, however, and initially, neither goddess nor god seems associated with this tree of life. Antoinette begins to fear the forest when a dream and other premonitions predict the Caribbean fire and all future disasters, including the fate Bertha meets in *Jane Eyre.* While she is still a child and her playmate Tia calls her a "white nigger," that night Antoinette dreams the first of three dreams forewarning her, and readers, of her destiny: walking in the forest, "Someone who hated me was with me, out of sight. I could hear heavy footsteps coming closer and though I struggled and screamed I could not move." Going to parts of Coulibri without road, path, or track and thinking of nothing, "It was if a door opened and I was somewhere else, something else. Not myself any longer" (25, 27–28). It is Tia who physically stains Antoinette as the white cockroach, both colonizer and colonized, one who historically, by race and class, victimizes. In addition, the implied affair with Sandi that later gender-marks her an "unchaste woman" is prefigured when she stains both her palm and a convent book right before she first meets Sandi outside the convent. The dress she exchanges with Tia as a child, the white dress of the second dream, in which she enters an enclosed garden and clings to a tree to avoid ascending steps, and the dresses of a servant in Granbois are, in the eyes of the English, all soiled or marked as dirty, as belonging to the white cockroach or nigger. Although her Aunt Cora assures her that the mark from the rock Tia threw "won't spoil [her] on [her] wedding day" (48), Antoinette later recognizes that it has: She wonders "who I am and where is my country and where do I belong and why was I ever born at all" (103). For Rochester, she is marked as Creole other and thus Bluebeard's victim.

The doors Antoinette initially fears are open, the first to sunlight, but she is sure that implements of obeah are hidden in Christophine's room and imagines hearing drops of blood: "No one had ever spoken to me about obeah—but I knew what I would find if I dared to look" (32). Later, when Antoinette ignores Christophine's warnings, it is obeah that Rochester appropriates to turn her into a marionette zombie named Bertha. The door to the house where Annette is confined is also open, but Antoinette's mother looks for Pierre in the house, not her, and flings her away. Next, Antoinette is again outside a door where she does not feel she belongs, the convent. Soon, she learns "to gabble without thinking as the others did" (58). Later, after Rochester crushes the frangipani wreaths and reads Daniel's first letter, she bolts the door between his dressing room and her room while he reads about obeah, and she fears the house where she will be cold and dream the end of her dream (107, 111). Again and again, as Rochester passes her closed door and she drinks and sleeps, he calls out, "Goodnight, Bertha" (113).

Forest, secret, trickery, stain, disguise, house, and room motifs all occur early in Rochester's narration, too. From the minute that he arrives in Jamaica, without identity as in some Bluebeard stories, he is feverish and sick; and he, too, fears the forest. Entering the forest or jungle of Dominica on the way to the honeymoon house in Granbois, he discovers that the village is named Massacre. Reversing the Perrault "Blue Beard" in feeling superior to her "alien" characteristics (67), he feels increasingly cut off from secrets he cannot penetrate. In the first part of the book, the secrets are Antoinette's as well as those his family has kept from him, and he quickly begins to suspect the stain (infidelity or a woman's sexual independence) of the fairy tale. When he sees Antoinette and her room reflected in the looking-glass, Amelie says he looks as if he has seen a zombie (100). The minute he feels that Antoinette has been "disguised," that he may be a cuckold, and that his family has sold him for thirty pieces of silver (30,000 pounds), his "disguise" as a gentleman falls away and readers recognize the ogre or devil underneath. The house Antoinette loves seems to shrink from the "hostile" forest and to be "swallowed" by it (71, 89, 105); but as Rochester prepares to exchange it and the forest for the English house and walled garden, he still recognizes that it holds—and keeps—the secret beauty and magic he most desires but represses and then murders.

Like other Victorian Englishmen, Rochester becomes the colonizer who continually crushes, dirties, or kills whatever no longer appears profitable but must still be owned: the magical flowers, the pool's crab king, the culture he refuses to understand, the girl Amelie (whose skin seems darker after he has sex with her), and Antoinette. When Christophine suggests that she take Antoinette to Martinique, where Antoinette could marry someone else and be happy, he plans his Bluebeard castle. As in many Caribbean Bluebeard tales, a cock crows, in this case as he draws an English house surrounded by English trees. In a room on the third floor he draws a woman "with a dot for a head" (164). The forbidden, locked room in which he later confines Antoinette thus becomes both figural and literal. Since Antoinette is part of Granbois's magic, this Bluebeard decides that "Very soon she'll join all the others who know the secret and will not tell it. . . . [the] long, long line. She's one of them. I too can wait—for the day when she is only a memory to be avoided, locked away, and like all memories a legend. Or a lie" (173).

Ironically, both Antoinette and Rochester recognize the parts they are playing but seem unable to escape both *Jane Eyre* and "Bluebeard" plots. After he has sex with Amelie and arranges for the arrest of Christophine, he opens the door of Antoinette's room and is shocked at the effects of his trickery, what Antoinette calls "obeah too." He, too, has a *Jane Eyre* vision: "it was like a dream in the large unfurnished room with the candles flickering and this red-eyed wild-haired stranger who was my wife shouting obscenities at me" (149). Christophine warns him that, although he is not using a machete, he is breaking Antoinette up, symbolically dismembering her, and that if he forsakes her, others, too, would "tear her in pieces" (157–59). By giving her a different name and calling her a doll or marionette, he turns her into a zombie that resembles the ornamented skull substitute of "Fitcher's Bird" and literally represents the marriage to death of the "Bluebeard" tale. Although he admits that she has the secret and that he is a stranger, he later thinks of her as an animal, what might be called a "Fitcher's Bird." The next locked door is the most important one: the room in England where he confines her and treats her the way her mother had been, as mad.

In the forbidden room without a looking-glass, no longer able to kiss her image and wondering who she is, Antoinette takes the keys and opens the door into the external world: "It is, as I always knew, made of cardboard. . . . As I walk along the passages I wish I could see what is behind the cardboard. They tell me I am in England but I don't believe them. We lost our way to England" (181). In keeping with what seems more like surrealism than magical realism in blurring any borders between fictional realities, Antoinette has a third dream from which both she and readers wake and do not wake as it suggests the volume's end. After holding her red dress and remembering Richard Mason's visit and the last time she saw Sandi, she has a dream and says it ends. In the dream, she remembers her wedding in a predominantly red room where "gold is the idol they worship," lights a fire in Aunt Cora's room, and sees and knows herself as the ghost, "the woman with streaming hair" surrounded by the "gilt frame": the hall mirror. Escaping outside to the battlements at the top of the house, she sees "all her life" in the red sky and achieves reconciliation with the tree of life, the picture of the Miller's daughter, the parrot, Christophine, Tia, herself and, as Emery suggests, the entire community of women and the history of people on the islands (59–60). Feeling her hair stream out "like wings," she jumps away from the colonizer who calls her "Bertha" into the pool at Coulibri and wakes, apparently ready to open the final door to the fire in which Bertha of *Jane Eyre* dies and Rochester is maimed (188–90). Significantly, however, Antoinette's end is not Bertha's, and, literally, she does not die within this novel. The film *Wide Sargasso Sea* ends with Antoinette dancing in flames (Duigan). Although both film and novel are open to multiple readings, the novel also seems to end triumphantly, in the way that Chopin's *The Awakening* is now generally read, with a culturally silenced woman attaining her only possible freedom, in this case ready to fly to freedom from the area of battle (battlements). Without a rescuing brother, as in the Perrault tale, Antoinette plays the role of the third sister in "Fitcher's Bird" and of the Great Goddess Isis: She puts together the dismembered pieces and rescues or heals herself. In *Wide Sargasso Sea,* too, it is possible to see a mythic rebirth, with Antoinette becoming both an Anancy flying trickster (Emery 57) and a phoenix under the tree of life signifying inexhaustible life or immortality. As discussed in chapter 4 in reference to *Beloved,* the tree of life is important in goddess myth and most of the major world religions, and when linked to water (the pool at Coulibri), snakes, and the color red, the life and regenerative goddess associations are even stronger (see Cirlot 328–32). In addition, as Emery suggests, "That it now flames signals a return in Antoinette's imagination to. . . . the ancient Arawak legend of the flaming tree," an Amerindian story about the transformation of the Arawaks into the Pleides (58). According to Wilson Harris, the colonized and killed Arawaks, the black West Indian presence in the tree, speaks in Antionette's dreams. "Jean Rhys implies in *Wide Sargasso Sea* that Antoinette flies home to herself in the end" (153–55). Antoinette continues to exist in readers' minds and in a postmodern reality that is not framed by a resolution (see also DuPlessis 45–46).

What this conclusion means in reference to postcolonial identity should be no less clear than the novel's postmodern techniques and feminist implications. Resembling a few critics who feel that the Canadian writer Margaret Atwood and Native American Louise Erdrich have sold-out their cultures not only by using postmodern techniques but also by having the impertinence to attract international audiences (Mathews, Silko 10–11), numerous Caribbean scholars resent the application of terms such as *postmodern* and *postcolonial* to Caribbean writers (e.g., Paravisini-Gebert 161–68). Some readers will point to what they consider racist statements in Rhys's autobiography (Ciolkowski 353; *Smile* 39–40), may overlook the novel's references to Jamaica's and Dominica's indigenous populations, and may find overcoming childhood conditioning like swimming through the gulfweed-clogged Sargasso Sea of the title. Despite the independence of most West Indian nations, some may doubt the likelihood of lasting reconciliation either between white, brown, and black Caribbeans or between Creoles, Amerindians, the Spanish, and the English. Nevertheless, as Christophine recognizes, it is clear that the master's blindness and cruelty are punished. As former slaves once burned down the childhood home that represents Creole colonization, Antoinette is ready to burn down the house that symbolizes colonial as well as patriarchal exploitation. Appearing in 1966 right before Rhys's native Dominica became one of the West Indies Associated States and achieved internal autonomy (1967, becoming an independent republic within the British Commonwealth in 1978), and right after Jamaica attained full independence from Britain, *Wide Sargasso Sea* predicts and celebrates the destruction of all houses of colonization.

CHAPTER 9

FAIRY TALES AND MYTH IN KERI HULME'S *THE BONE PEOPLE*

"RAPUNZEL," MOTHER PAPA, MAUI, THE FISHER KING, INDIANA JONES, AND GRAIL LEGEND

One of the writers of the New Zealand Maori Renaissance since the seventies, Keri Hulme is of English, Orkney Scots, and Maori descent and was born in 1947 and raised in Otautahi, Christchurch, New Zealand, and from 1986 to 1988 was appointed Cultural Ambassador. Winner of the Booker Prize, the Pegasus Award for Maori writers, and the New Zealand Book Award for Fiction, she has worked as a tobacco picker and a fisherman. Hulme revisions mythology to create a new family and a new beginning for humanity in her apocalyptic and utopian novel, *The Bone People* (1984). Through her fairy-tale and mythic intertexts, Hulme again realizes Homi Bhabha's conception of hybridization.

Like Atwood, Ferre, and Lessing's artist narrators, Kerewin Holmes is initially divided and alienated. Like *Memoirs'* watcher, Kerewin journeys from chaos and disorder, disease, and the end of a world, to order, healing, rebirth and a new beginning that is, on different levels, the novel we read and a future beyond what human beings can achieve now. Some critics say that, because she has a mixed genetic inheritance like Erdrich, Hulme cannot or should not speak as an indigenous person (Stead 103–4). Hulme uses many of the techniques, themes and motifs Atwood and Lessing do,[1] including italicized special passages, cycles, spirals, hands, mirrors and a turned around mirror, the divided and alien self, survival, fairy-tale archetypes, goddess and other mythic images, and the quest for home, order, and pattern. Both Hulme and Atwood write poetry, librettos, and short stories as well as novels, have designed their own book covers, and have strong feelings about retaining language that editors would change. Like several Atwood characters, Kerewin even feels as if Dracula or other vampires are draining her, and, like *Oryx and Crake,* this novel parodies and revisions canonical intertexts, in this case *The Tempest, Ulysses, The Waste Land, Alice in Wonderland,* and *Robinson Crusoe.* As Keri Hulme says in an interview, she draws on old stories and ancestors: "You can't ever be alone: the air you breathe is full of other people, other beings—and all their breathing—and you yourself are a knit and weaving of a thousand generations" ("Keri Hulme" 212). The English Maori term for this is "Carrying your ghosts on your shoulders" (Bryson 131).

In *The Bone People,* Hulme builds on the tower imagery of the Grimms' "Rapunzel" (Zipes, *Complete* 46–49) and other fairy tales and of such writers as Yeats, Joyce, Peake, and Woolf. Embedding and intertwining Maori, goddess, Fisher King, Grail, Buddhist, Sufi, and Christian myth (especially creation myth) and fish, hook, stone, spider, web, spiral, maze, crucifix, rosary, phoenix, whirling dervish,[2] Aikido, I-Ching, Yarrowsticks, and Tarot images in a multicultural text that uses both English and Maori languages, she opposes and then synthesizes and hybridizes eastern, Maori, and western religion, folklore, and literary traditions that may challenge readers.[3] Surprisingly, although Benediktsson comments on *The Bone People*'s "plot redolent of fairy tale" in order to discuss ruptures in realism (126), no one follows up on the importance of the fairy-tale and folklore context. When folklore, primarily myth, is discussed, critics refer to Hulme's bicultural rather than multicultural orientation.

As we have seen, fairy tales are not just European but occur with variations in numerous cultures around the world. The Maiden in the Tower type (AT 310) is distinguished by a virgin's captivity in a tower, where she is prevented from knowledge of men, marriage, or impregnation (motifs R41.2, T381; see chapter 7). Kerewin is the kind of archetypal Rapunzel that Margaret Atwood describes: an Ice-Virgin-Hecate figure,[4] symbolically imprisoned alone in a tower that, in this case, classically symbolizes her alienation from rather than incorporation of the attitudes of society. As is usual in this archetype, she and her tower are one, and the "rescuer" is absent (*Survival* 209–10). If a sorceress has enclosed Kerewin in her tower, the sorceress is Kerewin, who appears to know and be good at everything but is unable to achieve wholeness and happiness. Although she is not beautiful and fails to have hair like spun gold, she sings like Rapunzel in her symbolically desolate wasteland. At the beginning of *The Bone People,* Kerewin has built a spiral stairway exclusively for her own use, has cut herself off from everyone, including her "ex-family," seems to have no friends, and certainly is not waiting for a rescuing prince or the birth of twins to resolve her story. Like nearly all of Atwood's characters and most of Lessing's, Kerewin is split or internally divided as we first see her, alone in a bar and alone in her tower, cut off from the Maori value of community that she had cherished because she mistakenly believed that "she was self-fulfilling, delighted with the pre-eminence of her art" (7).

The evolving female artist who paints, sculpts, designs, composes and plays music, writes, and builds clever objects such as her suneater as well as homes and meeting halls, Kerewin is mythic in both wrecked and reborn states. Web and spider images, which indicate interconnectedness of all, the web of Fate, and the goddess as spinner (B. Walker, *Woman's Encyclopedia* 957), ironically show Kerewin's tower isolation. Kerewin is unable to transfer the drawing of a spider shadow in her mind to paper, as if it, too, is imprisoned (63, 73). Although she wishes for a pattern to life and again dreams of a spider shadow, her drawing refuses to come out. Her interior monologue is rife with the voice of her wise-cracking but self-demeaning snark; in her "unjoy," in her "haggard ashdead world," she hides a "screaming" painting behind her desk and thinks:

"You are nothing," says Kerewin coldly. "You are nobody, and will never be anything, anyone." And her inner voice, the snark, which comes into its own during depressions like this, says, And you have never been anything at anytime, remember? And the next line is. . . . I am worn, down to the raw nub of my soul. (91–92)

Like Iris of *The Blind Assassin* and Atwood's many "handless" characters initially unable to touch, be touched (S. Wilson, *Margaret Atwood's Fairy* 136–228), or, like Simon, subjected to "dismembering" touch, Kerewin uses her still poetic voice to deconstruct rather than to create. Significantly, rather than a Disney fairy-tale female who is an object in a story, however, Kerewin is the creator of story and, like Lessing's creators of *The Story* and *Memoirs* and Atwood's of *The Robber Bride, Oryx and Crake,* and *The Penelopiad,* symbolically writes the story we read at the end of the novel. As in the Grimms' "The Girl Without Hands," Kerewin, Simon, and Joe symbolically regrow cut-off hands. Although we do not know Kerewin's exact age, she is certainly not young, and if she is just "thirty odd" at the beginning (24), she appears to age in magical time as the book proceeds, experiencing, like the other main characters, a symbolic death and rebirth. Kerewin, whose name is a pun meaning "Keri win home," also connects to the detective Sherlock Holmes and ironically to the solitary wise person Tiaki Mira (the kaumatua, who is named after Hulme's grandfather) as well as her author (Hulme and Turcotte 137; 139–40).

According to Hulme, Kerewin is well aware that she has built a prison, a symbol of isolation for herself. . . . By the end of the book, she's ready to take up her responsibilities, and indeed she does list them in her book that she puts on the fire. . . . so she turns her home into an appropriate symbol. (Hulme and Turcotte 143)

In addition to "Rapunzel," Hulme uses biblical, Tarot—traditionally considered the Egyptian "Book of Thoth" (Leach and Fried 1104)— Akido, I Ching, Sufi, and Yarrowstick folklore in reference to Kerewin's imprisonment in the tower. Initially and ironically thinking of the Tower of Babel (The Holy Bible, Genesis 11:1–9) rather than her tower, in this polyphonic text Kerewin is isolated partly because she also exists in a world of confused languages, where people cannot communicate. Although she often seems to read Simon's mind when she looks at his eyes, Simon, Kerewin, and Joe frequently misinterpret one another, as when Joe thinks she might want to marry and she thinks he is eager to leave the beach. The tower struck by lightning is a well-known card in the Tarot pack, and Kerewin prophetically associates this card with several other Tarot images:

The pair chained to the column in the card called The Devil shifted and stretched and became The Lovers. The Fool stepped lightly forever towards the abyss, but the little dog snapping at his heels became hollow-eyed, bone cheeked, and Death rode scything the people at his horse's feet. . . . one card glowed . . . in that second she was drawn into the card. The sky split and thunderbolts rained down, and she started falling, wailing in final despair from the lightning struck tower. (267)

Kerewin later reduces her tower to rubble, sets fire to it and the image of herself within it, and symbolically falls, destroying the lies she held about herself. In this case, in addition to playing Rapunzel and the Fisher King in an Eliot wasteland, Kerewin is the Tarot Fool who believed herself self-sufficient and better than others (see The Tower) and uses ancient specialized knowledge (Le Cam 68–69)—Aikido, dervishs, I Ching, Yarrowsticks, runes, mandalas—she cannot understand except as part of a holistic system. Thus, the runes on her knife are ironic since the runic alphabet was invented by "wise women," including the goddess Idun, of northern Europe, and heroes died to acquire the runes for men (B. Walker, *Woman's Encyclopedia* 870). Since Kerewin, Joe, and Simon can be seen to represent mind, body, and spirit, which, according to Aikido, "must be unified if humankind is ever to achieve perfection" (Webby 20), Kerewin must experience a spiritual death in order to regain her sense of community and her relationship to the land and to rise like the phoenix from her ashes.

The tower also alludes to and parodies the great modernists, Joyce, Yeats, and Woolf, with whom tower images are so closely associated and who frequently do "portraits of the artist." In this context, the tower symbolizes the creative impulse:

The tower and the shell are both spirals, and spirals are used in both [Western and Maori] cultures to indicate spiritual values. Yeats envisages the spiral as a gyre which signifies eternally recurring patterns in history and in the individual man. . . . Yeats sees the past as something to which he has access." (Hughes 60)

Hulme says that Maoris "see the past before us" (Peek 9, Interview). This does not mean, as During and Huggan suggest, that she privileges western traditions, especially European high modernism, uses western narrative patterns, and thus re-inscribes colonization (During 373; Huggan 32, 34). As Hughes points out, the three separate introductory pieces which tie the end to the beginning are "reminiscent of oral structures. . . . Such oral structures are closer to an oral tradition—and the Maori cultural tradition is an oral one (65). Nor does her postmodernism absorb postcolonialism (During 373–74; Huggan 28). Instead, Hulme engages in postcolonial hybridization. Her multicultural, utopian vision is in a sense a new myth. The book

suggested that the pain of unbelonging experienced by both Maori and Pakeha—for which the book's horrifying domestic violence becomes emblematic—might be healed through mutual trust, shared spirituality, and the joint guardianship of the land and its inhabitants. . . . One of the most readily available keys to the novel's vision of biculturalism is that it appears to offer an imaginative resolution to—via a synthesis of—the putative binary oppositions which dictate the shape of life in contemporary Aotearoa. . . . Hence, the novel imagines a world in which hybrid identities based on choice rather than "race" might replace hard distinctions between Maori and Pakeha, where groups of caring individuals might replace biological families,

where alternative therapies and holistic approaches might complement Western medicine, where korero [talk] might replace violence, and where spirals
might replace towers. (Shieff 47, 51)

In addition to revisioning fairy tales and offering a new myth of belonging for New Zealanders, and by implication, all human beings,
Hulme, whose best-known book has been called an urban legend
(Shieff 48), also demythologizes, re-genders, and re-centers local legends, such as the literary myth of "Man Alone," the hobo or social
outcast based on fiction of the thirties and forties, to a myth of
woman alone (J. Wilson 278–79) and ironically alludes to nursery
rimes, "Simple Simon" and "Mary, Mary Quite Contrary," and the
children's games "Simon Says" and "All Fall Down." Kerewin, who
enjoys playing with language, is certainly contrary to what women are
expected to be and even to what she wants and does, and, like the
other characters, "falls down." Simon is neither simple nor autistic
nor able to say anything. In addition to being emotionally disturbed
(Hulme and Turcotte 145), he is marginalized in the way the other
main characters are. Although Atwood sees the Rapunzel Syndrome
as characteristically Canadian, other cultures, especially colonized
ones, illustrate the same kind of repressive conditioning that effects
self-esteem and creates victims rather than heroes. Doubly or triply
colonized as a Maori—Pakeha hybrid and a woman, Kerewin represents all New Zealanders' internalization of negative stereotypes, including those Joe and Simon internalize. Hulmes's deconstructive,
decolonizing, and postcolonial techniques center on her use of revisioned folklore: fairy-tale and mythic intertexts.

As well as "Rapunzel," the book parodies "Cinderella," "Sleeping
Beauty," and all gendered, heterosexual stories that resolve female
quests with a kiss or marriage and implicitly draws on tales with active
or heroic females, such as the Grimms' "The Robber Bridegroom"
(see previous chapters for summaries). Because she is not interested in
sexual relationships and does not conform to notions of a female as
weak, demure, petite, emotional, passive, and "feminine," Kerewin
actually sees herself as genderless, neuter rather than female, and
wants to escape being either "mizzed or mistered" (47). The shadow
self or ghost that helps to heal her is also androgynous, and Simon's
gender is not clear to everyone. Although a few critics seem to read
"deviance" and androgyny as evidence of the book's homophobia (J.
Wilson on Huggan 277), the world of the book, showing bisexual,
homosexual, and celibate characters as well as heterosexual ones, is far
more diverse than that of most novels. Kerewin initially thinks of the

child Simon, whom she eventually adopts, as "it." Her many valuable rings, some of them mystical greenstone so important in New Zealand mythology, have nothing to do with adorning herself to look attractive or performing as "feminine" in either the Maori or Pakeha cultures she straddles; and, like her author, she rejects even a regular telephone to keep her in contact with the outside world. Hulme seems deliberately to parody reader expectations of female characters, novel plots, sexual orientation, and gender roles. Because Kerewin is not submissive to desire and not seducible, some readers will think that she poses the traditional threat of the terrifying, castrating bitch; and her beating of Joe might support this view. At the end, she explicitly defies patriarchy by giving her name to both Simon and Joe, and we must recognize the book's feminism. Because the novel withholds a conventional "happy ending" and frustrates readers' desires for a marriage resolution to a plot about a woman, man, and child, some may miss how radical Kerewin's spiral journey and transformation are.

Kerewin is an artist rather than muse or tongueless, handless maiden, but initially a "non-painting painter" who loses her art and, along with Joe, their Maori selves in the way that they live (62). Although Hulme's fairy-tale references are usually ironic and parodic, *The Bone People* also uses "Rapunzel" and other folk tales in their traditional sense as agents of maturation (Bettleheim, Von Franz cited S. Wilson, *Margaret Atwood's Fairy* xiv) and transformation. At the same time as *The Bone People* parodies fairy tales, it also embeds fairy-tale characters, such as Joe as ogre and Kerewin as wish-fulfillment character (Hulme and Turcotte 138, 140), motifs—such as imprisonment, disguise, and escape from an ogre—and themes, such as transformation. As in the Grimms' "The Robber Bridegroom," Kerewin saves herself and others by exposing injustice and acting. As in Baum's literary fairy tale, *The Wizard of Oz,* the characters embark on an archetypal quest and reach community and home through qualities they already possess.

As we have seen, myths are often entwined with fairy tales and folklore, and Hulme uses Great Goddess, other Maori, hero, and Christian myths in *The Bone People*. In addition to being a central symbol in fairy tales and Maori culture, the spiral structure of the book, the spiral staircase of Kerewin's tower and art, and other spiral images suggest Great Goddess mythology all over the world, including among the Maori, probably one reason the novel was published by the feminist Spiral Collective. Maoris use spiral tattoos (Skin Stories), carve spirals on meeting houses, storehouses, rock paintings, war canoes, and door lintels, and create other art (Maori Art). Kerewin is aware that her engraved double spiral on the floor is a mandala (44), a meditation image supposed to lead to insight, and that spirals, unlike crosses, suggest joy (273). She says that "the old people found inspiration for the double spirals they carved so skill-fully, in uncurling fern fronds: perhaps. But it was an old symbol of rebirth, and the outward-inward nature of things" (45). Spirals sug-gest the wholeness of everything at the beginning of the universe, the spiral labyrinth of the Mother Goddess, serpent guardians, death and rebirth through the underground womb, and Kundalini energy (B. Walker, *Woman's Dictionary* 2, 14, 26). In most mythology, the Great Goddess is the creator of the universe, the giver of all life, sometimes, as in *Memoirs,* the world egg. Traditionally, the Great Goddess is viewed as a trinity, another major symbol in the book, or sometimes in seven aspects, like Kerewin's seven directions for her life; but particular goddesses are always part of a whole, as previously indicated: the maiden or new moon, the mother or full moon, and the Crone or old moon. Some of the best known Maori goddess fig-ures are Papatuanuku or Papa the earth mother, Hinetitama girl of the dawn, Hinenuitipo the goddess of night or death, Hinete iwaiwa the goddess of women, childbirth, and creativity, Apakura the venge-ful mother, Hine Moa the passionate princess, Hine Moana the lady of the sea, Hine Manu the goddess of birds, and Hine Ulu Rangi the goddess of clay.

Certainly Kerewin, a knife-carrying, heavy, muscular "pirate," whose face is eczema-scarred and who has yellowed eyes, has never thought of herself as Nature or as either nurturing or mothering. Ironically, although Kerewin is initially a parody of a goddess and of societal conceptions of the feminine, as Joe is when she thinks of him as a harpy, she is unified with Papatuanuku, the earth mother, through several dreams in which she subconsciously heals her rift. In one she dreams of entering a hole in the ground, hears the island breathing, and is called. In another, at "the hour when dreams are real," she touches the threshold and sees a wrecked building replaced with ones that fit the land. Then, when touched by welcoming peo-ple, she feels herself dissolving into bones and the bones sinking into the earth, which again speaks (428). Joe associates Hana with the Maori Persephone and also dreams of Hana in different goddess as-pects as an earth-mother, with milk-swollen breasts and a stream flow-ing from her vagina, and as a moth. The kaumatua, Tiaki Mira, tells him about three possible journeys of the soul to death, one of which is to stay with mother Papa (344, 351, 354). Before he dies, this guardian of the mauri stone, the heart of the land and the country, tells Joe that "we changed. We ceased to nurture the land. We fought among ourselves. We were overcome by those white people in their hordes. We were broken and diminished. We forgot what we could have been, that Aotearoa [New Zealand] was the shining land" (364). As LeCam states, to be successful, "Exploring the self means becoming one with the Earth" (70–72).

Many goddesses, including the Hindu Sita, the Greek Persephone, and the Mauri Hinetatama, descend into the earth and the under-world. As Hulme explains, "Maori cosmology opposed the world of the dark, the night, the place of the Great Lady of Death, with the world of Dawn, of the light, of the living." When she realizes that her father, Tane, has committed incest, Hinetatama, the goddess of dawn, descends to the underworld and becomes Hinenuitepo, the goddess of night and death ("Myth" 36, 31). People who recover from severe illness or wounds are said to have crossed the boundary between life and death at Cape Reinga on the North Island, and there is even an untrustworthy ferryman. Because she had not eaten food, Hine marama was able to return to the world of the living (A. W. Reed 13–18). Kerewin, Joe, and Simon all symbolically fall, die, descend, make contact with the earth, and return; and all three are guided by either a *wairua,* "an unseen double, a soul shadow, your own spirit" or a ghost. If a *wairua* becomes detached from the body, it can be seen as a *kehua* or ghost. A *wairua* can go to the realm of the dead and return with a message, and dreams are also messages ("Myth" 33). For Simon the *wairua* or *kehua* is a little brown man with blue lines across his face who is on the floor of the bach; for Kerewin it is the androgynous figure in the hut; and for Joe it is the kaumatua. Kerewin actually calls to Papa (the earth), the stars, and the sea when the figure asks her what she loves; and when she returns home, she fulfills the messages of her dreams by gardening and building in harmony with the earth.

In the Maori creation myth, there is no light in the beginning because Father Rangi, the sky, is in the arms of Mother Papa, the land. Their children want space and light, so their son, Tane, forcibly separates them and while other children take care of the waves, growing things, and war, he plants the forests and places the sun, the moon, and the stars on the chest of Rangi (A. W. Reed 4–6).

After the prefatory three unnamed characters walk down the street and open their hands, *The Bone People,* a book in which "The End [is] at the Beginning," starts with a creation myth: "In The Beginning, it was darkness" (5). Many creation myths, including also the biblical and Greek ones, begin with darkness, often coupled with or preceded by chaos: "Verily, very first of all Chaos came into being, but then Gaia wide-bosomed, secure foundation of all forever, and dark Tartarus in the depth of the broad land and Eros, the most beautiful of all the immortal gods" (Morford and Lenardon 36). Other Maori creation myths explain the origin of New Zealand, knowledge, life, death, sweet potatoes, greenstone, geological features, and the woman in the moon; and many are about various monsters or ogres, who often become part of the land (see A. W. Reed). The myths about Maui, the trickster, are especially relevant since Simon is sometimes considered a Maui figure (e.g., Hughes 61–62). Since Maui fishes up New Zealand, complete with people, animals, and buildings from the bottom of the sea, one might be reminded of him when Simon hooks the large shark. Maui also tames the Sun, Te Ra, so that he limps rather than races, and when there is perpetual daylight followed by perpetual darkness, ties the sun to the moon so that there would always be some light (A. W. Reed 19–21). Among the myths that Hulme explains is the one about Maui trying to conquer death so that all humans could be immortal:

Surrounded by his friends of the bird kingdom, he attempted to murder the sleeping Hinenuitepo by entering her vagina and—reversing birth—making his way to her heart to stop it. Unfortunately for him, Piwakawaka the fantail found the sight of Maui's legs wriggling round so funny that he burst out laughing. Hinenuitepo woke, squashed her legs together, and that was the end of Maui. ("Myth" 31)

Maori myth personifies stones, mountains, hot springs, rain, lightening, the sea, and land, among other parts of nature; and Hulme considers the land and sea to be characters in *The Bone People* (Hulme and Turcotte 140). According to Maori myth, the gods "have not yet vanished from the land of the Maori for beliefs that are as germane to the land as the vegetation that covers it cannot be completely banished from the mind" (A. W. Reed 84).

Janet Wilson thinks that Hulme specifically and ironically references the Christian creation myth in Genesis to suggest "that a Fall from Maori spiritual plentitude has occurred because of European occupation" (274). Hulme is well aware of the injustice of land confiscation (Hulme and Turcotte 149). In a book that uses a cross-cultural comparative method (Brydon and Tiffin 22–24), however, there is no reason that *Christian* should be privileged or equated with *European*, and doing so does not explain how other "Christian" images associated with the goddess, such as the rosary, the crucifix, the trinity, and the Virgin birth, are paralleled with Maori or non-Christian ones, such as Buddhism and Sufism. For example, Kerewin wears Simon's rosary, the instrument for worship of the Rose (the flower of Venus, later the Virgin Mary)—which in this instance contains a signet ring with a phoenix coat of arms—on top of the Sufi knotted necklace (the knot of Fate). The trinity is important in goddess, Hindu, Germanic, and Norse religion as well as Christianity and is the image Kerewin celebrates in her tricephalos sculpture of the three characters' heads. Virgin birth occurs in other religions, too, as among the vestal "virgins" and Ishtar's harlot-priestesses (B. Walker, *Woman's Encyclopedia* 866, 511, 1046, 1048–49). Assuming that Simon is a saint or Christ symbol is even less persuasive than thinking that Kerewin privileges Christian religion:

By enduring increasing physical pain through his beatings, Simon is taking the sins of the world upon himself. . . . His "sacrifice"—the ultimate bashing-cum-crucifixation which sends him into a coma—is necessary to *redeem* the threesome, and beyond the threesome, to redeem New Zealand. (Le Cam 74; see also Dale 419–21)

A pagan symbol before Christians accepted it, an effigy of a man hanging on the cross represented the sacred king whose blood was supposed to fertilize the earth. This image was set in fields to protect the crops and was replaced by scarecrows (B. Walker, *Woman's Encyclopedia* 188). Hulme actually wrote to Judith Dale objecting to her comparison of Simon to Christ and identifying Simon's " 'provenance' as the Celtic 'marvelous stranger' or marvelous child' " (qtd. Dale 427–28), yet another kind of folklore. Far from rationalizing child abuse, Hulme wishes readers to recognize it as a problem, historically especially in "white" New Zealand (Hulme and Turcotte 139, 146–47, 152–53). It is part of the sickness that afflicts all three characters and their country. The only Maori myth to deal with child abuse is that of *Hatu Patu*, about a boy, beaten up by his brothers, who "sicked" the cannibalistic "bird woman" onto his family. "It seemed to me that there had been a breakdown of a strongly hierarchical, strongly spiritual system, that had dispossessed Maori men from what was seen as their main functions, basically protector and nurturer of other members of the extended family group" (Hulme and Turcotte 139). First seeing Simon standing "like some weird saint in a stained gold window . . . haloed in hair shrouded in the dying sunlight" and with a puncture wound in his foot (16) seems a parody, similar to the parody of *Robinson Crusoe* when Kerewin finds Simon's sandal. On the other hand, when not pushed into allegory, use of Christian sacred stories in *The Bone People* parallels uses of other mythologies to revive the sacred and build a healing utopian myth.

In reference to hero myth, Kerewin is again both a parody of a hero and a real one. As Henke suggests, a "heroine is almost always defined by sexual difference, in contrast or in relation to a correlative hero" (89). Perhaps part of the problem is even using the diminutive suffix *ine*, as in *feminine*:

> In a highly self-conscious, lyrical, and polyglottic prose style, the author rede-fines the mythic circle of heroism to include the marginalised Other—the fe-male, the Aboriginal, the wounded, the obsessed, the enraged, and the mute. The protagonist Kerewin . . . emerges as Arthurian knight in search of the Holy Grail—a modern-day Percival who retreats to the Chapel Perilous for a "dark night of the soul" from which she arises victorious . . . [She] amalga-mates an anti-heroic subject-position with traditionally masculine characteris-tics of bravery, courage, self-sufficiency, and gallantry in the face of an abusive patriarchal authority. (Henke 89–90)

Rather than just having masculine characteristics, the traditional classical hero "must reject, tame, or even kill the women in his life, lest he be tamed (and thus psychologically destroyed) or killed by them" (Harris and Platzner 231). Thus, again overturning gender binary oppositions, Hulme exposes the sexual politics inherent in the heroic pattern. Of archetypal patterns Lord Raglan identifies for the classical hero, most relevant to Kerewin on a symbolic level is the journey to the underworld and the victory over a giant, dragon, or wild beast. Joseph Campbell refers to the hero's separation from familiar sur-roundings, a journey alone, a mysterious initiation, "during which he grapples with supernatural powers and gains a new understanding of himself in relation to his community and the gods." Finally, the hero returns to share the new vision. The hero is divided, isolated yet craves human companionship and love, may redeem humanity, and ultimately protects society (Harris and Platzner 229–31).

Just as Kerewin is her own tower, her ego, false sense of self-sufficiency, and urge to fight constitute the wild beast she must fight; and Joe and Simon face similar "beasts," with Joe's trials in finding and guarding the marae particularly reminiscent of the search for the Grail, including that of Indiana Jones in pop culture. Although patri-archal myth often pits the hero against Great-Goddess serpents, who must be decapitated because of fear of castration (Harris and Platzner 233; S. Wilson, *Margaret Atwood's Fairy* 18), the hero's journey to the underworld can be interpreted as a descent into the womb of the Earth Goddess (Harris and Platzner 230), a feat Kerewin performs through dreams. A Maori hero was preeminently a warrior, and in addition to enemy tribes, monsters, giants, and ogresses were always threats in Maori mythology. Kerewin possesses the Maori joy in fighting but recognizes the need to replace fighting with peace or discussion. Bragging in the pub that "I could take on any or all of you right now, and have a neat time, stomping you to mush," her snark adds, for her ears only, "Great, Holmes! An old lady, a tiny woman, a wee man, and a good fat fellow, placid as the day is long . . . kick 'em all to death eh? O mighty work, hero stuff that! (286–87). Deconstructing the usual white, gendered, heterosexual, misogynist hero, Kerewin models a new kind of hero for a new kind of country and world. Kerewin, Joe, and Simon

are nothing more than people, by themselves. . . . But all together, they have become the heart and muscles and mind of something perilous and new, something strange and growing and great. Together, all together, they are the instruments of change." (4)

Phoenix images and web images help structure the characters' rebirth. The Phoenix, usually considered part of Greek mythology, is also Egyptian, Arab, Indian, Hindu, and Christian and is generally a bird initially symbolizing the regenerated sun and later rebirth and resurrection (Leach and Fried 869). Many women writers, including Atwood and Rhys, refer to the Phoenix to indicate their characters' transformation. The crest of Simon's ancient Irish family is a Phoenix, and all three characters are Phoenix-like: They undergo archetypal journeys from being broken, diseased, lost, lonely, and internally and externally divided to being whole, well, found, and part of the family of humankind. By the end of the novel, web imagery, evident also in Erdrich and Atwood, also suggests rebirth. Kerewin is "painting easily, fluently, profoundly. . . . I am weaving webs and building dreams" (431). She decides on a shell shape (a spiral) for the meeting hall she is rebuilding. After writing what could be the story we read in her journal, her Book of the Soul, she places it in its chest and sets fire to both, suggesting that story—and *the* story—is also Phoenix-like, beginning from its ashes, at the same time as it emerges from the Chinese funeral pyre of dead selves and Kerewin's meeting with the goddess of death (437). Accompanied by her eyeless cat, Kerewin knows without eyes as Simon speaks without words. Like Atwood's *The Blind Assassin,* which finishes as its writer dies, and Lessing's

Memoirs, which "ends" with the re-creation of the world, Hulme's mythic text and intertexts signify beginnings from endings.

As Homi Bhabha says, "It is in the emergence of the interstices—the overlap and displacement of domains of difference—that the intersubjective and collective experience of *nationness,* community interest, or cultural value are negotiated" (*Location* 2).

As Ashcroft, Griffiths, and Tiffin suggest,

Most post-colonial writing. . . . emphasizes how hybridity and the power it releases may well be seen to be the characteristic feature and contribution of the post-colonial, allowing a means of evading the replication of the binary categories of the past, and developing new anti-monolithic models of cultural exchange and growth. (183)

As a hybridized, postcolonial Kunstlerroman, *The Bone People* uses multicultural folkore intertexts to show how stories continue to heal rifts within individuals and societies and to depict other ways of being in the world. Like Atwood, Lessing, Morrison, Erdrich, Ferre, Murdoch, and Rhys, Hulme uses mythic and fairy-tale intertexts to re-mythify old stories.

CONCLUSION

As demonstrated in the works of Atwood, Lessing, Morrison, Ferre, Erdrich, Murdoch, Rhys, and Hulme, contemporary women's metafiction embeds and sometimes parodies the plot, structure, themes, images, motifs, characterization, and even language of its fairy-tale and myth intertexts. Viewed broadly, these novels are about the timeless things that myths and fairy tales are about. Major themes of women's postcolonial metafiction and of texts that embed fairy-tale and mythic intertexts include the constructions of reality, struggle for survival, the possible end of the world, power and sexual politics, body politics, colonialism and postcolonialism, dehumanization, class conflict, the woman artist, amputation and return of senses, self-deception versus enlightenment, the quest for home and identity, quest for a better society, quest for the good, quest for wholeness, quest for independence and community, quest for the word, quest for the story and a way of passing it on, and art as a way of ordering "reality" or at least the predominant stories of characters' lives, or, alternatively, the impossibility of finding or saying the word. Such texts are about creation against and in the midst of destruction. They are about heroism against all that would deny human projects and value.

Although there is little recognition that magical realism is usually generated by mythic and fairy-tale intertexts, such is the case in works including Mikhail Bulgakov's *Master and Margarita,* Salman Rushdie's *Shalimar the Clown,* and *Haroun and the Sea of Stories,* Gabriel Garcia Marquez's *One Hundred Years of Solitude,* Margaret Atwood's *Cat's Eye* and *Alias Grace,* Isabel Allende's *House of the Spirits,* Ben Okri's *The Famished Road,* Michael Ondaatje's *In the Skin of a Lion,* Angela Carter's *The Bloody Chamber and Other Stories,*

Jorge Luis Borges's "The Garden of Forking Paths" and other stories in *Labyrinths,* and Julio Cortazar's *Blow-Up and Other Stories,* as well as the works discussed here. That magical realism is often postcolonial and metafiction is only beginning to be discussed. In addition, myth and fairy-tale intertexts generally produce metafiction—both straight or traditional and antifiction—again as illustrated in the above texts and those covered in this book. Indeed, fairy-tale, folklore, and myth intertexts appear in many of this and the previous century's most significant literary works. Virginia Woolf's *To the Lighthouse,* Zore Neale Hurston's *Their Eyes Are Watching God,* Doris Lessing's *The Golden Notebook,* John Fowles's *The French Lieutenant's Woman,* Louise Erdrich's *Tracks,* Joy Kogawa's *Obasan,* Margaret Laurence's *The Diviners,* Toni Morrison's *The Bluest Eye,* Amy Tan's *The Joy Luck Club,* Marie-Claire Blais's *Mad Shadows,* Anne Hebert's *Kamouraska,* Michael Ondaatje's *In the Skin of a Lion* and *The English Patient,* Ben Okri's *The Famished Road,* and A. S. Byatt's *Possession: A Romance* are self-conscious about themselves and stories or art (metafiction). Salmon Rushdie's *Haroun and the Sea of Stories,* Barbara Comyns's *The Juniper Tree,* Laura Esquivel's *Like Water for Chocolate,* Joyce Carol Oates's *Do With Me What You Will,* Eudora Welty's *The Robber Bridegroom,* Kurt Vonnegut's *Bluebeard,* Donald Barthelme's *Snow White,* Robert Coover's *Pinocchio in Venice,* John *Barth's Chimera,* John Fowle's *The Collector,* Marge Piercy's *He, She, It,* and Gail Godwin's "A Sorrowful Woman" are also about fairy tales and/ or myths. Some women's fiction embedding myth and fairy-tale intertexts and deserving of further study includes Marie-Claire Blais's *Mad Shadows,* Joy Kogawa's *Obasan,* and Maryse Conde's *I, Tituba, Black Witch of Salem.*

Metafiction that radically parodies traditional fiction, sometimes using antilanguage that erases what has been asserted or even doodling in the text like its forefather, Laurence Sterne, may also be antifiction, including anti–fairy tales (*The Robber Bride, Beloved,* Ferre's "Sleeping Beauty"*)* and antimyths *The Penelopiad).* Such work parodies readers' expectations by interrupting or changing the story, sometimes even refusing to present an illusion of reality. Most antifiction also embeds fairy-tale and/ or mythic intertexts: Joyce's *Ulysses* and *Portrait of the Artist as a Young Man,* Lessing's *The Golden Notebook,* Atwood's *Surfacing,* and "There Was Once," Beckett's *Molloy, Malone Dies,* and *The Unnamable,* Morrison's *The Bluest Eye,* Vonnegut's *Bluebeard* and *Cat's Cradle,* Robbe-Grillet's *The Erasers,* Nabokov's *Lolita,* and Barth's stories, including "Title" and "Night Sea Journey."

Many of the mythic and fairy-tale intertexts evident in the works examined in this volume include in several texts: "Fitcher's Bird" or "Blue Beard," "The Robber Bridegroom," "Sleeping Beauty" or "Briar Rose," "Cinderella," "Snow White," "Hansel and Gretel," "Rapunzel," and "The Red Shoes" and Great Goddess, Fisher King, and hero myth, including that about Odysseus. Literary fairy tales such as *Alice in Wonderland* and *Through the Looking-Glass*, "Scheherazade" from *One Thousand and One Nights*, and *The Wizard of Oz* also recur. Several literary allusions, as to Shelley's *Frankenstein*, Bram Stoker's *Dracula*, and Defoe's *Robinson Crusoe*, and biblical ones, such as Eden or Eve, also occur frequently in women's metafiction. In addition, many metafiction writers use quest patterns, trickster and shadow-self characters, and cannibalism and amputation images associated with folklore. The "Fitcher's Bird" fairy tale, subject of Atwood's watercolor, *Fitcher's Bird* (1970) on this book's cover, particularly suggests fairy tales' and myths' focus on human resourcefulness and survival.

These myth and fairy-tale intertexts generally serve at least four connected purposes: one, to indicate the quality and nature of characters' cultural contexts; two, to signify characters'—and readers'— entrapment in preexisting patterns; and three, to comment self-consciously on these patterns—including the embedded fairy tales, myths, and related popular traditional stories—often by deconstructing constricting literary, folkloric, and cultural plots with transgressive language and filling in the gaps of female narrative. Fairy-tale and myth intertexts comment self-consciously on the frame story, on themselves, and on other intertexts. When used in metafiction, these intertexts call attention to themselves as intertexts, highlighting their shortcomings or celebrating the power of language and story. Finally, they structure the characters' imaginative or "magical" release from externally imposed patterns, offering the possibility of transformation for the novel's characters, for the country they partly represent, and for all human beings (S. Wilson, *Margaret Atwood's Fairy* 34). Even when this release is death, as in Ferre's "Sleeping Beauty," the consciousness of the character(s) and readers has still transformed. Often, the text has been opened so that we become engaged in writing beyond the ending (DuPlessis 6), as in Rhys's *Wide Sargasso Sea* and Atwood's two re-visioned *Odysseys*, *The Penelopiad* and *Circe/ Mud Poems*.

Regardless of nationality, metafairy tales and metamyths typically possess identifiable features and reveal similar techniques of intertextuality. Although this listing includes interdependent techniques and is by no means exhaustive, it offers an overview of intertextual tactics I first observed in Margaret Atwood's work. Although writers of other genres also use many of these tactics, I am concerned here with how feminist, postcolonial writers use intertexts in their metafairy tales and metamyths. First, and especially frequent, an author of a feminist, postcolonial metafairy tale or metamyth may build a scene on one or more powerful images. For example, the scene in which *Beloved* in Morrison's novel first appears shows her rising from the water, adult and fully dressed, like the Lady of the Lake, being "born" with "new skin" as her "water" breaks (recalling Hathor), voraciously drinking like the vampire she partly becomes, and sleeping and waking as "sleepy beauty" or Sleeping Beauty (Morrison, *Beloved* 50–53). Second, an author may reverse the gender of the hero, "heroine," or other characters to shift females from object to subject. She sometimes doubles roles so that the same person may be both rescuer and rescuee and, in terms of divided archetypes or foils, princess and stepmother or witch. Sometimes men comically play roles assigned to women or even objects in the intertexts, as when Erdrich makes Wallace a male fairy godmother in *The Beet Queen* or the men become the loot in Atwood's *The Robber Bride*.

Third, displacing the "truth" of traditional texts and inherited patterns and giving voice to the silenced, metafairy tales and metamyths may shift the point of view from traditional, privileged, reliable, third-person narration to unreliable third-person centers of consciousness (reflectors), as in *The Robber Bride* or sections of *Beloved,* or use unreliable first-person narration. Fourth, they may use tropes and symbols to enlarge the meaning of the ordinary, especially to make the literal—the robbery in "The Robber Bridegroom," the awakening in Ferre's "Sleeping Beauty"—symbolic. Fifth, retaining the magical transformations of fairy-tale and mythic plots, metafairy tales and metamyths often displace the original plot line of such tales as "The Girl Without Hands" so that the silent or marginalized subtext of female amputation, such as the symbolic ones of Morrison's Beloved, Sethe, and Denver or those of Atwood's Robber Brides, are central.

Sixth, keeping something of the fairy tale's binary opposition and its archetypal, structural movement from "negative" to "positive," the feminist, postcolonialist metafairy tale and metamyth often change the intertext's resolution so that marriage or heterosexual relationship does not complete the woman's story (*The Robber Bride, The Bone People*); or, more commonly, they explode and open the resolution (what DuPlessis calls "writing beyond the ending" (6), as in *Beloved* and *Wide Sargasso Sea*. Seventh, these intertexts frequently transform, bend, or blend either tones or genres (e.g., making "The Robber Bridegroom" comic). Eighth, as in the works of Erdrich, Morrison, and Atwood, they tend to use irony as a subversive doubled or split discourse. Ninth, although they sometimes retain fairy-tale and mythic costumes (e.g., Offred's red clothing and basket in Atwood's *The Handmaid's Tale*), settings, props, and events—thereby aiding readers' unconscious recognition of fairy-tale and mythic intertexts—, they often use language to defamiliarize (Shklovsky 13–22), transgress, and parody these elements. Tenth, using decolonization in a transition toward a postcolonial and harmonious society, the metafairy tale or metamyth generally revises or "reverses" the norms or ideology of an intertext. For example, in *Beloved,* instead of awakening to adolescence, heterosexual love, or the female role in society; listening to the anima; or exercising a passive potential outside the world of action; Sleeping Beauty listens to ancestral images dormant in the unconscious (Cirlot 285) in order to confront history directly. Eleventh, by transgressing the conventions of language and culture through puns, word play, figures of speech, and irony; using what DuPlessis calls "delegitimation" (creating an unexpected story, 29), in addition to writing beyond the ending, the feminist, postcolonial metafairy tale and metamyth engage readers in the kind of joint creation of the text that Morrison and Atwood call for. Finally, metafairy tales and metamyths remythify intertexts distorted or amputated by colonization, racism, and patriarchy, potentially healing societies. Fairy-tale and mythic intertexts thus foreground sexual politics and other political issues, including those of the postcolonial condition (adapted from S. Wilson, *Margaret Atwood's Fairy* 31–33).

Intertexts in metafairy tales and metamyths are much more than allusions: "frame narratives echo inner narratives' images, motifs, themes, characterization, structures, and even plots, self-consciously reflecting, and reflecting upon, intertexts" (S. Wilson, *Margaret Atwood's Fairy* 3–4). In addition, metafairy tales and metamyths use or parody intertexts' scenes, point of view, symbols, and costumes to shape ironic postmodern and postcolonial texts that undermine essentialist, colonial, and sexist assumptions. Perhaps most meaningful, whether or not readers consciously recognize intertexts, their reading experience of texts embedding myths and fairy tales is heightened and enriched: They connect to the old, wise stories where magical transformation, rebirth, and healing are again possible.

NOTES

INTRODUCTION

1. Although Iris Murdoch is not usually considered postcolonial, she was born in Ireland, sometimes deals with postcolonial issues, and even sets one of her novels, *The Red and the Green,* at the time of the Easter Uprising.
2. Films, music, and other popular culture, particularly postmodernist varieties, also illustrate metaform. Madonna is frequently cited as a musician who calls attention not only to musical tradition but also to herself as performer and construction (see E. Ann Kaplan and Michael Dunne). Wayne Surijik's *Wayne's World I,* Penelope Spheeris's *Wayne's World II,* and Quentin Tarrantino's *Pulp Fiction* use titles and techniques calling attention to and parodying themselves as films. Many films, such as Wayne Wang's and Paul Auster's *Smoke* (1995) and Billy Crystal's and Mickey Gilbert's *Forget Paris* (1995), also call attention to storytelling or use oral tales to comment on the film as a whole. Film is, of course, usually both an auditory and visual medium and most films use dialogue.
3. Iris Murdoch's work, especially, has been limited by oversimplified expectations that she always uses realism and refers to objective reality, is antifeminist or nonfeminist, and is English and colonial rather than postcolonial. Although Fiander says that "Murdoch almost never portrays liberated women in her novels" (10), she "feels very strongly about the liberation of women" (Sagare interview 707).
4. Despite considerable evidence to the contrary, Greene surprisingly calls the mode of feminist writers, including Atwood, "realism" (4) and amazingly finds "no feminist metafiction by black women writers that relates the rewriting of old plots specifically to women's search for freedom" (*Changing* 24).
5. See S.Wilson's *Margaret Atwood's Fairy,* xii-xv, for an expanded critique of such oversimplification.
6. Although the Grimm brothers based their tales on oral informants such as Dorothea Viehmann and Marie Hassenpflug, these contributors were mostly from educated members of the middle and aristocratic classes. The Grimms also stylistically altered and sometimes, as in "The Girl Without Hands," combined tales (Zipes, *The Complete* 715, 728). See Ellis.

CHAPTER 1

1. For example, St. Andrew's head was divided into three pieces placed in three locations, including the Cathedral of St. Andrew in Patros, Greece, to suggest the power of his presence in each division of the early Christian church.

2. Other intertexts include Mnemosyne (Goddess of memory) and the devouring mother; other Greek and Egyptian myths, including those of Orpheus and Eurydice, Helen of Troy, Proteus, and the Golden Apples; the biblical stories of Jezebel, the Whore of Babylon, and the Good Samaritan; nursery rimes and stories, including "Goldilocks and the Three Bears" (Atwood, *Book Group Companion* 12), "The Three Little Pigs," "Mary Had a Little Lamb," "Humpty Dumpty"; Dodgson's *Alice in Wonderland* and *Through the Looking Glass;* Barrie's *Peter Pan;* Shelley's *Frankenstein;* mummy lore, mummy films such as *The Mummy,* and vampire legend (see S. Wilson, "Atwood's Intertextual" 59); historical legend, including the Empress Theophano and Dame Giraude; the radio show "The Shadow"; and Nancy Drew mysteries. In Book XVIII of Homer's *The Iliad,* Charis is the wife of the lame craftsman, Hephaestus, maker of magical things. In *The Odyssey* (Book VIII), his wife is the goddess Aphrodite (Stapleton 93), who, unlike Atwood's Charis, is unfaithful to her husband.

3. This quotation is at the beginning of the "Tale of Mr. Todd," announcing that now she is going to make a story about disagreeable people (Claudia Hill-Norton fax to Sarah Cooper, Collection 335, Box 2 RB Correspondence 1993–94. Margaret Atwood Papers).

4. This chapter is based on three papers, presented at the Popular Culture Association Conference in Philadelphia, Apr. 1995; the International Popular Culture Association Conference in Oxford, England, July 1995; and the Association for Canadian Studies in the U.S. Conference, Seattle, Nov.1995; and one section is based on an article in Stephen Benson's *Contemporary Fiction and the Fairy Tale* (Wayne SUP).

5. Folklorists classify all kinds of traditional narratives and their elements (motifs) and indicate geographical distribution. In the text, tale-types are indicated in parentheses following AT (Aarne-Thompson) and motifs in parentheses following Motif (Thompson, *Motif*).

6. Hunt and Stern 202–4; Magoun and Krappe 153–54; Zipes 156–57. Summary from S. Wilson, *Margaret Atwood's Fairy* 86–88.

7. Carter, *The Old* 8–10; Grace, "Courting" f.n. 250; S. Wilson, *Margaret Atwood's Fairy* 86–88.

8. See, for example, Rev. *Catholic New Times;* Potts, "The White Goddess" 230; Potts, "The Old Maps" 284; Bouson 159; Stein 97; Staels 198. Staels does note the importance of glowing eggs that contain the life force and of Zenia as a trickster and goddess (199–201).

9. If we recognize a post-enlightenment binary opposition of homosexual and heterosexual based on gender (Warner 549–65), the narrative manages to exist "in the space in between" the constructed poles.

10. The situation is similar among minor characters. The homosexual rela-
    tionship of the witty Boyce and his partner Larry seems far less warlike
    than its heterosexual corollary. Mitch, like Chris in *Life Before Man*, is
    unable to survive the sex war, and Billy, a war dodger, tries unsuccessfully
    to escape.

11. Other examples include characters from Du Maurier, Huxley, Flaubert,
    Poe, Hawthorne, Wharton, James, Fitzgerald, and Chandler, and some
    from ballet, opera, visual art, and film (Collection 335, Box 2 RB Notes,
    Margaret Atwood Papers).

12. She is not, as Jennifer Murray (79), Robert Graves, and patriarchal tradi-
    tion suggest, simply a muse. See Atwood's critique of Graves in *Survival*.

CHAPTER 2

1. When Atwood discusses fairy tales, she often uses an archetypal approach
   associated with one of her professors at the University of Toronto,
   Northrop Frye, author of *An Anatomy of Criticism*.

2. The "brown box" of clippings containing background research for the
   novel refers to a human-mouse hybrid that may form from stem cell mix-
   ing. The idea of breeding strawberries and flounder is also being considered (Margaret Atwood Papers, 335, Box 145, *Oryx and Crake*
   manuscripts.

3. Like the reference to Orwell, the idea of "The Three Pigs" as an intertextual cautionary tale was suggested to me by Shuli Barzilai, Hebrew
   University of Jerusalem, during the "Margaret Atwood: The Open Eye"
   symposium in Ottawa, April, 2004.

4. Although Atwood does not see *Oryx and Crake* as a classic dystopia, such
   as *The Handmaid's Tale*, because readers do not get an overview of the
   structure of society and what they do know is suspect because edited, this
   is true of the earlier novel as well. Her definition of dystopia does appear
   to apply to *Oryx and Crake* ("*The Handmaid's Tale*" 517).

5. Crake might appreciate current self-parodying Web sites such as Mad-
   SciNet, "a collective cranium of scientists providing answers to your
   questions."

6. Research Atwood considered for the book includes a reference to DNA
   social issues, including a 200 percent increase in autism among techie
   parents and a questioning of whether there is a Geek Syndome (Atwood
   Papers, 335, Box 145, *Oryx and Crake* manuscripts).

7. Other topics are brain regeneration, evolution of skin color, fuel-cell cars,
   Asperger's Syndrome, repairing hymens, unmanned air combat vehicles,
   animal rights violations, Mad Cow Disease, West Nile Virus, automated
   farming, the Earth Liberation Front, global warming, environmental
   damage, computer hacking, slavery, child sex trade, stem cell research,
   surveillance, endangered species, an artificial womb, vaccine and other
   testing that has killed volunteers, videogames, water, nanotechnology,

Internet crime, targeted commercials, the Kyoto Protocol, Proteomes (proteins), marijuana, globalization, DNA tampering, and wearable computers. In addition to the list of books, including Edmund Osborne Wilson's *The Future of Life,* that she published on the Internet (http://www .randomhouse.com/features/atwood/oryxandcrake/links.html), Atwood consulted *Time, Newsweek, Macleans, US News and World Report, Wired, The New Yorker, Harpers, Listener, Guardian Weekly, The Globe and Mail, The Toronto Star, The New York Times, World Link, Scientific American, The Observer,* the Sierra Club, the Temagami Wilderness Society, *Report on a Material Recovery Plan for the City of Toronto,* and Project C.A.N.O.E. Surya Bhattacharya of Atwood's O. W. Toad Ltd. company extracted passages from *Oryx and Crake* and arranged them in folders with the selected articles (Margaret Atwood Papers. 335, Boxes 98, 108, 111, 113–117).

CHAPTER 3

1. One of Atwood's editors, Louise Dennys, recognizes *The Penelopiad* as a "reinvention of the myth" and comments that the text "will make great theatre too" (Margaret Atwood Papers, 335, Box 151 Editorial Correspondence with Louise Dennys, 21 Oct., 2004). In addition to Homer's *The Odyssey* and Great Goddess myth, Atwood also uses Ovid's *Heroides* (Reader's Notes, Margaret Atwood Papers, 335, Box 153, Folder One), Baudelaire, the "Mistress Mary Quite Contrary" nursery rime, the Grimms' "Fitcher's Bird" fairy tale, and general mythological reference (e.g., Sisyphus) as intertexts. An unidentified reader well-versed in the classics finds Atwood's Penelope closer to Ovid's Helen in tone and voice than to Homer's (Reader's Notes Margaret Atwood Papers, 335, Box 153, Folder One).

2. In the handwritten first manuscript of the novel, much closer to the finished novel than were drafts of *Alias Grace* and *The Blind Assassin,* Penelope is handed over like "a package of meat in a magpie of gold . . . [she is a] gilded word pudding" (Margaret Atwood Papers, 335, Box 149, Folder 6, Thomas Fisher Rare Book Library). While I might prefer the "word pudding" for its emphasis on Penelope as existing in and through words, at this point in her story she is silenced and objectified.

3. In *The Cleft* (2006), life begins with women, and Lessing draws on goddess myth. See also Lessing's poems about wolves on playing cards (Inpopa) and scholarship on Sufiism. Critics who discuss myth in Lessing include Marianthe Colakis on the Cupid and Psyche myth, Lisa Tyler on Demeter in "Flavors of Exile,"and Kathleen Wall and Larry W. Hurtado on the goddess in *Marriages.*

4. Sage, G. Green (*Doris*), J. Walker, Duyfhuizen, Fishburn, Whittaker, and Raschke do not mention the egg. Rubenstein sees the One as a symbol of wholeness suggesting the archetypal Great Mother and "the unitary state of undifferentiated consciousness that precedes psychic separation from

the mother or characterizes symbiosis with her" (237–38). Whittaker recognizes the affirmation of the ending and "the numinous presence—goddess, Muse, Earth Mother" as the same person that the narrator saw briefly at the novel's beginning (96). Sage mentions the apparition of "a tutelary being (a cosmic mother) from the 'other side,'" Lessing's "future Muse" (77), but none of these critics relates the "She" to the Cosmic Egg. G. Greene mentions the narrator's putting her ear to the wall, as to a fertile egg, as an image of gestation that connotes life, but she does not interpret the black egg. She does, however, speak of the "One" as the Good Mother, nurturing, hatching out the world of her creatures (*Doris* 146, 156–57). Although Sullivan does not discuss the "she" of the conclusion, he identifies the wall with the patient's dream screen in psychoanalysis—the mother's breast—("*Memoirs*" 160).

5. Bettelheim suggests that "Hansel and Gretel" may also suggest a child's fear of independence (98).

6. Although she goes a long way toward disproving her own argument, according to Rubenstein, *Memoirs* "is Lessing's most pessimistic pronouncement so far. There seems no way to truly begin 'from scratch' that would not carry with it the seed of its own destruction" (233).

7. Sullivan feels the central symbol, used as a metalinguistic sign, is the yellow spot on the wall that becomes identified with the egg "whose shell is the world frame of space" ("Ideology" 76).

8. Creation myths reflect cultural values. In "The Creation of the Universe," a Chinese creation myth dating from 200–500 A.D., an egg creates the universe; and the first being, Pangu, breaks it open. The dragon-tailed Mother Goddess, Nugua, creates people from clay, men impregnated with yang, the masculine, aggressive principle, and women with yin, the female, submissive principle (Rosenberg 359–62). See also the Japanese creation myth, "The Creation of the Universe and Japan" (712–20 A.D.), in which, after heaven and earth separate from the egg-shaped mass, a disobedient goddess is punished with an abnormal child for not knowing "her proper place" (Rosenberg 370–73). Because of these cultural values, Lessing may not only be returning to older, matriarchal versions of myths, such as Goddess tales, but may also be re-mythologizing recent ones.

9. DuPlessis later discusses Lessing's *Children of Violence* and *The Golden Notebook* (186–96, 101–3).

CHAPTER 4

The Morrison section grew from a short paper, "Fairy Tales in Feminist, Postcolonial Fiction: Atwood and Other Writers." International Popular Culture Association Conference. Oxford, England, July 1995.

1. *The Bluest Eye* (1970) is an anti–fairy tale (Blake 197) in which the ugly duckling does not become the beautiful swan. Critics have commented on Morrison's ironic use of blues lyrics, allusions to Eliot's "The Waste Land," the Dick and Jane primer story, and the Horatio Alger success story in this

novel (T. Harris 11). They also note fairy-tale structure, ballad formulas, and African American jokes and music in *Sula* (1974) (T. Harris 12); "Hansel and Gretel," "Rumpelstiltskin," "The King of the Golden Mountain," "Jack and the Beanstalk," and Hans Christian Andersen's "The Swineherd" alongside the Circe and Daedalus-Icarus myths and the biblical Pilate-Jesus story in *Song of Solomon* (1977) (De Weever 133–35, 138, 140–42); and "Snow White," "Sleeping Beauty" (Harris 13), and of course "Tar Baby" tales in Tar Baby (1981). Critics also observe that Morrison uses traditional flight and quest narratives, sometimes inverting patterns (Bowman 13), and trickster characters throughout her work.

2. Mayer thinks Sethe's name is partly derived from the Egyptian god Set, who murders his brother Osiris from jealousy, is banished to the desert, and is identified with destruction, alienation, death, and self-destruction (192–93). Set or Seth also tears the body of Osiris into sixteen pieces and scatters them (Larrington 32).

3. Although Stave sees Sethe as Lilith (49), Beloved seems more closely associated with the demonic aspects of the patriarchal version of the Lilith-Osiris-Horus story. Stave discusses Sethe as Mother Goddess but seems to privilege the destructive aspects of the cycle (51–52). When Paul D enters Sethe's house, haunted with Sethe's sorrow over her dead Beloved, he enters "a pool of red and undulating light" (Morrison 8). When Adonis, the "beloved" of Astarte, is mourned, the river runs red (Stapleton 10).

4. Trace does not include Amy as a goddess figure but credits Morrison's contribution to Black feminist theology in *Beloved* and suggests that, in the religion of the future, "the symbol of the Goddess may displace patriarchal absolutism" (15).

5. Although Trace recognizes this circling as a mandala and a Jungian symbol of the Self (22), she does not explicitly link the image to the goddess.

6. According to Cirlot, Sleeping Beauty represents the anima and also ancestral images dormant in the unconscious. Princesses dreaming in their palaces outside the world of action stand for human beings' passive potential (285).

Chapter 5

1. Like Ben Okri, another postmodern, postcolonial writer who uses magical realism, Erdrich insists that the events others see as magical "don't seem unreal to me" (qtd. Rosenthal 108). Magical realism is, however, both magical and real.

Chapter 6

This chapter grew from two short papers, "Rosario Ferre's *The Youngest Doll* as Postcolonial Metafairy Tales." International Conference on Caribbean Literature, Nassau, Bahamas. Nov. 4–6, 1998, and " 'The Poisoned Story' and Other Postcolonial Metafairy Tales in Rosario Ferre's *The Youngest Doll*," presented at the 2000 International Conference on Caribbean Literature, Ponce, Puerto Rico and published in *Horizontes: Revista de la Universidad Catolica de Puerto Rico*. 43.84 (2001): 143–63.

1. According to Patricia Hart, magic feminism is "that particularly irreverent brand of magic realism inextricably interwoven with feminism practiced by some of Latin America's leading writers, including Isabel Allende, Luisa Valenzuela, . . . and Rosario Ferre" (98).

2. Ferre used cotranslators for some of the stories: Diane Velez, Nancy Taylor, Nancy Beutel, Claire Ashman, and Cindy Ventura.

3. In addition to "Cinderella," and "Sleeping Beauty," Patricia Hart also finds parallels with *Aesop's Fables*, Wilde's *The Portrait of Dorian Gray*, and Sarton's *Mrs. Stevens Hears the Mermaids Singing* (97–107).

4. Many of these stories overtly depict choices women must make, and many also function as intertexts in Margaret Atwood's metafairy tales.

5. See chapter 2 for other examples of Caribbean tales.

CHAPTER 7

1. Fiander says that "Murdoch almost never portrays liberated women in her novels" (10), but ironic writers rarely use characters as author surrogates. For an analysis of Murdoch's questioning of gender identity and trangressing gender boundaries, see Johnson (1); for feminist themes, see Weese (634). Murdoch actually "feels very strongly about the liberation of women" (Sagare interview 707). Murdoch was born in Ireland and even sets one of her novels, *The Red and the Green*, at the time of the Easter Uprising.

2. Margaret Moan Rowe admires Murdoch's talent for concealing as much as she reveals in interviews, often being "guarded and gnomic" in her responses (Rev. 351).

3. Jack in the Green was part of a May Day pageant in England and probably a relic of tree worship, resembling Eastern European Green George on St. George's Day (Leach and Fried 534).

CHAPTER 8

A shorter version of this article was first presented at the International Conference on Caribbean Literature in Bermuda, November 1999, and was published as "Bluebeard's Forbidden Room in Rhys's *Wide Sargasso Sea*." Jean Rhys Issue, ed. Mary Lou Emery. *The Journal of Caribbean Literature* (Summer 2003) 3.3: 111–22.

1. As she explains in a 1979 interview,

> When I read *Jane Eyre* as a child, I thought, why should she think Creole women are lunatics and all that? What a shame to make Rochester's first wife, Bertha, the awful madwoman, and I immedi-

ately thought I'd write the story as it might really have been. She seemed such a poor ghost. I thought I'd try to write her a life." (qtd. in Vreeland 235)

2. As indicated earlier, the four main divisions of West Indian folk tales are the animal-tickster (Anansi), the etiological, the picaresque, and the magic. The West Indian story is also distinguished by its focus on petty and puny phenomena rather than grand natural forms such as the earth and the sun, widespread magic powers, love for vivid detail, use of song, frequent ending with a nonsense tag, and respect for family and friendship (Flowers 601–607). *Anansy* is the old Jamaican spelling for tales about a spider trickster hero originating in Ghana and other parts of West Africa, where they are now referred to as *Anansi* stories about the Ashana Spider God (Berry v-vi). Almost as familiar to white children as to Negroes, Anansy is also called Kwaku Ananse, Nansi, Miss Nancy, Aunt Nancy, and 'Ti Malice, and is closely associated with Brer Rabbit. In Jamaica, the stories are now told chiefly at wakes (Leach and Fried 52–53).

3. For example, "The Singing Bag" type (311B) is about a green man who captures a girl in a bag. Her mother rescues the girl when she recognizes her singing, and the man is imprisoned (Jaffe, "Sing, Little Sack!"). "A Boarhog for a Husband" is about marriage to a disguised beast (Motif B651) who is himself dismembered and eaten (Abrahams 108–10). Note, however, that some scholars dispute the appropriateness of Aarne-Thompson numbers for some folktales originating outside of Europe, as in Africa. See, for example, Abrahams (313).

4. See also Hansen, Three Sisters Rescued from the Mountain from the Power of an Ogre, Rescue by Their Sister (Type 311) and Type 312 for versions from the Dominican Republic, Puerto Rico, and Cuba (27–28) and Parsons for French and English tales, many named "Bluebeard," all over the Antilles.

5. Like other Bluebeards, Mr. Fox cuts up his women, in this case including cutting off the hand that points to him as murderer. Appropriately, Lady Mary's brothers and friends cut him "into a thousand pieces" (Carter 8–10).

6. See also Kloepfer, who agrees that this scene restages "Little Red Riding Hood" and refers to Rhys's use of the tale in her autobiography as well (149–50). Rhys and her siblings were going to act out the story together, but, significantly, when the woodcutter gets bored and leaves the stage, the Red Riding Hood figure is silent (*Smile* 23–24).

CHAPTER 9

A few passages of this chapter are from an article, "Through the 'Wall': Crone Journeys of Enlightenment and Creativity in the Works of Doris Lessing, Margaret Atwood, and Other Women Writers." *Adventures of the Spirit: the Older Woman in the Works of Doris Lessing, Margaret Atwood, and Other Contemporary Women Writers*. Ed, Phyllis Sternberg Perrakis. Columbus: Ohio State UP, 2007.

1. According to Hulme, rather than a Christ figure, Simon is "the natural dervish, a (self-contradictive) wise zany, a trickster learning his trade, the apprentice magician" (qtd. in Dale 428).

2. Because students generally expect realism and traditional structure, are unfamiliar with Maori culture and folklore, and initially find confusing a text that integrates Maori language into English, when teaching this text it is useful to distribute Xeroxes of selected Maori myths, such as the Papa and Rangi and Maui creation myths, and to introduce discussion of these elements before the students have read more than the beginning of the book. A media presentation with a document camera or power point can provide an overview of major cultural elements, including the Maori traditional reverence for the land. Pictures of rocks, including greenstone, should be presented along with the stories of how gods, goddesses, or ogres transformed into rocks. Then, discussion of the Grimms' "Rapunzel" fairy tale, usually familiar to students, offers insight into the character Kerewin's self-imposed isolation in a tower she has built. Since Hulme parodies many of the intertexts she embeds, discussion of this and related popular tales ending with a prince and marriage also illuminate this "neuter," eczema-scarred character's distance from expected gender roles. Depending upon the background of the students and the nature of the course, some discussion of postcolonialism and postmodernism is probably also necessary. I teach this text in English 335 World Literature by and about Women and in a graduate seminar, Magical Realism and Antifiction.

3. Benediktsson comments on *The Bone People*'s "plot redolent of fairy tale" in order to discuss ruptures in realism (126), but no one follows up on the importance of the fairy-tale and folklore context. When folklore, primarily myth, is discussed, critics refer to Hulme's bicultural rather than multicultural orientation.

4. In Hulme's poem, "He Hoha" "[What a Fuss]," Hulme uses old, nearly infertile female bodies to hope "impossible things" through a "cuckoo child" who helps return rather than displace family (*Strands* 41–43). A "cuckoo child" haunts the aging persona and causes her to bleed inside. According to Fee, cuckoos "lay their eggs in those of other, usually smaller birds; the chick hatches, pushes the natural chicks out, and is fed by the coopted adoptive parents." Contrary to Fee's view that Simon does not displace another child, it could be argued that he does displace Joe's birth child. Still, Simon may perform a symbolic function: He "ultimately returns Kerewin to her family and to her art" (Fee 59).

WORKS CITED

Aarne, Antti, and Stith Thompson. *The Types of the Folktale: A Classification and Bibliography*. Helsinki: Academia Scientiarum Fennica, 1987.

Abel, Elizabeth. "Resisting the Exchange: Brother-Sister Incest in Fiction by Doris Lessing." In Carey Kaplan and Ellen Cronan Rose. Ed. *Doris Lessing: The Alchemy of Survival*. Athens: Ohio UP, 1988. 15–26.

Abrahams, Roger D. *African American Folktales: Stories from Black Traditions in the New World*. New York: Pantheon, 1985.

"African Goddesses." <http://dickinsg.intrsun.tcnj.edu/diaspora/african-goddesses.html> 9 Jan. 2007.

"The Algonquin Cinderella." *QPB Treasury of North American Folktales*. Ed. Catherine Peck, Introduction Charles Johnson. New York: Quality Paperback Book Club, 1998. 299–301.

Anderson, William. *Green Man: The Archetype of Our Oneness with the Earth*. New York: Harper Collins, 1990.

Ashcroft, Bill, Gareth Griffiths, and Helen Tiffin, eds. *The Post-Colonial Studies Reader*. London and New York: Routledge, 1995.

Ashliman, D. L. "Incest in Indo-European Folktales." <http://www.pitt.edu/~dash/incest.html> 20 June 2006.

Atwood, Margaret. *Alias Grace*. New York: Nan A. Talese Doubleday, 1996.

———. *The Animals in That Country*. Toronto: Oxford UP, 1968.

———. "Bad News." *Good Bones*. Toronto: Coach House, 1992.

———. *The Blind Assassin*. Toronto: McClelland and Stewart, 2000.

———. *Bodily Harm*. New York: Simon and Schuster, 1982.

———. "Bottle II." *Bottle*. Hay, UK: Hay Festival Press, 2004. 51–54.

———. *Cat's Eye*. Toronto: McClelland and Stewart, 1988.

———. "Circe/Mud Poems." *You Are Happy*. Toronto: Oxford UP, 1974. 45–70.

———. *The Edible Woman*. New York: Popular Library, 1976.

———. *Good Bones*. Toronto: Coach House, 1992.

———. *Good Bones and Simple Murders*. New York: Nan A. Talese Doubleday, 1994.

———. *The Handmaid's Tale*. Boston: Houghton Mifflin, 1986.

———. "The Handmaid's Tale and *Oryx and Crake* in Context." Special Topic: Science Fiction and Literary Studies: The Next Millennium. *PMLA* 119.3 (May 2004).

———. *Lady Oracle*. New York: Avon, 1976.

———. *Life Before Man*. New York: Simon and Schuster, 1979.

———. "Margaret Atwood's Address to the American Booksellers Association Conference." *The Book Group Companion to Margaret Atwood's The Robber Bride*. New York: Nan A. Talese Doubleday, 1993. 7–13.

———. Margaret Atwood Papers. Collections 200, 335. RB Holographs Box 131, Thomas Fisher Rare Book Library, University of Toronto. Toronto, Canada.

———. *Moving Targets: Writing with Intent 1982–2004*. Toronto: Anansi, 2004.

———. *Murder in the Dark: Short Fictions and Prose Poems*. Toronto: Coach House, 1983.

———. "Of Souls as Birds." *Mirror, Mirror on the Wall: Women Writers Explore Their Favorite Fairy Tales*. Ed. Kate Bernheimer. New York: Anchor/Doubleday, 1998. 22–38.

———. *Oryx and Crake*. New York: Nan A. Talese Doubleday, 2003.

———. *The Penelopiad: The Myth of Penelope and Odysseus*. New York: Canongate, 2005.

———. *The Robber Bride*. Toronto: McClelland and Stewart, 1993.

———. "Siren Song." *You Are Happy*. Toronto: Oxford UP, 1974. 38–39.

———. *Speeches for Doctor Frankenstein*. Illus. and printed by Charles Pachter. Bloomfield Hill, MI: Cranbrook Academy of Art, 1965.

———. *Surfacing*. New York: Popular Library, 1976.

———. *Survival: A Thematic Guide to Canadian Literature*. Toronto: Anansi, 1972.

———. " 'You Can't Do without Your Shadow': An Interview with Margaret Atwood." *Margaret Atwood's Novels: A Study of Narrative Discourse*. Ed. Hilda Staels. Tubingen and Basel: A. Francke Verlag, 1995. 207–14.

Atwood, Margaret, and Victor-Levy Beaulieu. *Two Solicitudes: Conversations*. Trans. Phyllis Aronoff and Howard Scott. Toronto: McClelland and Stewart, 1998.

Bacchilega, Cristina. *Postmodern Fairy Tales: Gender and Narrative Strategies*. Philadelphia: U of Pennsylvania P, 1997.

Baer, Elizabeth. "The Sisterhood of Jane Eyre and Antoinette Cosway." *The Voyage in: Fictions of Female Development*. Ed. Elizabeth Abel, Marianne Hirsch, and Elizabeth Langland. Hanover: UP of New England, 1983. 131–48.

Bakhtin, M[ikhail] M. *The Dialogic Imagination: Four Essays*. Ed. Michael Holquist. Trans. Caryl Emerson and Michael Holquist. Austin: U of Texas P, 1981.

Barth, John. "The Literature of Exhaustion." *Atlantic* 220 (Aug. 1967): 29–34.

Barthes, Roland. *Mythologies*. Trans. Annette Lavers. New York: Hill and Wang, 1999.

Barzilai, Shuli. Comment during the "Margaret Atwood: The Open Eye" symposium in Ottawa, Apr. 2004. <http://www.behindthename.com> 2 May 2007.

Bellamy, Michael. "An Interview with Iris Murdoch." *Contemporary Literature* 18.2 (Spring 1977): 129–40.

Benediktsson, Thomas E. "The Reawakening of the Gods: Realism and the Supernatural in Silko and Hulme." *Critique* 33.2 (Winter 1992): 121–31.

Benson, Stephen, ed. *Contemporary Fiction and the Fairy Tale.* Detroit, MI: Wayne SUP, 2008..

Benson, Stephen. *Cycles of Influence: Fiction, Folktale, Theory.* Detroit, MI: Wayne SUP, 2003.

Beran, Carol. "Strangers within the Gates: Margaret Atwood's *Wilderness Tips.*" *Margaret Atwood's Textual Assassinations: Recent Poetry and Fiction.* Ed. Sharon Rose Wilson. Columbus: Ohio SUP, 2003. 74–87.

Berry, James. *Spiderman Anancy.* Illus. Joseph Olubo. New York: Henry Holt, 1988.

Bethune, Brian. "Atwood Apocalyptic." *Maclean's* 116.17: 44–49.

Bettelheim, Bruno. *The Uses of Enchantment: The Meaning and Importance of Fairy Tales.* New York: Knopf, 1976.

Bhabha, Homi K. "Introduction." *Nation and Narration.* London: Routledge, 1995. 1–7.

———. *The Location of Culture.* London and New York: Routledge, 1994.

The Holy Bible. King James Version. Cleveland and New York: World, n.d.

Blake, Susan L. "Toni Morrison." *Dictionary of Literary Biography: Afro-American Fiction Writers After 1955.* Ed. Thadious M. Davis and Trudier Harris. Vol. 33. Detroit, MI: Gale, 1984. 187–99.

Boemer, qtd. Stephen M. Hart and Wen-chin Ouyang, ed. *Companion to Magical Realism.* Chippenham, UK: Tamesis, 2005. 6.

Bontatibus, Donna. "Reconnecting with the Past: Personal Hauntings in Margaret Atwood's *The Robber Bride.*" *Papers on Language and Literature* (Fall 1998): 358+8 June 2000. <http://web2.infotrac.galegroup.com>.

Bordo, Susan. "The Empire of Images in Our World of Bodies." *Chronicle of Higher Education* 50.17 (19 Dec. 2003): B6-B9. EBSCO Host. 1–6. 1 June 2006.

Bouson, J. Brooks. "Slipping Sideways in the Dreams of Women: The Female Dream Work of Power Feminism in Margaret Atwood's *The Robber Bride.*" *Literature Interpretation Theory* 6.3–4 (Dec. 1995): 149–66.

Bowers, Maggie Ann. *Magic(al) Realism: The New Critical Idiom.* London Routledge, 2004.

Bowman, Diane Kim. "Flying High: The American Icarus in Morrison, Roth, and Updike." *Perspectives on Contemporary Literature* 8 (1982): 10–17.

Bronte, Charlotte. *Charlotte Bronte Jane Eyre: An Authoritative Text Backgrounds Criticism.* Ed. Richard J. Dunn. Norton Critical Edition. New York: Norton, 1971.

Brydon, Diana, and Helen Tiffin. *Decolonizing Fictions.* Sydney: Dangaroo, 1993.

Bryson, John. "Keri Hulme in Conversation with John Bryson." *Antipodes: A North American Journal of Australian Literature* 8.2 (Dec. 1994): 131–35.

Caldwell, Gail. "Author Toni Morrison Discusses Her Latest Novel *Beloved*." In Danille Taylor-Guthrie. Ed. *Conversations with Toni Morrison*. Literary Conversations Series. Jackson: UP of Mississippi, 1994. 239–45.

Camus, Albert. *The Myth of Sisyphus and Other Essays*. New York: Vintage, 1955.

Carter, Angela. *The Bloody Chamber and Other Adult Tales*. New York: Harper and Row, 1979.

———, ed. *The Old Wives' Fairy Tale Book*. New York: Pantheon, 1990.

Castillo, Debra A. *Talking Back: Toward a Latin American Feminist Literary Criticism*. Ithaca, NY: Cornell UP, 1992.

Castillo, Susan Perez. "Postmodernism, Native American Literature and the Real: The Silko-Erdrich Controversy." *Massachusetts Review* 32.2 (Summer 1991): 1–6. EBSCO Host 14 Jan. 2005.

Catt, Catherine M. "Ancient Myth in Modern America: The Trickster in the Fiction of Louise Erdrich." *Platte Valley Review* 19.1 (Winter 1991): 71–81.

Chapman, Douglas. "To a New World of Gods and Monsters: Mad Scientists and the Movies." <www.strangemag.com/madscientists.html> 12 Feb. 2004.

Chase, Elise. Rev. of *The Beet Queen*, by Louise Erdrich. *Library Journal* (Aug. 1986): 168–69.

Ciolkowski, Laura E. "Navigating the 'Wide Sargasso Sea': Colonial History, English Fiction, and British Empire." *Twentieth Century Literature* 43.3 (Fall 1997): 339–59.

Cirlot, J.E. *A Dictionary of Symbols*. Trans. Jack Sage. New York: Philosophical Library, 1962.

Cixous, Helene. "Castration or Decapitation?" *Contemporary Literary Criticism: Literary and Cultural Studies*. Ed. Robert Con Davis and Ronald Schliefer. 2nd ed. Trans. Annette Kuhn. New York: Longman, 1989. 479–91.

———. "The Laugh of the Medusa." Ed. Robyn R. Warhol and Diane Price Herndl. *Feminisms: An Anthology of Literary Theory and Criticism*. New Brunswick, NJ: Rutgers UP, 1997. 347–62.

The Complete Grimm's Fairy Tales. Trans. Margaret Hunt and James Sterne. Introduction Padraic Colum and Commentary Joseph Campbell. New York: Pantheon, 1972.

The Complete Hans Christian Andersen Fairy Tales. Ed. Lily Owens. New York: Avenel, 1981.

Colakis, Marianthe. "Doris Lessing's New Cupid and Psyche: A Platonic Myth Foretold." *Classical and Modern Literature: A Quarterly* 12.2 (Winter 1992): 153–60.

Conradi, Peter. *Iris Murdoch: The Saint and the Artist*. New York: St. Martin's, 1986.

Conran, Kelly, dir. *Sky Captain and the World of Tomorrow*. ISA, Brooklyn Films II, 2004. 106 min.

Cowley, Malcolm. "Future Notebook." *Saturday Review* (28 June 1975): 23–24.

Cranny-Francis, Anne. *Feminist Fiction: Feminist Uses of Generic Fiction*. New York: St. Martin's, 1990.

Crater, Theresa. "Temporal Temptations in Lessing's *Mara and Dann:* Arriving at the Present Moment." *DLS* 23.2 (Winter 2004): 17–20.

Cronenberg, David, dir. *The Fly*. Brooks Films, 1986. 95 min.

Crystal, Billy, dir. *Forget Paris*. Castle Rock Entertainment, 1995. 101 min.

Dale, Judith. "*The Bone People* (Not) Having It Both Ways." *Landfall* 39 (1985): 413–28.

Daly, Mary. *Gyn/ecology: The Metaethics of Radical Feminism*. Boston: Beacon Press, 1978.

Davidson, Arnold. Margaret Atwood Society Session. San Diego: MLA Paper, 1994.

De Beaumont, Jeanne-Marie Leprince. "Beauty and the Beast." *Beauties, Beasts, and Enchantments: Classic French Fairy Tales*. Trans. and Intro. Jack Zipes. New York: NAL, 1989. 233–45.

Defoe, Daniel. *The Life and Adventures of Robinson Crusoe*. London: W. Clowes, [1890?].

De Villeneuve, Gabrielle-Suzanne. "The Story of Beauty and the Beast." *Beauties, Beasts, and Enchantments: Classic French Fairy Tales*. Trans. and Intro. Jack Zipes. New York: NAL, 1989. 153–229.

De Weever, Jacqueline. "Toni Morrison's Use of Fairy Tale, Folk Tale, and Myth in Song of Soloman." *Southern Folklore Quarterly* 44 (1980): 131–44.

Dipple, Elizabeth. *Iris Murdoch: Work for the Spirit*. Chicago: U of Chicago P, 1982.

Dorson, Richard M. *Folktales Told Around the World*. Chicago: U of Chicago P, 1975.

———. *Folklore of the Santal Parganas*, no. 50. Cited in Ashliman.

Drabble, Margaret, ed. *The Oxford Companion to English Literature*. 5th ed. Oxford: Oxford UP, 1985.

Duddy, Thomas. "Iris Murdoch (1919–1999)." *Continuum Encyclopedia of British Philosophy*. Vol. 3. 2006. 2286–87.

Duigan, John, dir. *Wide Sargasso Sea* film, Laughing Kookaburra Prod., 1993. Color, 98 min.

Dundes, Alan, ed. *Cinderella: A Casebook*. New York: Wildman, 1983.

Dunn, Richard J., ed. *Charlotte Bronte Jane Eyre: An Authoritative Text Backgrounds Criticism*. Norton Critical Edition. 2nd ed. New York: Norton, 1987.

Dunne, Michael. *Metapop: Self-Referentiality in Contemporary American Popular Culture*. Jackson: UP of Mississippi, ca. 1992.

DuPlessis, Rachel Blau. *Writing Beyond the Ending: Narrative Strategies Women Writers*. Bloomington: Indiana UP, 1985.

During, Simon. "Postmodernism or Postcolonialism?" *Landfall* 39.3 (1985): 366–80.

Duyfhuizen, Bernard. "On the Writing of Future History: Beginning the Ending in Doris Lessing's *The Memoirs of a Survivor*." Spec. issue of *Modern Fiction Studies* 26.1 (Spring 1980): 147–56.

Dworkin, Andrea. *Woman Hating*. New York: Dutton, 1974.

Editor. "Introduction to *The Beet Queen* Review." *SAIL* 10.4 (1986): 178–84.

Eisler, Riane. *The Chalice and the Blade: Our History, Our Future*. San Francisco: Harper and Row, 1987.

Eliade, Mircea. *Myth and Reality*. Trans. William R. Trask. New York: Harper and Row, 1963.

Ellis, John M. *One Fairy Story Too Many: The Brothers Grimm and Their Tales*. Chicago and London: U of Chicago P, 1983.

Emery, Mary Lou. *Jean Rhys at 'World's End': Novels of Colonial and Sexual Exile*. Austin: U of Texas P, 1990.

Erdoes, Richard and Alfonso Ortiz, ed. *American Indian Myths and Legends*. New York: Pantheon, 1984. 154–55.

Erdrich, Louise. *The Beet Queen*. New York: Bantam, 1989.

———. *The Blue Jay's Dance*. New York: Harper Collins, 1995.

Farris, Wendy B. *Ordinary Enchantments: Magical Realism and the Remystification of Narrative*. Nashville: Vanderbuilt UP, 2004.

Fee, Margery. "Keri Hulme." *International Literature in English: Essays on the Major Writers*. Ed. Robert L. Ross. New York: Garland, 1991. 53–62.

Ferre, Rosario. *Eccentric Neighborhoods*. New York: Farrar, Straus, and Giroux, 1998.

———. *The House on the Lagoon*. New York: Farrar, Straus, and Giroux, 1995.

———. "On Destiny, Language, and Translation; or, Ophelia Adrift in the C. & O. Canal." *The Youngest Doll*. 153–65.

———. "Sleeping Beauty." Trans. Rosario Ferre and Diana Velez. *Reclaiming Medusa*. Ed. Diana Velez. San Francisco: Spinsters/Aunt Lute, 1988.

———. *The Youngest Doll*. Foreword by Jean Franco. Lincoln: U of Nebraska P, 1991.

Fiander, Lisa M. *Fairy Tales and the Fiction of Iris Murdoch, Margaret Drabble, and A.S. Byatt*. Studies on Themes and Motifs in Literature. Vol. 70. New York: Peter Lang, 2004.

Fishburn, Katherine. *The Unexpected Universe of Doris Lessing: A Study in Narrative Technique*. Contributions to the Study of Science Fiction and Fantasy. 17. Westport, CT: Greenwood Press, 1985.

Fleming, Victor, dir. *Dr. Jekyll and Mr. Hyde*. Metro-Goldwyn-Mayer, 1941. 113 min.

———, dir. *The Wizard of Oz*. MGM, 1939. 101 min.

Flowers, Helen L. *A Classification of the Folktale of the West Indies by Types and Motifs*. New York: Arno, 1980.

Franco, Jean. Foreword. *The Youngest Doll*. Lincoln: U of Nebraska P, 1991.

Frankenheimer, John, dir. *The Island of Dr. Moreau*, 1996. New Line Cinema. 96 min.

Frankova, Milada. "The Green Knight and The Myth of the Green Man." *Brno Studies in English* 21 (1995): 77–83.

Gerstenberger, Donna. *Irish Murdoch*. Irish Writers Ser. Lewisburg, PA: Bucknell UP, 1975.

Gilbert, Sandra M. "A Dialogue of Self and Soul: Plain Jane's Progress." In Dunn. 2nd ed. 476–83.

Gilbert, Sandra M., and Susan Gubar. *The Madwoman in the Attic: The Woman Writer and the Nineteenth-Century Literary Imagination*. New Haven, CT: Yale UP, 1979.

Gimbutas, Maria. *The Civilization of the Goddess: The World of Old Europe*. Ed. Joan Marler. San Francisco: Harper, 1991.

Glendinning, Victoria. Rev. of *Memoirs of a Survivor*, by Doris Lessing. *TLS* (13 Dec. 1974): 1405.

Gordon, David J. "Iris Murdoch's Comedies of Unselfing." *Twentieth Century Literature* 36.2 (Summer 1990): 115–36.

Grace, Sherrill. "Courting Bluebeard with Bartok, Atwood, and Fowles: Modern Treatment of the Bluebeard Theme." *Journal of Modern Literature* 11.2 (1984): 245–62.

Graves, Robert. *The White Goddess: A Historic Grammar of Poetic Mythology*. Amended and enlarged edition. New York: Farrar, Straus, and Giroux, 1966.

Green, Martin. "Politics and Patterns: The Doom of Empire: Memoirs of a Survivor." *Critical Essays on Doris Lessing*. Ed. Claire Sprague and Virginia Tiger. Boston: G. K. Hall, 1986. 31–37.

Greene, Gayle. *Changing the Story: Feminist Fiction and the Tradition*. Bloomington and Indianapolis: Indiana UP, 1991.

———. *Doris Lessing: The Poetics of Change*. Ann Arbor: U of Michigan P, 1994.

Greenway, Gina Nicole. "Into the Wood: The Image of the Chokecherry Tree in Toni Morrison's *Beloved*." *Proteus* 21.2 (1 Sept. 2004): 3–7.

Gussow, Mel. "Handwringer's Tale of Tomorrow." *New York Times*. 24 June 2003. <http://NYTimes.com> 24 June 2003.

Haase, Donald, ed. *Fairy Tales and Feminism: New Approaches*. Detroit, MI: Wayne SUP, 2004.

Hamilton, Edith. *Mythology: Timeless Tales of Gods and Heroes*. New York: Meredian, 1969.

Hammond, Carla. Interview with Margaret Atwood. "Articulting the Mute." Rpt. Earl G. Ingersoll.

Hansen, Terrance Leslie. *The Types of the Folktale in Cuba, Puerto Rico, the Dominican Republic, and Spanish South America*. Folklore Studies 8. Berkeley: U of California P, 1957.

Harris, Elizabeth Warring. *Twice Upon a Time: Woman Writers and the History of the Fairy Tale*. Princeton, NJ: Princeton UP, 2001.

Harris, Stephen L., and Gloria Platzner. *Classical Mythology: Images and Insights*. 2nd ed. Mountain View, CA: Mayfield, 1998.

Harris, Trudier. *Fiction and Folklore: The Novels of Toni Morrison*. Knoxville: U of Tennessee P, 1991.

Harris, Wilson. "Jean Rhys's Tree of Life." *Journal of Caribbean Literatures* 3.3: 151–55.

Hart, Patricia. "Rosario Ferre's *The Youngest Doll*." *Studies in Honor of Maria A. Salgado*. Ed. Millicent A. Bolden and Luis A. Jimenez. Hispanic Monographs. Newark: Juan de la Cuesta, 1995.

Hart, Stephen M., and Wen-chin Ouyang, ed. *Companion to Magical Realism*. Chippenham, UK: Tamesis, 2005.

"Hathor." <http://en.wikipedia.org/wiki/Hathor> 9 Jan. 2007.

Henderson, Mae G. "Toni Morrison's *Beloved:* Re-Membering the Body as Historical Text." In *Toni Morrison's Beloved: A Casebook*. Ed. William L. Andrews and Nellie Y. McKay. Oxford: Oxford UP, 1999. 79–106.

Hengen, Shannon. "Zenia's Foreignness." *Various Atwood's: Essays on the Later Poems, Short Fiction, and Novels*. Ed. Lorraine M. York. Concord, Ontario: Anansi, 1955.

Henke, Suzette. "Constructing the Female Hero: Keri Hulme's *The Bone People*." *Myths, Heroes and Anti-Heroes: Essays on the Literature and Culture of the Asia-Pacific Region*. Ed. Bruce Bennett and Dennis Haskell. Nedlands, WA: Centre for Studies in Australian Literature, University of Western Australia, 1992. 89–97.

Hintz, Suzanne S. *Rosario Ferre, A Search for Identity*. Wor(l)ds of Change: Latin American and Iberian Literature.Vol. 12. New York: Peter Lang, 1995.

"Holistic Qualities of Gems." <www.fruitsofthesea.com/Gems.htm> 10 Aug. 2007.

Holman, C. Hugh, and William Harmon. *A Handbook to Literature*. 5th ed. New York: Macmillan, 1986.

Howells, Coral Ann. "The Robber Bride; or, Who Is a True Canadian." *Margaret Atwood's Textual Assassinations*. Ed. Sharon Rose Wilson. 88–101.

Huggan, Graham. "Opting Out of the (Critical) Common Market: Creolization and the Post-Colonial Text." *After Europe*. Ed. Stephen Slemon and Helen Tiffin. Sydney: Mundelstrup, 1989. 27–40.

Hughes, Mary Ann. "Transgressing Boundaries." *Span* 39 (1 Oct. 1994): 56–68.

Hulme, Keri. *The Bone People*. New York: Penguin, 1983.

———. *Strands*. Auckland: Auckland UP, 1992.

Hulme, Keri A. L. "Myth, Omen, Ghost and Dream." *Poetry of the Pacific Region: Proceedings of the CRNLA/SPACLALS Conference* (1984): 31–38.

Hulme, Keri, and Gerry Turcotte. "Reconsidering *The Bone People*." *Australian and New Zealand Studies in Canada* 12 (1 Dec. 1994): 135–54.

Hunt, Margaret, and James Stern, trans. *The Complete Grimm's Fairy Tales*. New York: Pantheon, 1972.

Hyde, Lewis. *Trickster Makes This World: Mischief, Myth, and Art*. New York: Farrar, Straus, and Giroux, 1998.

Ingersoll, Earl G., ed. *Doris Lessing Conversations*. Princeton, NJ: Ontario Review Press, 1994.

———. *Margaret Atwood Conversations*. Princeton, NJ: Ontario Review Press, 1990. 109–20.

———. "Myth in Margaret Atwood's *The Penelopiad*." *Myth and Intertextuality in the Works of Margaret Atwood*. Margaret Atwood Society Session, MLA. Philadelphia, 2006.

Inpopa. "Doris Lessing." "The Wolf People," "Cave Wolves." Inpopa (The Institute of Poetic Patience) Anthology 2002: Poems by Doris Lessing,

Robert Twigger and TH Benson. Ed. M. P. Gould. <http://www.dorisless-ing.org/the wolf.html. and http.//www.inpopa.org/decks/index.html> 24 July 2007.

Isis. <http://en.wikipedia.org/wiki/Isis> 9 Jan. 2007.

Jacobsen, Sally A. "Daughters of the Dark Goddess: Tales of Hoffman, 'Pop Goes the Weasel,' and the Manuscript of *The Robber Bride*." San Diego: MLA Paper, 1994.

Jaffe, Nina. *Sing, Little Sack! Canta, Saquito!: A Folktale from Puerto Rico*. Retold and Adapted by Nina Jaffe; Illustrated by Ray Cruz. New York: Bantam, c1993.

Jameson, Fredric. Foreword. Jean-Francois Lyotard. vii-xxi.

Johnson, Deborah. *Iris Murdoch*. Key Women Writers Series. Brighton, UK: Harvester P, 1987.

Jones, Dorothy. "Narrative Enclosures." In Turcotte. 47–67.

Kaplan, Carey, and Ellen Cronan Rose, ed. *Doris Lessing: The Alchemy of Survival*. Athens: Ohio UP, 1988.

Kaplan, E. Ann. "Madonna Politics: Perversion, Repression, or Subversion? Or Masks and/as Master-y." *The Madonna Connection: Representational Politics, Subcultural Identities, and Cultural Theory*. Ed. Cathy Schwicht-enberg. Boulder, CO: Westview, 1993. 149–66.

Kenton, Earl C., dir. *Island of Lost Souls*. Paramount, 1933. 71 min.

"Keri Hulme." *Contemporary Authors*. Detroit, MI: Gale, 1989. 125: 209–15.

Kloepfer, Deborah Kelly. "The Syntax of Stained Glass." *Forbidden Discourse in Jean Rhys and H. D*. Ithaca, NY: Cornell UP, 1989.

Knapp, Mona. Rev. of *Mara and Dann*. *World Literature Today* 74.2 (Spring 2000) 366.

Korenowsky, Christopher. Rev. of *The Story of General Dann and Mara's Daughter, Griot and the Snow Dog*. *Library Journal* (Dec. 2005): 113–14.

Kristeva, Julia. *Desire in Language: A Semiotic Approach to Literature and Art*. Ed. Leon S. Roudirz. Trans. Thomas Goa, Alice Jardine, and Leon S. Roudiez. European Perspectives. New York: Columbia UP, 1980.

Kubrick, Stanley, dir. *Dr. Strangelove: Or How I Learned to Stop Worrying and Love the Bomb*. Hawk Films, GB, 1964. 96 min.

Lacan, Jacques. *Ecrits: A Selection*. Trans. Alan Sheridan. New York: Norton, 1977.

Larrington, Carolyne, ed. *The Feminist Companion to Mythology*. London: Pandora, 1992.

Leach, Maria, ed. and Jerome Fried, asst. ed. *Funk and Wagnalls Standard Dictionary of Folklore, Mythology, and Legend*. San Francisco: Harper and Row, 1984.

Le Cam, Georges-Goulven Ven. "The Quest for Archetypal Self-Truth in Keri Hulme's *The Bone People*: Towards a Western Re-Definition of Maori Culture?" *Commonwealth* 15.2 (1993): 66–79.

Ledbetter, Mark. *Victims and the Postmodern Narrative or Doing Violence to the Body: An Ethic of Reading and Writing*. New York: St. Martin's, 1996.

Lesser, Wendy. "Interview with Iris Murdoch." *Threepenny Review* 19 (1 Jan. 1985): 13–15.

Lessing, Doris. Address. Tenth International Conference on the Fantastic in the Arts. Dania, Florida. Mar. 1989.

———. "Author's Note." *Mara and Dann: An Adventure.* New York: HarperFlamingo, 1999. vii-viii.

———. *Mara and Dann: An Adventure.* New York: HarperFlamingo, 1999.

———. *The Memoirs of a Survivor.* New York: Knopf, 1975.

———. *The Story of General Dann and Mara's Daughter, Griot and the Snow Dog.* London: HarperCollins, 2005.

Lyotard, Jean-Francois. *The Postmodern Condition: A Report on Knowledge.* Trans. Geoff Bennington and Brian Massumi. Vol. 10, Theory and History of Literature. Minneapolis: U of Minnesota P, 1993.

MadSciNet. <http://www.madsci.org> 12 Feb. 2004.

Magoun, Francis P., Jr., and Alexander H. Krappe, trans. *Grimms' German Folk Tales.* Carbondale: Southern Illinois UP, 1960. 151–52.

"Maori Art—Meaning and Symbolism." <http://www.maori.info/maori art .htm> 13 Feb. 2007.

"Margaret Atwood." Video. Ovation Arts Network.

Mathews, Robin. Opening Address. XI Annual Commonwealth Literature and Language Conference in German-Speaking Countries. Aachen, Germany. 16 June1988.

Mayer, Elsie F. "Morrison's *Beloved.*" *Explicator* 51.3 (Spring 1993): 192–94.

McCombs, Judith. "Rewriting *Crusoe:* Atwood's Cautionary: Future-Shock *Oryx and Crake.*" Paper presented at ACSUS. Portland, 2003.

———. "*The Robber Bride:* Atwood's Pre-Modern Feminist Bildungsroman." San Diego: MLA Paper, 1994.

Meisenhelder, Susan. "Race and Gender in Louise Erdrich's 'The Beet Queen'." *Ariel: A Review of International English Literature* 25.1 (Jan. 1994): 45–57.

Melville, Herman. *Moby-Dick or, The Whale.* Ed. Alfred Kazin. Boston: Houghton Mifflin, 1956.

Memoirs of a Survivor. Dir. David Gladwell. VHS Color. 116 minutes. National Film Trustee Co., 1981.

Middleton, David L. *Toni Morrison: An Annotated Bibliography.* New York and London: Garland, 1987.

Miller, Kathy. "Cultural Geography—Nomadism, Friendship and War in Margaret Atwood's *The Robber Bride.*" *Dedalus* 6 (1996): 71–80.

Mitchell, Carol. "Feminine Metaphors of Cosmogony: Parthenogenesis." American Folklore Society Conference. 1996.

Mitchell, Carolyn. "I Love to Tell the Story: Biblical Revisions in *Beloved.*" *Religion and Literature* 23.3 (Autumn 1991): 27–42.

Miyares, Ruben Valdes. "Sir Gawain and the Great Goddess." *English Studies* 83.3 (June 2002): 185–206.

Morford, Mark P. O., and Robert J. Lenardon. *Classical Mythology.* 6th ed. New York: Longman, 1999.

Morgan, Emily. "Iron Age Apocalypse, or Rebirth of a Goddess Golden Age?: Reading the Iron Egg in Doris Lessing's *Memoirs of a Survivor.*" MLA Paper, Philadelphia, Dec. 2006.

Morrison, Toni. *Beloved.* New York: Knopf, 1987.

———. "Memory, Creation, and Writing." *Thought* 59.235 (Dec. 1984): 385–90.

———. "Rootedness: The Ancestor as Foundation." *Black Women Writers (1950–1980); A Critical Evaluation.* Ed. Mari Evans. New York: Anchor/Doubleday, 1984. 339–45.

Mulvey, Laura. "Visual Pleasure and Narrative Cinema." Warhol and Herndl. 438–48.

Murdoch, Iris. *The Green Knight.* New York: Penguin, 1993.

———. *The Unicorn.* New York: Viking, 1963.

Murray, Jennifer. "Questioning the Triple Goddess: Myth and Meaning in Margaret Atwood's *The Robber Bride.*" *Canadian Literature* 173 (1 June 2002): 72–90.

The Mwindo Epic. World Mythology: An Anthology of the Great Myths and Epics. Ed. Donna Rosenberg. 2nd ed. Lincolnwood, IL.: NTC, 1994.

Neumann, Kurt, dir. *The Fly.* Fox. 1958. 94 min.

Newman, Robert D. "Doris Lessing's Mythological Egg in *The Memoirs of a Survivor.*" *Notes on Contemporary Literature* 14.3 (May 1984): 3–4.

Nicholson, Linda J., ed. "Introductions." *Feminism/Postmodernism.* London: Routledge, 1990.

Owens, Lily, ed. *The Complete Hans Christian Andersen Fairy Tales.* New York: Avenel, 1981.

Paravisini-Gebert, Lizabeth. "Women against the Grain: The Pitfalls of Theorizing Caribbean Women's Writing." *Winds of Change: The Transforming Voices of Caribbean Women Writers and Scholars.* Ed. Adele S. Newson and Linda Strong-Leek. New York: Lang, 1998.

Parsons, Elsie Clews. *Folk-lore of the Antilles, French and English.* Part II. New York: American Folk-lore Society, G. E. Stechert, 1936.

Peek, Andrew. "An Interview with Keri Hulme." *New Literatures Review* 20 (1990): 1–11.

Perrakis, Phyllis Sternberg. "Journeys of the Spirit: The Older Woman in Doris Lessing's Works." *Doris Lessing Studies* 24.1 & 2 (2004): 39–43.

———. Letter to Wilson. 21 June 2002.

Piercy, Marge. *Woman on the Edge of Time.* New York: Knopf, 1976.

Petersen, Nancy J. "History, Postmodernism, and Louise Erdrich's *Tracks.*" *PMLA* 109.5 (Oct. 1994): 982–94.

Potts, Donna L. " 'The Old Maps are Dissolving': Intertextuality and Identity in Atwood's *The Robber Bride.*" *Tulsa Studies in Women's Literature* 18.2 (Fall 1999): 281–98.

———. "The White Goddess Displaced: National/Sexual Parallels in Atwood's *The Robber Bride.*" *Literature of Region and Nation: Proceedings of the 6th International Literature of Region and Nation Conference, 2–7 August 1996.* Saint John: University of New Brunswick, 1998.

Pourrat, Henri. *French Folktales*. Selected by C. G. Bjurstrom, Trans. Royall Tyler. New York: Pantheon, 1989.

Powell, Michael, and Emeric Pressburger. Directors, producers, and scriptwriters. *The Red Shoes*. Great Britain, 1948.

Pratt, Annis. *Dancing with Goddesses: Archetypes, Poetry, and Empowerment*. Bloomington: Indiana UP, 1994.

Rabinovitz, Paula. "Naming, Magic and Documentary: The Subversion of Narrative in *Song of Solomon, Ceremony*, and *China Men*." *Feminist Re-Visions: What Has Been and Might Be*. Ed. Vivian Patraka and Lopuise A. Tilly. Ann Arbor: Women's Studies, U of Michigan P, 1983. 26–42.

Raffel, Burton, trans. and intro. *Sir Gawain and the Green Knight*. Afterword Neil D. Isaacs. New York: New American Library, 1970.

Rainwater, Catherine. "Reading between Worlds: Narrativity in the Fiction of Louise Erdrich." *American Literature* 62.3 (Sept. 1990): 405–22.

Rao, Eleonora. "Immigrants and Other Aliens: Encounters in the 'Wild Zone' in Margaret Atwood's Recent Fiction." *Intersections: la narrative canadese tra storia e geigrafia*. Bologna: Cisalpion, c1999.

Raschke, Debrah. "Cabalistic Gardens: Lessing's *Memoirs of a Survivor*." *Spiritual Exploration in the Works of Doris Lessing*. Contributions to the Study of Science Fiction and Fantasy. 81. Ed. Phyllis Sternberg Perrakis.Westport, CT, 1999. 43–54.

Reed, A. W. *Maori Myth and Legend*. Illus. Roger Hart. Auckland: Reed, 1996.

Reed, Carol, dir. *The Third Man*. Starring Joseph Cotton, Alida Valli, Orson Welles. England, 1949.

Rev. of *The Robber Bride*, by Margaret Atwood. *Catholic New Times* 19.20 (19 Nov. 1995): 1, 3.

Rev. of *The Story of General Dann and Mara's Daughter, Griot and the Snow Dog*. *Kirkus* 73.23 (21 Jan. 2005): 1249.

Rhys, Jean. *Smile Please: An Unfinished Autobiography*. New York: Harper and Row, 1980.

———. *Voyage in the Dark*. Harmondsworth, UK: Penguin, 1969.

———. *Wide Sargasso Sea*. New York: Popular Library, 1966.

Ridley, Chauncey A. "Sethe's 'Big, Bad' Love." *Understanding Others: Cultural and Cross-Cultural Studies and the Teaching of Literature*. Ed. Joseph Trimmer and Tilly Warnock. Urbana, IL: NCTE, 1992. 153–64.

Rochman, Hazel. Rev. of *The Story of General Dann and Mara's Daughter, Griot and the Snow Dog*. *Booklist* (1 Dec. 2005): 31–32.

Roemer, Danielle, and Cristina Bacchilega, ed. *Angela Carter and the Fairy Tale*. Detroit, MI: Wayne SUP, 2000.

Rooth, Anna Birgitta. *The Cinderella Cycle*. New York: Arno, 1980.

Rosenberg, Donna. *World Mythology: An Anthology of the Great Myths and Epics*. Lincolnwood, IL.: NTC Publishing, 1993.

Rosenthal, Caroline. *Narrative Deconstructions of Gender in Works by Audrey Thomas, Daphne Marlett, and Louise Erdrich*, Rochester: Camden House, 2003.

Rousseau, Francois-Olivier. "The Habit of Observing." Ingersoll, NJ. 146–54.

Rowe, John Carlos. "Buried Alive: The Native American Political Unconscious in Louise Erdrich's Fiction." *Postcolonial Studies* 7.2 (2004): 197–210.

Rowe, Margaret Moan. "Dame Iris Murdoch" [also listed as "Dame Irish Murdoch."] *A Companion to the British and Irish Novel 1945–2000.* Ed. Brian W. Shaffer. Malden, MA: Blackwell, 2005.

———. Rev. of *From a Tiny Corner in the House of Fiction: Conversations with Iris Murdoch.* Ed. Gillian Dooley. *Studies in the Novel* 37.3 (Fall 2005): 351–52.

Rubenstein, Roberta. *The Novelistic Vision of Doris Lessing: Breaking the Forms of Consciousness.* Urbana: U of Illinois P, 1979.

Rubins, Josh. Rev. of *The Beet Queen,* by Louise Erdrich. *New York Review of Books* (15 Jan. 1987): 14–15.

Rusoff, Marly, and Nan A.Talese, ed. *The Book Group Companion to Margaret Atwood's The Robber Bride.* New York: Nan A.Talese Doubleday, 1993.

"Russian Crafts." <http://www. russiancrafts.com/tales/alionushka.html> 14 Aug. 2007.

Sagare, S. B. "An Interview with Irish Murdoch." *Modern Fiction Studies* 47.3 (Fall 2001): 696–714.

Sage, Lorna. *Doris Lessing.* London: Methuen, 1983.

San Souci, Robert D. *Cendrillon: A Caribbean Cinderella.* Illus. Brian Pinkney. New York: Simon and Schuster, 1998.

Sarton, May. *Mrs. Stevens Hears the Mermaids Singing.* New York: Norton, 1965.

———. "The Muse as Medusa." Gilbert and Gubar. 1690–1691.

Scholes, Robert. *Semiotics and Interpretation.* New Haven, CT: Yale UP, 1982.

Sedgwick, Eve Kosofsky. "Gender Asymmetry and Erotic Triangles." Warhol and Herndl. 524–31.

Sellers, Susan. *Myth and Fairy Tale in Contemporary Women's Fiction.* Houndmills, Hampshire, and New York: Palgrave, 2001.

Shelley, Mary Wollstonecraft. *Frankenstein or the Modern Prometheus.* New York: Macmillan, 1973.

Shieff, Sarah. "The Bone People; Myths of Belonging." *New Literature Review* 41 (Apr. 2004): 47–63.

Shklovsky, Victor. "Art as Technique." *Russian Formalist Criticism: Four Essays.* Trans. Lee T. Lemon and Marion J. Reis. Lincoln: U of Nebraska P, 1965. 3–24.

Silko, Leslie Marmon. "Here's an Odd Artifact for the Fairy-Tale Shelf." Rev. of *The Beet Queen,* by Louise Erdrich. *Impact/Albuquerque Journal* 17 Oct. 1986: 10–11. Rpt. *SAIL* 10.4:178–184.

"Skin Stories: The Art and Culture of Polynesian Tattoo." <http://www.pbs .org/skinstories/culture/role2.html> 13 Feb. 2007.

Slaymaker, William. "Myths, Mystery and the Mechanisms of Determinism: Aesthetics of Freedom in Murdoch's Fiction." *Papers on Language and Literature* 18.2 (Spring 1982): 166–80.

Sontag, Susan. *On Photography.* New York: Farrar, Straus, and Giroux, 1977.

Spheeris, Penelope, dir. *Wayne's World.* Paramount. 1992. 95 min.

Spivak, Gayatri Chakravorty. *"Wide Sargasso Sea* and a Critique of Imperialism." *Wide Sargasso Sea: Backgrounds, Criticism.* Ed. Judith Raiskin. New York: Norton, 1999.

Staels, Hilda. *Margaret Atwood's Novels: A Study of Narrative Discourse.* Tubingen and Basel: A. Francke Verlag, 1995.

Stapleton, Michael. *The Illustrated Dictionary of Greek and Roman Mythology.* Library of the World's Myths and Legends. New York: Peter Bedrick Books, 1986.

Stave, Shirley A. "Toni Morrison's *Beloved* and the Vindication of Lilith." *South Atlantic Review* 58.1 (Jan. 1993): 49–66.

Stead, C. K. "Keri Hulme's *The Bone People* and the Pegasus Award for Maori Literature." *Ariel* 16.4 (1985): 101–8.

Stein, Karen F. *Margaret Atwood Revisited.* Twayne's World Authors Series. New York: Twayne, 1999.

Stevenson, Robert Louis. *The Strange Case of Dr. Jekyll and Mr. Hyde.* 1886.

Storhoff, Gary. "Family Systems in Louise Erdrich's *The Beet Queen.*" *Summer* 39.4 (1998): 341–52.

Sullivan, Alvin. "Ideology and Form: Decentrism in *The Golden Notebook, Memoirs of a Survivor,* and *Shikasta.*" *The Alchemy of Survival.* Ed. Carey Kaplan and Ellen Cronan Rose. Columbus: Ohio UP, 1988. 71–79.

———. "*The Memoirs of a Survivor:* Lessing's Notes toward a Supreme Fiction." Special issue of *Modern Fiction Studies.* 157–62.

Surjik, Stephen, dir. *Wayne's World II.* Paramount, 1993. 95 min.

Swift, Jonathan. *Gulliver's Travels. An Annotated Text with Critical Essays.* Ed. Robert A. Greenberg. New York: Norton, 1961.

Tarrantino, Quentin, dir. *Pulp Fiction.* 1994. 154 min.

Taylor, Don, dir. *The Island of Dr. Moreau.* AIP, 1977. 99 min.

Taylor-Guthrie, Danille. *Conversations with Toni Morrison.* Literary Conversations Series. Jackson: UP of Mississippi, 1994.

Tennyson, Lord Alfred. "Ulysses." *Norton Anthology of English Literature: The Victorian Age.* 7th ed. Ed. M. H. Abrams and Stephen Greenblatt. Vol. 2B. New York: Norton, 2006. 1213–14.

Thompson, Stith. *The Folktale.* Berkeley: U of Ca P, 1977.

———. *Motif-Index of Folk-Literature: A Classification of Narrative Elements in Folktales, Ballads, Myths, Fables, Mediaval Romances, Exempla, Fabliaux. Jest-Books, and Local Legends.* Rev. and enlarged ed. Six Volumes. Bloomington and Indianapolis: Indiana UP, 1955.

Tiger, Virginia. "Ages of Anxiety: *The Diaries of Jane Somers.*" Perrakis. 1–16.

———. "'Our Chroniclers Tell Us': Lessing's Sequel to *Mara and Dann.*" *Doris Lessing Studies* 25.2 (Winter 2006): 23–25.

Tomalin, Claire. "Watching the Angry and Destructive Hoards Go By." Interview with Doris Lessing. Ingersoll. 173–77.

Toni Morrison: Profile of a Writer Video. "A London Weekend Television 'South Bank Show' Co-produced with RM Arts." 1987. 52 minutes.

Toni Morrison: A Writer's Work. Parts One and Two. 60 minutes.

Torrents, Nissa. "Testimony to Mysticism." Ingersoll. 64–69.

The Tower. <http://www.aeclectic.net/basics/tower.html> 31 Jan. 2007.

Trace, Jacqueline. "Dark Goddesses: Black Feminist Theology in Morrison's *Beloved.*" *Obsidian* II 6.3 (1991): 14–30.

Turcotte, Gerry, ed. *Margaret Atwood. Entering the Labyrinth: The Blind Assassin.* Second Annual Nortel Networks Canadian Studies Address. Wollongong: U of Wollongong P, 2003.

Tyler, Lisa. "Classical, Bublical, and Modernist Myth: Doris Lessing's Flavours of Exile." *Doris Lessing Newsletter* 15.2 (1993): 3, 10, 11, 13.

Von Franz, Marie-Louise. *An Introduction to the Interpretation of Fairytales.* Dallas, TX: Spring Publications, 1970.

———. *Problems of the Feminine in Fairy Tales.* Irving, RX: Spring Publications, 1972.

———. *Shadow and Evil in Fairy Tales.* Dallas: Spring, 1987.

Vonnegut, Kurt. *Cat's Cradle.* New York: Dell, 1963.

Vreeland, Elizabeth. "Jean Rhys: The Art of Fiction LXIV." *Paris Review* 21.76 (Fall 1979): 218–37.

Walker, Barbara G. *The Woman's Dictionary of Symbols and Sacred Objects.* San Francisco: Harper and Row, 1988.

———. *The Woman's Encyclopedia of Myths and Secrets.* San Francisco: Harper and Row, 1983.

Walker, Jeanne Murray. "Memory and Culture within the Individual: The Breakdown of Social Exchange in *Memoirs of a Survivor.*" *Doris Lessing: The Alchemy of Survival.* Ed. Carey Kaplan and Ellen Cronan Rose. Athens: Ohio UP, 1988.

Wall, Kathleen, and Larry W. Hurtado. *Healing the Divisions: Goddess Figures in Two Works of Twentieth-Century Literature.* Atlanta: Scholars P, 1990.

Wang, Wayne, and Paul Auster, dir. *Smoke.* Miramax, 1995. 112 min.

Warhol, Robyn R., and Diane Price Herndl, ed. *Feminisms: An Anthology of Literary Theory and Criticism.* New Brunswick, NJ: Rutgers UP, 1997.

Warner, Michael. "Homo-Narcissism; or, Heterosexuality." *Contemporary Literary Criticism: Literary and Cultural Studies.* Ed. Robert Con Davis and Ronald Schleifer. 3rd ed. New York: Longman, 1990. 549–65.

Webby, Elizabeth. "Keri Hulme: Spiralling to Success." *Meanjin* 44.1 (1985): 14–23.

Weese, Katherine. "Feminist Uses of the Fantastic in Iris Murdoch's *The Sea, The Sea.*" *Modern Fiction Studies* 47.3 (Fall 2001): 630–56.

Whale, James, dir. *Frankenstein.* Universal, 1931. 71 min.

———, dir. *The Invisible Man.* Universal, 1933. 71 min.

Whittaker, Ruth. *Modern Novelists: Doris Lessing.* New York: St. Martin's, 1988.

Wilcox, Fred M., dir. *Forbidden Planet.* MGM, 1956. 98 min.

Wilson, Janet. "Intertextual Strategies: Reinventing the Myths of Aotearoa in Contemporary New Zealand Fiction." *Across the Lines: Intertextuality and*

Transcultural Communication in the New Literatures in English. Ed. Wolf-gang Klooss. Amsterdam: Rodolpi, 1988. 271–90.

Wilson, Sharon R. "Atwood's Eyes and I's." *International Literature in English: Essays on the Major Writers.* Ed. Robert L. Ross. Garland Reference Library of the Humanities Vol. 1159. New York: Garland, 1991. 225–39.

———. "Atwood's Feminist Metafairy Tale, *The Robber Bride.*" Popular Culture Association Conference. Philadelphia, Apr. 1995.

———. "Atwood's Intertextual/Sexual Politics." *Approaches to Teaching Atwood's The Handmaid's Tale and Other Works.* Ed. Sharon R. Wilson, Thomas B. Friedman, and Shannon Hengen. New York: Modern Language Association, 1996.

———. "Atwood's Metafairy Tale, *The Robber Bride:* Feminist, Postmodern, and Postcolonial Contexts." Association for Canadian Studies in the US Conference. Seattle, Nov. 1995.

———. "Camera Images in Margaret Atwood's Novels." *Margaret Atwood: Reflection and Reality.* Ed. Beatrice Mendez-Egle, General ed. James M. Haule. Living Authors Series No. 6. Edinburg, TX: Pan American U, 1987. 29–57.

———. "Deconstructing Text and Self: Mirroring in Atwood's *Surfacing* and Beckett's *Molloy.*" *Journal of Popular Literature* 3 (Spring/Summer 1987): 53–69.

———. "Fairy Tales in Feminist, Postcolonial Fiction: Atwood and Other Writers." Paper. International Popular Culture Association Conference. Oxford, England, July 1995.

———. "Through the 'Wall': Crone Journeys of Enlightenment and Creativity in the Works of Doris Lessing, Margaret Atwood, and Other Women Writers." *Adventures of the Spirit: the Older Woman in the Works of Doris Lessing, Margaret Atwood, and Other Contemporary Women Writers.* Ed. Phyllis Sternberg Perrakis. Columbus: Ohio State UP, 2007.

Wilson, Sharon Rose. "Fiction Flashes: Genre and Intertexts in *Good Bones.*" *Margaret Atwood's Textual Assassinations: Recent Poetry and Fiction.* Ed. Sharon Rose Wilson. Columbus: OSUP, 2003. 18–41.

———. *Margaret Atwood's Fairy-Tale Sexual Politics.* Jackson: UP of Mississippi, 1993.

———, ed. *Margaret Atwood's Textual Assassinations.* Columbus: Ohio SUP, 2003.

———. The Self-Conscious Narrator and His Twentieth-Century Faces. PhD Diss.,University of Wisconsin, 1976. Ann Arbor, MI: UMI, 1976.

Woolf, Virginia. *A Room of One's Own.* New York: Harcourt and Brace, 1929.

———. *To the Lighthouse.* New York: Harcourt, Brace, and World, 1955.

Zamora, Lois Parkinson, and Wendy B. Farris, eds. "Introduction: Daiquiri Birds and Flaubertian Parrot(ie)s." *Magical Realism: Theory, History, Community.* Durham: Duke UP, 1995. 1–11.

Zimmerman, Barbara. "Shadow Play: Zenia, the Archetypal Feminine Shadow in Margaret Atwood's *The Robber Bride.*" *Pleiades* 15.2 (1995): 70–82.

Zipes, Jack. *Fairy Tales as Myth/Myth as Fairy Tale.* The Thomas D. Clark Lectures. Lexington: UP of Kentucky, 1993.

——, ed. *Arabian Nights: The Marvels and Wonders of the Thousand and One Nights.* Adapted from Richard F. Burton's trans. New York: New American Library, 1991.

——. *Don't Bet on the Prince: Contemporary Feminist Fairy Tales in North America and England.* New York: Methuen, 1986.

——, trans. and ed. *Beauties, Beast, and Enchantment: Classic French Fairy Tales.* New York: New American Library, 1989.

——, trans. and ed. *"Blue Beard." Beauties, Beasts and Enchantment.* 31–35.

——, trans. and ed. *The Complete Fairy Tales of the Brothers Grimm.* Toronto, New York: Bantam, 1987.

——, ed. *Spells of Enchantment: The Wondrous Fairy Tales of Western Culture.* New York : Viking, 1991.

INDEX

Printed in the United States
154007LV00003B/27/P